Flirting with danger . . .

"God, you're beautiful," he said as he rubbed his thumb gently over her cheekbone.

"Lake," she said; it came out as a breathy little rush of sound.

He moved again, and her eyes closed involuntarily as he tilted her head slightly. She knew, she could feel it coming, but she still gave a little start when his lips touched hers.

He was hot and strong and powerful, and it was as if he were pouring every bit of all three into this kiss. Yet it was restrained, and she thought again of a wolf on a thin leash.

And then he swept the tip of his tongue over her lips, and thoughts about anything else fled. All that was left her was sensation. . . .

Dangerous Games

Justine Dare

A SIGNET BOOK

SIGNET
Published by New American Library, a division of
Penguin Putnam Inc., 375 Hudson Street,
New York, New York 10014, U.S.A.
Penguin Books Ltd, 27 Wrights Lane,
London W8 5TZ, England
Penguin Books Australia Ltd, Ringwood,
Victoria, Australia
Penguin Books Canada Ltd, 10 Alcorn Avenue,
Toronto, Ontario, Canada M4V 3B2
Penguin Books (N.Z.) Ltd, 182–190 Wairau Road,
Auckland 10, New Zealand

Penguin Books Ltd, Registered Offices:
Harmondsworth, Middlesex, England

First published by Signet, an imprint of New American Library,
a division of Penguin Putnam Inc.

First Printing, June, 1999
10 9 8 7 6 5 4 3 2 1

Copyright © Janice Davis Smith, 1999

As always, for Tom—
For the patience,
For the support,
For surviving the changes,
But most of all for the love . . .
even though.

ACKNOWLEDGMENTS

Elia de la Cova, for her willing help
when my Spanish failed me.
Yo te amo, mamacita.

Julie Hamburg, for the Jewel
when I needed it.

Prologue

He curled up around the pain, uttering a low curse with every breath.

"I'll kill both of you," he promised vehemently.

It was their fault he was holed up like an animal, trapped, not daring to move for fear they'd find him. He would not be satisfied until they were all dead, those bastards who had set themselves up as judges and deemed him not worthy. They'd gone on to glory as the Wolf Pack, to become legends among covert operations teams, when all the time it should have been him. He was the one who should have led their missions, those deep cover clandestine operations. He was the one who would have understood the international importance of what they were sent to do, not those narrow-sighted idiots who naively only wanted to know they were in the right.

"Bastards," he hissed through clenched teeth.

He knew what had happened. He was too good, better than all of them, and they hadn't wanted to risk having him around, to show them up. Oh, they'd left it to Ian Russell to do it, to make up that pile of psychological crap about him not having the right mind-set for the pack, but he knew the truth. He knew the real reason why they'd kicked him out of that very exclusive club. He'd had a very long time to figure it out.

But now he would show them. He'd had to wait for his revenge, but he would have it at last. He had gotten one of them, and he would get the last two. He would kill them, and he would do it long and slow and hard. He'd have them both screaming, begging him to end it. And he would. Eventually. After they'd admitted he was the better man, that he'd won, against the vaunted, legendary Wolf Pack.

*The names marched through his fevered mind. Ian Russell—
already long buried, robbing him of the chance for revenge.
Jess Harper. Lake McGregor. Rob Cordero. The Alpha Wolf,
the Lone Wolf, the Gray Wolf, and the . . . dead wolf, he
thought, grinning despite his pain. He'd already sent Cordero
to hell. He would have got Harper, too, if he hadn't caught
this damn bullet, but no matter, he'd take care of him later.
And very soon he would have McGregor. On his knees.*

*Pain shot through him again. He whimpered involuntarily,
then hated himself for it; that was the kind of sound they'd be
making, not him. Before he was through with them, he'd have
the satisfaction of seeing tears of pain streaming down their
faces. But first he had to heal, he had to be strong, at his best,
so there would be no chance of escape for them. He'd have to
work harder than he'd planned, since that idiot coward Duran
had crumpled and given away the game. He should have
known better, should have taken things out of Wayne Duran's
hands the moment he'd realized what a useless weasel he was,
but it was too late to worry about that now. He had to con-
serve his energy, he would need it all to finish the job. But
he'd do it. No matter how long it took. He'd waited a long time
for this. He could wait a little longer.*

*Let them think he'd given up, let them think perhaps that
lucky shot had taken him out. It would just be that much
sweeter when he had them on their knees, knowing they were
going to die, slowly and painfully, at the hands of the man
they'd dared to pronounce not* fit *for their damned Wolf Pack.*

It would be very, very sweet.

Chapter 1

He'd found the lair, but the killer was gone.

Lake McGregor swore silently as he looked around. The small room had been cleaned—as cleaned as a room in a dingy, urban hotel got, anyway—but luckily, and perhaps not surprisingly, it had been unoccupied since the killer had left.

His quarry was too smart to have left many traces, but there was enough. The faint smell of antiseptic lingering in the rather grim bathroom, a reddish brown smear on the flimsy shower curtain, a heavy, broken rubber band in the toilet tank, indicating something—gun or stash?—had been hidden there. That, coupled with the abandoned brown sedan just like the one Lake knew the killer had been driving out back, and the description given by the clerk downstairs, clinched it.

With what he hoped was a coaxing smile Lake handed over the promised twenty to the overworked and sour-faced maid who had let him into the room.

"When was he last here?" he asked.

"Three days," she said, stuffing the twenty in the pocket of a smock that was none too clean itself. "But he is paid until the end of the week. The manager, he says clean the room."

She muttered something under her breath, in Spanish, that Lake didn't catch. He lifted a brow at her. She repeated it, he assumed, in English.

"He left behind many towels that are ruined."

"Ruined?"

"Sangre," she told him flatly, and then, apparently considering the implications of what she'd said, firmly closed her mouth without translating. Lake considered what he might get

for another ten, or even more, but she hurried away and he let it go. He already had what he needed, anyway.

The man he was hunting had been staying here.

He'd left in a hurry, without settling up, even though they owed him money.

And he'd been wounded.

Sangre. Blood. Bloody towels.

He silently thanked Rob for the crash course in Spanish. Genial, good-hearted Rob Cordero, murdered by the man who had left behind those bloody towels.

"You'll be needing more than towels when I catch up with you, Joplin," Lake muttered.

Of course, how he was going to do that escaped him right at the moment. The man already had nearly a week's head start, because it had taken Lake so long to find this place. Jess Harper would have done it in a day, he thought. The Lone Wolf of the Wolf Pack could track a mosquito through a rainstorm. It was his talent just as explosives had been Rob's, and leadership had been Ian Russell's. Together they'd been the Wolf Pack, and they'd pulled off missions no one thought possible.

But the pack was no more, Jess was safely out of this, and just as well; there was little doubt that at the end of the trail would come a killing, and that was his department, not Jess's. It always had been. Jess was tough, quick, and the best at what he did. But he was no killer.

He's found another place to hole up, a place to hide, Lake thought. And chances were he'd stay there until he was strong again; the man he was hunting was many things—vicious, cold, and probably crazy, but he was not stupid. He knew if you didn't move, you didn't leave a trail. And he knew Lake didn't have Jess's uncanny ability as a tracker. He knew too damn much about the Wolf Pack. It had almost gotten Jess and the woman he loved killed.

And it was up to Lake to make sure the man didn't get a second chance.

Lake left the drab room and the drabber hotel behind, walking briskly. This older, run-down area was at odds with the sunny, prosperous image of southern California; even the golden sunlight of this late summer day couldn't save it. But it was the kind of place he was all too used to; the Wolf Pack had done its work out of places a lot worse than this. But that was long ago, the pack was ten years scattered, their leader ten years dead.

He paused before a newsstand in front of an office building, a more modern structure that seemed to be the demarcation between the dinginess of the hotel he'd left and a more prosperous business district. He was, he guessed, somewhere near the county courthouse; no doubt that was the reason for the change. Courthouses meant lawyers, and lawyers meant fancy offices and secure parking garages for the fancy cars that went with the territory.

It also apparently meant every newspaper in the country and most from abroad, he thought, scanning the stacks.

He had *The Wall Street Journal* and was handing over a dollar bill before he realized he didn't need to look for the moment; there was no one to call for help. For ten years he'd checked every issue of the ubiquitous paper, carefully reading the Marketplace section, looking for the call. And for ten years, it had never come. Never had the Wolf Pack been summoned out of hiding, until the widow of Ian Russell, its founder and leader, the man who had been the heart and soul of them all, had called for their help.

Lake stifled the reflexive surge of disgust that the one time he was weeks late in checking, the one time he'd allowed himself time away from the memories, had been the one time when he'd been needed. And he hadn't been there for Jess, or Ian's widow and son, when they'd needed him.

But he could clean up the mess. They were safe now, out at sea on Jess's boat, sailing Puget Sound with no set schedule or timetable—a moving, unpredictable target even someone as clever and determined as Lake's quarry was would have trouble finding right now.

And that, he thought, brought him to the true bottom line. It didn't really matter if he found his quarry now or not. Because Lake knew perfectly well that eventually his prey would come to him. Because he knew that he was the hunted as well as the hunter.

He bought a cup of coffee from the shop next door to the newsstand, smiling wryly at the trouble it was to convince the young woman behind the counter that yes, he wanted a plain, simple black coffee.

"We have great espresso!"

"No, thank you."

"How about a latte?" Her voice was so bright he nearly winced, and she was watching him very intently.

"No, thanks."

"At least try our special hazelnut blend. I promise you'll like it." She smiled, and he could have sworn he heard a giggle.

"Just black coffee. Please."

She was trying too hard, he thought as he took the cup she at last handed him and sat down at a small table with a single chair, by habit moving it so that his back was to the wall and he faced the door. All that smiling, dimpling, and the breathy little "Great hair" as he'd turned away were a bit much to sell a double mocha latte.

Unless she'd been selling something else, he thought suddenly. Startled, he glanced back at her. She caught the movement and smiled. He got the strongest impression she was about to wink, but the customer she was serving said something, rather loudly, and she turned back to business.

Flirting? Had she been flirting with him?

He was suddenly bemused, not so much by the idea as by the fact that it was such a revelation. Had he really been that isolated that the very idea of a woman flirting was so unusual? He dismissed the subject with the ease of long practice; he knew better than to dwell on the solitude of his life.

But the woman's attentions did bring to mind something else. He ran a hand through his hair; it was past time for a haircut. The thick, silver locks were enough of an attention-getter without adding shoulder length to the equation. More than once on a mission he'd clipped it short, or even darkened it, knowing he couldn't afford to be as distinctive as that combination of hair and his oddly colored eyes made him.

He stopped the motion, letting the long strands fall back to his shoulders. Maybe he'd postpone that haircut. Perhaps the distinctive silver would serve a useful purpose, making him easy to track, to find. Maybe he couldn't track like Jess, but he could give his quarry a chance too good to pass up. If he could find the right way to lure him out, with himself as bait, it would no doubt be a lot quicker than continuing to try to hunt the man down.

Once he had the right setup, all he had to do was wait. And while waiting was not going to be easy—the image of Rob, a gentle, generous man he had laughed with, drunk with, and fought beside, lying broken and dying, was not easily ignored—he was a very patient man.

The best predators always were.

A moment later he was staring in shock at the newspaper spread out before him, the newspaper he'd bought out of habit rather than need, the newspaper that couldn't possibly hold anything for him.

But it did.

He closed his eyes for a moment, then read it again.

It was obviously a trap, that black-rimmed death notice. Especially in *this* newspaper. He knew it instinctively, would have known it even if it had not come at this particular time, when the last of the Wolf Pack was being hunted down, when Rob had already been murdered, and Jess nearly so. But it had come now, and it was far too coincidental for him to accept at face value. It might appear to be only the notice of the death of a man in some distant, small Colorado town, but he knew there was more to it, knew there was something else at work here. Only this time he had no coded message to spell it out for him. There were only the routine, cold words announcing a death.

His mind raced through the possible ramifications. Perhaps his quarry wasn't as badly wounded as it seemed, and had been able to set this up. Or perhaps Joplin had set this in motion before his confrontation with Jess, before he'd been injured. Or perhaps it wasn't him at all . . .

That possibility sparked a hot interest in Lake, and he set down the coffee that seemed cool now by comparison. Could it be not Joplin but the man who'd started it all, that slime who'd decided that for his own political aspirations the Wolf Pack must die, hadn't crawled deep into a hole after all? Was he not convinced disappearing was the only way he would stay alive? Was he stupid enough to try again?

Lake almost hoped so. Jess had made a bargain with the man, and Lake had to respect that; he even tended to agree with Jess that the public ruination was the worst possible punishment that could be inflicted on a man like Wayne Duran, who had aspired to the highest halls of power. But if Duran was fool enough to break that bargain, all bets—and deals— were off.

Either way, it was still a trap. But he'd walked knowingly into traps before, when it suited him. And if it would end this now, he wasn't averse to doing it again. His record of turning traps against the trapper was untarnished. The thought wasn't arrogance; it was simply a cool, rational acceptance of what he was, and how well he'd been honed to do what he did best.

Kill.

That was his unique talent. It was what had made him invaluable to the Wolf Pack. But for all his lethal abilities, he hadn't been able to save Ian, the one man who had understood. He hadn't been able to save Rob, the one man in whose pure goodness of heart he believed. Two of the three men on this planet he would have not only killed for but died for were dead, and he'd done nothing.

Quashing the useless regrets, he tossed the dregs of the coffee into the trash, folded the paper up neatly, and headed out the door.

Colorado, he thought with an unexpected sense of longing.

It seemed he was going home.

Alison Carlyle was used to people stopping dead in front of her gallery window, so she merely smiled when this one did. It happened whenever she put an unusual or particularly beautiful piece there, but never as often as it had since she'd hung that painting.

She knew just how they felt; she'd felt the same way the first time she'd seen it. Her father had had a term for it; poleaxed, he'd called it. It was as good a description as any for the complex rush of feelings she'd felt when she'd first looked at the piece. Now she found herself judging people by how they reacted to the painting—discounting the locals who came to stare out of sheer amazement at her temerity in hanging it.

Of the others, some didn't look at all. Some glanced at it and kept on moving as if it were nothing more than a pretty local landscape. Some stopped, looked, then moved on. Some even hastened their steps, as if anxious to get away.

And some came back, as if the glimpse they'd gotten had just played back in their heads, and they had come back for a second, longer look. A few, as this one had, simply stopped dead in their tracks, staring, the myriad of expressions crossing their faces a blatant display of the emotions the painting evoked. It was these two kinds of people Alison made an effort to approach, knowing they would likely appreciate the kind of art she presented inside.

Alison set down the clipboard holding the shipping form she'd been filling out, and walked toward the front of the gallery, toward the man who had come to an immediate halt on spotting the painting. The last time this had happened, she'd sold the odd little twisted iron sculpture that had sat near her office door for nearly a year. She'd put it there simply because it made her smile; the first time she'd looked at it she'd seen the suggestion of a whimsical fox in the curved iron, head cocked at a quizzical angle, as if bemused by the all too human world in which it found itself. The fact that no one else had seemed to see the creature in the piece didn't bother her; she knew her eye, as well as her sense of style and design, was different.

That time, the woman who stopped had tried to talk her into selling the painting, despite the NOT FOR SALE tag clearly displayed. And when Alison had as graciously as possible refused yet again, she had said she'd take the metal fox instead. Alison had wanted to hug her for seeing the fox. She would have laughed at her own protective feeling toward an inanimate iron sculpture, but she'd long ago accepted that it was part of her makeup, this deeply personal reaction to the art that moved her.

She held on to the smile that the thought of the sculpture had brought as she stepped outside. A moment later that smile was gone as she stared—all right, she admitted, gaped—at the man standing there.

He was the most striking man she'd ever seen, and she'd seen a lot among the artists she dealt with. A very few who were naturally dramatic, intense in that way the purest of artists have, and many more who struck the pose, as if adopting the exterior could cause the talent on the interior.

It was partly the hair, she realized. She'd never seen hair quite like that on man or woman: silken, thick, and a pure shining silver. Not gray, not white, but silver. She knew, logically, it had to be just a combination of gray and white and the way the light played on it, and here in the Rockies the light was as pure and gilding as anywhere on earth, but it was still silver. It hadn't always been, she could tell; his brows were as raven-dark as her own hair. But it had obviously happened young; he wasn't that old now.

She had an instant more to notice, with her trained eye, a profile that lived up to the promise of the striking hair; high forehead, neatly shaped nose, steady chin on a strong jaw. But she had only that instant, for then he turned on her. And she found nothing extreme in the words that came to her, for indeed he turned on her, like an attacking wild thing.

It took all the self-control at her command not to stagger back before the sudden threat. She was imagining things, of course, Lord knows she'd done it before; her father had always said her vivid imagination would get her into trouble someday. But not today, she told herself. It was broad daylight in peaceful little Jewel, there was no threat. Talk, she ordered herself. Say what you've said a hundred times. *If you'd like to come in, we have . . .*

The thought ended incomplete. Even the idea of inviting this man inside made her shiver. It was something about his eyes. Not just the oddly metallic color, as if they had gone silver just as his hair had, but the ferocity in them. The stark black jeans, boots, and long-sleeved pullover shirt he wore did nothing to alleviate the menacing picture.

"Is . . . something wrong?" she asked, rather inanely. Of course something was wrong, or this total stranger wouldn't be looking at her as if she'd murdered his best friend. As if he were about to leap at her throat.

That fit, she thought. There was a touch of wildness about him. Or perhaps it was a sense of solitariness, of a man closer to the wild things, and lonelier because of it.

God, Dad was right, she thought. That imagination of hers. She was facing a man who looked like he wanted her head on a platter, and she was trying to figure out what he was instead of diffusing the situation. Or perhaps wiser still, simply getting out of his way.

"You work here?"

She could tell nothing about his natural voice; the words came from behind clenched teeth. She again had that sensation of facing a wild animal. A barely restrained one. A tiger by the tail, a wolf on a leash. A very thin leash.

Normally, her rather proud answer would be "I'm the owner." She'd worked long and hard to be able to say that. But this situation seemed anything but normal.

"Yes," she said slowly, figuring it was both safe enough and the truth. "If you need any help . . ." she began, all the while thinking that whatever he needed help with, it was way out of her league. Her degree was in art, not anger management. And her minor was in business not . . . guerrilla warfare. The analogy should have been funny, she knew, but it wasn't; she could too easily see this man in camouflage with paint on his face, synchronizing some kind of jungle mission with that complicated watch that would have looked like an affectation on any other man, and carrying a weapon that fired faster than she could count.

"Where did you get that?"

She knew perfectly well what he meant, but she didn't like knowing he could make her feel this way; whoever he was, he was damned intimidating, and she didn't let herself be intimidated often. Besides, they were outside on the public sidewalk, there were people around, he wasn't about to do anything to her here.

"Which piece were you interested in?" she said in her best helpful salesperson voice.

She thought he swore, but it was so quiet, so low and under

his breath she couldn't be sure. Perhaps that leash was a bit stronger than she'd thought.

"That one," he said, the teeth tightening again as he jerked a thumb over his shoulder toward the painting without looking at it. Odd, she thought. He looked as if he were struggling with . . . something.

"I'm afraid that one's not for sale. If you'll notice the tag, it's clearly marked that—"

She was sure about the curse this time; it was audible, and short, although no less emphatic for its brevity.

"Where the hell did you get that painting?"

It burst from him, words that were low, harsh, and barely controlled. That leash seemed to have vanished, and she again had to fight the involuntary urge to step back, to get away from him.

He saw it, she could tell by the way his eyes narrowed slightly. And suddenly the leash was back, almost visible, as if her slight shrinking from him had brought the beast back to civilization.

"I'm sorry. I didn't mean to upset you. Maybe I should talk to the owner," he said.

She wasn't sure she liked the cool steel in his tone now any better than she'd liked the bewildering rage. Nor did she like his assumptions. She drew herself up straight, and looked at him steadily, in what her friend Yvette had once called her most regal way. There was no point in denying what had been so obvious, so instead she turned it back on him. It wasn't like her to do that to a potential customer, but she wasn't at all sure she'd want to sell any of her pieces to this man anyway.

"You've already upset the owner," she said, her tone cool.

He blinked. Those eyes were really quite remarkable, she thought. Metallic was the only word she could think of to describe them, a sort of burnished pewter color that defied traditional description.

He looked her up and down in a way that was more assessing than insulting. She knew she didn't fit the idea some people had of a gallery owner. Her pale gray suit was trim, businesslike, set off by a rich, royal blue silk blouse that turned her eyes the same shade. The strand of hand-carved

blue beads at her throat was unique, the product of a local arti-
san, and her hair was neatly up in its usual French twist,
smooth and tidy.

More than once her friends had suggested she should wear
something flowing and artsy, let her hair down, to fit the imag-
inative and sometimes fey atmosphere of Phoenix. They didn't
realize she was projecting exactly the image she wanted to
project; the pieces she sold were unique, and expensive, and
when dealing—and parting with—those amounts of money,
people felt more comfortable with a familiar, businesslike
look. Besides, her art spoke for itself, it didn't need a shill.

"Why are you avoiding the question?"

He asked it mildly, almost gently. It should have been
soothing, this switch to normalcy, but instead it made the hair
on the back of her neck stand up. She liked this voice least of
all, she thought and, irritated at herself, answered sharply.

"I have a tendency to not answer questions that sound like
accusations."

"Is that out of guilt, or just an effort to deflect attention?"

Her eyes widened; she'd spoken out of irritation, but he was
reacting as if his words truly had been an accusation.

"I don't know what you're implying, Mr. . . . ?"

He ignored the nicety. "I'm not implying anything. I'm stat-
ing that there is no honest way you could have come by that
painting."

Alison's breath caught. She stared at him, unable to stop
herself even as her mind told her it must seem by her reaction
that what he said was true and she'd been caught out. But the
only logical explanation for why he would say what he had
just said was something she'd almost given up on. She called
up in her mind the photos she'd seen, compared them to the
striking face before her, mentally darkening his hair . . .

"It was . . . given to me by the artist's father," she said,
keeping her gaze fastened on his face, watching those eyes for
any sign that the leap she'd made was valid. She saw only the
slightest tightening of the skin around his eyes. And there was
only the barest hint of emotion beneath the flat words he
spoke, in that same low, dangerous voice.

"You're a liar. A good one, I'll concede—that was just the right touch of ingenuous sincerity—but a liar, just the same."

She knew then. She was certain; she didn't need to ask, so she didn't.

She merely said, "Welcome home, Lachlan McGregor."

Chapter 2

Lake bit back the sharp words that rose to his lips. He wasn't often thrown so off stride, but this had done it, and he struggled to think, instead of just demand furiously how the hell she knew who he was. And why she was looking at him with such emotion; her face held the strangest combination of awe and joy and relief, none of which made any sense when he'd never laid eyes on her before.

There was no damn way she could have simply recognized him. She couldn't be much more than thirty, which meant even if she'd been born here—and few people were—she would have been little more than a toddler when he'd left town. And he didn't look a thing like the gangly, dark-haired, scared-eyed kid he'd been then.

Nor had he ever been back. At least not to town in daylight, where he could have been seen by anyone who would have recognized him, although he doubted there was anyone left who would now that his father was dead. If, of course, he was dead. If the death notice in the paper was genuine, not just bait to lure him here. But it was so easily verifiable that he had to assume it was true.

It was proof, he supposed, of how icy cold he'd become that the news barely caused a flicker of feeling, other than a slight sense of relief that the last possible lever for the world to try and use against him was gone. It now no longer mattered if he led anyone here, because there was no one left in Jewel with any connection to him. It wasn't much of a reaction, but all he seemed able to manage.

But the sight of this painting, hanging in a window, openly visible to anyone who passed by, had filled him with a rage he'd not felt in a long time, and a sense of intimate violation he'd never felt in his life.

He suddenly realized they were standing outside on the sidewalk, and that people passing by were looking at them . . . and then at the painting. He wanted to smash the window down and grab it, destroy it, anything rather than have it exposed to more prying eyes.

"Inside," he suggested shortly, aware his jaw was still clenched, but knowing it was the only thing keeping him from doing what his gut was screaming at him to do.

"I don't think so."

He stared at her; she'd said it so calmly, almost regretfully, in contrast to that gratified expression on her face. "What?"

"I said no. I don't think I want to be alone with you out of public view just now."

Lake drew back slightly, still staring at her. She clearly thought he was dangerous, and was wary enough of him that she didn't want to be alone with him, but still she held his gaze steadily, refusing to flinch or back down. And he'd intimidated men—and women—far more battle-hardened than she with the look Ian had called glacial.

Or perhaps she was more battle-hardened than he thought. Obviously she was tougher than she looked. Sophisticated, coolly attractive, smooth, charming . . . and with a core of steel beneath the silken surface, Lake thought. He'd seen the type before. The last one had been married to a South American jungle lord who'd kept her in diamonds paid for with the blood of his people.

Although this woman was hardly dripping in gems; the necklace of richly colored, intricately carved blue beads at her throat looked unique, but not necessarily expensive. And she wore no earrings, no other jewelry to detract from either the necklace or the simplicity of her sleek gray suit. No rings, Lake mentally cataloged, including on the left hand. No sign of a recently taken off wedding band on the ring finger, either, which meant she either hadn't been married at all, or it had been over long enough for any mark to fade. But there had to be someone in her life; a woman who looked like this didn't stay alone for long.

Unless she wanted to, he amended, looking once more at the set of her small chin, the straightness of her spine.

He wasn't going to get anywhere by trying to scare her, he realized. Not that he'd been trying. He didn't have to actually try very often; he seemed to scare people with very little effort. But not this woman. She was indeed wary, a bit tense, but not afraid.

"I'd rather we didn't discuss this out here."

"If you're going to continue with unfounded accusations, I'd rather we didn't discuss it at all."

No, definitely not afraid. He reined in emotions he'd thought long dead, wondering what cave they'd been hiding in for the past thirty years. And he wondered at himself, at the fact that he was still able to feel anything this strongly. Strongly enough that he'd been unable to hide it from this woman, when usually his friends, what few there were, couldn't even begin to guess what he was thinking.

Or perhaps she was just exceptionally perceptive. No, he made himself admit, he'd lost it. He'd taken one look at that painting hanging there, and he'd lost it. But clearly, if he wanted answers out of this woman, he was going to have to keep it under control.

"I . . ." He had to stop, swallow, and start again. "I'm sorry. I just want to . . . talk. Can we go inside?"

She looked at him consideringly, as if she wasn't certain he'd really put the trappings of civil behavior back on.

"Please?" he added. An easy enough word to say. Sometimes manners, sometimes merely a formality, sometimes a genuine plea, often issued to some higher power from the depths of a soul. Lake had not used it in that way in years. Not since he had worn himself out pleading with the God his mother had believed in so strongly, and it had gained him nothing. Nor had it saved his soul.

As if weighing his new attitude, she looked him up and down much the way he had her. It was hardly something new. He'd been assessed and gauged by men who had nothing more than his death in their minds. It hadn't even ruffled him. But now he found himself wanting to move before her steady gaze, to shift his feet in a nervous way totally unlike him. Oddly, it wasn't the wariness in her expression that bothered him. It was whatever made her look as if she'd just found buried treasure that made him uncomfortable. And he wasn't used to feeling uncomfortable.

"My office," she said abruptly, and he heard the echo of his own sharp words in hers.

And without another word she turned and walked back through the door that was propped open to allow the fresh air in. He paused for a moment to look at the large oval panel of leaded stained glass that made up the top half of the door; it was exquisite work, he noted, the smallest bits of glass tiny, and the lines of lead thin and delicate. The green of firs, the gold of changing aspens, and the gray and snow of the Rockies all blended together in a piece that delineated nothing yet suggested everything that was grand and beautiful about this part of the country.

Lake felt an odd qualm; he'd grown up in Jewel, and despite the tragedy that had ended his time here, he'd loved it. And this piece reminded him of why, and made him feel the loss all over again.

Jess was right, he thought grimly. *He'd said too damn many memories started stirring when you went poking around in the past. Just concentrate on now,* Lake told himself. *And on the future—and making sure Joplin's was short.*

He turned away from the door and found the woman watching him rather intently.

"Lovely work, isn't it? She's a local artist. She was hurt rather badly in an accident and was back east for a year, in a rehab clinic. That was the first piece she did when she got home. The love of this place is all there, isn't it?"

"Who—" He barely stopped himself from asking who the artist was. It didn't matter. It wasn't likely it was anyone he'd known; the voluble old man at Murphy's gas station where he'd filled up his rental car had gone on and on about all the "artsy types" who had moved to Jewel in the past few years. "Somethin' in the water, I guess," he'd said.

Lake could have told him it went much, much deeper than that, but didn't. The man was looking at him rather oddly, and he was afraid at any minute old man Murphy was going to rec-

ognize the boy who'd toppled his proudest accomplishment, a
stack of old used tires piled in a pyramid higher than the roof
of the old station building. Of course, it had been Douglas's
idea, but—

Too damn many memories.

He shook himself out of it and followed her inside. His
nostrils flared slightly as a faint waft of perfume drifted back
to him; fruity, sweet . . . peach, he thought. A light, mouth-
watering scent that to him seemed at odds with the sleek sophistication he'd seen thus far. The way she moved, he thought
as he watched her walk, could make a man's mouth water, too.

He was wasting recon time, he thought, and made himself
look around instead of at her.

The high-ceilinged main room was neatly divided into three
different levels, each of the two upper levels accessed by
curved oak stairways that looked to be from the same fine
hand as the beautifully hand-carved mantelpiece that graced
one wall. Each level had several pieces of art, and he wondered what the pattern was, what made her decide what went
where and with what.

Assuming she did decide, he thought as she led the way toward the back of the building. She could simply be the bean
counter around here, or more likely, the one looking for a tax
write-off. That would fit, he thought. Some rich woman,
maybe a refugee from overtouristed Aspen or Vail, looking for
something to lose money on to keep the IRS's fingers out of a
deep set of pockets.

She walked easily, confidently, with the unstudied control
of a person in perfect balance. Her stride was long and graceful, her simple pumps with just enough heel to curve her legs,
and not enough to be uncomfortable—or to keep her from running if she had to.

His mouth twisted slightly; it truly hadn't taken long for
him to slip back into the old habits of assessing everything and
everyone by the standards of the dark, grim world he'd once
lived in. It wasn't very likely that the sophisticated owner of
this place in this quaint little town would ever have to worry
about whether she could run fast enough to escape a pursuer,
no matter how many tourists were now drawn here by her

gallery and the others that were, according to old man Murphy, springing up overnight like mushrooms, as people cashed in on the sudden emergence of Jewel as the biggest haven for the arts north of Taos and Santa Fe.

But he had to admit, he thought as he glanced around, she had an eye. Or else she had a buyer with an eye, he amended. More likely the latter; he couldn't quite connect the businesslike, polished woman with the rather eclectic collection of work housed here. From the stained-glass door to the one-of-a-kind mantel, to a painting that seemed too impossibly bright and vivid to have really been done in the soft wash of watercolor, to a whimsical sculpture depicting a standoff between a bear cub and a porcupine, everything had a quality that made it different, some aspect that made it stand out from the usual.

A young woman packing something into a box watched their progress with interest, and since he obviously wasn't a customer or a casual browser, was clearly wondering who he was.

Which brought him back to the reason he was here. He felt the tension between his shoulder blades tighten another notch, and he picked up his pace. He caught up with her at the door to a small office in the back of the main room. Even if she was the one with the unerring eye, even if she was the heart and soul of this unique collection, it still didn't explain how she'd gotten that painting. He didn't believe what she'd said for an instant, which left only some kind of duplicitous method she felt compelled to lie about.

When he closed the door behind them, she raised a brow at him. "Should I tell Yvette to call 911 if I'm not out in ten minutes?"

She was a cool one, all right. "This is going to take more than ten minutes," he said flatly.

"I imagine so," she said. "But I have a lunch date."

"I'm sure you do," he said, in a tone that earned him another lifted brow. While he was sure she was quick-thinking enough to plant the idea that someone would be waiting for her, he didn't doubt it was the truth; he couldn't imagine her going without company for anything she wanted to do.

Instead of going around to the desk chair that sat at an

askew angle, implying a rushed exit—or someone too busy to spend much time sitting—she took one of the two cushioned wing chairs in front of the desk, gesturing to him to take the other. They were cleverly carved so that the arms ended in spread, wooden wing tips that provided a rest for the sitter's hands. The feathers were done in delicate, minute detail, and the regal head of an eagle was carved into the chair's back.

The rest of the office, he noticed as he sat down, was done in the same inventive way, each piece appealing to a different emotion, yet all blending together to provide a total that was fascinating, yet comfortable. As if the care that had gone into the selection of each piece clung to them, and somehow enveloped whoever came in.

It was disarming, he thought. And right now he wasn't about to let himself be disarmed.

"That painting isn't signed," he said.

"No," she agreed.

"How did you know who I am?"

She leaned back in her matching chair. "I recognized you."

"You couldn't have."

"But I did. You haven't changed so very much."

His eyes narrowed. "Changed? I don't know you."

"No."

"I left here over twenty-five years ago. Even if you were here when I was, you were what, maybe five? You couldn't remember me."

"I'll take that as a compliment," she said, her tone rather dry, "since I would have been pushing fifteen. But no, I wasn't here. I opened Phoenix five years ago."

She was nearly forty? He barely kept himself from showing his surprise. He supposed it was there, in fine lines around her eyes, a trace of creases at the corners of her mouth, but those could just have easily been signs of living in the dry air and pure sun of Colorado.

He made himself turn back to the more crucial matter. "Changed from what?" he asked, his voice quiet, as it got when he was deadly intent on getting an answer. She looked wary again, as if she'd somehow sensed this softer, gentler tone was more dangerous than his visible anger.

"Your pictures," she said carefully, watching him as if waiting for him to pounce.

He sat back. He had her now. Surprising how bitter the taste still was. "Been reading old newspapers?"

She blinked, surprised. "Newspapers? No. Why would you think—"

She stopped suddenly, her eyes widening as she looked at him. So she did know. He chalked up the expected reaction, wondering why he was feeling almost disappointed; what else had he expected?

"Oh, dear, I'd almost forgotten. Newspapers. That's why you're here, isn't it? I'm so sorry, Mr. McGregor, that you had to learn about your father that way, but we couldn't think what else to do."

He'd thought she was about to confess that she had seen the old newspapers with his photo—usually side by side with Douglas's—so it took him a second to make the leap; he sat up straight in the eagle chair.

"You had something to do with that notice? The one in the *Journal*?"

She nodded, and he could have sworn the troubled look in her eyes was genuine. "Your father and John Thompson, his attorney, had tried all the other national and regional papers."

"Why?" Every old instinct he had ever had came screamingly alert, and it was an effort to keep the single syllable from sounding like an inquisition at gunpoint. She didn't seem to notice.

"Colin didn't know where you were, or how to reach you."

"Colin?" he asked, his voice even quieter now.

She nodded. "I . . . we became friends, before he died."

He let out a breath he hadn't really been aware of holding. "He really is dead, then?"

Her head tilted slightly, puzzlement crossing her face. "I thought . . . you saw the notice?"

"I saw it."

"But then you know . . ."

"How?" he asked, not because he particularly wanted to know, but to divert her from wondering why he'd doubted the truth of the notice she'd placed. If she was in this up to those pretty carved beads, then she already knew. And if by some slim chance she wasn't, she was better off not knowing.

"It was an accident," she said, her voice gentle. "A fall from a roof, on a job site. He'd always been afraid of that, falling." She gave an embarrassed smile. "But then, you'd know that already."

He did, vaguely. His father had always been hands-on in his development business, down to inspecting construction sites personally. And he remembered his father always being extra careful when up high. And he had reacted rather strongly when Lake had fallen from the roof that time. He'd been worried, he'd cared then . . .

He veered away from the memory. Maybe it hadn't been such a great idea, to come back here.

"The end . . . It was rather quick, really," Alison said. "He didn't linger. But he was concerned about you—"

He laughed, low and harsh. "Don't even think about playing that tune," he said. "Just explain how you got that painting."

"He . . . your father . . . brought it to me, six months ago. For an opinion, at first." He stared at her in disbelief. "I have fifteen years experience in appraising, Mr. McGregor. Before I came here I worked in—"

He waved her off. "I'm not questioning your credentials, Ms. Carlyle. I'm just trying to figure out why you're lying about this."

She stood up suddenly. "I've wanted for a very long time to meet you, Mr. McGregor. Now I'm beginning to wonder why. You're rude, abrasive, contemptuous of someone you don't even know, and—"

He held up a hand to stop the tirade that he was afraid was all too accurate. "Agreed." She looked startled and before she could speak again he asked, "You wanted to meet me?"

"Ever since your father brought me that painting."

"Why?"

"I wanted to meet the mind that produced it."

Oh, no, you don't, lady, Lake silently told her. *You truly don't.*

He leaned back in his chair. He was certain she thought being on her feet gave her some sort of advantage, that towering over him for the moment—she was a tall woman, he noticed, tall enough even for those legs—made her less vulnerable. But he knew too much about hitting low and hard to accede that to her. He merely looked up, faint traces of a cold smile curving his lips.

"You sure you want to stick to that story?"

Her generous mouth tightened. Odd time to notice that mouth, he thought inanely. But it was lovely. Full and soft. But not now, as she glared down at him. "He did bring it to me, as I said. And then he allowed me to hang it. Why do you have such trouble believing—"

"Because it's impossible. My father never cared one iota about my . . . painting. I figured he'd burned that one long ago."

"You're wrong!" she exclaimed. "He was very proud of you—"

Laughter burst from him, cold and harsh. "Maybe that pitch will work to sell your overpriced art, but you'll never in a million years sell that to me."

She gave him a look now that was full of nothing but disgust. Unexpectedly, he found he missed the other emotions that had been there, the ones that went with that odd declaration that she had wanted to meet him for a long time.

"Your father was a kind, caring, generous man. How he ever had such an ill-mannered son is beyond me."

Kind. Caring. Generous. Colin McGregor had been all of those. Just not to his oldest son. Not after that sunny, innocent summer day when with a careless blow dealt in anger he'd destroyed a family. But he wasn't about to discuss his relationship with his father—or lack thereof—with her.

"Just lucky, I guess," he muttered.

The sarcasm only fueled her ire. "And your gift only excuses so much, no matter how great it is."

That made him blink. "Gift?"

"The world will make a lot of allowances for the kind of talent you have, Mr. McGregor. But even an artist like you—"

"I am not," he said as he rose slowly, "an artist."

He'd shut her up at last. She simply stared at him.

"Now," he said, "I want the truth about where you got that picture and how you know who I am."

For a long, silent moment she continued to stare at him. Then she slowly shook her head. "You don't want the truth, because I gave it to you and you rejected it. You've already decided on your version of the truth." She paused, took a deep breath, and added, "But that doesn't change what it is. Any more than denying that the man who painted that painting is an artist changes that truth."

"Is that a quote from Art Appreciation 101?"

"Making jokes about it doesn't change the fact, either. The person who painted that is an artist. A very complex, talented, and . . . unique artist."

He caught the hesitation in her voice, caught the sudden flicker in her eyes, a look as if she'd suddenly remembered something disturbing.

"Or, perhaps," he suggested mildly, "just a little bit crazy?"

He heard her breath catch, and knew he'd struck home. She was more perceptive that he'd given her credit for, he thought, if she'd realized the man behind that painting was crazy.

Chapter 3

"It's just not going to work out. I'll give you a recommendation for some other kind of—"

"I don't want your damned recommendation! You can't cut me! I've worked my ass off for you, I'm the best man here and you know it!"

"You're good, Joplin. In some ways you are the best. But you don't function as part of a team. You have tunnel vision. You don't see the big picture."

He shifted in his sleep, pain lancing through him, but not quite enough to wake him out of the fevered dream of the day when all he'd planned, all he'd worked so hard for, had been crushed and handed back to him by a man too soft to lead the Wolf Pack.

"You going to give me another load of 'team player' bullshit?"

"That's what the Wolf Pack is all about. Trusting your team, and gaining their trust. On every level, even life and death. Especially life and death."

Russell had no real guts of his own, he knew that. It infuriated him that this man was in charge. That this man had the power to cut him—him!—from the team.

"If it was your life on the line," he said acidly, "who would you want coming for you? That bumbling Mexican, Cordero, who can't find his way out of a square room with one door? Your pet, Harper, who might find you but wouldn't have a clue what to do? Or maybe McGregor? Hell, if you could buy him, anybody could, and he'd probably kill you as easily as anybody else."

"That Mexican can fly any aircraft ever built, and blow up

a shoe box without marking the shoes. Jess could track you no matter where you tried to hide, under any conditions, even if he'd never set foot on the terrain before. And Lake . . ."

He glared at Ian Russell, challenging him to defend the man they both knew was already earmarked as the killer wolf, the assassin of the team. The position that should have been given to him, the place on the team that was his by right of superior skills and intelligence.

"If you think Lake McGregor can be bought," Russell said softly, "then you're a fool as well as out of control."

He heard the finality in Russell's voice, knew his cause was lost. "You bastard! You'll pay for this, Russell. Someday you'll pay. Nobody cuts me like I was a second string player."

"You're worse than a loose cannon, Joplin. You're not just ruthless, you're vicious. You're cruel without cause. I don't trust you not to lose it one day, and take that rage of yours out on innocents in some crazed rampage."

He swore again; stupid bastard didn't even realize there aren't any innocents.

There aren't any innocents.

There aren't any—

He sat up with the words still ringing in his ears. Pain stabbed at him, and he swore. But bad as it was, it wasn't the gut-deep pain he'd had before. He was healing. It was taking too damned long, but he was healing. He'd be on his feet again soon, and then he'd work as hard as he had to to get his strength back.

He had time. He was safe here. That doctor he'd picked up outside that hospital had been nearly useless; he had little equipment with him, and was so frightened he trembled like a woman as he bandaged the wound. But he got all he needed from him, eventually, including meds, especially the painkillers. And the world wouldn't miss the sniveling whiner; he probably killed more patients than he saved. He belonged rotting in the trunk of that fancy car of his.

After he dispensed with the doctor, he knew he had to keep moving, trying to treat himself along the way. He found the woman just in time. She was thoroughly charmed, completely under his control. She took him in, was convinced he was a

*cop on an undercover mission, heroically wounded, and was
so excited at the idea of helping him she could hardly contain
herself. She'd probably be crawling into bed with him before it
was over.*

*He smiled at the thought. He'd let her. Because she saw him
as the hero of some brave adventure, she'd let him do anything. He could even hurt her, and she'd think it was just part
of who he was, a man who lived on the edge. He played the
role to the hilt from the moment he kidnapped her in her own
car, and although she was frightened at first, she bought it,
hook and all. Women, he thought, were easy. You just had to
know what buttons to push. And he did.*

*She would help him until he was ready to leave. It wouldn't
be much longer, because he had a job to do. A job he'd waited
a very long time to finish.*

*Too bad; she was attractive enough, if a bit of a wallflower
type.*

Too bad he'd have to kill her when he was done with her.

Alison held her breath as Lake McGregor watched her.
He'd stated it so calmly, so coolly, as if he indeed thought
himself crazy. But what she had wondered about from the moment she'd first seen the painting was what hells had the artist
seen, to be able to portray the range of feeling on that canvas?
What emotions had been unleashed in the wild yet controlled
brush strokes? Had he used acrylics because he didn't have the
patience for the drying time of oils? How did his mind work?

From the beginning she'd been fascinated by the different
layers of emotion evident in the work, in the seeming calm im-
posed over chaos that it evoked, the serenity hiding turmoil.
She'd even named it *Layers*. She'd been just as fascinated by
the mind behind the work, wondering if it, too, was as complex as the painting was, beneath the deceptively smooth surface.

"I thought about that," she said quietly, leaning back against
her desk in front of the man she'd thought never to find.

He was still watching her. Carefully. She saw many things
in those oddly metallic eyes; traces of his earlier rage, cool in-
solence, a predatory gleam—but not madness. She knew as

well, on some level she didn't quite understand, that she was seeing those things because he let her.

At last she spoke again, slowly, thoughtfully, trying to explain why his painting had struck her so hard.

"I thought about it for a very long time. I'd stare at that painting, looking for more and more layers. I'd see how cleverly the light plays up the normal, while the shadows hold the unusual, frightening things you have to search for, like turning over a rock or looking behind a door. And the light itself, that incredible luminescence . . . is it sunlight, or the glow from a raging fire just out of sight? Those downed trees, are those edges too sharp, have they been mowed down rather than just died a natural—"

"And you wondered," he broke in, cutting her off as her enthusiasm built, "what sort of insanity could produce such a scene?"

Making herself hold his gaze, she shook her head. "I wondered what sort of insanity the artist was saving himself from."

For an instant, a moment so brief she wouldn't have been sure had she not been looking right at him, shock showed in his face. It vanished immediately, but she knew she'd seen it. She also somehow knew he did not often betray such things.

What she didn't know was why he was shocked. At her guess? Had she struck close to the bone? Or simply at her temerity in saying it? Or perhaps her temerity in discussing his work at all; some artists were like that, unable to bear any kind of analysis. But she somehow didn't think this man's skin was so thin; again she had that vision of him armed to the teeth and clawing his way through a perilous jungle.

But then, she wouldn't have expected the kind of reaction he'd had to seeing his work in the front window of a gallery, either. She would have expected him to be surprised, perhaps even excited, but never furious.

In fact, Lachlan McGregor wasn't what she'd expected at all.

She'd meant what she'd said, he hadn't changed so much from the pictures Colin had showed her. It was the silver hair that had thrown her off, the hair and the unexpected rage. And the hundred years of knowledge she saw in his eyes.

There you go again, she told herself. *That imagination. No wonder you were so fascinated with the story Colin told you—*

Colin.

Lord, she'd forgotten. She'd been focused for so long on the seemingly fruitless task of trying to locate him, and on what it would mean to her personally to finally find the man who'd done the painting that so fascinated her, that she'd forgotten the other reason why it was crucial.

She had to tell him. She had to tell him, and she hadn't the slightest idea how to even begin.

"I'm sorry about your father," she began.

"Don't be," he said, any sign of his previous shock vanished now, and his icy tone making it impossible for her to continue. He studied her for a moment, then seemed to reach a decision.

"All right," he said, "give me your story. The one for publication, about Colin McGregor giving you *that.*" He gestured over his shoulder in the general direction of the front of the store, as if he couldn't bring himself to name it.

"So you can insult me again?"

"Is it an insult if it's true?"

"This is America, Mr. McGregor. Last I heard it was still innocent until proven guilty."

He gave her an odd look, and for a moment it seemed as if he'd gone away somewhere, as if he were seeing something long ago or perhaps far away.

"Point taken," he said softly. "Maybe I've spent too much time in places where that isn't true."

There was something in his voice that reminded her vividly of her first sight of the painting. She hadn't expected much when the quiet, sad-looking man brought it in to her, especially when he said it had been painted by his son. But the moment the wrapping began to come off, and she saw the gleam of light that seemed to emanate from the canvas, her heart began to pick up speed. She tried to tamp it down, reminding herself of past disappointments when what had seemed to be special had turned out to be ordinary, or worse, a lesser copy of someone else's distinctiveness.

But by the time it was unwrapped and propped on her office chair, she knew. She knew, and her heart was racing with the elation she always felt when she knew she was facing a piece of unique vision. Those pieces weren't always pretty, and they weren't always comfortable, but the sheer power was what filled her with the joy of discovery.

She instantly asked to meet the artist. Colin—although she didn't call him that until later—sadly said he had no idea where his son was, or even if he was still alive.

And now here that son was, in front of her. In the face of his unexpected acrimony, she'd lost sight of how much she'd wanted this day. She wasn't about to let all those months of searching and hoping be for naught. If he was the epitome of the mercurial, temperamental artist—which seemed evident at this point, despite his denial that he was an artist at all—then so be it. If it came in proportion to the talent, then he had only his fair share.

"I told you," she said, her emotions in check now. "He brought it to me for an opinion." She leaned forward slightly. "He *did* care, Mr. McGregor. He cared very much. He handled that painting as if it were blown glass. And when I told him what a prize he had, he was so proud—"

"Why?"

"Because you were his son, of course."

"There's no 'of course' about it," he said, and Alison thought she heard the slightest tinge of bitterness in his tone. "I meant why did he want . . . your opinion?" She stiffened. He saw it, and shook his head. "I didn't mean you specifically. Why . . . any trained opinion?"

She relaxed, and said simply, "I think he wanted to know if it was . . . as good as he thought it was. I told him it was better."

He stared at her as if no one had ever told him of the quality of his work. She couldn't believe that; anybody with any knowledge or background at all couldn't miss it. True, the technique was a little rough, as if he'd taught himself to handle color and texture, but it suited the work perfectly; there were rough edges to the world he portrayed, and it fit that there be rough edges in the work itself.

"He certainly didn't want to sell it," she assured him. "Although I told him he could put a hefty price on it. But he said

no, that it was about all he had of you. Did you really do that
when you were seventeen?" she asked suddenly, still unable to
quite believe what Colin had told her.

"About then," he said, looking oddly distracted, as if he
weren't even aware of answering.

"Do you have more?" It had been the first thing she'd
wanted to ask if she ever found him; she didn't encounter such
prizes often enough not to be greedy for more. "Your father
showed me some of your early pencil sketches, and framed up
and properly set they'd be the perfect counterpoint to a series
of paintings."

"He did what?"

"Showed me some sketches," she repeated. "But what we
need are more paintings."

Eagerness filled her voice now; this was what she loved,
being able to offer the gold ring to an unknown, knowing her
long, hard years of work had resulted in her being able to almost single-handedly launch a career. Her reputation for spotting genius was stellar, she knew with a quiet pride, and she
liked nothing better than the excitement of helping the world
discover an artist who could speak so deeply, so universally, to
so many.

"Tell me what you have ready, and I'll start setting things
up. It's going to be wonderful, Mr. McGregor."

He just stared at her, and she smiled widely. Yes, she loved
this, when an artist who was struggling, had perhaps even
given up—maybe that was the explanation for his anger, she
thought suddenly—realized his dream was about to come true.
Her enthusiasm grew.

"I'd say by fall, if you have enough pieces. We can draw in
the crowds who come to watch the aspens change. Or if that's
too soon, then perhaps before Christmas, if the weather coop-
erates. Just enough snow to bring in the ski crowd, and the
right time for people to think of gift-giving." She grinned at
him then. "And close enough to tax time for them to think of
investing."

She paused, waiting for him to say something, anything.
Not to thank her, she wasn't in this for gratitude or effusive
thanks. Nor was she a frustrated artist herself; she'd long ago

realized and accepted that her talents lay elsewhere. She quite simply loved art that reached her, and admired and—when possible—respected the people who produced it. And was delighted that her eye and her knack for business had combined to enable her to spread that love to others.

"Mr. McGregor?" she said when he still hadn't reacted to what should have been glorious news.

"What," he said slowly, "are you talking about?"

She laughed gaily. "A show, Mr. McGregor. A first-class, A-list show. Champagne, caviar, high prices, the works."

She got up and went to the oak file cabinet behind her desk and pulled out a copy of the press kit Yvette had put together for their last exclusive showing a couple of years ago; her friend and assistant had a flair for PR, and the brochure was impressive. She handed it to Lachlan McGregor, who took it without taking his eyes from her face.

"That's from our last one. We don't do them often, because I'm not into the flavor of the month. But when we do hold a showing, it's special. We promote across the country, heaviest in the West, and it gets noticed. I can pretty well guarantee you attendance of at least a hundred, and we're talking a nice percentage of buyers, not just lookers."

"Buyers." Tension rang in his voice, and Alison wondered if it was just now sinking in.

"I'm not bragging, Mr. McGregor," she said honestly. "It's simple fact that Phoenix has launched more than one artist to national acclaim. Of the three artists' showings we've done since we opened, one is now wildly rich and famous, and the other two are happily working at their own pace and delighted to be living comfortably doing it. That part is up to you."

This time when he looked at her she saw understanding finally register, and began to smile again.

"You do have more pieces, don't you? Do you know how many?"

"You're talking about a showing . . . of *my* paintings?"

"Of course," she said, certain now that he'd just been too stunned to take in the good news. "I'd like a minimum of ten pieces, more if possible—"

She broke off when he stood up, suddenly, as if the chair's

eagle had begun to sink hot talons into his flesh. He spoke, his voice hot and barely controlled. It wasn't even in English, so Alison wasn't sure how she was so certain, but she knew he was swearing violently. She drew back slightly, confused.

"I want that painting out of your damned window, now," he spat out. "He had no business even looking at it, let alone bringing it here, for the public to gawk at."

What was this, some father/son dysfunctional thing she'd stumbled into? Alison wondered. And then it hit her again, hard, the memory of Colin's horrible tale of that long-ago summer, and a family destroyed by the one who had once been its cornerstone.

And the weight of what she had to tell him pressed down on her again. She wished Colin had picked someone else, anyone else, for this task, but he'd chosen her on his deathbed, and left her an unwilling messenger with no choice in the matter.

And she was tired of waiting. All her life she'd been a doer; she'd only been able to get through many challenges and unpleasant situations by knowing she was doing all she could about it. So it was time to do this.

"Mr. McGregor . . . Lachlan . . ."

"My work," he said, his dark brows looking suddenly demonic beneath the bright silver of his hair, "is private. It is not to be shared, with *anyone*. He had no right."

She didn't understand what was going on, not exactly, but she tried her best to get through his rage. She certainly couldn't bring up his father's last wish when he was in a fury with the man over something else.

"Your work is masterful," she said. "It should be shared, people should be able to see it—"

"People," he said sharply, "can go straight to hell."

He didn't say "including you," but Alison felt the implication hanging there as if he had.

He walked out of her office before she could say another word. She sank down into the chair he'd vacated in such a rush. She heard noises from outside in the gallery, but didn't dare look. She simply sat there, trying to regain some calm, feeling a bit like she'd weathered a tornado's passing.

*   *   *

Lake walked down streets that were both familiar yet greatly changed. He ignored passersby, never succumbing to the urge to see if he recognized anyone from his past, and not wanting to know if anyone recognized him. He'd had enough recognition for one day.

Damn his father anyway. He'd had no right to do that, to take that old piece of history out of the attic and drag it into the sunlight for the world to see.

"I should have burned it myself," he muttered, only peripherally aware of the look he got from an elderly woman on the sidewalk. She quickly turned into the next open doorway, which, since it was a record store blaring some rather cacophonous alternative rock, he doubted she had business in.

Hell, for all you know, she's into speed metal, he told himself.

His opinion of his own perceptiveness was pretty low at the moment. He'd thought if nothing else that he knew himself fairly well. It had been necessary, to run with the Wolf Pack. You had to know yourself, and the others in the pack, down to predicting what any of the group would do under any circumstances. It was a big part of what had kept them alive.

The irony of it all bit deep. They'd survived seven years of hellish missions nobody else would take on. They'd rescued hostages from terrorists, children from mass murderers, and the world from biological weapons of the nastiest kind. And now half the pack was dead, not because of the dangerous missions they undertook, but because some slimy politician had had his own lethal agenda, had used them to accomplish it, and then had decided they had to be disposed of. They'd been attacked by their own, from the top, and had discovered that they had still had some illusions left only by their destruction.

But he'd believed all strong emotions had been crushed out in him long ago. He knew others believed it too; his coldness was legendary. He'd cultivated it, knowing it essential to his work, to being who he was, to being the Gray Wolf of the pack, the one who closed in and did the killing.

So he was at a loss to understand his reactions to seeing his painting in that window. He didn't like the idea that he had an Achilles' heel, yet it seemed he did. His reaction had been violent and uncontrolled, and both were against his nature. He never got agitated, never lost control, and here he'd done both.

Jess had warned him that ten years had taken the edge off, had made even his ferocious tracking skills rusty. Lake wondered now if Jess had been hinting that other things got rusty, too, like that icy coolness that came with his own unique talent. He had to trust that it hadn't; he would need all his skills before this was over.

But he doubted he would ever lose the ability to kill and walk away clean. It was ingrained deep inside him, born on the day he'd destroyed his life with his own reckless hands. Killing should move you in *some* way, should leave some trace, but it never left a scar on his soul—because his soul had been lost long ago, long before he'd ever killed a man with official sanction.

So why was he so rattled over this?

It was just that his work was never meant to be seen by anyone else, he told himself. The very idea of anyone else seeing those charred and bloody remnants of what had once been his soul felt like a violation of the worst kind. And that he could feel that way at all stunned him.

And Alison Carlyle had looked at him as if she'd handed him the keys to a sports car on his sixteenth birthday, as if she were waiting for him to light up with joy.

Alison Carlyle.

Her image formed in his mind again, tall, sleek, beautiful, poised . . . with those eyes that gave away the emotion beneath the composed surface. Eyes the deep blue of the mountain lakes, or the sky over the Rockies in the moments just before sunrise.

Eyes that made him wax idiotically poetic, he thought wryly.

Did he believe her? Did he believe one word of her unlikely story? Or was she part of the trap, her innocent eyes and enthusiastic words a front for a conniving, calculating mind?

He knew better than to believe his father gave a damn about him or his painting, but he supposed it was possible he might have put on a front for a stranger, especially a charming one like Ms. Carlyle. But that still didn't answer the question of why he'd taken it to her in the first place.

I told him he could put a hefty price on it.

She couldn't be serious, of course. No one would pay good money for his . . . purging. For that was how he thought of it. A purging of his mind and heart, of the evils undreamed of until seen in the flesh. A purging of the wickedness he'd seen, of the malignancies of the world masquerading as human beings, inflicting their tortures and twisted desires on innocents, until the only thing that would keep the world alive another day was to excise them completely. And permanently.

That had been his job. And then he'd come home to pour the hell out onto canvas, not because it was too much for him to carry, but because he needed to be free of it so he could go out and do it again the next time the Wolf Pack was summoned. Sometimes it worked. Sometimes it didn't, and the only thing that helped was knowing he was doing the single worthwhile thing left to him in this world; enabling the three men who were as close to family as he allowed himself to keep their own souls.

Two young boys dodged out of a doorway at a run, and he had to stop suddenly to avoid a collision. The old pharmacy, he realized; they must still have the cheapest candy bars in town. He wondered if Mr. Grimes was still behind the raised counter, running his domain of white coats and shelves of medicines with an iron fist minus the velvet glove. He'd be about sixty-five by now, Lake thought. Same age as his father . . .

As his father would have been, next month, he amended.

He waited, wondering if deep down there would be at least a small prick of pain. There wasn't. Somewhat reassured that this emotion, at least, was staying nicely dead, he stepped inside.

Once there, he looked around, not really sure why he'd come in. In front of the candy counter was another, older boy, although he seemed more interested in the cigarettes just out of his reach. Lake glanced to his right, at the brightly lit pharmacy area. Mr. Grimes was nowhere in sight. Behind the counter was a young woman he didn't know. He read MELINDA

NORWOOD on her name tag, and relaxed slightly when the name didn't ring any bells either. She gave him a bright smile.

"Can I help you?"

"No, thanks," he said, waving her off.

"Phoenix?" she asked.

He tensed, staring at her until he realized he was still holding the brochure Alison Carlyle had given him, crumpled in his hand. He stuffed it into his pocket.

"They have the most wonderful things in there," Melinda said. "Someday I'm going to buy something. Alison has wonderful taste, don't you think?"

Questionable taste, Lake thought, if she meant half of what she said.

"She volunteers at the elementary school on Wednesdays, teaching an art class. My little girl just loves her."

Lake was wary of anyone who did anything for free, because most of the time he'd found there was a hidden price more costly than an open one would have been. He wondered what her angle was. Wondered what she got out of this. Perhaps it was simply a move to build up goodwill, so people like Melinda would send customers enthusiastically her way. That was the most innocent explanation he could come up with. That he could believe, anyway.

"You like her, too, then?" he asked; as long as the woman was willing to chat, he might as well pump her for what he could get. If Ms. Carlyle was in on some plan to draw him here with the news of his father's death, if she'd been recruited by Joplin, or Duran, or some other, still hidden enemy, she might have unknowingly given herself away to someone.

"I like her a lot," Melinda agreed easily. "She's always so willing to explain things to me, about art and all, even though I'm hopeless." She gave him an ingenuous smile. "And she's done wonders for this town. It's been good for everyone, how she's brought people in from all over, just to see her gallery."

"Is that why you came here?" he asked.

She laughed, a cheerful, unhaunted laugh. "Me? Heavens no, I grew up here."

"Really?" He'd better search his memory again for that name, he thought. Then again, maybe not, he amended as he noticed the wedding band on her left hand. "Is your whole family still here?"

"All except my brother, Ronnie." She paused as the phone rang, but the woman at the front cash register picked it up and she went on. "My grandmother practically runs the place, although my father's the mayor. That's my nephew, Willie, over there," she said, gesturing at the boy who shifted his gaze from the boxes of cigarettes to Lake, curiously. "He's only visiting, though," Melinda said. "But there have been McCrays in Jewel almost since it was founded."

The name registered with almost an audible click. McCray. Second only to the McGregors in longevity in Jewel. Her grandmother must be Althea McCray, the iron-fisted woman he remembered from his childhood. And her brother, Ronnie, he'd been a big wheel in town, captain of the high school football team the year they'd won the conference championship. So this must be the baby sister who had so embarrassed Ronnie when she'd arrived when he was sixteen; everyone knew parents were supposed to be beyond fooling around by then.

But Lake was grateful for the gap; at least she wouldn't recognize him, maybe wouldn't even know about him.

"Mrs. Langley's coming in for her heart medication, Melinda," the woman who had answered the phone said as she walked toward them.

Lake's mouth twitched; how many times had that name been a signal for the pack? Mr. Langley. Mrs. Langley. Either one indicating they were about to get a handoff from the CIA, that the Langley, Virginia headquartered agency had run into another one they couldn't—or wouldn't—handle.

But here, in peaceful, pastoral Jewel, Langley meant only the white-haired, gentle woman who gave piano lessons to all the youngsters who couldn't talk their parents out of it.

"—ready right away," Melinda was saying.

"Good, you know she always waits until she runs out, and that's dangerous for her . . ."

The woman's voice trailed off as she looked at Lake. And he braced himself; she was older, a little heavier, her face more deeply lined, but there was no mistaking Evelyn Grimes, wife of the pharmacy owner.

And there was no mistaking the shocked recognition in her face.

"My God," she whispered, staring at him. "I never thought you'd have the nerve to show yourself here again."

He'd never paid much attention to the adults who talked about him after that awful day, he'd had enough to do to deal with the vicious cruelty of his peers. But there was little doubt which faction Mrs. Grimes had belonged to.

"You're not welcome in here, Lachlan McGregor. And I think you'll find I speak for most of Jewel."

He let her outrage roll over him; it would take more than this to rattle the Gray Wolf. He was aware of Melinda's shocked stare, and of the boy Willie's suddenly increased attention. He looked at neither of them, and spoke mildly.

"I'm sure you do."

"Why are you here? You didn't bother to come back when we buried your poor mother, and we've already buried your father this month past, so why have you come?"

Years of practice in living in situations where the outward betrayal of anything could get you killed let Lake keep his expression unchanged.

"Just to give you the joy of something to gossip about, Mrs. Grimes," he said smoothly. He thought he heard Melinda stifle a sound that could have been a gasp or a chuckle. He glanced at her, nodded, ignored the gaping boy, turned, and walked out.

Hearing Mrs. Grimes say it made it somehow more real. His father was dead. His mother was dead.

At long last, it was over.

At long last, there was no one left to torture him by their very existence.

At long last, he was truly the orphan he'd felt like since the sunlit afternoon that had turned out to be his first view of hell.

Chapter 4

Alison stared at the painting she'd moved from the window into her office. She hadn't wanted to take it down, but she always had a healthy respect for the wishes of the artist.

Even, she thought wryly, when he was barely civilized.

She chastised herself silently for the thought. If ever a man had the right to be . . . surly, it was this man. She should have told him, should have gotten rid of the message that had weighed her down for so long.

"Like when?" she muttered under her breath. "After his outrage at having this one work displayed at all, or after his blowup at the suggestion of a full showing?"

It made no sense; she'd been a long-time supporter of local artisans, and an offer to simply display pieces was usually met with great enthusiasm. And a large dose of gratitude, which she tried to fend off; it should be the other way around, she kept telling them all, but wasn't sure anyone believed her, really.

But she hadn't been kidding when she'd told him a showing at Phoenix could make his career; she had the track record to prove it. She hadn't ever considered he might not want his career made.

I am not an artist.

He'd said it so coldly, in a tone that left no room for argument. Could he really not know, could he really not see what he was, what the man who'd produced that painting had to be?

She would have been willing to consider that he'd been a one-shot wonder, someone who had poured what there was of heart and soul and gut into one piece of work, and then had nothing left. She would have, had she not seen the drawings Colin had shown her, the youthful pencil sketches, the charcoals, all with that same sense of energy and talent, but without the turmoil.

She had wondered what the difference had been, what had happened to change the fledgling talent into pure, raw, emotional power far too stark and grim for a seventeen-year-old.

And then Colin had told her, and she wished she had never asked.

"Ali? You all right?"

Yvette Munoz stood in the doorway, concern furrowing her forehead. Alison had often thought the young woman looked like the paintings of old Spanish royalty with her aristocratic features and thick, wavy black hair. The thoroughly Americanized Yvette herself preferred the image of a fiery flamenco dancer, although she ruefully admitted she was an utter failure with castanets.

"I'm fine," Alison assured her.

"Who *was* that man?"

"A dissatisfied customer?" Alison suggested wryly.

Yvette snorted inelegantly. "Like you ever have such a thing."

Alison sighed. "In this case, it was a thoroughly dissatisfied artist."

Yvette's dark eyes narrowed, then widened with realization. "It was him? Lachlan McGregor? The one who did *the* painting?"

Alison nodded. Yvette was aware of her effort to find the man, although she knew only the surface reasons for it; her fascination with the painting that now sat propped on one of the eagle chairs, and her equal fascination with the unknown artist.

"Guess he finally got the message, huh?"

Yvette was studying the painting, and her tone was neutral. Alison knew she saw the scope of the work, but Yvette didn't understand Alison's need to know more about the artist. She was perfectly capable of being enthralled by the work, but was also capable of letting it end there. Alison could not. She never had been able to. Yvette said it was a holdover from one too many psych classes in college, having to understand the why of things.

"Yes, he did," she answered. "In *The Wall Street Journal*."

Yvette looked at her then, one arched brow lifted. "Not the usual artist's reading material, is it?"

"He claims not to be an artist."

Yvette blinked. Her gaze flicked to the painting, then back to Alison. "And you claim you're just average-looking. That don't make it so."

Alison's mouth twisted wryly. It was good to have friends, she supposed, even when they embarrassed you.

"For as long as you've been hoping to find that man, you don't look nearly as happy as you should that he finally turned up," Yvette said.

Alison shrugged, knowing Yvette read her too well for her to try to deny it. "He just . . . wasn't what I expected."

"Girl, who on earth *would* have expected a six-foot, built, silver-haired, bottomless-eyed hunk with a tendency toward the ice age?"

Alison laughed in spite of herself. And didn't dispute Yvette's succinct—and accurate—assessment. "Ice age? More like volcanic."

"Well, the two aren't mutually exclusive, after all."

No, they weren't, Alison thought. However, most of the good artists she'd dealt with had had an abundance of the fire, but lacked the cool control. It seemed to come with the territory. But she had no doubts that Lachlan McGregor could be as cold as that ice age Yvette had mentioned, if it was necessary.

How different from his father; Colin had been a gentle, quiet man, a man, Alison suspected, who had been rather cowed by a wife she'd gathered was mostly fire and brimstone, and in the worst way.

She was honest enough to admit there had been self-interest involved in her friendship with Colin; she wanted to know about this artist, wanted to find him, wanted to be the one who got him the recognition he deserved. But she had also become aware there was a great sadness in Colin about his son. She had thought it simply because there was obviously no contact between them, had thought it sadness over the permanent estrangement of a family. But it had been as Colin lay dying that she'd found out the real, horrible truth.

She hadn't wanted the knowledge, or the responsibility that went with it. And she especially hadn't wanted to be bound by a deathbed promise. But there had been no one else, Colin had told her. No one else he trusted to make a genuine effort to find his son, and tell him the truth. She was someone who didn't sit around waiting, but got out and did something, Colin had said. And he had faith that she would do this.

Left to carry alone the secrets of a family not even hers, Alison had felt even more compelled to find Lachlan McGregor. She'd had no luck. Neither had Colin's attorney; in his attempts to deal with the will, he had been the one to suggest advertising widely. It had been a friend of Colin's who had suggested *The Wall Street Journal*. It had seemed odd, and she didn't care for Peter Clarkson very much, or the way he seemed to try to manipulate things, but nobody had a better idea. And at least it made her feel like they were doing something, trying.

And now she was wondering if she should have done it at all; there was a lot of anger in Lachlan McGregor. But it was out of her hands now; he was here. Although he'd been right in front of her, and she'd barely thought of her promise. He'd been here for—had it really only been minutes? It seemed as if they'd been locked in some kind of battle for hours. But still, she hadn't done what she should have done in the first instant.

And now it seemed he wasn't going to be particularly happy to hear from her again.

But he would. He had to. She would discharge her promise; she didn't take such things lightly. Maybe then she could work on the rest. After he'd calmed down from whatever had set him off when he'd seen his work hanging in her window. What she had to tell him, after all, would no doubt resolve a lot of that anger he was carrying around.

It would do more than that, she thought. It would, she was certain, change his life. And she owed, if not him, his father that much.

"Ali?"

She focused suddenly on Yvette, who was looking at her warily. "Sorry, I was . . . thinking."

"Yeah, and you've got that 'hell or high water' look again. What are you planning?"

"Nothing."

"Uh-huh. Sure."

"Don't you have to catch a plane for L.A.?"

"Not until tonight. What are you plotting?"

"No plot. Just keeping a promise," she said.

"Alison Carlyle? Of course I know her, everybody knows her. I gather you've already spoken to her? I know she was anxious to talk to you."

Lake didn't want to discuss that, so he commented only on the man's first words. "And I suppose everybody loves her, too," he said dryly.

John J. Thompson, attorney at law—and, Lake thought ironically, a dead ringer for a clean-shaven Abe Lincoln—leaned back in his chair. Lake heard the sound of the flexing of genuine leather; Jewel might be a small town, but lawyering seemed to pay well anywhere. Or perhaps this solid, expensive office decor was left over from a prior life; Thompson had told him he'd moved here ten years ago from Chicago, tired of city life.

And with enough tucked away from his feeding on that city life to make it possible, Lake thought cynically. He knew he wasn't cutting the man much slack, especially considering he was staying late to see him, but he wasn't in a forgiving mood this evening. The illustrious Ms. Carlyle had taken care of that.

"A lot of people do admire her," Thompson said. "She does a lot of good around here. Volunteers at the local schools that can't afford a full-time art teacher, established a market for local crafts that helped some folks get through some dark times. Not to mention having sent careers skyrocketing for a couple of proverbial starving artists. Heard she even helped support one of them until it happened for him."

All admirable things. And probably, Lake thought cynically again, carefully calculated to make her look good in the eyes of the town, who in turn would send every well-heeled tourist they could her way.

"But?" he prompted when the man didn't go on.

"I wouldn't say everyone loves her," Thompson answered after a moment. "There are those here who don't like the fact that she almost single-handedly put Jewel on the society map, right behind Aspen and Vail. We have our share, as every place does, who are opposed to change in any form."

"And you?"

He chuckled. "I'm all for progress. But I'm still a new kid to those folks, too. They don't like me much either, but I'm the only lawyer in town."

Lake wasn't sure he'd equate change with progress, but he merely said, "Monopoly does have its benefits."

Thompson shrugged. "They have options. There's a three-person practice down in Hotchkiss, and several lawyers up in Carbondale."

Lake held the man's slightly amused gaze. "So their dislike of the newcomer was outweighed by the inconvenience of leaving Jewel."

Thompson nodded. "So it seems. I do the occasional civil claim or minor arrest—usually from a drunken brawl over at Callahan's—but mostly their wills and trusts. I think they enjoy dictating the terms to me, that they want their property so tied up no newcomer could ever get his hands on it."

Lake smiled to himself; so Callahan's was as rowdy as ever. He'd once looked forward to being old cnough to go into the place, to partake of that particular rite of passage. But by the time he'd turned twenty-one, he'd been long gone, Callahan's and Jewel nothing but a painful memory. And then, eventually, even the pain had gone, as he'd learned to bury it so deep it couldn't be felt anymore. He called himself orphan and meant it; only Ian had known any different, and Ian had understood.

"Which brings us back to why you're here," Thompson said, indicating the folder he'd gotten out when Lake had identified himself. He hadn't opened it yet, being distracted by Lake's query about Ms. Carlyle, but he did now. "As I said, everything's pretty cut and dried."

Thompson hesitated, and Lake spoke quickly, understanding that this probably wasn't a pleasant position to be in no matter the circumstances, telling a son he wasn't in his father's will. Unless maybe the old man had damned him to hell one last time.

"I'm sure it is. I only came because there was one . . .personal thing I'd like from the house, if that's possible."

Thompson looked at him quizzically. "Of course. I see no reason why you can't pick up a personal item right away. Do you plan to keep the house, or sell it?"

Lake blinked. "What?"

"It's in a good neighborhood, and could bring a nice price, if you wanted to sell. But since you grew up there, I thought you might want to . . ."

Thompson's voice faded away as Lake stared at him. "Are you saying . . . he left me the house?"

"Why, yes. The estate consists of the house and contents, some stocks, a car, and some money, although that's been depleted slightly for upkeep on the property, until we located you."

"Are you saying he . . . left me everything?"

"I understand your surprise," Thompson said quietly. "Your father said there had been a . . . falling-out."

Lake would have laughed had he been able to find any emotion to spark it in him. *A falling-out.* What a fine euphemism for it.

"We hadn't spoken in seventeen years, and I hadn't seen him face-to-face in over twenty. I suppose you could call it a falling-out."

"Yes. Well." Thompson cleared his throat. "He remade his will about six months after . . . his wife died." He'd hesitated, Lake guessed, over calling her "your mother." And wisely decided against it. "I'll need to prepare some papers for you to sign, but you can take possession as soon as—"

"Sell the house."

"Excuse me?"

"Sell the house. And everything else. You do handle that kind of thing?"

"I . . . can, yes. You're certain?"

"Yes. I'll pick up the one thing I want, the rest can be sold. Or trashed. I don't care."

Thompson didn't turn a hair; Lake supposed this was not

new to him. Chicago was a big town, he must have dealt with this kind of thing before.

"Very well. I have people who can handle that for you. The car as well—?"

"Everything. As soon as possible."

"And the proceeds?"

He hadn't thought that far ahead. "I don't know. Give it away."

"I see. Well. I suppose an escrow account could be set up until you decide—"

"Fine."

"All right. Let me know when you have what you want from the house—I'll need to take it off the inventory, of course—and then we can proceed." Thompson cleared his throat rather delicately. "I presume you won't be staying at the house?"

"No." *I'm not tough enough for that*, Lake said to himself sourly. *If I was, I'd move in and make myself live with it.*

"Then where can I reach you?"

An image shot through his mind, of the one place he'd ever found a sort of peace. And suddenly the need to go there was strong. He'd allow himself that, he thought. He'd let himself indulge in some time there; it had been a while.

Still, he wasn't about to advertise it. "I'll contact you in a couple of days."

Thompson hesitated, then nodded. "Please do."

Lake stood up. Thompson held out his hand. For a moment Lake just looked at it; it had been so long since he'd dealt with a stranger on strictly a . . . civilized basis. Then he held out his own hand, warily.

Thompson's grip was firm but not challenging. And after a brief moment of contact, Thompson spoke again. "It's not my place, Mr. McGregor, to inject myself into a family situation. But I think you should know that your father was quite genuine in his . . . desire for you to have everything. In direct opposition to the old terms of his and . . . your mother's wills."

Lake smiled at the hesitation. "You don't have to walk on eggshells, Mr. Thompson. I'm quite aware of how my mother felt about me. I'm sure she excluded me in no uncertain terms and condemned me to everlasting hell the same way."

Mr. Thompson's expression told him he'd struck close to the truth. "Your father said that she was . . . wrong."

His father had never said his mother was wrong in the entire time he had lived at home. Lake studied the lanky man. Perhaps it was the Lincoln resemblance, but he found himself believing his words despite the unlikelihood of them.

"Question is, why now?" he muttered.

He was still asking himself that when he pulled his rented sedan, selected for its nondescript looks, into the driveway he'd run down, played basketball on, ridden a bicycle across, so many times. He'd never valued those idyllic days enough when he'd had them, never guessing they'd come to such a sudden and ugly end.

He used the key Thompson had given him, although he supposed he could have resorted to his old way of getting in, up over the roof of the laundry room and into his old bedroom window. He'd done it many times, in the days when his worst fear had been getting caught sneaking out at night.

He'd known so little of real fear, then. But he'd learned fast. Very, very fast.

He was startled when he stepped inside. Somehow he'd expected a preserved version of the house as he'd last seen it, just after he'd left the Army Rangers to join the Wolf Pack. He'd come, late one night, not really knowing why, only knowing the life expectancy of any member of the pack wasn't going to be anything to brag about. But he'd walked away without even knocking on the door, never to return. He'd seen them sitting inside, looking just as they always had, and he'd walked away.

He'd thought the house would never change. And it wasn't simply naivete; his mother had allowed no changes in her pastel, flowery decor for as long as he could remember. His father had not cared to dispute her authority when she was alive, and Lake had figured he wouldn't have when she died, either. But it was unexpectedly gone now, almost every trace of his mother's influence replaced by a darker, more masculine tone.

It was still somehow bland, yet at the same time, the change was shocking.

It was hard to believe they were both gone. Lake had always carried in the back of his mind, although he wouldn't admit it, an image of them here, in this unchanged house, bonded in the way only decades of marriage could make them, and united in their faith—and their hatred of their single surviving son.

But the house was changed. And his father had changed his will after she had died.

And he was left with that question he couldn't answer. Why?

He made his way upstairs, slowly, wondering if the ninth step still creaked. It did, and it was somehow reassuring. It was only the surface appearance that had changed; the foundation of this house remained the same. Whatever motive his father had had for changing his will, Lake was sure it wasn't meant to please. Pile on the guilt, perhaps. As if anything anyone could do could make him hate himself any more than he already did.

His own room—or what had been his room—was now a giant closet, it seemed. Cluttered with boxes, piles of old clothing, and the accumulation of things common to those who lived in the same residence for more than four decades. A dumping ground, Lake thought. Fitting. That's how they felt about him anyway.

And across the hall was the shrine.

He knew it would be the same as it had always been. A hundred and fifty square feet of space frozen in time, at that moment twenty-seven years ago when a young life had ended. Nothing would have been removed, nothing changed; his mother would never have allowed it. She'd sworn to keep it that way forever, and his mother had never unbent once her mind was set.

The door was locked. It took him barely ten seconds to have the simple lock undone. The door yawned open, and he stepped inside.

A thick layer of dust clouded all the flat surfaces, and he wondered if anyone had been in here at all since she died. His father had told him years ago, on one of the few occasions

they'd spoken before the Wolf Pack, that she alone went inside
on holidays, on Douglas's birthday, and on the anniversary of
the day he had died. His mother had refused, as usual, to speak
to him at all.

He stepped into the room, coughing slightly at the stuffy,
musty smell. It looked as he remembered, the room of a boy
still held by childhood but within sight of adulthood, a boy in
that adolescent stage of discovery marked by science fiction
posters on the walls, but toys still within reach on shelves.
Douglas had wanted to write science fiction someday, had
read the otherworldly tales voraciously. And the books still sat
on his bookshelf, in some order only Douglas had understood,
the one he'd been reading still on the bedside table, another
open, facedown, on the small wooden desk.

He was wrong. There had been a change made.

Lake looked at the picture frame that sat on the desk. The
thing he had come for. He knew the photo it held, he'd had a
copy of it himself until he'd lost it on that Middle Eastern mission when he'd let himself be taken to give the others a chance
to get past the enemy perimeter and rescue the hostages; he'd
been stripped and beaten and his few possessions burned, including this photo.

He'd carried it all that time, as a reminder, as a badge of
shame, as a goad. Taken at a school fair, it was a twelve-year-
old Lake and his seven-year-old brother, side by side on a car-
nival ride, both of them laughing and mugging for the camera.

At least, that's what the photo had originally been. This
copy was only Douglas. Lake's image had been blotted out by
repeated, angry strokes of a broad black marker, until the
emulsion had been worn off the paper and there was nothing
left of him. Nothing left in the photograph but Douglas. The
brother who, five years after this photo was taken, was dead.

The brother Lake had killed with his own hands.

Chapter 5

"You can't have anyone come over here. I can't be seen."

"But my sister—"

"No one. You can't tell anyone either, not even your sister. Especially not your sister."

"She'd never—"

"No one. These bad guys I'm after mean business, and they'll go after anybody they think could help them find me. Do you want to be responsible for that happening to your sister?"

She stared at him, wide-eyed, shocked. Even after the tale he'd spun her about low-life drug dealers and a crooked cop who prevented him from calling for help, all of which she'd eaten up like someone whose sole source of excitement was exaggerated police dramas on television, she could still be shocked.

What idiots people are, he thought. They live in their safe, quiet little circles, and are shocked and frightened when the real world intrudes. They can't deal with it, they're fools and cowards, and wouldn't survive a day in his world. It took somebody special to survive out there. Not the oblivious, soft, naive clowns who thought they were important, thought they did meant something. It meant nothing. Had nothing to do with the real world, where everything came down to power, and the people who ran things either had it or could buy it. Nothing else mattered. And most of the world was too stupid to see that.

And women were the worst. They insisted on believing people were good at heart, that all children are born innocent, and that love could fix anything.

Love.

He nearly spat it aloud. Then he realized her face had changed, she was looking at him warily. He couldn't afford for her to get suspicious, or become afraid of him, not yet. He still had a use for her. He needed this place to hide, until he was back in top shape. He'd underestimated Jess Harper, and it had cost him, but he wasn't about to do the same with Lachlan McGregor. Of all the Wolf Pack, it was McGregor who was the most dangerous, McGregor who was the most lethal.

And it was McGregor he hated the most. He'd wanted to save him for last, wanted to be able to take his time killing him, with no worrying about another wolf coming after him. He would still take his sweet time carving McGregor to pieces, he'd just have to watch his back at the same time. But not too carefully; he doubted Harper would be eager for more, after his narrow escape.

He would have to hunt Harper down later, but McGregor would be looking for him now. And he supposed there would be a certain satisfaction in showing McGregor how badly he'd failed, in telling him how Harper—and maybe the widow and the brat, too—would die because McGregor hadn't been good enough to stop him.

Yes, that might just be the sweetest torture for McGregor. Not that the man gave a damn, he was a killer, just like he himself was. But he'd hate to die a failure. That was unacceptable for one of the vaunted, glorious Wolf Pack.

So he would go after McGregor now, and deal with Harper later. It had perhaps been a mistake to try to work two fronts simultaneously, he could admit that. But when Duran had come up with the plan to lure the Wolf Pack out of hiding, he couldn't put him off, not when Duran was the one providing the cash and the information he needed.

That plan, probably because it had been Duran's and the man was a fool, had fallen apart. But Joplin knew he would win in the end. He could find McGregor. And before McGregor could find him. The man was no tracker, at least, not the kind Harper was. He could follow a trail, but only if there was one. So he had to stay here, hidden, leaving no tracks to find.

Which meant, he thought, turning his attention back to the woman, that he had to keep her believing.

He schooled his expression to a pained weariness. "I'm sorry, honey," he said in the gentle voice that never failed to soften her mouth. "It's just that these men are ruthless, and they'll kill anyone who gets in their way. We can't risk your sister's safety."

He studied her face, gauging her acceptance. The "we" should do it, he thought, even more than the "honey." Women were such suckers for that kind of thing. Let her imagine he was thinking of them as a unit, a couple, implying a future together, and she'd do anything. He saw the change in her, saw the softening, the warmth coming into her gaze, and decided to sew her up good and tight.

"They might even kill you just for helping me, and if anything happened to you because of me, I couldn't live with it." He looked away, letting his mouth twist as if with too much emotion, letting his voice crack artistically. "I've put you in danger. Maybe . . . maybe I should leave. Get out of here, out of your life—"

"No!"

The side of his mouth she couldn't see quirked up into a smile.

"No," she repeated, less strident this time. "You're still hurting, you can't leave. You're not well enough to be moving around. And maybe . . . fighting."

Ah, yes, so very manageable. Useful. For all their foolishness, very useful.

Tonight, perhaps. He would make certain she wouldn't even begin to think of betraying him. She'd given him enough signs, she was captivated, it wouldn't take much to seduce her. He'd learned she was shy, retiring, had rarely dated, wasn't used to having a man around, was a tiny bit scared of them, yet attracted at the same time. He'd also seen that she was thrilled that something exciting was finally happening to brighten up her drab days. And he'd been able to use it, all of it, until she was firmly in his control.

He was feeling well enough. He planned on increasing his workouts tomorrow, to get his stamina back. But tonight . . . well, that might just be a good test of his regained strength.

And finish the job of tying her to him, completely, unquestioningly.

He reached out and pulled her into his arms, murmuring softly all the things he knew she wanted to hear, a scene worthy of the finest of television undercover cops. And felt her go soft in his embrace as she ate it up.

Little fool, he thought once more. She should have run the first time he'd gone to sleep. Or at the least been on the phone, verifying his identity, the minute she'd had a chance. But she hadn't. And in his mind, that meant she deserved what she got.

He couldn't wait to see the look on her face when she finally realized he was really going to kill her.

As he had been all night long, Lake McGregor was in the back of Alison's mind as she unlocked the rear door to the gallery and went inside. But the instant she walked into her office, he leaped to the forefront again; the painting was where she'd left it, propped on the chair he'd sat in.

She shook her head ruefully; for months she'd helped Colin try to find his son. She'd commiserated when each new effort came to nothing. She'd listened to stories of a bright, happy, energetic child with a knack for drawing lively, clever pictures, then of a mildly moody teen, who channeled adolescent angst into athletics and hikes in the mountains above their home and more serious drawings. And finally, this painting, which seemed far too much to have come from such a young hand.

What she hadn't heard then was what had made that supremely normal-sounding boy run away at seventeen. Colin would only say that something awful had happened, and their lives had never been the same.

When Alison had come here five years ago, it had been when Cora McGregor had been in the last stages of her illness. She'd never met the woman; she'd already been confined to the small clinic, after refusing to be moved to a bigger hospital in some city far away from Jewel. Alison had heard people talk, as was normal in a town where everybody knew everybody. And what they talked about in the most hushed of tones was not her impending death, but that the life had truly been taken out of her over twenty-five years ago, when *It* happened. They said it like that, as if it were capitalized, and they didn't expand on it, even if asked. If you should know, you did, and if you didn't know, you shouldn't; if you'd lived here when it happened, you had the right to know, and if you hadn't, you had no business prying.

Alison supposed it was their way of protecting their own from outsiders, and she couldn't say she disagreed with it. It was a far cry from the life she'd been used to in L.A. There, too many people didn't—and didn't want to—know their neighbors, and instead peopled their lives with celebrities they'd never met and probably wouldn't like much if they did. In Jewel, they had enough to do keeping up with the local population.

Cora McGregor had been an upstanding, God-fearing woman, those who'd known her had agreed. A woman who had never been the same since *It* had happened. And Colin McGregor hadn't been the same since she died. And that's all they had to say on the matter, they informed newcomers, inferring that they of course knew all the gruesome details, but were above gossiping about them. Not that that stopped them from saying "Good riddance" whenever Lake McGregor was mentioned. Which he never was, by name, he was just "that boy," or worse, "that devil's child."

The irony was, Alison thought, not for the first time, that it was she, the relative newcomer, who had the truth.

It would be easier, she thought, if she hadn't gotten her emotions all tangled up in finding, not the son who needed to hear his father's last words, but the creator of the painting that had held her in thrall for half a year now. She had known, had sensed from the work itself, that he would not be an easy man to know or deal with. But she hadn't expected the monumental rudeness of Lake McGregor.

But perhaps she should have. She more than anyone should have realized what he would be like, a man who had unfairly carried the burden she alone knew he had most of his life.

And she alone could rid him—and herself in the process—
of that burden.

But to do that, she had to find him.

At least there weren't that many places to check. *It could be
worse*, she told herself as she reached for the phone. *You could
be looking for him in L.A.*

When her calls to the two motels and one bed and breakfast
in town had accomplished nothing but setting the Jewel
grapevine to humming, she had the thought to call John
Thompson. He was her lawyer as well as the McGregors'—
she'd decided it would be good business to use a local man—
and they'd spent some time together when Colin had asked
him to help in the search for his son. So perhaps he would tell
her where to find him. It had been John's business address and
number that had run in the ads, so she was sure Lake must
have gone to him. Perhaps he had been on his way there—
John's office was just up Aspen Street a couple of blocks—
when he'd spotted her window.

Moments later, she had her guess confirmed.

"Yes, he was here yesterday evening," John told her. "I
must say, it was quite a shock when he just . . . walked in and
announced himself."

"And?"

"You know I can't divulge what we discussed."

Alison smiled. "I *know* that, John." They'd probably discussed the will, disposition of property . . . Her smile wobbled
as she thought of Colin; it had surprised her how much she
missed him, for the short time she'd known him. "I just want
to know if you know where to reach him."

"As a matter of fact, I don't. I told him there were papers
he'd need to sign, but he insisted he would contact me." Curiosity crept into his voice. "He asked about you."

Did he now? She could only imagine what he might have
said. John's voice betrayed nothing, but then, he was a very
good lawyer. "Isn't that giving me confidential information?"
she asked dryly.

"No. We hadn't begun talking about business yet."

"Mighty fine lines in your business, John."

His chuckle echoed in her ear. "How did you find him, before he even got here to me?"

"I didn't. He found me."

"Oh?"

"He saw the painting."

"Ah."

"Yes." She left it at that; it seemed beyond her at the moment to explain McGregor's unexpected and volatile reaction. Even to herself.

"Did you . . . get Colin's message delivered?" John asked gently. She hesitated; John knew there was something crucial she'd been carrying around since Colin's death, but not what it was.

"No. There . . . wasn't time. That's why I'm looking for him. He's not staying at the house?"

"No," John answered. "Definitely not. I got the feeling . . ." She could almost hear him debating whether to tell her, deciding if this violated attorney-client privilege. She kept silent, hoping that would tip the scales more than trying to persuade the man. It worked. "I got the feeling that he didn't want anything to do with it. Any of it."

I'm not surprised, she thought. "Thanks, John. Would you let me know if you hear from him again?"

"Unless he asks me not to," he said in his best attorney's tone.

Alison thanked him, hung up, briefly contemplated the oddities of being a lawyer, then turned her mind back to business. Clearly her renegade artist would be around for a while, and she had things to do. Third-quarter inventory was less than two weeks away. And her quarterly taxes were coming up; she needed to transfer some funds to deal with that. Someday maybe she'd turn those smaller tasks over to her accountant, but right now she was convinced they were the only thing keeping her left brain operating at all, so she kept doing them.

She finally got to the taxes three days later. And she still hadn't found Lachlan McGregor.

He seemed to have vanished. He'd not been seen or heard from, by anyone. All she'd managed to do was start a buzz around town with her inquiries. She sensed no one quite believed she'd seen him, because no one believed he would ever really come back to Jewel. This was said in the same hushed tones they used when talking about *It*, and Alison was beginning to find it irritating.

That blazing encounter at her gallery was taking on, in memory, the proportions of a bad dream, and with Yvette gone to visit her family in Arizona, if it hadn't been for John Thompson having seen him as well, she might have thought she'd dreamed the whole thing.

The point on her pencil broke for the fourth time this morning, and she tossed it down in disgust. She glanced at her wrist, and an image of Lake McGregor's big, complex-looking watch, with that odd flap that covered the face, shot through her mind. Colin had said he'd joined the army after he'd run away, and now she was wondering just what he'd done there.

She was wondering, she thought tiredly, too darn much about him. And it was taking too darn much of her time and energy.

She flexed her shoulders, considering. It wasn't quite noon, but she supposed it was close enough to justify lunch. She sometimes forgot, without Yvette here to ride herd on her, about things like eating.

Of course, Yvette's idea of eating was some sprout-laden sandwich on one-hundred-grain bread, while hers was a cheeseburger and fries from the Silver Spoon, the diner half of Jewel's main restaurant. The other half was the elegantly appointed Columbine Room; the fact that they used the same kitchen was a fact the locals carefully ignored.

Her stomach growled at the thought of the fries, and she grinned. While the cat's away . . .

Sure she'd found the perfect distraction, she grabbed up her purse. Yvette always laughed at the huge bag, but Alison sometimes worked so late that she was too tired to go home. Then she slept on the Victorian daybed on the third level, and she needed all this stuff for those mornings.

She'd walk the five blocks to the diner and back; surely, she thought, that would burn off most of the fat? At the least it would assuage her guilt.

Her stomach growled again the moment she walked in and

the smells hit her. Her mind went on alert the moment the sudden silence registered; was everyone really staring at her? That hadn't happened since the first year she'd been here.

Then the usual chatter started again, and she told herself she was imagining things. Although, she thought as Gertrude Langley's granddaughter led her to the window booth she requested—with some vague idea of maybe seeing McGregor strolling casually down the street—perhaps she really had rattled enough cages with her search for where he was staying to cause this.

She had an answer to that rhetorical question much sooner than she would have thought.

She didn't see the man she was looking for strolling along, but she did see a green county sheriff uniform, and the man wearing it spotted her through the window, waved, and headed for the Spoon's door. Alison sighed; Ray Tinsley was a very nice man, and she knew he had a soft spot for Yvette somewhere behind that badge he wore, but he also had a network in this town that wouldn't quit, and she knew perfectly well why he'd zeroed in on her just now. And she didn't want to talk about it, not when she couldn't explain why she needed to find the apparent town bad boy.

"I talked to Yvette this morning. She said to say hello from Arizona," she told him as he sat down, hoping to head him off even though she knew better; Ray was a bulldog when he wanted to be. Or had to be.

He did brighten, though. "Did she? Say hello for me next time you talk to her. She's due back next week, right?"

"Yes. So, are you going to ask her out finally, or what?"

Amazingly, he blushed. It was surprisingly charming on him; while he was in good shape, he was losing his dark brown hair at a rapid clip, and was self-conscious about it, wearing his uniform hat whenever he could, and a ball cap or cowboy hat when off-duty. And he was certain a woman like Yvette would never consider going out with him.

"Don't underestimate her, Ray. Yvette isn't at all shallow. And I happen to know she thinks Captain Picard is the epitome of sexiness."

The reference to the much-balder fictional starship captain

made him blush even more, and Alison thought maybe she'd pulled off her diversion. Ray was a hometown boy, come back to be the hometown sheriff's deputy, and despite the years in law enforcement he'd kept a shyness she found sweet.

"She wouldn't let you eat that," Ray said as her wonderfully greasy cheeseburger arrived.

"I know," Alison whispered. "That's why I sneak them when she's gone."

Ray grinned. It lit up his face, and Alison thought suddenly Yvette would be a fool to turn him down. And then, that quickly, he turned on her.

"Hear you've been stirring things up around town."

She wondered if it was a technique all cops perfected, lulling someone and then suddenly going in for the surprise attack.

"Why do I feel like that should be followed with 'Get out of town by sundown,' Sheriff?"

He had the grace to look abashed. "Didn't mean it that way. I'm just curious why you're stirring up those particular waters again."

She decided to cut to the chase. "Because he's here, and I need to talk to him."

Ray blinked. "It's true? Lake really came back?"

"He did." Her mouth quirked. "Or somebody doing a heck of an imitation did."

Ray shook his head. "He's pretty . . . unmistakable."

"Well, since it has been nearly thirty years since anybody's seen him, I suppose . . ."

She let her voice trail off when Ray shook his head again. "I last saw him . . . maybe seventeen years ago. When I was still in the service."

"Really?"

He nodded. "He'd changed from when we were in high school, the hair mostly, but I knew him."

"The hair?"

He eyed her speculatively. "Six-foot, strong-looking, dark hair with a lot of gray, eyes . . ."

"Pewter," she suggested when he stopped. "And the hair's all silver now."

Ray sighed. "It must be him, then. He was already half gray
when he was twenty-five. We crossed paths a few times when
we were both in Special Forces."

"Special Forces?" She didn't know much about that kind of
thing, other than what she saw in the movies, which she immediately discounted half of.

"Rangers."

"Rangers?" She was surprised; Ray didn't seem the type.
But then she chastised herself for thinking that quiet equaled
weak; Ray did an excellent job as a cop here, and even in a
place like Jewel that occasionally took some toughness.
"They're the real tough guys, right, like the Navy SEALS?"

Ray laughed and held up a hand. "Oh, no, you're not going
to suck me into that debate. It's bad enough my brother was in
the navy and the Army-Navy game is civil war time."

"Do those men usually . . . have a temper?"

"If they do, they learn to control it pretty damn fast." He
frowned at her. "Why?"

"No reason."

Ray was suddenly leaning forward, all joviality gone; she
was facing the cop now, and he wasn't happy with whatever
he was thinking.

"What did he do?"

"Nothing, really."

"Tell me," Ray said warningly. "Did he threaten you, hurt
you in any way?"

"No," she said hastily. "Really, Ray, it's nothing."

"Alison," he said quietly, "don't take this lightly. I grew up
with Lake, and I knew him in the service, but I also heard rum-
bles about where he went when he left."

"When he left the army?"

Ray nodded. "The Rangers are tough enough, but rumor had
it he left to join some private, ultra-covert operations team.
The kind of guys who do the really deep and dirty stuff no one
else will touch. The kind of guys you don't mess with, no matter who you are."

She stared at him, seeing the sudden hardness in the warm
brown eyes, and knowing he was deadly serious.

"You mean he was some kind of . . . spy or something?"

"Nobody had any details. Just scuttlebutt, that a few men had been approached. Only the best. Joke was they were looking specifically for orphans."

Alison blinked. "Orphans? But he wasn't an—"

"Might as well have been," Ray cut in. "His folks disowned him. I tried to tell his mother back then I'd seen him and he was okay, thought she might be worried, but she just told me she had no son and slammed the door."

Alison felt herself pale, felt the sudden chill at his words, and the ramifications of them. And then anger filled her, anger toward a family—and a town—that could have done this to one of their own.

"I know it sounds cold," Ray said, mistaking the reason for her sudden upset, "but you have to realize where they were coming from."

"And where was that?" she asked, her voice sounding as chilly as she felt. She knew, but she wanted, at last, to hear someone say it.

"People don't talk about it much, especially to—"

"Strangers," she supplied when he stopped. "Believe me, I know I'm still an outsider to the old guard around here."

"Well, this is kind of . . . personal," Ray said defensively.

"I got the idea it was more a scandal everyone rather salaciously enjoyed."

He didn't deny it, just lifted a brow. "So you do know?"

"Colin told me," she said, barely controlling her fury enough to carefully choose her words, "what he's been blamed for."

Ray looked puzzled. "Lake admitted to it. And there were several people who had heard them arguing earlier, and a couple who saw Douglas's face afterward, all bruised, and his nose broken. Lake really clobbered him."

"But he was still walking around, after? Doesn't that seem strange to you?" she asked, barely keeping a rein on her temper. She knew she had to, she couldn't blow up, couldn't let loose the words piling up behind her teeth, she had no right. She was bound by her promise to Colin McGregor and she would hold her tongue.

Ray shrugged. "Head injuries are funny things. You just never know."

"Is that what the autopsy said?"

She'd startled him with that. "There was no autopsy. Mrs. McGregor wouldn't allow it. But the X rays they took at the clinic showed a sizable hemorrhage and a skull fracture. It was pretty obvious what had happened. It just took a few hours for it to go sour. It happens."

"And Lake McGregor is blamed for it."

"Alison, I know you're defending him because of Colin, but there was never any question. He *said* he did it."

It was much more complex than that, but Alison let the assumption pass. "Killed his own brother?"

"Well, now, I don't think he *meant* to kill him, you know how brothers get sometimes. They fight. That's why Lake didn't end up in jail." Ray grimaced. "Contrary to what his mother said, the DA didn't believe there was malicious intent. He just didn't know his own strength, and hit Douglas hard enough to make him fall and hit his head. A murder or even a manslaughter charge wouldn't have been fair."

"Fair?" she said, sarcasm dripping from the single syllable. "I didn't think that word was in the Jewel vocabulary."

"It wasn't in his parents'. Or in Lake's, really. He blamed himself as much as anybody, for losing his temper, and striking out in anger."

"And so did the rest of the town. He may not have gone to jail, but they tried and convicted him."

"It's hard to explain, what it was like. His mom, especially. She really thought Douglas was perfect. And she was kind of . . . preachy, I guess you'd call it."

"Fire and brimstone, I heard."

Ray looked relieved, as if glad he didn't have to paint an unflattering picture of a woman dead and buried. "Anyway, she blamed him, pretty much publicly, called him a murderer to the world. And everybody was angry. Douglas was a really sweet kid, almost pretty, you know? He had really good manners, all the parents loved him."

"And the kids?"

Ray grimaced. "Honestly? All those manners annoyed us.

And we thought he was a little . . . simple. But Lake'd take our heads off if we said that. Said Douglas was just smart in a different way."

She looked at him steadily. "Doesn't sound like a kid out to kill his brother."

"He didn't mean to, I know he didn't," Ray said. "But there was no convincing his mother. She ranted on all the time about his evil, and her friends joined the chorus. Acted like they were afraid he'd come after them anytime they saw him. She dragged him to church to be prayed over, and then when he finally said he wouldn't go anymore, she disowned him."

Alison had a word in mind for such a mother, but she kept it to herself.

"I remember that day," Ray said, his expression troubled. "In front of everybody in that church, she stood up and said she was giving him up to his master, the devil. That as a God-fearing woman she could do no less, since he bore the mark of Cain."

Alison's breath caught, and again words bubbled up inside her, words she had to tamp back down. She had promised she would tell only Lake, that he had to be the one to decide what to do with that knowledge. It was a promise she wished now she'd never made.

"Lake just stood there, looking at everyone stare at him. Listening to them call him evil, a murderer, and worse. He left Jewel that night." Ray rubbed his forehead as if he were suddenly weary. "And I never set foot in that so-called church again."

"I'll give you credit for that," she said, knowing she sounded snappish and not caring.

"I don't blame you," he said. "If it had been anyone but Cora McGregor I would have told Lake to ride it out, that it would have passed. But she never got off her holy horse, and I knew he wouldn't make it. I wasn't surprised when he split."

"Sounds like good riddance to me."

"People did relax a bit after he left," Ray said.

"I meant," she said coldly, "to this town."

Ray sighed, that sigh she heard when the locals tried to explain something to an outsider. Something she still was after five years, and John Thompson still was after ten.

And something Lake had been since he'd been seventeen. Never mind that he was a direct descendant of one of Jewel's founders. Colin had told her that his great-grandfather had been a partner in the silver mine that had been the life's blood of the town for its first fifty years, until the ore played out. He'd begun the town, and named it and the mine after his wife.

That history also meant the good people of Jewel had cast out the great-great-grandson of said founder, but they seemed quite able to overlook that.

"Just be careful, will you?" Ray asked. "Who knows where Lake's been or what he's done. And what he might do now. Bitterness can build up in a man."

"Sure," Alison muttered. Right now she wasn't sure she'd care if Lake McGregor took a nuke to the whole town of Jewel.

And he might want to, when she finally told him what she had to say.

Chapter 6

Ray Tinsdale yawned as he drove, glad he was nearing the end of his shift. Staying awake on a late shift was difficult in a town where the sidewalks were generally rolled up by ten, and well put away by midnight. But he felt he should at least be out on the street until then. After his shift, he was either in the station or at home and available by phone. Some people thought he took his responsibilities too seriously, but there was just as many who thought of him as their own personal cop, who should be at their beck and call at all hours.

He made the turn onto Aspen and drove past the Silver Spoon. He glanced that way; it was dark and peaceful, all as it should be.

So, are you going to ask her out finally, or what?

Alison's words came back to him, along with her comment about Yvette thinking the bald Captain Picard was sexy. He'd never thought Yvette was shallow, but he could see Alison's point. It almost seemed like he must think she was, to fear she wouldn't date him because of his hair. Or lack thereof.

Maybe he *would* ask her. He knew Yvette well enough to know that even if she turned him down, she would do it gently, with class. He could live with that.

But he wouldn't like it. He hadn't dated that much since he'd come back to Jewel. At first he'd been too busy, and it was awkward trying to see people who had known him all his life as romantic interests. When Alison had first come here, he'd wondered if a stranger might be better—but then he'd seen Yvette, and quit wondering about anything except how he was going to get her to like him enough to go out with him. He'd been alternately afraid of her big-city sophistication, and drawn by her down-to-earth personality, and the tug-of-war had been going on far too long already.

And then there was Alison and Lake McGregor. Her spirited defense of the man when he'd only meant to gently warn her had surprised him; he wondered if perhaps there wasn't something else going on, or if perhaps Colin McGregor hadn't had some last-minute conversion regarding his son and some of it had rubbed off on Alison. Although come to think of it, Colin had, after his wife had died, gotten off the condemnation train. Everyone had just thought he was too angry to talk about it, but perhaps it had been something else.

He yawned again, then glanced at his watch and realized he'd gone past midnight. And he was already a mile out of the city limits. He pulled to the right, then made a U-turn and headed back, the unit's headlights almost unnecessary in the silver light of a nearly full moon.

It would be after one by the time he got to bed, he thought, stifling another yawn. And he needed to be up early to talk to Charlie before he came on in the morning; the deputy had managed to generate another irate female, a high-powered attorney from Aspen who didn't appreciate his condescending approach to women he stopped for traffic violations. He was going to have to do something about Charlie soon, and he wasn't looking forward to it. As the senior deputy, he had some rank on him, but—

He hit the brakes as a small shadow broke loose from the larger shadow of the buildings on the east side of the road. A boy dressed in dark clothing darted into the alley just past Alison's gallery, disappearing into the black shadows. Abandoning his unit, knowing it was safe enough at this hour, Ray took off after the boy, even knowing it was unlikely he'd catch up with him. He heard a faint metallic sound in the distance, but by the time he reached the alley all was silent. He walked through the nearly pitch-black passageway, listening carefully.

Nothing disturbed the night stillness but his own quiet footsteps. He reached the end of the alley and looked at the chain-link fence that separated the alley behind the commercial area from the residential district beyond it. The fence was obviously what he'd heard, or rather the boy going over it. He could be anywhere by now, Ray thought, and acknowledged the futility of further pursuit alone. Instead, he walked back into the darkness of the alley, as if giving up. When he reached the shadows, he stopped. He turned, looked back the way the boy had run, and waited, knowing he'd be virtually invisible here in the alley, while the moon lit the landscape beyond like a stage.

He waited, and waited, knowing as any trained warrior knew that patience was indeed a virtue, and at its most valuable when you most wanted to forgo it.

His patience paid off. After ten minutes, he saw a small, dark-clad shape dash out from behind a house and head up the hill at a run. Ray stayed still and watched, grateful again for the wash of moonlight that lit the boy's progress for him. He watched until the runner reached the high brick wall at the end of McCray Road. Rather than try and scale it, the boy went for the gate, which oddly—or perhaps not—swung open at his touch, as if it had never been closed.

Speaking of folks who considered him their own personal cop, he thought as he made his way back to his unit, checking the buildings for any sign of a problem as he went, what was Althea McCray's great-nephew Willie doing out at this hour, skulking around in the dark downtown? He knew the boy had come to live with his great-aunt because of some trouble with his father, but none of the details.

Perhaps he needed to find out just what kind of trouble Willie McCray had been in.

For the first time, Lake wished there was a phone at the cabin. Money wasn't really a worry; he'd been paid exorbitantly for his Wolf Pack years and he'd never spent much, but he still hated to think what a bill he was running up on the cellular, and for lousy reception here on this hillside, too. Nor did his gut care for the knowledge of how easily cellular calls were monitored. He kept reminding himself that he wasn't hiding now, that there was no need for a low profile, not when he *wanted* the coming confrontation, and the sooner the better.

But the instinct for the low profile was strong, reinforced by training, honed by years of living in a world of shadows. An instinct that, he admitted, was probably born out of the wish to never, ever have people stare at him the way they had when Douglas had died.

And an instinct that was especially strong here, in the cabin his grandfather had built and then willed to him. It had been too small and remote for his father, and his mother had hated it for the lack of conveniences, the very things Lake liked about it; no radio, phone, television, a propane stove, the only electricity from a generator, and the only contact with the world a CB radio in case of emergency.

She would have hated it even more if she'd known he'd used it, visited it, at least a dozen times in the past seventeen years. He'd come here after returning from the Wolf Pack's first mission, when the reality of the life he'd chosen had been weighing on him heavily. He had found a sort of peace, and after that had returned after almost all the pack's missions. And he had come here and stayed for a very long time after Ian's death, searching for answers, looking for reasons, anything to help him deal with the loss of the man who had been the one to give him reasons.

Since then, he'd come whenever the nightmares got too ugly to bear.

And that, he thought with an anger that was steadily growing colder and more implacable, was even before he'd known Ian hadn't died because of some misstep or bit of bad luck. Before he'd known Ian hadn't just been sacrificed for the completion of the mission, that he'd been set up to die from the beginning, betrayed by a man he had trusted.

He got up and walked to the large front picture window, the one extravagance his grandfather had yielded to in building the cabin. It was obvious why; the expansive view stretching up to the towering Rockies, their lower flanks covered thickly with fir trees that, in a couple of months, would serve as a rich, deep setting for the blazing gold of aspens changing color. Like a handful of yellow diamonds tossed on a green velvet cloth, the patches of aspens would glow bright and beautiful, a last flare of color before the whiteness of winter set in.

He stood looking out at the serenity, wishing it could be absorbed as easily as admired. Before, he had always come here on foot from the south, a day-long hike over some interesting terrain, from the town where he bought supplies. It kept him in shape, and it had been worth it to never set foot in Jewel; the last thing he wanted was to be seen and recognized as the lead actor in the town's most memorable tragedy.

Nor did he want to risk encountering his parents. That one late-night trip had been enough. Odd, he thought suddenly; the last time he'd been here to the cabin, his mother had been already dead, although he hadn't learned of it until much later; it had filtered down to him through a convoluted grapevine that had begun with his old commanding officer in the Rangers and ended with a blue-suited messenger who had thought he was delivering bad news instead of relief; the shrill, didactic presence that had been the voice of Lake's conscience had been silenced forever.

Not that it mattered, really; he carried the echo with him every step of his life. And there wasn't a thing she had ever said to him that he hadn't said to himself first, not a single accusation he hadn't already pled guilty to before the harshest of judges: himself.

A rabbit burst from the brush just beyond the cabin clearing. Instinctively, Lake looked up. In a moment he'd found her, circling lazily on a thermal. The hawk must not be hungry, for she didn't dive; the rabbit had panicked for nothing. A rare enough occurrence in their world. And in his, for that matter.

He stared out at the pastoral scene that hid more violence than most people cared to admit, and wondered again why he found a peace here that he found nowhere else. Perhaps it was because his grandfather had died when he was fifteen, before he'd killed Douglas. Angus McGregor had never known his firstborn grandson was a murderer; maybe that was what kept Lake coming here. Maybe he was trying to recapture the innocence he'd destroyed. He didn't think he was that much of a fool, but he had no other explanation for why he kept coming back. Somehow the pure, golden light didn't seem enough reason.

But he had done most of his painting here, in this place his parents had forgotten existed. They were stored here, those exorcisms of his grim memories. Stacked facing the walls in the loft of this small cabin, where they would stay, all of them, forever hidden.

Except for the one that was now in the possession of Ms. Alison Carlyle.

Tension coiled low and tight in him. He felt like he had on a mission, when there was more than one front to deal with, when the focus on the goal had to widen to include possible flank attacks, when flexibility was crucial, when he had to be ready at any moment to deal with a blindside that might get in the way of the mission.

But the painting, this town—including Alison Carlyle— were personal demons he had no right to deal with until he had taken care of the primary goal. And the primary goal was still Joplin. He could only consider Alison in as far as the very real possibility that she was working with Joplin. Or was being used by him.

He looked at the cell phone again. He'd called all his old contacts, those that were still alive, anyway. No one had known, or admitted to knowing, anything about Joplin now, but had promised to check and get back to him. He'd not bothered to disguise himself with any code name, although he'd had to mention the pack and the Gray Wolf to those who'd known him in no other guise. If one of them was lying, and reported his whereabouts to Joplin, that was fine with him.

And after what Rob had learned, Lake wouldn't be in the least surprised. Ian had been betrayed at the highest level, and had died a torturous death on the Wolf Pack's last mission because of it, so why should things be any different now? Betrayal at every level seemed possible, even probable now.

Ian had been on that highest level. He'd walked the halls of power, and the men who resided there listened to him. He'd numbered heads of government agencies and CEOs of *Fortune* 500 companies among his circle. He'd been tough enough to first put together, then lead the pack, and polished enough to be the diplomat when he had to be; it had been his greatest strength that the smooth, refined exterior hid a core of unbreakable steel.

An image came to Lake, of a man from one of those *Fortune* 500 companies, caught up in an unexpected South American coup, a businessman trapped behind what had once been friendly lines. George Gillespie had been held by the rebel faction, paraded before cameras as a hostage, as an example of American imperialism and a decadent capitalist, a huge bargaining chip in a war conducted in the media as well as the sweltering jungle.

The U.S. government had demanded his release and been refused. When diplomatic channels failed, they'd mounted three rescue missions, which had also failed, rather miserably. When the ransom was declared to be sidearms, rifles, rocket launchers, and one small nuclear bomb, they'd called Ian. And the Wolf Pack had done what no one had been able to do; they'd gotten the man out of the country before the rebel faction even knew he was no longer in the cave they'd had him chained in.

Gillespie had been tough enough, for a man not trained to it, and Lake had admired the way he'd handled himself, never buckling, never giving in to his captors. He'd kept up with them with minimal help, considering the shape he was in after some brutal beatings. And he'd told them, with tears moistening his eyes as they'd landed back in the U.S., that if there was ever anything any of them needed . . .

It took him a moment to get the number, and when he did he dialed it before he could change his mind. Secrecy no longer mattered; half the Wolf Pack was already dead, murdered, and Lake wasn't about to let Joplin get away with that. And he would handle it himself; he had nothing to lose. Jess did. Now.

It was odd to think of Jess married to Ian's widow. Lake had always had a suspicion there had been a past between them before Beth had married Ian, but it had ended there; Jess and Beth both had too much respect for Ian for it to be otherwise. Lake hadn't thought much more about it after that; if Jess was hurting, it hadn't shown. But then, he was the Lone Wolf, and rarely showed anything. Or hadn't then.

What a jolt it must have been for Jess, Lake thought, to get that summons and find out it was from the girl he'd once loved but had surrendered to another man, thinking it for her own good. Probably the only man, Lake thought, that none of the pack would ever have fought. For anything.

But Jess had Beth now, and Jamie, Ian's son. There was more love there than Lake had seen in a very long time. The three of them were a family now, and Jess had reasons to live.

And Lake would make damn sure all of them did just that.

Eventually, through stubborn perseverance, he got through to Gillespie's office. Before the woman who answered the phone could give him the usual spiel that Mr. Gillespie didn't take unscheduled calls, he cut her off.

"I suggest that you give him this message as soon as possible."

"Oh?" Wariness had suddenly come into her voice, and he knew his ominous tone had gotten through.

"Yes. Have you got it?"

" 'A friend of Ian Russell's,' " she quoted back to him, the name clearly meaning nothing to her. She read the number off, then, her voice taking on a suspicious note, said, "And that's the whole message? 'Gray Wolf'?"

"Yes." He read her easily. "And don't write this off as a crank call. I can promise you Mr. Gillespie would not be pleased."

He wondered if she would do it, or if he'd lost the knack of coercion over the phone in the past ten years. He thought again of what Jess had said, that he was worse than rusty, and that it had nearly gotten him killed.

And Rob. Rob who could fly any aircraft ever built, who could finesse explosives better than anyone Lake had ever seen, yet had been taken out by a car crash. A crash plotted and engineered by Joplin.

But Joplin wasn't as good as he thought he was. He'd only been able to get as far as he had because of the rust. He'd never have gotten to Rob, or nearly to Jess, if the pack had still been running. They'd been the best. And Lake knew he'd have to become that good again, to stop Joplin.

He'd have to—

The shrill ring of the cell phone cut off his thoughts. Three minutes, he thought with a satisfied glance at his watch. He flipped the phone open.

"McGregor."

There was a pause. "This is George Gillespie."

"Mr. Gillespie. Thank you for returning my call so quickly."

"Is this . . . really you? The . . . Gray Wolf of Ian's pack?"

He said it as if that painful episode in his life were long past and he had expected it to stay that way. Lake couldn't blame him.

"It is," he confirmed. "The hair's pure gray now, but I'm still the one who hooked that charming guard of yours into his own shackles, choking on his own stinking sock."

The laugh was unexpected, but genuine. "It *is* you. I'll never forget that vivid illustration of the phrase 'Put a sock in it.'" The laugh faded away. "I . . . was sorry, truly sorry about Ian's death."

He had been there, Lake remembered suddenly. "I saw you, at the funeral."

"I felt it only right, to show my respects. He—you all—pulled me out of hell. You saved my life, at considerable risk to your own."

"How did you know?"

"Know what?"

"Ian's death. The funeral. It wasn't exactly front page news."

"I have a sizable research department here at TechCorp. I have several . . . standing inquiries."

Bull's-eye, Lake thought. "I know you would probably rather forget that incident," he began, not sure how to approach a man in this position; that had been Ian's forte.

"I told you then that if any of you ever needed anything I could provide, you had it. I meant it then, I mean it now." This was the man Lake remembered, brusque, to the point, and utterly honest. "Now, this isn't just a social call, not after all this time. What can I do?"

"Ian wasn't just murdered," he said abruptly; bluntness seemed to be the right approach.

"What?"

"He was set up. Not even just sacrificed, but set up to be taken, tortured, and killed."

Lake heard a quick intake of breath. "Go on," Gillespie said.

"The mission he died on was completely politically motivated. A rescue of a man with a high political profile, planned to directly influence that year's elections here, to benefit one man's political career, and build another's."

"Ten years ago," Gillespie murmured thoughtfully. Then, in an awed tone, "Bendegas? That loudmouth who lived high on drug money while his people starved, then claimed he was a political prisoner when they finally rebelled and threw him in his own jail?"

Gillespie, Lake thought, was a very smart man. "Yes."

"Whew." A pause, then, "I'd heard he . . . wasn't functioning real well anymore."

A kind way to put it, Lake thought. When Jess had told him Bendegas was in a fancy nursing home, his mind drifting in and out of reality, Lake had felt oddly disappointed; you couldn't take revenge on a man in that condition. And he wanted revenge—no, justice—for Ian.

"No, he's not. He's . . . pretty much out of the picture."

"Then paint the rest for me."

He was liking Gillespie more and more. "Ian's death was a . . . diversion," he said, "to insure the rebels were distracted enough for us to get Bendegas out. Ian was chosen as the sacrifice because they knew he'd hold out the longest, and that he'd die before he gave us up."

Gillespie swore, low and harsh, and the sound of it did Lake good. "You just found this out?"

"Rob . . ." Lake stopped, remembering Gillespie had only known their code names. "You remember our pilot? He found out. And now he's dead, too."

"You think it's connected?"

"I know it is. They used Ian's son, to lure us out into the open." Gillespie whistled lowly. "If it hadn't been for Jess— the tracker who led us to you—the boy might be . . ." Lake stopped again, but the man clearly needed no further explanation.

"They?"

"The men who decided the Wolf Pack is now a liability."

"But I thought you'd broken up after Ian's death."

Lake's mouth twisted. "That is quite a research department you have there."

"They're the best," he said briefly. "So why did you suddenly become a liability that had to be removed?"

"Because somebody couldn't risk his connection to us, to some of our more . . . unofficial, unsanctioned missions being found out."

"Why?" Gillespie asked, but Lake got the feeling his mind had already raced ahead.

"Same reason as before. Elections," he answered shortly.

"Son of a bitch," Gillespie spat out.

"We've . . . neutralized the two top players, for the moment. But the muscle . . . he's still out there. Hunting. He's a loose cannon."

"Those two top players have names?"

The edge in his voice made Lake wonder if perhaps he should have checked on Gillespie's political affiliations before starting this; if he was in the wrong camp—

"It's Sloan Harvey, isn't it? And his flunky, that smooth-faced, oily college boy hanging on his coattails?"

Lake blinked, stunned at the leap to the truth Gillespie had made.

"I'm right, aren't I? It all fits, Harvey withdrawing from the presidential race when he was a shoo-in, and his sleazy protégé—Duran, was it?—disappearing like that, when a week before you couldn't open a paper or turn on the news and not see him? And it was Harvey that Bendegas helped get elected, with all that 'free the oppressed' oratory of his, when all the time he was the oppressor."

Lake breathed a sigh of relief. It somehow made him feel a little better to know that not everyone bought into Bendegas's public image as the liberated dissident, or Harvey's as the reincarnated father of the country.

"I'd say," he told the man admiringly, "you don't need that research department most of the time."

Gillespie laughed, but it wasn't particularly lighthearted. "So it was Harvey's idea to go in for Bendegas, to assure his election ten years ago, and his little Duran buddy was going to step into his shoes when Harvey moved on to the White House, is that it?"

"Pretty much all of it. Except for one other little fact."

"Which is?"

"Duran was the control who ran the Wolf Pack."

Gillespie swore again, low and ugly, and Lake knew he'd quickly grasped the ramifications of that. "He was the one who set Ian up? All to insure Bendegas got out, Harvey got elected, so he could polish his own political apple?"

"Yes."

"I hope when you said neutralized, you meant dead."

It startled Lake a little, such fierceness coming from the businessman, but then he realized you probably didn't become the head of a *Fortune* 500 company by being a wimp. Nor would a wimp have survived the kind of captivity Gillespie had endured, with his psyche intact.

"No. He would be, if it had been me. But Jess made a deal with him, and I have to keep to that," he said.

"Too bad. But I understand."

"But that's part of what I wanted to ask you. I need to know he's keeping his word, that I'm not going to have to watch out for him. And I may have to use him to get a line on the loose cannon. But I don't have the resources Ian did, and I don't trust anybody in that chain anymore anyway—"

"You've got whatever you need here. I'll find him."

"He could be hiding real deep."

"My people love the occasional real challenge. And something different gives them a thrill, after doing pure business research for too long."

The man's confidence heartened Lake. "I won't use your information to go after him unless I have to," he assured him.

"It's yours to do what you need with. What about that muscle you mentioned?" Gillespie asked. "I assume that's who you're dealing with now, so can I help there?"

"Maybe. He was in training for the Wolf Pack, but Ian booted him off at the final cut. He didn't take it very well."

"And he's been waiting all this time to get back at all of you?"

"Seems that way."

"That," Gillespie said frankly, "is crazy."

"Exactly. He always was on the edge. Too vicious, no restraint. A real 'the end justifies any and all means' kind of guy. That's why Ian cut him. And I'd like to know what he's been doing since then."

Lake heard movement, then a brisk, "Give me what you have on him." He gave what little he could remember, and said he hoped it was enough. "It will be," Gillespie said.

"Thanks," he said. "Anything will help, any kind of patterns or habits."

"I'll have a history for you in a couple of days." Lake didn't doubt it. "Need help with him? I have a really good private security man here—"

"No, thanks. I want to handle that . . . personally."

"Don't blame you," Gillespie said, sounding approving. "But if you need anything, you got it. And here, take down my private number, so you don't have to wrestle your way through corporate America again. It's forwarded to my home if I'm not here, so you can reach me anytime."

Lake wrote the number down in the margin of the notepad he'd been scribbling on. "Thanks, Mr. Gillespie. I—"

"Gil. Call me Gil. And no thanks necessary. It does my heart good to be able to do something for you."

It was, Lake thought as he hung up, probably foolish, but he trusted the man. And he suspected that whatever obscure corner of the world Duran had run to after Jess had brought his slick plan crashing down around him, Gillespie would find him. As he'd told Gillespie, he'd rather the man were out of it permanently, but Jess had made the deal, and he couldn't cross that. It would be enough for the moment to be sure he wasn't going to be blindsided by an attack from a different quarter. If Joplin was as far over that crumbling edge he'd once walked as Lake suspected, he was going to have enough on his plate to deal with him.

It was odd, though, he thought. Joplin, wanting revenge for some slight, real or imagined, he could understand. But Duran . . . to manipulate, then betray a good man who trusted you, and kill repeatedly, just to be elected . . . he didn't, couldn't understand that, couldn't understand what lack in themselves made some people need that kind of power, need it so much they would barter away whatever passed for their souls.

He nearly laughed at the bitter irony of it; who was he to talk about souls?

Perhaps you had to lose it, had to live year upon endless year without it, before you realized that once lost, a soul could never be regained.

He was almost ready to move. He had to get closer, where he could watch. Then all he had to do was wait.

But first he had to get back to his stash of gear. He'd need all the weapons; he'd lost his Beretta when Harper had pulled that crazy stunt of his. He'd make him pay for that, but later. Now he'd pick up the Uzi, and the baseball grenades he had secreted away. But he'd need more; if he was going to play the game right, he had to have all the options open to him. He'd twist that whiny little arms dealer for what he wanted. The man had bitched when he'd liberated that shipment a couple of years ago, but he'd wisely been more afraid of him than of his Middle Eastern customers. They'd kill him later, but the little ferret knew Joplin would kill him now. And not quickly.

But when it came right down to it, all the equipment was just insurance. He wanted his final encounter with Lake McGregor to be up close and personal. With his weapon of choice for murder, his long, lethal Ka-Bar knife. He'd skin the bastard, and keep his ears as a souvenir. And maybe some other, more personal body parts as well. But he'd slice those off before he killed him, and immerse himself in the screams.

The sound of a key in the door warned him, and he quickly got to his feet. Not much longer, he thought. Soon he'd be slashing McGregor's throat. It would be such a rush, give him a thrill beyond any he'd ever known.

And certainly far beyond anything this pitiful excuse for a woman could give him.

Nevertheless, he turned to greet her with a loving smile.

Chapter 7

Had he really just the other day thought of himself as patient? Lake wondered wryly. Hard to believe that he'd once been able to lie in wait endlessly, either to attack or be attacked. Now he'd managed barely a week, and was so antsy that when Gil Gillespie called him back with a report on Duran's whereabouts, he jumped at the chance to do something. Anything. He'd been on the next plane south.

He slung the battered leather duffel bag over his shoulder as he stepped out of the bus into the blazing Mexican sunlight. The bag was lighter than he was used to, but then he hadn't dared risk bringing a weapon, not even a knife, into the country. He couldn't spare the time it would take to explain if he got caught, and the Mexican authorities weren't always understanding.

Not, he thought, that he really thought he'd need a weapon. It wouldn't take one to intimidate the kind of man who fought with manipulation and power plays, with backroom bargains and betrayals.

And he wasn't going to kill the guy, even though his gut was telling him he should. Jess had made a deal, had given Duran this head start and told him never to show his face in public again, and Lake knew he couldn't break Jess's word. But it wouldn't hurt, he supposed, to prove to Duran that he could be found at any time and exterminated like the betraying slime he was.

Besides, he was going stir crazy, just sitting waiting for Joplin to make a move. The man had truly gone to ground, not leaving a trace since he'd vanished from that dingy hotel room. And the slow, steady burn of anger at both Duran and

Joplin was making it impossible for him to just stay put and wait.

So here he was in Cozumel, the once quiet Mexican coastal town now converted to a tourist and cruise ship Mecca with the requisite tourist lures lined up along the waterfront. The global community was represented by the Hard Rock Cafe, the locals by the stalls selling rugs, silver jewelry, and knock-off T-shirts for that same Hard Rock Cafe.

He didn't linger in the commercial tourist area. Finding a visiting American there would be worse than problematical; he was only willing to allot this so much time. Instead he headed inland, hoping his admittedly rusty Spanish would hold up. *"Claro y dispacio,"* he muttered, practicing, figuring if he could just get people to speak clearly and slowly, he might have a prayer. It was an island, after all.

He fought down the ever-hovering memory of Rob, of the cheerful, good-hearted man who had been more than friend, who had been buried by the two survivors of the annihilation attempt on the Wolf Pack. He'd promised Rob over his fresh grave that Joplin would pay. And Duran, for what he'd done to Ian. And if he had to put himself in the role of bogeyman, if he had to haunt Duran for the rest of his days, he'd do it. He owed that much to the men who had become the only family he had.

He walked on, and within just a few blocks, he was out of the tidy waterfront area, peopled with locals lying in wait for the passengers of the cruise ship that had pulled in during the night, and into the quieter, less commercial area. He knew the only thing that would get him what he wanted here was green, folded neatly, and bore various presidential portraits, and he'd come prepared with what he hoped was sufficient amounts. He had it secreted in various pockets; he wasn't crazy enough to pull out a big bankroll in a foreign country. Not that he was worried about being mugged, but he didn't want to waste time dealing with the intricacies of the Mexican judicial system after he took out the unwary fool who might try it.

Still, he was down the price of several parasail rides, and was sitting with a group of laughing fishermen, refusing their offer of yet another beer, by the time he finally found someone who knew something. Surprisingly, it was a big-eyed little girl, daughter of one of the fishermen. The ten-year-old seemed fascinated by his appearance and had asked him if all *Norte Americanos* had such strange hair. At first he'd talked to her because she reminded him of Rob, who'd always been a sucker for big-eyed kids. But when it finally penetrated that she was talking about another light-haired one, who had come here a few weeks ago but did not act like a tourist, he began to pay closer attention; that matched what Gillespie had told him.

Duran had been in a little town farther inland for a while, Gillespie had said, but apparently the isolation had been too much for him, and he'd decided to risk a move. Perhaps hungry for the sight of such people as he had once hoped to govern, he'd gravitated to the tourist town that attracted the occasional high roller and those wealthy enough to travel in style.

Lake looked at the child's father, who nodded and explained that when Lake had first asked, he'd forgotten about the man staying behind one of the shops farther up the road, a place that rented gear for crazy *turistas* who wanted to look at fish rather than catch them.

Lake pulled the last picture of President Jackson out of his right front pocket, then looked at the girl's father.

"*¿Puedo?*" he asked, acknowledging the father's right to decide if he should do this; he'd learned well in many places that pride was a fierce thing. "She has helped me."

The man nodded, a flicker of respect in his eyes. Lake handed the bill to the child. Her eyes widened; she might be only ten, but she knew well the value of American dollars. Her giggle lightened his heart, and he began belatedly to realize what had driven Rob to his many acts of kindness toward children.

Barely five minutes later, he was standing in the back doorway of an old building painted a rather bilious shade of pink, like a tube of deep rose acrylic that had been left uncapped to dry up. He stared down at the man snoring on a flimsy cot in a shadowy corner, empty beer bottles and food wrappers strewn about him like debris from a three-day Superbowl party.

He wasn't even sure it was Duran. All he'd seen were a couple of rather blurry newspaper photos, and this guy certainly didn't match Jess's description. Tall and tan he'd give him, blue-eyed he couldn't tell, but bright blond hair carefully styled, and a body honed in an expensive gym somewhere?

Polished and elegant, Jess had said, making him feel a bit too rough around the edges. But the man lying here snoring ungracefully, his clothes dirty and ill-fitting, one shoe on, one off, his hair dirty brown and hanging in lank strands against his skull, looked like he had more rough edges than Jess had ever thought about having. Nor did he look anything like the smooth charmer Beth had ruefully told him about.

And most of all, he didn't look like a man capable of planning the downfall of the Wolf Pack.

Lake crossed the small room in a single stride, and without much forethought kicked the flimsy cot. It collapsed with barely a sound, just a slight *thwap* and a big puff of dust kicked up from the floor.

A belching grunt came from the man, and a muttered protest.

"Wake up."

He nudged the man with a foot. Another grunt. He upped the volume.

"Wake up."

This time it was a cross between a snore and a snort. Progress, Lake thought. And then, with a tone of command he rarely used anymore, he snapped out a name.

"Duran!"

The shape on the floor went very still. *Bulls-eye,* Lake thought. The man's eyes opened slowly. Blue, Lake confirmed, at least what wasn't bloodshot red. Not that he'd needed confirmation. Not now that the man was looking at him.

Because he was looking at Lake as if the gates of hell had just yawned open before him. It didn't matter if he recognized this man as Duran, because the man obviously recognized him. Recognized him for who and what he was. And that made him Duran.

Duran, who knew exactly what he'd created in Lachlan McGregor.

Duran, who knew what he'd done to bring the trained killer down on him.

Duran, who was starting to whimper. And scramble backward across the floor while staring up at Lake like a man who has seen his nightmares come to life. Lake had been away from it so long that it almost took him aback, but once he realized what the man was thinking, he had no hesitation about using it.

"This is no dream, Duran," Lake said softly. "Did you think I would let you get away so easily? I'm not as generous as the Lone Wolf."

Unintelligible sounds came from the man, terror-stricken sounds. Lake took a step closer, until his boots were practically touching Duran's belly. He towered over the supine man, looking down at him with the expression Ian had described as glacial.

"Oh, God," Duran whined.

"No," Lake said coldly, "but I'll be happy to send you to him. He may have some mercy on you. The Gray Wolf won't."

The man whimpered, and Lake felt a squirm of distaste. This was what had brought down the Wolf Pack? It didn't seem possible. Jess had said that Duran had once been different, that he'd been corrupted by the promise of power, but it was hard to picture. But he knew it had to be true; Ian was no fool, and Ian had once trusted him.

And that trust had gotten him killed.

"You have to understand," Duran babbled, "I couldn't risk being connected to the Wolf Pack, not in politics, I—"

Lake didn't speak, in fact barely moved, just a slight motion of his right hand, but Duran shrank back as if he were wielding an ax. *If this is what the halls of power in this country are filled with,* he thought, *we're in big trouble.*

"Harper said if I just went away, if I never came back—"

Lake cut him off. "You're dealing with me now. And you know what I am, you made me."

"Please, don't. Don't kill me."

Damn, the man was going to start blubbering any second, Lake thought. "Why not? You betrayed Ian. You planned to wipe the rest of us out so nobody could connect you to what you'd sent us to do. You cut loose that mad dog on us."

"I didn't know he was a lunatic," Duran wailed.

"You should have. Just like you should have known I'd never let you walk away."

"I tried to call him off, I swear I did. But there's no stopping him. He's crazy."

"I'm supposed to believe you tried to stop him?"

"I did," Duran said, his voice rising to a pleading whine. "You think I wanted you always behind me? That I wanted to live always looking over my shoulder for you?"

"Prove it."

Hope flared in the bloodshot eyes, and Lake grimaced. He'd never had qualms over doing what was necessary before, but he'd always drawn the line at killing a man already broken. And Wayne Duran was clearly that; Jess had been right when he'd said taking his cushy, powerful life away from him was the worst punishment this man could be dealt.

"Anything," Duran said, the words tumbling out in haste. "I'll do anything."

Lake let himself appear to be considering it, relaxing his posture slightly, rubbing one hand over his unshaven jaw. "Joplin," he said at last.

Duran's crimson-rimmed eyes widened. "What?"

"Save me some time, and I might reconsider. Where is he?"

"He was in a hotel near the courthouse in—"

"Nice try. He left there the night Jess put a round in him. Where is he now, Duran?"

"I don't know."

Lake drew himself up straight again, flexing his hand again. "Your choice," he said with a shrug.

"No, no! I mean it, I swear, I don't know where he is! He called me, and I told him Harper wasn't dead like he'd said. He blew up and that was the last time I heard from him!"

"As usual, he overestimated his effectiveness," Lake said coldly. He could only imagine Duran's shock when the supposedly dead Jess Harper had walked into his office and smashed all his careful plans to bits.

"I don't know where he is," Duran repeated helplessly. "I don't know."

Maybe he was getting soft, Lake thought, but he believed him. The man was too terrified to lie.

"What *do* you know?" Lake asked.

"What do you mean?"

"Where's he getting his info?" The fear that flashed across the puffy face answered him. "I suppose you paid him in cash? And a lot, so he doesn't have to surface to get money?"

Duran rolled over onto his side, as if to avoid looking at Lake any longer.

"What's he going to do next? What was the plan?"

"I . . . don't know. It all fell apart, and he went crazy, I told you."

He should have expected as much, Lake thought. He was back to square one, and this trip had been for nothing. Except, perhaps, to prove to Duran he was living on borrowed time. And to tell himself that Joplin was well over the edge.

Lake swore in frustration. At the curse Duran moaned. He moved, curling in on himself, into a fetal ball. He lay there quivering, and Lake heard muffled sobs. And he knew that stepping on this already half-squashed insect was beyond him.

It wasn't until he was on a plane back to Colorado that he had the thought that the Gray Wolf might well have killed Duran anyway. And he wasn't quite sure what it meant that the man he was now hadn't.

Alison packed up the dancer with the same sense of regret she always felt when a piece she loved was sold. And this had been a particular favorite; the clear, heavy crystal with the graceful, slender figure of a dancer hollowed out of the center, making it a sort of reverse sculpture viewable from all sides, and beautiful from each angle, was unique.

But it was going to a good place; the man who had bought

it had been scarcely able to conceal his delight. His daughter had just been accepted at a premier dance academy in New York, and he'd been searching for the perfect gift. He'd shown Alison a photo of the girl; seventeen, luminous, eyes wide with life and joy, in a dance pose Alison couldn't imagine holding for more than ten seconds. She'd immediately thought of the crystal piece, and led him up to the middle level where it sat on a simple black pedestal, lit from beneath so that the dancer seemed to shimmer with her own light. She tried to do that for every piece, give it its own setting, designed for it alone, to show it off fully.

The man's decision had been instantaneous, and Alison had known it was right. She did sell pieces that were bought for investment, but she much preferred the personal sales, like this one. So her regret faded as she sealed the box, replaced by the sense of satisfaction that was one of the best parts of her work.

Finished with the packing, she went to her office to get the mailing address. And came face-to-face with the painting again.

She'd left it here still, not sure what else to do with it. Colin had told her to keep it, but she knew it hadn't really been his to give. He'd known it too, but he'd been so doubtful that his son would ever show up to claim it that he'd said she would probably have it forever.

And she'd come to think of the painting as hers. She felt a connection to all the pieces she gathered here, but she knew she was only a temporary custodian. But this painting . . . she'd felt possessive about it in a way that was very unusual for her. Which could be painful if McGregor showed up as she'd been half expecting and demanded its return.

But she had to hope he would show up, since she'd had little luck finding him herself. John Thompson had promised to contact her if he heard from him, but he hadn't called. After a couple of days she had called him, to discover that the papers to be signed were still on his desk, waiting. After a week, he had called her, asking if she'd seen him again.

Even the gossip had died down, and the town seemed divided between those who had seen or thought they had seen him and those who thought the others had been mistaken, simply because Lake McGregor would never have the nerve to show his face in Jewel again. And anytime she asked if anyone had seen him, she was met with either outrage or a kindly explanation of why she didn't really want to find him, and they were all better off if he'd simply vanished again. Assuming he'd ever really been here at all; there was only her word and that lawyer's, and they didn't know the McGregors like the rest of the town did, being newcomers and all, so they could easily be mistaken.

"And what about Melinda Norwood, and Mrs. Grimes?" she finally asked someone; Melinda, mother of one of the kids she taught at the local elementary school, had told her about the icy encounter between Lake McGregor and the pharmacy owner's wife.

"Why, Evelyn hasn't said a word, and you know how flighty and silly that Melinda is. Always has been."

Alison was relatively certain flighty and silly were not solid qualifications for a pharmacist, and had gathered that Melinda's occasional refusal to obey the edicts of her grandmother, the self-appointed matriarch of the entire town, was behind that assessment, but she had given up the argument. She had felt a pang of longing for the anonymity of L.A.; in a small town, it seemed you never quite outgrow everyone's memories of your youth. Lake McGregor was walking proof of that.

She wanted to grab them all and shake them, scream the truth at them, and she couldn't. She'd never realized just how much she hated injustice until now, when she had the means to right one, but not the permission.

"Get used to it," she muttered as she dug into her in-tray for the address for the dancer. "The world just isn't fair, never has been nor ever will be fair, so you might as well—"

"Bad day?"

She sucked in a startled breath. She whirled toward the voice.

Lachlan McGregor stood in her office doorway. He was again dressed in black jeans, but this time with a gray band-collared shirt that slightly lightened the dark effect, and his shoulder was propped nonchalantly against the doorjamb as casually as if he'd been expected.

Well, he had been. Sort of, she thought inanely; she really had half expected him to show up, after all.

"You . . . startled me. I didn't hear you."

Nor had she heard the bell—a small wind chime, handmade by a young man from the Special Education center, who seemed to have infused the chimes with his own sunny disposition—she'd adapted as a customer signal. She'd hung it just inside the doorway, and the only way to get in without activating its cheerful tones was to be very much smaller than this man was, or to purposefully squeeze in and avoid touching it with the door. Most people didn't even notice it was there until it rang.

In more ways than one, Lachlan McGregor was not most people.

And right now, Lachlan McGregor was smiling.

"Sorry," he said. "I didn't mean to . . . scare you."

She didn't trust that smile. It was lovely, and gave a new aspect to his face, one she'd not seen, but she didn't trust it.

"I said startled. There's a difference."

The smile widened. Curved creases bracketed his mouth, emphasizing the benevolence of his expression. It was . . . effective, she admitted. If she hadn't seen him furious, she would be charmed.

But she had. And she didn't trust this benevolence.

"That there is," he agreed cheerfully. "I imagine it would take a bit more to scare you . . . Ms. Carlyle."

It was on the tip of her tongue to say, as she usually did, to call her Alison. But the words wouldn't come out, and she wasn't sure why.

"Quite a bit," she said, eyeing him warily.

"I'm afraid I came fairly close the other day. I'd like to apologize for that."

Well, well, Alison thought. *Maybe he's civilized after all.* "Feel free," she said.

He chuckled. "I am sorry. I was . . . startled to see a painting I thought hidden safely away. And one I hadn't seen in years. I'd almost forgotten about it."

She should have been placated. But somehow she was only more suspicious. "You'll pardon me for noticing your reaction was a bit beyond startled."

He straightened up, as if he'd realized this was going to take more attention and effort than he'd thought. Perhaps she was supposed to have succumbed to the charm and the sweet smile and let it go at that.

"It was," he admitted. "I was . . . angry."

"I suppose that's one word for it," she said dryly.

If she'd expected further explanation of his reaction, she didn't get it.

"This is quite a place. Will you show me around?"

She still didn't trust him. But perhaps, if she could spend a few minutes with him calmly, she could manage to get out what she had to tell him. It wasn't the kind of thing you just blurted out, it needed some . . . preparation. It was going to be a shock—although if there was ever a man who looked as if nothing would ever rattle him, it was this one.

Besides, she never could resist showing off her pride and joy.

As they walked, she studied him as carefully as he studied the pieces they passed. She noted what moved him, and what didn't. By the time they reached the first upper level she realized that, unexpectedly, it wasn't the stark, dramatic pieces like his own that made him pause, it was the delicate, graceful works, the bronze and enamel butterfly perched on a single, impossibly slender blade of grass, the exotic fragility of a tiger lily painted amid a bunch of sturdy white carnations.

She thought of his own work, of how the pastoral appearance was so deceiving, masking but not quite hiding the violence and chaos underneath. She wondered if that was what he was looking for here, any trace of his own dual view. Or if perhaps he was drawn by the fact that there was no trace of the ugliness here, if he wished he could see things this way, without the darkness.

Her own words came back to her, when she had wondered what sort of insanity the painter had been trying to save himself from. And she had a sudden flash, a vivid image of an artist who, instead of following the path of others who descended into the blackness, their painting becoming darker and grimmer as their mind did the same, was struggling to go the other way, struggling to rid himself of the darkness and ghastly images, struggling to swim out of the morass and break through to the sunlight.

And you are truly losing control of your imagination, she chastised herself. *He's a talented man with a temperament to match, that's all.*

She led the way up the second staircase, to the level she reserved for the most unique of the collection. At the top, he paused before one of her favorites, an amazing piece of stone and blown glass, the heavy rock serving as timeworn cliff for the pure, crystal waterfall that poured over it. It was an exquisite piece of work, the main stream of glass water holding a hint of blue as it went over the edge, tiny drops of clear glass suspended by filaments almost too fine to see giving such a vivid effect of spray that you wanted to wipe your face dry.

As he studied it, she took a moment to wonder at herself instead of him. While she was always interested in her artists, what inspired them, their techniques, how their view of life was reflected in their work, the kind of thrall Lachlan McGregor had held her in since long before she'd met him, since the moment the incredible light and shadow of his work had reached out from the tattered wrapping and grabbed her, was singularly unusual.

All right, it was beyond unusual, she admitted to herself. It was . . . abnormal. Or she was.

"Beautiful, isn't it?" she said hastily, more to the waterfall than to him.

"Yes."

"It's a Degroot. One of the first of his I ever saw."

He looked at her then. "You discovered him, I hear."

"Yes," she said, wondering just where he'd heard. And from who. And why. Had he been asking others about her, besides the town lawyer? "He's done rather well for himself."

It was an understatement. Degroot had gone on from the

small show she'd launched him with to build a national reputation with his incredible work of combining unusual elements, complete with a touring exhibit that had just left for Europe. He'd insisted she keep the waterfall as thanks for all she'd done, hence the NOT FOR SALE tag discreetly adorning the strand. She had accepted because she loved it; now it was worth high into five figures. But the no sale tag remained, and always would, no matter that some of her colleagues in the business called her a sentimental fool for it.

"I saw a show of his in D.C.," he said, surprising her. "The centerpiece, an Indian warbonnet, was . . . amazing."

She knew the piece, a life-size replica done in copper and beads, Degroot's newest exploration of materials. It had caused quite a stir among the powerful in the capital, and Alison had remembered smiling with genuine satisfaction at this pinnacle of success for her friend.

"Do you go to art shows a lot?" she asked.

Something flickered in his eyes, hardening that metallic sheen, and for an instant she thought of that guerrilla fighter again. She stifled a shiver, wondering what had set him off, if something even as bland as her question was too personal for him.

"When I can," he said, his voice as smooth and even as if she'd imagined that flash of hardness. "Tell me about this place. You said you opened it five years ago? Not many last that long."

"No," she agreed proudly.

"Usually takes some solid backing. Got a partner or two?"

Instinctively she bridled at the suggestion. "No. It's mine, alone, and I own it, free and clear, building and all."

He lifted a brow at her. "Quite an investment. You must have had a nice chunk of change you needed to put somewhere."

"Yes," she hissed, truly irritated now. "My only *partner* was going to be my husband. He's dead. His life insurance bought this place. That's why I named it Phoenix. And I'd give it all up in an instant, if it would bring him back."

She'd disconcerted him now, as she'd meant to.

"I'm . . . sorry. I didn't know."

He sounded genuine, but she wasn't quite ready to forgive him. "Maybe you should think about what you don't know before you mouth off next time," she suggested.

"Maybe I need to go back to charm school."

"Do they let you back in after you flunk?" she asked sweetly.

To her amazement, he laughed. A rumbling belly sort of laugh that startled her with its depth. Surprisingly, after their exchange, she was charmed.

"Touché, Ms. Carlyle. Nicely done."

She smiled in spite of herself. "Thank you. You had it coming."

"No argument there," he said, and when he smiled Alison thought she'd vastly underestimated this man. He could obviously be as winning as he could be temperamental, and she imagined that being around him much would be a constant roller coaster with as many side turns as ups and downs.

"So why here, in Jewel?" he asked.

"My husband and I both grew up in Denver. We had been through here a couple of times, and really liked it. He loved the mountains, especially the Rockies. We'd talked about opening a gallery, and he wanted to do it here."

"So . . . you did it for him?"

"In a way," she said. "But it was for me, too. And I know it's what Steve would have wanted."

"What . . . happened to him?"

"Black ice and a mountain road at ten thousand feet."

His mouth twisted slightly. "Ugly. I'm sorry. You . . . must have loved him very much."

He said it as if he didn't believe any such thing. Whether it was her love for Steve he didn't believe in, or love itself, she couldn't tell. It made no difference to her answer.

"Yes, I did. I loved Steve from the first moment I saw him."

"Love at first sight?" he said, his cynical tone giving her the answer to her question.

"Yes," she said firmly. "For both of us. I met him in college. We knew the moment we both came up with the same sarcastic answer to one of Professor Hoyt's stupid questions. We were never apart long after that first class."

An odd sort of smile crossed his face, a wistful sort of expression that tugged at something inside her in a way she wasn't prepared for.

"Destiny?" he said softly.

"Maybe. We were married the day after we graduated, and we were happy for twelve years, until he was killed."

"Idyllic bliss?"

"No," she said, beginning to get irritated with the string of questions. "It was hard work. A good marriage takes that."

His mouth curled up at one corner. "So you worked at a good marriage for twelve years. And then he died. And you . . ."

"Went on. Is there a point to this Q and A?"

"Just wondering."

"Wondering what?"

"If that was what wasn't fair."

She blinked. "What?"

"What you were saying. That the world isn't fair, and never would be."

She had been saying that, she realized. But for once, she hadn't been talking about Steve's untimely and unfair death.

"I . . . no."

And there it was, right in front of her. The chance to unburden herself. Now was the time. He wasn't angry, he seemed amenable to talking . . . she had to do it now.

"Mr. McGregor—"

She stopped when he held up a hand. "Lake, please."

"All right. Lake. We need to talk."

"Yes, we do."

"Will you sit down?" she asked, gesturing at the restored sofa from the height of the silver boom era that she kept up here, often liking to come here and sit quietly among her favorites, reflecting, thinking, or working on whatever problems were besetting her at the moment.

He smiled and sat down, but she had the uneasy feeling the curve of his mouth was more amused than friendly. Had John said something to him, about the message she had to pass on?

Had he hinted at its seriousness, and McGregor—Lake—didn't believe it, was amused at the idea?

"This is . . . hard for me to say," she began slowly, folding her hands neatly in her lap. But in her mind she saw Colin's face, his desperation, felt the pang of sadness she always felt when she thought of him, and knew she would get it said.

"Don't bother."

Her gaze shot to his face in surprise. *Did* he know already? Had he somehow found out? Was this the reason for his light mood, had the horror he'd lived with most of his life already been removed by someone else?

"You don't need to do this," he assured her.

Alison let out a long, slow breath of relief. No matter how compelled she'd felt, she hadn't been looking forward to what was sure to be a highly emotional scene with a man essentially a stranger. But she was curious. More than curious. Who had told him? Who else had known, and kept it secret? Colin had said she was the only one, but obviously somebody else had to have known—

"I've decided," Lake said.

"Decided?" Alison asked, yanked out of her speculation.

"To let you go ahead."

He wanted to hear it again, from her? "You want me to . . . go ahead?"

He nodded. "I'm sure your pitch is . . . effective, but you don't need to sell me. As I said, I've decided."

Utterly confused now, she simply stared at him.

"That is what you wanted to talk to me about, isn't it? So don't waste time trying to sell me on the idea. I've checked and there are ten paintings. I believe you said that's enough?"

Her eyes widened. "Paintings?"

"As for the sketches, they seem pretty bad to me, but if you insist, you can use most of them . . ."

He trailed off as if only now aware of her gaping stare. She couldn't believe this turnaround, in the matter of two weeks. The man who had been enraged to the edge of violence at the mere suggestion was now offering to participate wholeheartedly in putting on a showing of his work?

"Let me get this right," she said carefully. "You now *want* me to put on a showing of your work? You who are not an artist?"

"Well," he said, with a charming tone of guilelessness, "you'd know that better than I, wouldn't you?"

As she sat staring at him, Alison was sure of three things.

He was an artist, no matter what he claimed.

He was turning on the charm because he truly wanted her to agree to putting on a show.

And he was up to a lot more than just that.

Chapter 8

This had been ridiculously easy, he thought. He'd barely been in town an hour before he overheard two old biddies gossiping, expressing their shock that the town disgrace had returned. No welcome prodigal son was Lake McGregor, it seemed.

He barely managed to keep from laughing; this was a benefit he hadn't anticipated, that McGregor coming home would mean he'd be subjected to ridicule and humiliation. How fitting, after what he himself had been through.

The old rage rose in him. He'd been the perfect one for the job, he could have done it so much better. The Wolf Pack had needed somebody who could kill whoever and whenever necessary, not somebody who had to know it was right.

He quashed the feelings thoughts of Ian Russell always caused. He'd wanted to be the one who killed him, and it was a constant annoyance that fate and that idiot Duran had taken that away from him. True, it was amusing to know that Russell had been set up to die like a sacrificial lamb, and that the Wolf Pack had been too dumb and naive to figure it out and save him. And the sweetest of ironies was that he'd died for the sake of getting Duran's boss elected, and putting Duran into the position of power that had enabled him to order the rest of the pack killed.

Joplin would have done that killing on his own, sooner, but the surviving members of the Wolf Pack had hidden deep and well. But eventually, when it suited his plans for his own political career, Duran had supplied what he'd needed to lure them out into the open. And the fool had never realized he was being used; Duran had thought he was using him.

He shook his head; he had to focus. Right now the goal was Lake McGregor. And it wouldn't do to underestimate the man. He had survived seven years with the Wolf Pack, seven years of dangerous and rough missions. And they'd both had the same training, the best the American taxpayer's dollar could buy, although the fools had no idea that along with the Special Forces, FBI, CIA, and dozens of spin-off little agencies, they'd been paying for the training of a team their beloved bureaucrats had no control over.

Fury spiked through him again, violently. He'd been reduced to a life well beneath his talents and intelligence. Working for slime, when by rights he should have been the hero, the kind those stuffed shirts looked up to, the kind they had to turn to when nothing else worked. Like the Wolf Pack had been.

He tamped down his rage. He needed to save it, hoard it, let it build. He would unleash it only at the right time.

He would unleash it on Lake McGregor.

"Why?"

Without answering her question Lake watched her, as he had been, albeit surreptitiously, since he'd come back to Phoenix. He'd been struck with several things; she loved this place, it was she who had the brilliant eye for distinctive art, she was rightfully proud of her accomplishment in opening this place and keeping it going for five years in a very itty business . . . and she didn't like anyone assuming she must have had help to do it.

He hadn't assumed that, really; he'd just wanted to see her reaction. She had been testy, but not enraged; she'd taken it personally, not as a testament to his view of women in general. He wasn't quite sure if that was good or bad; what skill he'd had at interpreting women's reactions was rusty at best.

She was sure of herself, but not arrogant, pleasant but not ingratiating, poised but not cold, quiet but not a pushover. And she wasn't quite beautiful, but somehow it didn't matter; it all came together in a way that made actual looks irrelevant. Any man with a brain stem would see that the most important thing about her was a lively, crackling intelligence. This was not a woman to be taken lightly, she would demand as much as she would give. And the man she chose to give to would have to know it would be well worth the effort it would take to keep up with her on all levels. He would have to—

He reined in his wayward thoughts, startled by the direction they'd taken. He didn't think about women that way, not anymore, they had no part in his life except in passing, small islands of human contact in the barren sea of his life. He'd lived with one once, Rachel, back in . . . he couldn't remember when. It was years before the Wolf Pack, anyway, when his life could have almost passed for normal. They'd lasted two years, before he'd been transferred overseas and she'd told him she liked him a lot, but not enough to continue moving around at the army's whim. He'd thought once later that if she thought the army was a bit abrupt with changing locations, she should have seen the Wolf Pack's pack-a-bag-and-run operation.

It hadn't been particularly painful to watch her go; he'd expected her to leave him a lot sooner than she had. Everyone did. As if they could sense what he was, as if some instinct told them they should get away from him, because he was corrupt, evil—

"Why?" Alison asked again. "Why the turnaround?"

He dragged himself back to the present; it wasn't like him to go woolgathering, either. Memories, he thought. Just like Jess had said, they were a distraction he couldn't afford.

"I got to thinking about what you said."

"You barely *listened* to what I said."

No, she was no pushover. "I did, no matter what it seemed like," he said. "I told you, I was just startled . . . and angry, to see that painting in your window. I never thought of it as . . . art. At least, not the kind you deal in."

"Why angry?"

He considered his answer. She was smart, too smart to be fooled by a facile lie. He was going to have to give her at least part of the truth. Probably a lot of the truth. As much as he could stand, anyway. And if it turned out he'd spilled his guts to the enemy, so be it. It was a price he'd just have to pay to get the job done.

"Because . . . my painting has always been a very, very private thing. For myself alone. Not for . . . the world to stare at. Not for anyone to stare at."

He couldn't quite keep the loathing of the idea from his voice, and she didn't miss it. But to his surprise, she didn't ask the logical next question: *Then why the showing?* Instead she said softly, "You said you never thought of it as art . . . so what is your painting to you?"

He couldn't *do* this, he thought. Somehow he who thought himself immune to such human turmoil, to the deep tear of emotions like this, was feeling caught in the steel jaws of a trap. And he suddenly understood why the wolf of legend and lore had been known to gnaw off its own foot to escape.

Why couldn't she just be happy that he'd agreed? It was what she'd wanted, wasn't it? Why did she have to probe like this, dig where she wasn't wanted, where he didn't want anyone, couldn't allow anyone, especially someone as perceptive as she?

But she remained quiet, waiting, and the pressure of the silence built up. If she was in league with Joplin, she was damn good. Or as he'd suspected in Mexico, he had truly forgotten everything he'd ever known about patience. With the Wolf Pack he'd spent hours on end waiting in tense silence, in much more dangerous places than here, and had never broken. Yet now, with her beside him, he couldn't stand it another moment.

Or maybe, he thought wryly, there *wasn't* a more dangerous place than here.

"Catharsis," he said suddenly.

Alison only nodded, as if his belated answer was only what she'd expected. "You're not the only person in the world who needs that kind of help, Lake, that kind of . . . cleansing of the soul, ridding it of ugliness. And your paintings will speak to those people, in a way no simpler work could."

"If they still have their souls, they don't need it . . . and if they don't, it won't help."

The words came from him in a rush, and he listened to them in shock even as he spoke them, wondering where in the depths of his hell they had risen from, and what quirk of his twisted psyche had let them escape.

For a long moment she stared at him, and there was such pain and sympathy in her eyes it made him shiver inside, as if he'd been given a load too heavy to carry. How could she look like that, if she was helping Joplin? But he didn't want her sympathy, and he sure as hell didn't want her pity. Even if—especially if—she was just what she seemed. She must know what he was, what he'd done—everybody in Jewel did—and this was her do-gooder way of offering help, he supposed. He didn't want her help, either, this had been a stupid idea, he'd think of something else, some other way—

But he'd spent days and sleepless nights trying to think of an alternative plan, and he hadn't come up with one. His desperation trip to Mexico hadn't yielded Joplin's current whereabouts. Which meant one of three things. Joplin could be dead—but Lake didn't believe in that much luck. Two, he'd given up the idea of annihilating the Wolf Pack and was running—Lake didn't believe that, either; he was too viciously determined. Third and most likely, he was holed up somewhere and not moving at all. And he wouldn't emerge until he was ready, until he was sure he could take Lake on and win.

And Lake wasn't about to give him that time. He needed whatever advantage he could get to offset his own rustiness. He had to make Joplin come out now, had to present him with an opportunity he didn't dare pass up. And if later there were others who wanted to come after the Wolf Pack after all this time, then they'd just have to deal with it. He was tired of hiding anyway, and he knew Jess was, too.

So he would stand out in the open and dare the man to come after him.

And despite his efforts, he hadn't been able to come up with a better way to do it than this.

He stood up suddenly. "Do you want to do the showing or not?"

"Of course I do, but—"

"All right, here are the parameters." He began to tick the items off. "It has to be as soon as possible."

For a moment he had the thought that perhaps dictating to her was not the best approach; from her expression he wondered if she was going to tell him in no uncertain terms what he could do with his parameters. But she seemed to conquer the urge, and after a bit of consideration, answered him.

"Six weeks. A month if we push."

It had to be sooner. He had to have this wrapped up by the time Jess and Beth came back, otherwise there would be no stopping Jess from joining in the hunt. He didn't want that. Both Jess and Beth had found something he never would, and he wanted them to live long and enjoy it.

"Not soon enough," he told Alison.

She lifted a brow at him. She had, he thought, a very expressive face. And she was clearly expressing doubts about him right now.

"All right. The bottom line is three weeks. It will cut down on attendance, because even if we jam, people will only have two weeks notice. A lot of the high rollers I deal with often aren't able to be that flexible in their scheduling. And that's not much time for word to get out to others."

"That doesn't matter." Nothing and no one mattered, Lake added silently, except that one particular person got word. And came. "You won't get much turnout from around here, anyway. And certainly not in Jewel."

"That's what you think," she said dryly. "They'll show up because they're ragingly curious. And because they'll want to see if you dare show up yourself."

She had a point, he thought. And he almost gave it up right there; the thought of the population of Jewel gaping at his paintings turned his stomach. But before he could put it into words, she was going on.

"That also means we have to get ready in a rush, design the setting, the lighting, work on framing, and matting—I assume they're not framed?"

"No." He hadn't thought of any of this, he'd had some vague idea that you just hung the stuff up on the wall and opened the doors.

"Those will have to be picked carefully. I'll have to see them to decide if they should all be different, or similar. We'll need to come up with the right arrangement, what order the guest should see them in, and arrange the floor plan accordingly with the portable display walls."

Ian had always said go to the experts, Lake thought, feeling a little numbed by the flood of details he'd never considered. It seemed he'd done just that.

"All right, what else?" she said. "I assume there's more on your list of . . . parameters?"

He ignored the edge of sarcasm in her voice. "It's to be small, as few as you can reasonably build a show around. As I said, you can have most of the sketches; I'll pull the ones I don't want used."

That was reasonable, he thought. Most of the sketches were harmless, full of early images from his childhood that were meaningless now.

"I see," Alison said, sounding rather amused now, which irritated him. She also remained sitting, when most people's instinct would have been to stand, to be more on his level. But Alison Carlyle didn't seem to react in any normal way. And he didn't like that.

He ignored the unfamiliar reaction and went on. "I want full regional press, especially in the Southwest. Including my name and a photo. And if you can manage it, a bit in the national papers, too. The same ones you used to announce my father's death."

He said it without change in expression or tone, but he saw the flicker of sadness in her eyes. It surprised him; she really had liked Colin, he thought.

"I don't know that *The Wall Street Journal* runs to local art show publicity," she said mildly.

"Think of something," he said brusquely. He knew she was getting warier by the minute, despite her calm tone, but he wanted out of here, now.

"I'll check. Anything else?" she asked in the tone of a person indulging another's outrageous list of demands.

"Yes," he said, knowing this would be the toughest part. "Nothing's for sale."

She drew back a little, staring at him. "Excuse me?"

"You heard me."

She stood up then. It was a smooth, easy movement that made him appreciate her fluid grace.

"Then I suggest, Mr. McGregor," she said coolly, emphasis

on the name, as if to point out he no longer deserved the familiarity of a first-name basis, "that you contact a museum. I'm in business."

She turned and walked toward the stairway. Lake stared after her, not quite sure what to do now. "I thought you wanted to do this," he said.

She halted. She turned slowly. She looked steadily at him. "I think your work is very powerful, and should be shared. I think people deserve, perhaps even need to see it."

He just managed to keep from grimacing at the thought. She went on as if she hadn't noticed, but he wasn't fooled; that expressive face told him she missed little, and was uncomfortably good at reading reactions.

"Over the years I've developed a lot of patience with artists' quirks and idiosyncrasies, which are innumerable. I can also understand the ideals that cause reluctance to sell one's art. There are grants of all kinds to enable those artists to keep working, although I tend to think that's merely a different way of selling."

Her honesty was refreshing, he thought; too many people kidded themselves, thinking that being one step away from what they were trying to avoid was enough, when in reality they'd only changed the course, not the destination.

"It's not ideals," he muttered.

She shrugged. "My goal is to help artists who want to make a living at it. Who want to be free to do as they see fit, and rise or fall on their best work. And that means selling."

"I . . . can't."

He was horrified at how broken the words sounded, at how shaken his voice was. But he couldn't call them back.

"Then you truly do need a museum, Mr. McGregor," she repeated, more gently this time. "It would take some time, but I'm sure you could find one—"

"It has to be now."

For a long silent moment she just looked at him. "Why do I get the feeling," she said finally, "that there's something going on here that has nothing to do with your work?"

Not this work, anyway, he thought as he warned himself once more that he was clearly dealing with a very perceptive person, as some part of his mind was registering that this was not the way a partner of Joplin's would react. He sensed if he denied there was anything else going on, she'd walk away. She had that much faith in her instincts—and apparently rightfully so. And he couldn't afford for her to quit on him now.

"It's nothing you need to worry about," he said instead.

"I don't like flying blind, Mr. McGregor."

And he didn't like the formal way she was addressing him; he liked it much better when she'd been calling him Lake. Then he realized he didn't like that he liked it, and gave up the ridiculous train of thought.

"It's nothing to do with the showing," he said. And that was true; he would head Joplin off before he ever got that far. The moment he got near Jewel, he would take him out the quickest, quietest, most effective way possible. With a little luck, before he ever even got anywhere close to Phoenix.

She stood watching him, waiting. And he had the thought that he'd faced armed men who wouldn't look him in the eye like this.

"All right," he said suddenly, knowing he had little choice. "Price tags. On some." It didn't really matter, he told himself. Nobody would shell out good money for his visions of hell at a masquerade. Besides, the worst was already a given: having the darkness within him displayed for eyes that could never understand.

"I still don't like flying blind," she said softly, and he knew she'd recognized his diversion for what it was. "But you have the right to control this, to some extent. It is your work, after all."

"Thank you," he said, meaning it more than he wanted to. "Shall I bring them in?"

"Bring them— They're here? You brought the paintings with you?"

It wasn't that she'd not been alert before, but now she had come to attention like a deer who had scented danger, every muscle taut, her eyes wide.

It's a wolf you're sensing, all right, he told her silently, warningly.

But he couldn't deny that her pure excitement over the presence of the paintings was somehow warming. She, at least, seemed to understand them, seemed to see all the levels, the layers . . .

He stifled another grimace, wondering how he could possibly think of this as a good thing. He didn't want her to understand, to see in his work everything he'd poured into it. That implied too much, it was an intimacy he didn't want to—or couldn't—deal with.

When he started down the curving staircase, he wondered if he wasn't going to regret this in more ways than he ever could have imagined.

It was worse once they'd brought the stack of canvases inside. He'd been mildly amused—and distracted—by Alison's horrified response to his casual handling of them; he'd simply stacked them in the backseat of his rental car, and had left it parked—albeit locked—in front of the gallery. She'd ranted at length about proper storage procedures and the danger of heat and sunlight, let alone theft, most of which he'd ignored except to note that he rather enjoyed her passionate enthusiasm. And wondered if it carried over into other areas.

He immediately warned himself to stop that line of thinking, but then she began to prop the paintings up to look at them, and he was able to think about nothing but the sudden violent churning in his gut.

She stood there, her gaze going from one canvas to the other. She'd gotten some easels and stands to set them all up at eye level, and placed them without looking at them, saying she wanted to get the impact of seeing them all at once, because that would tell her which one was to be the centerpiece.

He stood there, not looking at the paintings but watching her look at them, and the excitement in her eyes and the joy on her face warmed him in a way he'd never known before. It made no sense, that anyone could find joy in these outpourings of despair and ugly memories, no matter how cheerful and serene the setting he'd chosen to hide them in, but he couldn't deny that look on her face. And he stood there, waiting, with nothing in his mind but how much he both needed and dreaded her reaction. In this moment, nothing else mattered, not what had happened, not why he was here, nothing.

And when she chose her centerpiece, when she stopped before the painting on the far right and breathed, "This one," in hushed tones, he wasn't at all surprised. In fact he'd expected it, that she would somehow see, somehow know.

It was the piece he'd done after Ian's death. They'd known then that he'd died under torture, holding out long enough to give them the chance to escape, but this picture had been done long before they'd found out it had all been part of a plan, that Ian had never been meant to come home from that mission.

On the surface, the painting appeared to be a wildlife scene, with a big, heavily racked buck standing sunlit in a lovely meadow, off away from his herd, alone, noble, beautiful.

It was only when you looked closer that you saw the buck was being stalked by a stealthy mountain lion, almost hidden in the underbrush. And that the big cat had already drawn blood, barely noticeable on the deer's flank.

"Look at him," Alison whispered. "Look at the way he's looking back at the herd, and they at him. He's doomed, and he knows it, they know it, but they all know his death will give them the chance to get away, that they will survive because of him."

Her soft words struck him hard because of the awe her voice held, and deep because of the nerve they struck; she indeed saw everything he'd tried to portray in the animal's eyes, everything he'd felt when they'd learned that Ian had died long and hard and in agony, but he had never given them up.

She looked at him then, and delivered another blow when she said in that same awed tone, "They're wonderful, Lake. All of them, but this one especially."

He was Lake again, he thought inanely, reeling a little. "How can you . . . like them?"

"How can I not?"

"But they're . . . awful."

"Yes, they are." He winced inwardly at the bald agreement before she explained. "They're awful in the original sense of the word, that of inspiring awe," she said, as if she'd read him easily, "And they're powerful. Dynamic. Shocking. Emotional. Even painful."

He stared at her, feeling a bit bewildered. "And you . . . *like* that?"

She smiled slightly. "I do. What did you think, that art had to be pretty to be effective? That only great beauty moved people?"

He swallowed, trying to gather his scattered thoughts. "But . . . these aren't exactly what you'd hang in the living room."

"No. You'd hang them where you needed them." She gestured at the painting he'd mentally titled *Sacrifice*. "This one, anyplace you needed to be reminded of courage, and that it can be found anywhere, if you look hard enough. This one—" she gestured at the original painting that had stopped him in his tracks at her window—"anywhere people need to be reminded that peace doesn't come free, that it comes at great cost, and that if you have it, a price was paid, and you should thank those who paid it."

He stared at her. "You . . . see all that?"

She shook her head. "It's all there," she corrected. "I only see what you put there."

He shook his head in turn, more than a little stunned. He turned away from her, unable to look at her and deal with his conflicting emotions at the same time. He didn't know how to feel, if he should be glad or horrified that she saw so much. On top of his feelings about the paintings being seen at all, he felt like he was approaching overload, like he had once on a mission, full of the feeling that if one more thing went wrong, or one more thing popped up that he had to deal with, the whole thing was going to fall apart.

Only now, here, the only thing at risk was him. Whatever twisted part of him that produced the work that this woman saw and read and reacted to in precisely the way he did, seeing just what he'd tried to put in it.

He couldn't believe she was in on it. He simply could not make himself believe she was part of the trap. The old instincts warned him not to trust, but common sense also had its say; did it make any difference? Would he approach this any differently if he was convinced she was involved, that she was

consciously part of the bait that had drawn him here? He knew
the answer was no, but somehow it didn't bring him relief.

If he'd thought himself still capable of it, he would have
said it scared him to feel this way. That she scared him. But it
didn't seem possible, not in this tranquil place, not with this
woman. She fascinated him, that's all. She was different than
anyone he'd ever met, and he was intrigued.

Only natural, he told himself. Given her looks, add how
long he'd been alone, and he should have expected his reaction
to her to be rather strong. But it wasn't just that, it was much
more. It was everything he'd learned about her, her kindness
to those around her, her courage in going on after her husband's death, her determination in keeping this place going,
her passion about the art, her quick wit in dealing even with
someone like him, her quick emotions and her fearlessness in
showing them, and it was above all her perfect understanding
of his work, of what it meant and what it was meant to do and
show.

She was still looking at him, as if she were somehow able to
read the parade of his garbled thoughts.

And he realized with a little shock that he *was* scared. Not
because of how strong his response to her was. But because
for the first time in his life, it was for those reasons.

He'd seemed stunned by her reaction, and she saw the truth
of what he'd said in his eyes; he'd never thought of his work
as art, never considered that there might be a valid reason to
share it, that there might be others out there who could truly
understand.

They ended up in her office, where she busied herself fixing
coffee, giving him a chance to absorb it all. She understood the
need for retreat; even for her, the full blast of his work was
something to be taken in measured doses. Especially as he'd
progressed, learned more, made small changes in his technique
that added to the power of his work. Most artists did the same
thing over time, but few of them had started where he had, already far above most others, even at seventeen.

He held the cup she gave him as if he wanted the warmth,
despite the perfectly comfortable temperature, and she sensed

that this betrayal of need was foreign to him, and that he didn't like it. He didn't speak, just sat in the same eagle chair he'd been in before, staring into the dark liquid as if it held the answers he sought.

Now, she told herself. *Do it now.*

She didn't like the idea, she wanted to ease into it, but she wasn't sure she'd ever have a better chance.

"I . . . we still need to talk, Lake," she said, her tone gentle.

He looked up, dark brows furrowing beneath a wayward strand of silver hair. "What? You have the paintings, and—"

"Not about the show."

He didn't move, nor did his expression change, but she felt the sudden charge in the air just the same. Taking a deep breath she plunged ahead.

"About your father."

He didn't even hesitate. He simply stood up, setting the coffee cup down on her desk with precision. The faint sound of the front door chimes came through the closed door; Alison ignored them.

"Lake—"

"I'll bring the sketches by tomorrow. The ones I have, anyway."

"Lake, wait. I know you weren't on good terms with—"

"I believe you have a customer, Ms. Carlyle."

His use of her surname was purposeful, she was certain, a warning not to go any further. But once he heard what she had to say, he would change his mind, she knew he would. He turned away and started toward the door. Torn between anger at his rudeness and a sudden panic that she would never get her message delivered, she followed him.

"You *have* to hear this, Lake. Colin left a—"

"Good afternoon," he said formally.

With a quick step she slipped around him and blocked the doorway. He stopped, although Alison had the sudden impression that he wanted nothing more than to sweep her aside and keep right on going. And that he could have done it, and there would be nothing she could do to stop him.

She ignored her qualms, gathered up her nerve, and tried again. "Lake, you have to believe me, this is important."

He looked down at her with an expression so utterly emotionless she felt a chill. But she held her ground.

"I have nothing to say about, nor do I want to hear anything about or from my father."

"But you won't feel that way, if you just listen—"

"I have felt that way for over twenty-five years. Nothing you can say will change it."

"But I was with Colin when he died. He left you a message—"

"I don't want to hear anything he had to say, Ms. Carlyle." His voice was as cold as that emotionless expression had been. "I don't care if it was forgiveness from his deathbed."

With a motion that was so powerful she couldn't resist it but yet so subtle she was barely aware he'd done it, he moved her away from the door. Before she could open her mouth to get another word out, he was gone.

And she was left still holding the burden she'd carried since Colin McGregor had died.

Chapter 9

He hadn't meant to kill her so soon. He would have preferred to keep her alive; she'd been handy, had nursed him well enough, and in the past week she'd been an enthusiastic if not particularly talented bed partner. She'd devoured all the sweet words and promises, and he'd been content to let her make grandiose plans for their future; it kept her occupied and stopped her from asking too many questions.

It also kept her from complaining about some of his more . . . unique sexual tastes. He'd hurt her, bruised her, even drawn blood, but he'd painted it with the pretty words women wanted to hear, that he'd wanted her so badly he couldn't help himself. And she'd done just as he'd expected, ignored the pain while she reveled in the idea of being a temptress.

But now she'd disobeyed him. And he couldn't allow that. So he'd had to move his timetable up.

He didn't like it when that happened, didn't like his plans being altered by someone else's actions. But he didn't have any choice. She'd hinted about him to her sister, after he'd told her that nobody should know he existed. Not that she'd given the sister anything, she'd simply hinted that there was someone in her life and she'd tell her about it soon. But it was too much. And besides, he'd told her not to.

It was her own fault. She'd signed her own death warrant with those words. He'd given her a chance to live a little longer; if she'd behaved, he wouldn't have killed her until he was ready to leave.

She'd made it so easy. All he'd had to do was kiss her, and suggest that she tell everyone she'd be gone for a long week-

end. She'd been puzzled, but when he'd put his arms around her and whispered that he wanted her all to himself, she'd blushed and agreed.

She'd gone out to get food, her mail, and to pick up the things on the list he'd dictated to her. She'd been wary of some of them—she didn't know anything about buying bullets, she'd said—but he'd diverted her by hinting that there was something very important he wanted to ask her this weekend, and the sooner she got going the sooner they could be alone again. The mood had to be just right, he'd told her, and even added candles to the list to pound home the hint.

He knew she thought he was going to propose, just as he'd intended, and she'd done exactly as he asked so eagerly it was pitiful. When she'd returned, he'd graciously helped her put it all away; the easiest way to make sure she'd gotten everything he'd asked for. He set aside the mail and newspapers, telling her she wouldn't care about the rest of the world soon. She'd blushed again, never realizing he meant it literally.

She'd been shyly hesitant when he'd led her toward the bedroom in the middle of the day. She didn't fight him when he tied her hands to the headboard of the bed with the sexy nylons he'd found she had; she'd grown to trust him after the first few times he'd restrained her, teasing her lovingly about being naive. He used two of her scarves over his hands, stroking her body lovingly, so she would think the silk was simply to heighten the sensation for her, not to cover his hands.

He could have killed her so surreptitiously she'd never have known what happened. But he enjoyed the thrill of the struggle too much. He waited until he was deep inside her body before he began to close his hands around her neck.

She was late in realizing what he was doing. Even then she only made a murmur of protest, clearly expecting him to stop the moment he realized he was hurting her. He tightened his grip, concentrating on making her fight him, not killing her; he didn't want to leave any more evidence than he had to, and fingerprints lifted from the body were not what he had in mind. They were throughout the apartment anyway, but as long as he left none on her, he could work up a denial if he ever got caught.

Not that he ever would. He was too smart for that.

Instinctively she began to try to break free. Her body twisted, arched, and he smothered a groan of satisfaction as his own body responded to the thrill of her desperate struggle. He smiled down at her, for the first time letting the practiced mask drop. Her eyes widened in horror. He laughed, feeling more alive than at any other time as she stared at him as if she were seeing the devil himself.

The moment he came he didn't need her anymore, and he snapped her neck.

He discarded the condom, as he always did, in a bag to take directly to the Dumpster out back. The trash pickup was on Monday, so it would be long gone by the time anyone knew about her. Little fool; she'd thought he was taking care of her when he'd insisted on them.

He dumped her in the bathtub, becoming annoyed when he had to kick her right leg several times to get it out of the way. Then he strolled back into the living room and poured himself a cup of the coffee she'd made this morning. She did make good coffee.

Idly he began to scan the morning paper.

When he'd finished with the news—which only proved, he thought, that he was right about people being worse than idiots—he was closing the paper when a small teaser on the front of the second section caught his eye.

He froze, staring. Slowly he turned to the indicated page.

He smiled.

He would have had to kill her today anyway.

His smile widened. He folded the paper neatly. He rinsed out his coffee mug and left it to drain. He went into the bedroom and packed his things, folding his clothes carefully; he liked things tidy. Then he searched the apartment for anything helpful, taking a flashlight, a knit ski cap, and the small stash of money he'd found earlier in a desk drawer. He added them to the duffel.

Then he went into the bathroom and took a shower. It was a little difficult, having to dodge the body, but he liked to be

*clean. He pulled on the jeans she'd pressed for him, just like
he'd told her. Then came a pristine white shirt, and his highly
polished lace-up boots. They were the same boots he'd been
issued during training for the Wolf Pack, and he'd kept them,
taken assiduously good care of them, wearing them only when
on a mission. They were his constant reminder, and his private
goad. He would wear them when he killed the Gray Wolf.*

*But first he had to get ready. He would need his equipment,
his weapons. And he'd need a car, too, since he'd had to abandon the last of the fleet Duran had acquired to accomplish the
mission of exterminating the Wolf Pack. He'd have to steal
one; he could take hers, but he didn't want to betray his direction to the cops, when they eventually found her. In fact, he'd
take her car and dump it somewhere else, in the opposite direction, with a flat maybe, so they'd think he'd had to abandon
it and assume he was still headed in that direction. It would
take more time, but he knew where his quarry was now, he
could afford it.*

He carefully locked the door when he left.

Yvette watched, worried, as Alison stared at the mess.

The rough, lopsided letters were smeared across the window
in paint as red as fresh blood. It had dripped like blood as well,
running down the glass in thick, slow paths. Some of it was
still damp, and Yvette wondered how close she'd come to
walking up on the vandalism in progress by coming in early.

Yvette could almost feel the fury rising in her friend. And
she knew Alison well enough to know her anger was not at the
shock of seeing this, not even at the desecration of her property. But as she stared at the word emblazoned across
Phoenix's front window, for all the world to see, it was clear it
was the sheer injustice of it that roused such rage in her.

MURDERER.

"Over a quarter of a century, and they still won't let it go,"
Alison said through clenched teeth.

"If we get started now, we should have it mostly cleaned up
before too many see it," Yvette said, trying to divert Alison
with practicalities. It was her first day back after her family
visit, and she'd come in early to catch up, only to find this.

She'd immediately called Alison at home, who had arrived in a rush; it was still well before opening time for most of the neighboring businesses.

"I'm tempted to leave it there," Alison snapped. "And make them all look at it when they find out—"

She cut herself off, and Yvette had the feeling she'd had several times before, that there was something, something major, that her friend wasn't telling her. But she knew it would do no good to prod Alison; if she was keeping some secret, she had her reasons.

"I'll admit," Yvette said casually, "it would make a heck of an advertisement for the showing, but I'm not sure that's the approach you want to take."

Alison's head snapped around, and Yvette kept a mildly amused expression on her face, even under the stare of fierce blue eyes. And then she saw the twitch at the corners of Alison's mouth and knew everything would be all right.

"It would be quite a marketing ploy, wouldn't it?"

"If you were the type to take advantage of the kind of morbid mind-set that makes some people want to own Bonnie and Clyde's car."

Alison gave an eloquent shudder. "Let's get this cleaned up."

"You don't want to report it to Ray?"

"No. I don't want it to get around any more than it already will."

With a shrug, Yvette went inside to gather cleaning materials. When they'd finished the messy job, opened the gallery, and Alison had retired to her office to check on a delivery that hadn't gone as scheduled, Yvette began to work at getting the flakes of paint out from under her nails and the smell of turpentine from her hands.

She was peeling away a bit of red that had dried on her thumbnail when she heard a faint sound. She looked up and saw Lake McGregor approaching, and wondered yet again how he managed to come in without sounding the chimes.

He looked at her silently, and she recalled suddenly that this was the man that graffiti had been aimed at. She quickly hid her paint-marked hands and gave him her best effort at a smile.

It didn't work. "You cleaned the window already," he said, betraying no emotion at all.

"You saw it?" *Silly question,* she told herself. Obviously he had. "It was just some stupid kids or something, I'm sure," she said hastily, hoping to salve his feelings.

"Maybe," he said, his tone so even, those metallic eyes so unfathomable, that she wondered if he'd been disturbed by the epithet at all.

"Well, I admit some of the adults in this town aren't very . . . adult, but—"

He waved a hand at her. "If it's someone from town, it doesn't matter," he said cryptically. "Is Alison here?"

"In her office," Yvette confirmed. And as he headed that way, she wondered who he thought it could have been.

Later, over lunch, she asked Alison, "Is he demented, or what?"

Alison gave her a sideways look across the table. Today had been her turn to pick the place, and she had picked her favorite sandwich shop with the healthiest menu in town. She had endured Alison's wondering aloud if they ordered their sprouts—bean, alfalfa, and others whose origin she could only guess at—in fifty-five-gallon drums, and kept her attention on the matter at hand: Lake McGregor.

"Possibly," Alison said, sounding as if she wished she were sure it was a joke. "But he was perfectly nice to you all morning, wasn't he?"

It was true that the Lake who had shown up today bore no resemblance at all to the ice-cold man who had stalked out of Phoenix yesterday. Despite the fact that he knew about the graffiti, he had seemed quite normal. Even friendly. As long as, Alison had told her in a rather morose tone after he'd gone, the conversation stayed off forbidden ground.

"Yes," Yvette admitted. "And he didn't even let the . . . paint incident this morning bother him." A lingering anger flickered in Alison's eyes, and Yvette went on quickly. "But I still don't like that . . . look he gets sometimes. Gives me the shivers."

"And you haven't even seen that look at its peak," Alison said, sounding rueful.

Yvette noted that Alison had known exactly what look she'd meant, that distant, cold look, of a man who had disassociated himself from the world. With some it was because they had been ostracized by that world; with Lake McGregor, she sensed he'd ostracized himself. And it had only appeared now and then; most of the time he'd been polite, considerate, and occasionally charming.

And as if the angry man she'd seen that first day didn't exist.

"He's been . . . in some bad places, I think," Alison said tentatively.

"Or he carries them around with him," Yvette retorted. "But I admit, he's been pretty handy to have around, if he's done all you said. I didn't expect that."

He'd been more than that, he'd been indispensable. He'd explained to Yvette that since he'd put the rush on Alison, it was only fair that he do some of the work. And he'd turned out to be an adequate hand at carpentry and wiring, freeing Alison to work on the layout for the show and getting the paintings framed.

"He has been . . . handy," Alison agreed, sounding distracted as she took a spoonful of the French onion soup that was her favorite thing on the menu here. Which, Yvette knew, wasn't saying much, considering she wasn't into tofu, or cheeses of unknown origin, as she called them. But Yvette looked upon it as her duty to get her boss to eat something healthful at least once a week, whether she liked it or not. Because she needed it. Just like she needed to talk about whatever had been eating at her.

"So," Yvette said, more worried about her friend than she let on, "what is it that you've been hiding, that you started to say and stopped at least a dozen times today?"

Alison looked startled, then chagrined. "I . . . just something I have to tell him. About his father. But we need to be alone, and he made sure we never were." She sighed then, rather heavily. "I have to think of a way to get it out before he realizes what I'm talking about. Maybe I should just give up on the idea of breaking it gently."

Yvette had no idea what she was talking about, but Alison's expression was so distant and troubled she decided to let it pass for now.

"He sure doesn't paint the kind of stuff you want hanging in the dining room," Yvette said after a moment, recapturing a stray sprout from her vegetarian sandwich and popping it into her mouth. "Really put you off your feed."

Alison smiled. "Funny, that's almost exactly what he said."

Yvette wasn't sure she liked that bit of news. "He's on the edge, if not over, girlfriend. You watch yourself."

"I'm putting on a show of his work," Alison said, "not moving in with him."

"Too bad," Yvette drawled, "because, honey, no living woman could look at that man and not at least *think* some carnal thoughts."

Yvette could tell by Alison's blush that she wasn't going to argue with that. *Good,* she thought. *At least she was reacting to the man.*

Yvette had always known it would take somebody along the lines of Lake McGregor to break through that shell Alison had been living in since Steve had been killed. Yvette didn't quite trust him, sensed some dangerous depths to the man, but maybe that's what it would take to get through to Alison. No one else had had any luck, that was for sure.

"David Dylan is even better-looking, and I didn't fall for him," Alison pointed out, using one of the potato chips—the closest thing to evil food in the place—to gesture for emphasis.

"David is gay."

"Well, I didn't know that, until he brought his partner to the showing."

"Then why did you treat him from day one like he was your . . . brother or something?"

Alison seemed to consider that. "Because he reminded me of a brother?" she suggested.

"How would you know? You don't have a brother. Besides, you treat all the men you meet like that," Yvette said.

She saw by Alison's expression her friend knew what was coming. *Tough, girlfriend,* she thought. Alison hadn't heard this lecture in at least a month, so it was overdue. She shifted her gaze to look out the window, but that didn't stop Yvette. Alison was the strongest, toughest woman she knew, but Yvette could be just as determined.

"It's been nearly six years, Alison. You've done your grieving, and you know Steve wouldn't want you to go on like this forever. It's time to get on with it. It's time you worked on a social life, instead of letting Phoenix eat up every minute."

Alison turned back to her friend. "Wait a minute, aren't you the one who was just warning me off Lake McGregor?"

"Interesting," Yvette said blandly, "that that's the first name you mention."

Alison let out a tiny groan, and Yvette smothered a smile at the success of her little trap.

"Only because you mentioned it first," Alison pointed out rather feebly.

Yvette ignored her tone. "I wasn't warning you *off,* just warning you. Frankly, I think a little risk in your life would be a good thing. And believe me, honey, that artist of yours may be a lot of things, but gay ain't one of them."

"You can tell that just by looking, can you?" Alison asked dryly.

"I can tell," Yvette said just as dryly, "by the way he looks at you."

Alison blushed, and ignored her friend's cogent observation. "Running a small business, and an art gallery at that, isn't risk enough?"

"You know that's not what I meant and quit sending up a smoke screen."

"Friends who know you too well are a nuisance," Alison muttered, turning back to the window.

"Besides," Yvette said, ignoring her jibe, "if you ask me, I think you've been half in love with him ever since you laid eyes on that painting of his."

Alison turned back from the window. "Thank you so much for that assessment of my intelligence, falling for a man I've never even met."

Yvette dropped the last of her sandwich back on the plate and leaned forward. Then she relaxed. She knew she didn't have to remind Alison she had nothing but her best interests at heart; she'd been there for her during the worst of times, had hugged Alison during those endless weepy nights after Steve's death, had browbeat her into taking care of herself, and finally had abandoned her apartment and a job she admittedly didn't care much for anyway to come to Jewel and help Alison start Phoenix.

Alison had often lamented she had never been able to do much in return, that Yvette's cheerful outlook and wry humor rarely failed her, or left her in need of support. Yvette had told her she didn't need any repayment, that Alison had rescued her from nine-to-five hell and that was all the return favor she wanted.

A car pulling in across the street caught Yvette's eye; there were only two marked police units in town, and the four-wheel-drive one was Ray Tinsley's. She quickly turned her gaze away, hoping Alison hadn't seen it. No such luck.

"Speaking of social lives," Alison said, "when are you going to put our local law enforcement out of his misery and go out with him?"

As a diversion, it worked rather well, Yvette tried to stay cool, but knew she was betraying herself by her sudden nervousness.

"When he takes off the bashful shoes and asks me," she managed to say rather haughtily.

"This may be the day," Alison said as she made eye contact with Ray through the window, and he turned and headed toward the door. "Here he comes, and it looks like he has jump boots on."

Yvette blushed as she glanced toward the street in time to see the deputy pull open the door. He stopped to chat briefly with the hostess, who was the daughter of the owner of the place, then walked toward them. Yvette's fingers tapped out a staccato rhythm on the table, and Alison quickly finished her soda before gathering up her big purse and the small stack of envelopes beside it.

"Hi, Ray. Take my seat, I was just leaving. Post office," she said, gesturing with the mail.

"Hello, Alison." He glanced at her. "Yvette," he said with a nod. Yvette hoped she wasn't imagining the change in his tone.

"I'll see you later," Alison said, sliding toward the end of the booth's padded seat.

Yvette shot her friend a panicked look, and opened her mouth to tell her to stay, but knew when Alison gave her a huge wink that she was on her own. Then Ray sat down and smiled at her, and suddenly she felt better. About everything.

Alison pondered the scene she'd just left as she walked toward the small post office. She hoped Ray would finally get his tongue unstuck. Yvette deserved a nice, decent guy, and Ray was certainly that.

Unlike Lachlan McGregor, who was a mass of contradictions, it seemed. Friendly and charming when it suited him, but changing to that provoked wildness whenever she trespassed onto his precious privacy. And especially when she brought up his father. He'd told her simply that if she persisted, he would simply walk away. She'd tried repeatedly anyway, and he'd done just that, and nothing short of following him and screaming it down the street at him would have gotten it done.

And she was about to consider doing just that. *God, Colin, how do I tell him when he refuses to listen?*

As she got to the post office door she heard a male voice call her name, and glanced up to see John Thompson waving at her from just up the street. She waited until he trotted the last couple of yards toward her.

"I called the gallery, but got the machine. I wanted to let you know Lake McGregor finally came back to my office."

She smiled at him. "He paid me a visit as well."

"Did he?"

"We're going to do a showing of his work."

"Really?" Thompson looked surprised. "He didn't impress me as the type who would want something like that."

"Frankly," Alison said, "I don't think he is. He's

very . . . protective of his work. But apparently he has some reason he's allowing it." And he isn't about to reveal it, she added silently. "I hope you'll come," she said. "It's going to be in three weeks."

Thompson's brows were still raised as he listened to her. "I confess, I didn't think he'd be here that long. He seemed in such a hurry to sell everything, I presumed so he could leave."

"Even the house?" she asked; she knew Colin had changed his will shortly after his wife had died, leaving everything to his sole surviving son. Thompson hesitated, and Alison apologized quickly. "Sorry, John, I know you can't discuss that. But . . . he's not staying there, so I wondered."

She knew that because she'd driven by Colin's old house several times, hoping to catch the elusive Lake McGregor, without any luck.

"Actually, I did find out where he's living. His grandfather had a small cabin up in the foothills, at the end of Silver Creek Road, and apparently he left it to Lake many years ago."

She knew where the road was, although she'd never taken it all the way out to the end. "That's pretty remote, isn't it?"

"It's out there," John agreed.

That didn't surprise her, that he'd chosen that place instead of the old family house in town. She imagined any good memories he had of the place had long ago been eclipsed by painful ones.

After she had extracted a promise from John to come to the showing he went on his way, and she stepped into the post office. She had just dropped her mail—mostly bills, she thought with a sigh—into the slot when a blast of lavender warned her she was about to be cornered.

"Good morning, Miss Carlyle."

She pasted a bright smile on her face and turned around. "Hello, Mrs. McCray. How are you this morning? Arthritis leaving you alone?"

"It's not too bad today," the woman said. Her medical complaints were famous, part of the fabric of life in Jewel. Arthritis was only the beginning; if there was a disease of the month, Althea was the first to have it. Or think she had it. "I'm glad I ran into you," the rather large, imposing woman said.

Uh-oh, Alison thought. But there was no escape; she'd learned that early on in her time here. And she didn't dare offend the woman who could sink Phoenix with a few well-chosen words to her husband—who happened to be the mayor—and friends.

"Why is that?" she asked, determinedly keeping her tone cheerful.

"The ladies and I have been talking, and we've decided someone needed to speak to you."

Uh-oh, Alison thought, *was an understatement.*

The ladies, she knew, were the Ladies Auxiliary. What they were an auxiliary to, no one seemed to know; Alison thought they had just liked the sound of the name and used it without a clue as to what it really meant. They met every Tuesday afternoon in Althea's gingerbread-laden mansion, to solve all of Jewel's problems and drink tea the men suspected was laced with something a bit stronger than honey.

And when the ladies decided someone needed a talking to, it was inevitably unpleasant, and inevitably it was Althea McCray who did the talking.

"We know that you're new to Jewel," the woman said kindly, "and because of that you don't understand some of the . . . intricacies of life here."

Sensing where this was heading, Alison stayed silent. But inwardly she was cautioning herself not to lose her temper, no matter how tempting it would be to slice a large chunk of pomposity off this woman.

"You weren't here when *It* happened, so you can't be expected to know that . . . that boy is not welcome in Jewel."

"That boy?" Alison asked, proud that her tone was nicely innocent.

"The McGregor boy, as if you didn't know," Althea said sternly.

"Sorry," she said, purposely sounding confused, "the only McGregors I've known have both been grown men."

Althea waggled a finger at her. "Now don't you get smart with me, young lady, when I'm just trying to look out for you. We thought you were simply foolish, hanging that painting and saying it was his, when we all knew it wasn't possible. That boy's not an artist, he's a murderer!"

Alison went very still. Once again, it was all she could do to bite back the anger that bubbled up in her. "Been indulging in a little graffiti, Althea?"

The older woman gave her a puzzled look tinged with irritation, Alison was certain because she dared to use her first name so familiarly. "Whatever are you talking about?"

Alison had to admit she seemed genuinely puzzled. And she couldn't really picture the redoubtable Althea McCray doing such a thing—merely fostering the kind of atmosphere that encouraged it.

"Murderer's a bit harsh, don't you think?" she said, unwilling to let it drop entirely.

"Tell that to poor Cora McGregor. She was never the same after that boy killed her son."

"*He* was her son, too," Alison pointed out.

"Not after that day. She disowned him, as was right and proper. So did his father."

Not forever, she thought, again feeling the weight of being the one Colin McGregor had trusted with the truth.

"If you're smart, you'll stay away from him. Who knows but that he might up and do it again?"

I'm not sure I'd blame him if he did, and started with people like you, she thought. But she merely said, "Thank you for your concern, Mrs. McCray."

"You be on guard around him," the woman warned again.

"I already am," Alison said, and as she walked gratefully away from the woman, she thought it was more true than she wanted to admit.

Chapter 10

He was getting used to sleepless nights again. He'd spent a lot of them on end lately, while resigning himself to this plan. Sleep deprivation had been a significant part of the Wolf Pack's training, and he'd handled it well enough then. But it seemed more tiring than it once had been; he'd gotten out of the habit, eventually, after Ian had died and the pack had broken up.

After Ian had been betrayed, set up, and sacrificed, Lake reminded himself grimly.

And now Rob was gone too. He'd clung to life until Jess had been able to tell him they'd found the man who had set Ian up to die a torturous death. Only then, when he knew his message had gotten through, had Rob surrendered his tenuous hold on life, only then had he allowed himself to die.

Lake leaned back on the bench on the front porch of the cabin, staring out at the small, moonlit meadow, at the stark crags of the Rockies beyond painted in eerie silver light. He sipped at a small glass of amaretto, warmed by his palm. It was the single holdover from his relationship with Rachel; she'd taught him to like the sweet liquor and the starburst of warmth as it went down.

Alison had been true to her word, as he suspected she always was. She'd done exactly as he'd asked and wanted, even though Lake knew perfectly well she suspected there was something else going on, something he hadn't told her. As he'd guessed, she was very perceptive, and at times he'd been hard-pressed to keep her from pushing him for an answer he wasn't about to give.

He'd also been hard-pressed not to let the act he was putting on become real, and that shocked him.

He'd worked at keeping their relationship friendly, at allaying her suspicions, at keeping up at least a front of being enthusiastic about an idea he still loathed. He'd even smiled when he'd had the damned photograph taken for the press release. He'd worked harder at charming her than he had at anything in the past ten years, and possibly before that; he found planning an attack on a jungle stronghold or kidnapping a stockpile of biological weapons relatively clean and simple when compared to dealing with the complexities of Alison Carlyle.

"You're losing it, McGregor," he muttered, lifting the glass. "You'd better keep focused on Joplin, or you're going to wind up dead."

Easier said than done, he acknowledged. She was bright, quick, sharp, astute, and no one's fool, least of all his. She was the kind of person he'd always pictured as the reason for it all, the kind of person the Wolf Pack, in the corniest of all phrases, wanted to make the world safe for. When they were off in some blinding desert sandstorm, or sweltering in tropical heat, it was the knowledge that what they were doing had to be done so that people like her could exist safely and in peace that had kept him going. But it had always been an abstract idea, he'd never really known anyone like that.

And now that he did, he wasn't sure what to do about it. Were it not for the necessity of it all, he'd probably be gone, he admitted wryly. Because what he found hardest of all was dealing with the realization that it wasn't Alison who was the crux of the problem, it was him. He *never* got involved with anyone on a mission. Although he didn't like it, he used people when he had to, sometimes with their knowledge and cooperation, sometimes not, but it never went beyond the minimum required to get a job done.

But Alison was different. She had been from the moment he'd seen her, when she'd faced his anger with a composure that had surprised him, once he'd calmed down enough to recall it.

And to his amazement, he liked her. For all the things that made her the personification of that abstract idea of what the Wolf Pack had been all about, and more.

But he was equally wary of her; she saw things, in him, in his painting, that he'd thought forever hidden, and that made him nervous. It wasn't a fear of being revealed, it was a fear of her ability, of the way she read every detail, of how she so easily explained what he had put into paint because he could never, ever put it into words. It seemed a very short step from that to her seeing too deeply inside him, and recognizing that hollow, dark place inside him.

And that he didn't like that idea worried him even more.

While he didn't like using her, especially since his doubts about her involvement with Joplin were growing by the minute, he knew he had little choice. He'd tried every other way he could think of to track Joplin down. He was sure the bastard had gone into hiding, in some untraceable place.

Unless he was already here, and behind that bit of repainting at Phoenix. That had been his first thought when he'd gone by in the dawn hour and seen the blaring red letters. But both Alison and Yvette seemed certain it was some kid's prank. He might be inclined to think that, too, if it weren't for the fact that he had no damn idea where Joplin was—and he was very much afraid that meant he was closer than Lake wanted to think.

The cellular phone chirped. Reflexively he noted the time: well after midnight. He got up and went inside, catching the phone in the middle of a ring.

"Yes."

"McGregor?"

The brusque voice was now familiar, and Lake relaxed slightly. "Mr. Gillespie."

"Gil, please," the man insisted. "I know it's late there, but I just got the report in on . . . your friend, and thought you might want to hear it. No location, but some of this might be helpful."

Lake considered this. Cell phones were notoriously easy to monitor, and Joplin certainly had the know-how to do it. And the equipment wasn't that hard to come by. But did he care? He wanted Joplin to know he was here, and that he was hunting him even as the reverse was true. And Joplin obviously already knew Lake didn't know where he was or he would have gotten to him by now, so Gil hadn't given away much by saying he still didn't have a location on him.

Deciding there was really little to lose, he told Gil to go ahead.

"You want the history first?"

"Might as well start there," Lake agreed.

"It seems the feds have quite a file on him."

"And you have friends among the feds," Lake guessed.

"A few," Gil acknowledged. Lake guessed it was an understatement; the man traveled among the movers and shakers in a big way. "Anyway, according to this report, he's been knocking around on the fringes of organized crime ever since he was dropped from . . . that team of yours. Seems he was feeling pretty insulted."

"I know. I saw him right after Ian cut him. He tried to take my head off."

"So he's stupid, too," Gil observed, and Lake smiled in spite of himself.

"Let's just say he didn't succeed. What else?"

"As I said, he was insulted enough to offer his services to . . . what could loosely be called the other side, I suppose."

"As?"

"Tactician, point man, and, rumor has it, hit man on occasion."

"With the best training in the world," Lake muttered.

"He was in the vicinity at the times of several murders, but they were never able to really connect him to them. He's been investigated a couple of times, under various aliases, but never charged."

"I'm not surprised. He was booted out of the pack for that amoral streak of his, not because he wasn't damned good."

"Something else," Gil said. "It seems he has a habit of coercing innocent bystanders into helping him."

Lake grimaced. "That would explain why he's been untrackable. He's probably holed up with some civilian."

"Yes. His last known location was Nevada. Las Vegas. They don't know if he was doing some work for the unsavory types there or not."

"How long ago?"

"Six weeks ago."

Before Beth had had to call for help, Lake thought. Perhaps Joplin had recruited the lunkhead who'd been helping him with that plan in Vegas.

Gil read him the rest of the report, which contained nothing Lake didn't already know or hadn't guessed.

"Was the location on Duran . . . helpful?" Gil asked.

"Yes," Lake said; it wasn't Gil's fault Duran hadn't known a thing. "Thanks again."

"You didn't . . . finish it."

Lake was startled. "How did you know that?"

"I have somebody watching him. I figured you'd be better off with a warning if he moved; my guy says he's pretty jumpy."

"I . . . thank you."

Gillespie brushed off his thanks. "Did he have what you wanted, then?"

"No. But he's already among the living dead. Didn't seem any point to making it official."

"Then why's he so edgy?"

"Maybe he thinks I keep deals the same way he does." Lake didn't bother to hide his sarcasm, knowing Gillespie would understand. "Besides, he's used to running things from behind a nice safe desk."

"And ordering the death of good men from his ivory tower?"

The vehemence in Gillespie's tone surprised Lake. As if he'd read the meaning in Lake's silence, he added, "Ian Russell was a good man. He was honest, courageous, and honorable, and he deserved better than to be betrayed by someone he trusted."

"Yes," Lake agreed softly.

"If it's all right with you, I'll keep my man on him. He seems to think Duran's too scared to do anything but hide, but just in case . . ."

"Fine. Thanks."

"My pleasure," Gillespie said, sounding like he truly meant it.

Lake sat thinking for a while after the call. His mind went

back to the dripping red letters across Alison's window. She'd
been almost solicitous about it, assuring him that it was a
prank, that it didn't mean anything other than some kids had
too much free time and were bored. As if she thought it would
hurt his feelings. That amused him, but at the same time made
him feel rather odd inside, that she would be trying to protect
him. Him, of all people.

But the incident had more significance than she realized. If
she was wrong, if it had been Joplin, then the ball was already
in play. And it would be just like Joplin to make his first salvo
something so innocuous, so that he couldn't be sure.

But if she was right . . . well, he couldn't count on that. Assumptions like that got you killed. And got those around you
killed.

So, there were two choices: wait until Joplin emerged on his
own schedule, whatever it was, or make the man come to him.
He wasn't in the mood to wait any longer, which effectively
made the decision for him. He had to go ahead with the show.
He had to make the clever murderer abandon his own
timetable, had to dangle in front of him the only bait he'd
strike on. He had to give him a chance at what he wanted: taking down the Gray Wolf. And this was the only way Lake had
been able to think of to do it. His resources were limited, and
he had only himself to rely on; he had to use what was at hand.
And who.

He hated the idea. And not only because of his distaste
about exhibiting work that even he didn't care to look at once
that particular demon had been exorcised. He also hated it because there was the chance of drawing an innocent civilian
into the target zone. And Lake put a very high value on innocence. Ian had once told him it was because he'd lost his own
innocence so early in life, but then Ian had been given to making that kind of reflective observation. But Lake admitted he
could have been right.

And despite her polish and sophisticated looks, he had the
distinct feeling Alison Carlyle was an innocent, at least when
it came to the ways of his ugly world. He realized then he'd at
some point decided firmly that she wasn't in on it. He had to
trust that instinct, and since it wouldn't change anything he

did—only how he felt about it—it couldn't be allowed to matter.

And he couldn't deny the sense of relief that instinctive feeling gave him. He didn't stop to analyze why, didn't dare.

But at the same time, it made things worse, knowing she was innocent but he was dragging her down into darkness. He had to do it, he told himself yet again. This was the only plan that might give him at least some kind of an edge, the only plan that might put Joplin a little off guard, leave him wondering what was going on. The whole thing, the very idea of a highly publicized showing with his name and photo all over it was so outrageous, so utterly out of character, so against every bit of training for secrecy either of them had ever had, that he figured Joplin would either think he'd lost his mind, or recognize it for a trap.

But either way, Joplin would come. He wanted the Wolf Pack wiped out. He'd gotten halfway; Ian and Rob were dead. And right now he couldn't reach Jess; he and Beth were safely out at sea, out of his reach. All he had was Lake. So he would come.

And, Lake mused, tilting the small glass so that the moonlight was warmed by the amber liquid, he would just have to make sure Ms. Alison Carlyle stayed safe.

There was something about a man who could use a hammer, Alison mused idly as she watched Lake attach another of the simple display lights she'd chosen to one of the movable walls. And he handled it with an ease that indicated some familiarity, the same kind of grace with which she was certain he handled a brush.

He paused to shove that distinctive, long silver hair back out of his eyes. Alison felt her throat tighten a little, felt her pulse give a little kick; he was truly the most striking man she'd ever known.

He went back to hammering, and she watched as if mesmerized. Those long-fingered hands didn't lie, she thought; he was an artist, through and through. But no matter how mild he seemed now, Alison never lost the sense that there was an edge to him that could slice swiftly and viciously if turned loose.

It was that, she told herself, that put her on edge, that shook her usual poise. Even though she saw no trace of the angry self-declared nonartist of their first meeting, she didn't quite trust this charmer. He could too quickly turn into the cold, unmovable man he became whenever she so much as thought about bringing up his father.

Suddenly aware she was staring, she made herself look away. But the thought lingered; he *was* charming. Personable. Helpful. Attentive enough to make her the tiniest bit nervous, not being used to such things since Steve had died. And he was just as interesting as she'd always imagined the creator of her prize painting would be. Despite her uncharacteristic nervousness, she found herself looking forward to his presence, fascinated beyond the aspect of the painting that intrigued her so.

"Alison? Jerry says your car's ready."

She looked across the room to where Yvette was on the phone. "Tell him thank you. I'll be over later to pick it up."

As Yvette delivered the message and hung up, Alison turned back to find Lake's steady gaze on her. "Car trouble?"

"Sort of." She tried to turn her attention back to the framing materials she was selecting.

"If you call getting your tires slashed and names painted on it car trouble," Yvette put in, grimacing as she walked by them.

"Yvette," Alison said sharply; she hadn't wanted Lake to find out about this.

Unintimidated, the young woman shrugged. "He's got a right to know."

Lake looked from Alison to Yvette and then back again. "A right?"

"Get it from her," Yvette said, clearly knowing perfectly well Lake would do just that. "I need the job."

She continued on into Alison's office and closed the door. Alison let out a sigh of exasperation, then glanced at Lake.

"I suppose you want the whole story?"

"The *Reader's Digest* version will do." There was an odd

tone in his voice, as if he was much more tense than this deserved.

"It's nothing unfixable," she assured him. "I left my car here last night. When I came back this morning, my tires had been slashed."

"And?"

"I thought you wanted the short spin."

"But complete."

She sighed again. "Somebody painted on my hood, too."

"Yvette said names."

"Yvette doesn't know when to keep quiet."

"On the contrary, I think she knows exactly when to speak." He watched her steadily. So steadily that Alison felt badgered, and stubbornly set her jaw.

"Can I assume," Lake said in a tone so gentle it startled her, "that it was something like what was painted on your window? Perhaps the same paint, even?"

She should have known he'd guess. She didn't bother to answer, sure he could read it in her face.

"You don't have to protect me, Alison," he said in that same soft voice. "Believe me, being called names is nothing new."

She winced inwardly at the weary acceptance in his tone. But she couldn't deny he'd apparently been the catalyst for what had happened. "That painting hung there for months and nothing like this happened. I guess they finally believe it's really yours, and you're really here."

She thought he gave a negating shake of his head, but the movement was so slight she couldn't be sure that's what it had meant.

"I'll pay for the damages, of course," he said.

"Of course, nothing," she said, irritated for reasons she couldn't quite understand. "I have insurance."

"As you wish," he conceded easily, and it struck her that what was bothering her was his calmness. And then he made it worse by smoothly changing the subject as if it meant less than nothing to him. "You've decided on the frames?"

She thought about walking out on him as he did her every time she mentioned his father, but that thought reminded her she needed to keep him here, while they were alone for one of the only times he'd allowed it to happen.

"Yes," she said, "very simple, smooth, plain, in either the primary or brightest color of the individual work. Fairly narrow mats in the same color. Nothing to detract from the impact of the painting."

He glanced at the materials she'd gathered. "You do it yourself?"

She nodded. "I've got a table set up in the storage room out back. I worked at an art supply store for three years when I was in college, most of it framing."

"Art major, I presume?"

"Yes," she answered. Then, as had long been her habit, fueled by those who seemed to equate that fact with ineptitude at anything else, or looking for an easy way to a degree, she added, "With a minor in business."

He looked at her intently for a moment, as if he knew exactly why she'd said it that way. Then he smiled. It really was an amazing smile, she thought. "There are a lot of artists who would be better off if they thought that way, I imagine."

She felt oddly warmed by his reaction. She ran a finger around the knob of the mat cutter on the table. She didn't quite understand why his opinion had become so important to her, and she didn't want to think about it just now. And suddenly, she didn't want to spoil this moment of open exchange.

"Where did you learn to paint?" she asked.

He shrugged. "Around. I had some classes in school, even took some more later, when I'd be in one place long enough. That gave me the basics, but the rest? Mostly from studying others, some lectures at museums here and there around the world. I've . . . done some traveling." He grimaced as if he regretted saying that. Then added wryly, "But most of all by a hell of a lot of trial and error, mostly error."

She couldn't help smiling. He studied her for a moment before asking, "No desire to be an artist yourself?"

She'd been hit with the question before, and had long been used to the only answer there was.

"No talent."

He glanced around, taking in all of Phoenix with the gesture. "Then I guess," he said, "that what constitutes an artist is truly a matter of interpretation."

She couldn't miss the inference. And again, felt warmed by it. And again, still oddly; she didn't usually require the approval of people she barely knew. She didn't even usually require it of her family and close friends. She knew in her heart she'd done well, and had enough self-confidence to count her own judgment as paramount. But somehow this mattered. His opinion mattered. And it was that, she supposed, that was making her into a coward, afraid to break the spell by mentioning Colin and his final wish.

"Your family must be proud of you," he said.

"My mother is," she said. "My father died a few years ago."

"I'm sorry." It was automatic, without much feeling behind it, but she didn't blame him.

"He'd been ill for a long time. He was a cop in Denver, and it broke his heart when they medically retired him. He never quite got over it."

"That must have been tough, sometimes. Cop's kid, I mean."

"Sometimes. But he was the finest man I ever knew. He was a cop for all the right reasons."

"One of the good guys, huh? I am sorry, Alison," Lake said, and this time the words were genuine. and the look in his eyes was soft, warm, and comforting. She felt a tug deep inside her.

I think you've been half in love with him ever since you laid eyes on that painting of his.

Yvette's words came back to her in a rush, and for a moment she wondered if her assurance that she would never be so foolish as to fall in love with a man before she'd ever even met him had perhaps been a little too quick. Feeling flushed and flustered, she tried to change the object if not the subject.

"Whatever made you think you weren't an artist?" she asked abruptly.

"The source," he said, then looked as if he wished he hadn't spoken. She had the feeling he didn't often let things slip, and wasn't happy with himself when he did.

"The source of . . . your talent?"

He didn't meet her eyes, and she had the same feeling that

didn't happen often either. And then it struck her, as she looked at the thick sweep of lashes as dark as his brows, in contrast to the silver, what he had probably meant.

"You mean . . . where the pictures come from? The ones in your mind that drive you to put them here?"

She gestured at the painting she'd been preparing to frame, of a lovely meadow, full of wildflowers and birds and small wildlife, all gathered around a peaceful stream. An almost bucolic scene. Only when you spent some time with it did you notice the ominously dark clouds off to one side, with the thunderheads rising above them. And when you did, the bits of debris floating along the top of the swift water took on a whole new meaning to anyone who knew anything about flash floods. And again, the peaceful scene was merely a mask for something much darker, much more threatening.

This was one of the items he'd allowed her to list for sale. They'd finally agreed on seven of the ten—all but the most powerful of the collection, she'd noticed, which didn't surprise her. What did surprise her was that he hadn't protested the rather steep price she'd put on them. It took her a moment to figure out why, then she realized he didn't expect that anyone would pay that kind of money, so in a way he would be saved from selling them after all.

When he didn't answer her, Alison asked softly, "Is that why you don't sign them?"

His head came up sharply. But that was the only sign he was at all disturbed; he set the hammer and the box of finish nails he'd been using down on the framing table without any trace of haste or anger.

"I have some errands to run," he said, and was gone before Alison could even respond. And she'd wasted those few moments alone, when she should have been talking of Colin's wishes. She not only still carried that burden, but now she felt selfish about it, for not telling him in these moments alone.

She turned back to look at the paintings. Whatever Lake McGregor had done after he'd left the army, it hadn't been easy. Or pretty. Or taken lightly.

Her gaze shifted to the painting of the buck, and she saw again the pure, raw emotion there. It was shouted from every brush stroke, and virtually screamed from the tortured eyes of the wounded animal.

Whatever he'd been, or done, Lake McGregor had paid the price.

Chapter 11

"Hello, Lake."

Well, that was a switch, Lake thought as he set the small bag of groceries on the passenger seat of his rental car. Someone actually initiating a conversation with him, other than Alison. He'd begun to think she was the only one in this town with the nerve to look right at him, without any darting sideways glances as if looking for escape routes. But even that was better than the hushed whispering that seemed to trail behind him like a ship's wake everywhere he went.

He turned to see who the brave soul was. At first he saw only the uniform, the drab green of the county sheriff's office. Then the face registered, and he realized he knew the man. It had been many years, and he was losing his hair just like his dad, as he'd feared at sixteen, but Lake recognized him.

"Ray." It came out on an odd sort of breath that almost sounded relieved. And perhaps he was; Ray had been his friend, and had felt for him when things had gotten so bad in Jewel that Lake hadn't been able to stand it any longer. He'd heard that Ray had even quit going to the church his family attended after Lake's mother had passed judgment on him that snowy Sunday morning.

And later, when they'd both been in the service, he'd run into him on occasion, and they'd gotten along fine, although it had been tough to hear that *It*, as Ray told him people referred to his brother's death, was still a topic of discussion so long after the fact.

"I'm sorry about your father."

"Someone should be," he said neutrally.

Ray leaned against the fender of Lake's rental, obviously

planning to stay awhile. "He looked for you, you know. After your mother passed."

Was that supposed to make him feel something for the man? Lake wondered. He said nothing, but Ray didn't seem to be ready to abandon the subject.

"I tried to get a message to you, after she died," Ray said.

That surprised him. "It was you?"

Ray nodded. "I called my old CO in the Rangers, told him what I knew about where you'd gone. He said he'd see if he could get the news to you."

So Ray had initiated the message that, after passing through more hands than he knew to finally reach him, had informed him his mother had died. He supposed he should thank him for that.

"I figured it might do you good to know," Ray said, surprising Lake again. "I know you're not supposed to speak ill of the dead, but she was . . . a very difficult woman. And she was pretty tough on you."

"Be fair," Lake said. "I killed her favorite son. How was she supposed to feel?"

"You didn't mean to kill him."

"Didn't I?" He'd lost his certainty about that long ago, when he'd realized there was something in him that made him capable of killing on a regular basis. He'd begun on that path thinking he'd already taken those first steps, but it hadn't been long before he'd started to wonder if perhaps it had indeed been cause and effect, but not in the way he'd thought. If perhaps killing Douglas had been a symptom of something already there, not an incident that had set him upon this road.

"Boy, I'm glad he's not *my* brother! I'd be dead by now." Ray and Lake both looked at the two boys on the sidewalk, who took off running. Ray looked after them thoughtfully while Lake schooled his expression to impassivity, leaning on the open passenger door as if the taunt had meant nothing.

Ray turned back to face Lake. "Willie's got a mouth on him," he said with a shrug.

"Just repeating what he's heard, I'm sure," Lake said, his tone emotionless. And the something Ray had said belatedly registered. His gaze narrowed. "What did you mean . . . what you knew about where I'd gone?"

For the first time Ray looked a tiny bit uncomfortable. "Well . . . we heard some rumors, after you left the Rangers . . ."

"Rumors?"

Ray shrugged. "About some ultra-covert special missions team that was being formed. Private. A lot of the guys were saying they liked the idea, because they were tired of being the world's policemen but kept toothless."

"You mean constantly being pulled back before the job was really done."

Ray nodded. "A lot of them were tired of having to go to the same problem area over and over again—"

Ray broke off as an older man walked past them. Mr. Murphy, Lake noted. The man nodded at Ray, glanced at Lake, and did a classic, almost laughable double take. His expression turned fierce, and he looked back at Ray.

"I hope you're throwing him out of town!"

"Have a nice morning, Mr. Murphy," Ray said. The man harrumphed and walked on.

"So," Lake said as Ray watched the man go, "are you?"

Ray looked back at him. "What?"

"Throwing me out of town."

Ray gave him a speculative look. "Any reason I should?"

"No." *Not yet,* he amended silently. But the image of that "MURDERER" scrawled across Alison's window haunted him. And her slashed tires, and that word once more, slopped onto the hood of her car. He shook off the odd mood that seemed to have seized him; he *would* stop Joplin before he did any irreparable damage to Phoenix. Before he did any damage to anyone in Jewel.

And most importantly, before he did any damage to Alison.

As if he'd read his thoughts, Ray said, "Alison's taking a bit of heat over you."

"I . . . heard about the window. And the car."

"Window? I know about her car, but what about a window?"

"Just some creative painting."

"Hmm. She didn't report that. For that matter, she didn't report her car. I only know because Jerry over at Murphy's garage told me. I wonder why?"

"Busy?" Lake suggested, knowing Ray wouldn't believe it any more than he did.

"Maybe," Ray said, his voice proving Lake's speculation right. "But actually, the vandalism isn't what I was talking about. I'm working on that. But a lot of people aren't happy about this show you're putting on, and they're letting her know."

"It was her idea," he said, wondering why the truth of that didn't make him feel much better about it; he didn't like the idea of her being harassed because of him. "Letting her know how?"

"Well, they're generally being kind about it, explaining to her because she's an outsider. Most of the town likes her, so they're giving her the benefit of the doubt."

And they hadn't even given him the benefit of doubting that he'd meant to kill Douglas. Or if anyone had, they hadn't had the guts to stand up to his mother and Reverend Vaness and say so. Not that he'd expected them to. Nothing could change the bottom line, the simple fact—he *had* killed Douglas.

"But they're not giving up, either," Ray added.

"You mean until they've convinced her I'm the devil incarnate and she should run for her life?"

Ray studied him for a moment, as if to assure himself Lake was joking. He must have been satisfied, because he quipped, "I'm sure she's been warned to guard her immortal soul."

A chill swept him. "Advice she'd be wise to take. I just might try to steal it to replace the one I threw away."

Ray stared at him, as if the chill had expanded to brush him as well. As if what he'd said as a joke seemed suddenly very serious.

"I . . . warned her myself, Lake," he said.

Lake stepped back and slammed the passenger door shut. "Did you now?" he asked, turning to face Ray full on. He was taller than the deputy by a good two inches, and he knew his expression was cold, but Ray never blinked. Not that Lake would have expected the ex-Ranger to flinch; he'd been as tough as the outfit required and then some.

"I told her you were a Ranger, and gave her my best guess as to what you'd done after."

Something in the man's eyes told Lake that his best guess was pretty accurate. "Just when did you tell her this?"

"Shortly after you got here."

She'd known all week? Every day when he'd come into the gallery, she'd had Ray's warning about what he was in her mind? He was beyond startled; she'd never shown a sign of being nervous around him.

"I like Alison." Ray's voice was even, and he held Lake's gaze steadily. "I'd hate to see her hurt."

"Warning me, now?"

"If it's necessary. I hope it's not."

Lake knew it would be a mistake to underestimate the mild-mannered Ray. "I have no intention of hurting her."

"Unintentional still counts."

Definitely a mistake; Ray cut right to the crux of things, to Lake's biggest fear. It always had been. With the Wolf Pack, even when there'd been absolutely no doubt of the rightness and necessity of the mission, he'd always counted the cost too high if innocents paid it.

"Point taken." Then, before he could stop himself, he said, "Got a personal interest?"

Ray shifted slightly. "Not that it's any of your business if I did, but no. Not . . . like that."

He was right, Lake thought. It wasn't any of his business. He wasn't even sure why he'd asked.

Ray tossed the question right back at him. "Do you?"

"No," he said instantly, automatically. "I just . . . I've been taking up a lot of her time, and I wondered . . ." He trailed off, wondering why on earth he was suddenly explaining himself.

"If there was somebody who wouldn't like it?" Ray suggested.

"Yes." Somebody who wouldn't like it enough to slap the town's opinion of him across her front window. Enough to take a knife—Joplin's weapon of choice, as he recalled—to her tires. He wished he could believe those were really the only reasons he'd asked.

"Not that I'm aware of. She doesn't date, that I know of. Not that there aren't guys interested, but when she first came here, her husband had just died so everybody kept clear."

"That was five years ago."

Ray nodded. "But she's never shown an interest in changing things. She takes a bunch of kids to the movies, spends time just talking with the old folks over at the Blue Spruce, helps with the founder's day parade."

A regular candidate for sainthood, Lake thought.

"She even goes to the founder's banquet alone."

Lake's breath stopped. He'd forgotten about the founder's banquet, the highlight of Jewel's social year. The formal affair was, the denizens of Jewel told themselves, the equal of any big city gala. The ladies trotted out their glitziest formal wear, the men grumbled about wearing tuxedos, the children whined about not being old enough to go. The entire thing revolved around the day Jewel had been founded by silver miner Alexander McGregor. And there was nobody, Lake thought, who would be less welcome at that celebration than Alexander McGregor's great-great-grandson.

There was nobody who was less welcome in all of Jewel than Alexander McGregor's great-great-grandson. The town would never give up punishing the McGregor most of them thought had gotten away with murder.

If they only knew how many murders he *had* gotten away with.

He didn't look happy to be here.

Alison sighed. He wasn't making this easy. Not that anything could. But she'd gotten him this far, using the brochure for the showing as an excuse, telling him she wanted him to look at the layout before she had them printed.

When she'd suggested they look at them over dinner, he seemed startled. But she persisted; she wanted to do this someplace where they wouldn't be interrupted, and where he might not find it so easy to walk away from her.

"You sure you want to be seen with me on what could be

construed as a . . . social engagement? You're in enough trouble already having anything to do with me."

"Trouble?" she said airily. "I hadn't noticed. Shall we go?"

The silence when they walked into the Columbine was unmistakable, as was the hushed buzz that followed them to the private booth she'd requested in the back of the restaurant.

"You noticed enough to hide out back here," he remarked as they sat down.

She let him think so, mainly because she didn't dare tell him yet why she'd wanted the privacy. Didn't dare tell him that she refused to carry this alone any longer. She had no doubts he'd walk out; he'd made it clear every time she even mentioned his father that it was a subject he would not even discuss.

So, we won't discuss it. I'll just . . . tell him.

It sounded easy enough. And he was relaxing, finally. He even liked the brochure, which she'd had to struggle with, considering how little biographical information he'd given her to deal with. Of course, that was probably why he liked it, she thought as she looked at the sample on the table beside her dessert plate. The elegantly simple, muted silver cover with black lettering was her own selection. It suited him, she thought, matching his own distinctive coloring.

Inside, each painting was numbered and described, those for sale discreetly marked. He'd even had a few changes to make in her copy, and those he wanted were ones she could have predicted, in places where she'd given away a bit too much about him in her words about his work.

She couldn't put it off anymore. She'd been lugging this around far too long, and she wanted to be rid of the burden. And he needed to know, whether he wanted to or not.

She took a deep breath.

"Lake . . ."

He looked at her over the rim of his cup of coffee. His face didn't change, but somehow his expression darkened, as if he'd sensed what she was about to bring up.

"You *have* to hear this," she said. He set down the cup. Before he could make another move she spoke again. "And you're going to. So help me, you're going to, even if I have to

follow you to your grandfather's cabin if need be, and yell it
through the window. This is crucial."

His expression grew darker, as if he wasn't happy that she
knew where he was living. "Nothing you have to say about my
father is crucial to me."

She could feel him tensing to rise, and said quickly, "I have
nothing to say about your father." That slowed him down a little. "What I have to say is *from* your father."

"That interests me even less."

He folded his napkin neatly, although something about the
methodical movements told her he was more tense than he
probably wanted her to see.

"I'm not asking you to be interested. Just listen. I want to
be . . . rid of this."

The odd phrase made him look at her. "I'm sorry if my father laid this on you. He shouldn't have. But drop it, Alison.
Now."

There was no mistaking his tone, no misunderstanding the
look in those metallic eyes; she'd found again the angry man
she'd seen that first day.

Alison decided she'd had about enough of this. She'd dealt
with temperamental artists many, many times, but this one was
making her crazy. Why didn't matter; even if Yvette was right,
and she'd been half in love with him before she'd ever met
him, she'd had enough. This up and down ride was too much;
knowing how unfairly he'd been condemned made it no less
wearing, in fact only made it more urgent that she get this said,
and now.

"I can't," she said. "I—"

"Drop it," he repeated.

There was no other way to describe it; it was an order. And
Alison wasn't used to taking orders. That it was from him, a
man who made her a tiny bit frightened, made it even worse;
she wasn't used to being frightened of men, either. The two
things seemed to boil together, rising hotly within her. Then
she saw him give a short nod, as if her silence was proof she'd
acquiesced. He sat back in his chair, apparently willing to stay
now that she'd been dominated.

It was the match to her already tension-shortened fuse.

"In a minute," she said through clenched teeth, "I'll tell you to go straight to hell. But first you're going to hear this."

He didn't even blink at her words. Maybe people told him to go to hell all the time. She wouldn't be surprised.

Instead he said flatly, "I told you, I don't care if he forgave me with his dying breath. The subject is closed. Permanently."

"He didn't *forgive* you," she nearly hissed, "because there is nothing to forgive you *for*."

His eyes narrowed. He stared at her, but didn't speak.

You will never have a better chance, she told herself. *Get it out.*

"You didn't kill him, Lake. You didn't kill your brother."

He went utterly still.

"That was what your father made me promise to tell you."

She'd expected . . . something. Some reaction she could read. But there was nothing. Somewhat inanely, she realized how shocked he truly must have been to see the painting in her window, to have allowed so much anger to show. Because now, when he should be showing even more emotion, there was nothing.

Perhaps he hadn't understood, she thought. He'd been carrying this guilt around for most of his life, after all.

Instinctively she reached out a hand and laid it on top of his. The move was soon proven a mistake—he turned his hand and grabbed hers in a grip she didn't even try to break. It was not painful, simply inexorable.

"What are you up to?"

His voice was as cold as his flesh was hot beneath her fingers, his tone menacing, and she was certain it was not her sometimes expansive imagination. For an instant all she could think of was Ray's warning that this man had been a highly trained covert agent of some kind.

She felt herself shiver, and saw something flicker in his eyes, some acknowledgment of her fear. Somehow that, and the fact that he still did not release her hand, gave her the strength to steady herself.

"I am trying to do as Colin asked, what he made me promise with practically his last breath. To tell you Douglas's death was *not* at your hands."

She was making no headway, she could see that. It was her own fault, for blurting it out like that; she'd meant to lead up to it more gradually.

"I killed my brother, Ms. Carlyle. I've admitted that from the day it happened. So what do you hope to accomplish with this . . . tale?"

"To give you—and your father—peace."

"A lovely sentiment."

His tone was acid, and she had to take a deep breath before she could speak again. "I know I . . . went at this backward, but you have to believe—"

"What I believe isn't going to change. I know what I did, and Douglas died because of it. So you might as well give it up."

"Colin told me you wouldn't . . . believe easily, after all this time."

"My father knew I did it. He was second in line to call me a murderer."

"Right behind your mother," Alison said, a tinge of the outrage she'd felt often in the days since Colin had died.

"Yes."

"That's why he was so determined," she said. "He wasn't offering forgiveness, Lake, but absolution."

"Then while you're absolving me, explain one thing." She knew what was coming, and she swallowed tightly. "If I didn't kill Douglas . . . who did?"

She paused, took a deep breath, then said it.

"Your mother."

Chapter 12

He was staring at her as if he thought she was crazy. And then he muttered something under his breath, and Alison thought she actually caught the word.

"I'm not crazy," she said, and he looked startled, as if he'd only then realized he'd spoken aloud. "I know you argued with Douglas that day—"

"I hit him. Hard," Lake corrected, his voice grim.

"Yes, but you did *not* kill him."

"I hit him hard enough to break his nose. I can still . . . hear it."

She shivered, imagining the torture and the nightmares he'd been through. But she was going to relieve him of that hell now, finally, and she couldn't help but rejoice. She leaned forward over the table, speaking urgently.

"But you didn't kill him. Kids get their noses broken all the time—" She cut herself off this time. She had to tell him the most important thing, what Colin had told her, first. "Lake, listen to me. Your mother . . . she admitted she killed Douglas. With his own baseball bat."

He stared at her, disbelief clear on his face. Her words came then in a desperate rush.

"When she knew she didn't have much time left, she told Colin. She'd been carrying the guilt all these years, of letting you take the blame for something she'd done. She'd tried to protect herself, and had lost both her sons in the process. Your father tried so hard to find you, after she died, to tell you, but he couldn't locate you."

She had to take a breath, but made it quick for fear he was going to interrupt the flow.

"Everybody thought he'd changed after her death because he'd loved her so and couldn't bear the loss. But the truth was, he was weighed down with more guilt than he could bear. When he was hurt, when he realized he was dying, he made me promise to keep looking, to find you and tell you the truth."

She felt an incredible sense of relief. It was out. Done. She'd kept her promise. She sagged back in her chair, and drew in what seemed like the first breath she'd taken in hours.

Lake just looked at her. Time spun out, silently. The disbelief was still there, mixed with something else she couldn't recognize. At last he said, "I'm supposed to believe this?"

Alison sighed inwardly. She'd relaxed too soon. She drew herself upright again. "It's the truth."

"And just why would my father choose you to spill this . . . deep, dark family secret to?"

She met his gaze despite the uncomfortable feeling stirred by his utter lack of expression. And she answered him with blunt, utter honesty. "Because he didn't think anybody else in this town would believe you were innocent."

The truth of that struck home with him, she could see that in the faint tightening of the skin around his mouth.

"Douglas didn't die because of your fight, Lake. He died because your mother hit him with the bat."

He shook his head. "She would never have hit him. He was her . . ."

"Favorite? So your father said. But it's true. She did."

"But I hurt him." He sounded almost bewildered. "We fought over . . . God, it was so stupid, it was over my car, my first car . . . he'd sneaked out and sat in it, and let it roll out of the driveway and into the neighbor's car. I got in big trouble, they took the keys away from me, even though it wasn't my fault. I was so damn mad at him, I . . . slugged him."

"He died of a skull fracture. Did you strike him with anything other than your fist?"

"No—"

"Did you have anything in your hand?"

"No, but—"

"Your father had the X rays examined again, after your

mother died. There's no way you could have done that kind of damage with just your fist."

"But he was so much smaller, and I knocked him down. They said he hit his head then."

"Did he?"

He was starting to look a little dazed. "I . . . they said he must have. I don't remember, but they—"

"They? You mean your mother, perhaps? You were there, Lake. You were the *only* one there. Did he hit his head? Or were you just told that so often you believe it must have happened?"

"I . . . don't remember."

"The doctor your father had look at the X rays is a forensic expert, Lake. He said there was only a slight chance Douglas could have been conscious, let alone gotten up and walked away, after the delivery of the blow that actually killed him."

She was getting through at last, she could see it in the way his grip had tightened on his wineglass. But his eyes frightened her; something dark and smothering seemed to stir there, just where she would have expected to see relief.

"She wouldn't," he said, looking down as he shook his head again, but this time in the manner of a creature who had absorbed a crippling blow.

"She did," Alison insisted gently, knowing nothing less than the full story was going to convince him. "She'd found some kind of evidence that he'd been . . . masturbating. She was very angry, and that night she pulled him out of bed, to punish him, even with the broken nose. He tried to dodge her, which made her more furious. So she grabbed the bat and . . . swung it at him."

His head came up then, and when he stared at her this time it was with the stark realization of the possibility of it widening his eyes.

"My God," he whispered. "She . . . could have done that. She was . . . that would have set her off . . ."

So he knew his mother was capable of this, Alison thought. Perhaps he'd been punished himself as a boy, for some similar sin of the flesh; that seemed to be what Cora McGregor had

fixated on most. Which always made Alison wonder what pro-
clivities that person was trying to hide in themselves.

"That's why she wouldn't let them do an autopsy. She hid
behind her supposed religious beliefs to conceal what she'd
done. And she told the story over and over, that Douglas had
hit his head when you'd beaten him, until even you believed it
had to have happened that way. When the cause of death was
agreed to be a skull fracture, that was the end of it, because a
scared, seventeen-year-old boy admitted to whatever she told
them."

She tried to bite back the outrage that rose in her every time
she thought of it. But she couldn't swallow the words that rose
to her lips, words of anger and accusation.

"My . . . mother killed Douglas?"

He was hearing, really hearing, at last. Alison hastened to
pound the point home. "A good two or three hours after your
fight with him. Close enough that there was a chance even an
autopsy wouldn't have pinned it down close enough to make a
difference."

She saw the faintest tightening of the skin around his mouth.
She hesitated, then plunged on. "Maybe on some level she
even planned it that way, after you fought, knowing there was
a chance to let her own son take the blame. So she did it, let
you be called murderer by an entire town, to save herself."

For an instant, something flashed in his eyes, some bright
flicker of what could have been gladness, even joy. But it was
only a moment before darkness took over again and it died,
seemed to go out like an ember without enough oxygen for a
flame to catch. Alison spoke again, as if venting her own anger
could somehow help him.

"She let it go on and on, taking the role of bereaved martyr
to new heights, and never letting the story die, never letting
anyone forget her version, that it was you who murdered your
own brother."

He was staring at nothing, breathing quickly, audibly,
through parted lips, as if he couldn't quite get enough air.
She'd known this would shock him, but she couldn't understand why he wasn't relieved, why that brief flicker of glad-

ness hadn't lasted at the discovery that he hadn't caused his brother's death at all.

Not knowing what else to do in the face of his lack of response, Alison went on with the last of it. "Your father really did try to find you. He was told you were dead, then alive, then MIA, then that you'd never existed. But he never gave up trying. He said it had to be your decision, what to do about your mother's confession, since you were the one harmed by it."

Destroyed is more like it, she thought, watching him carefully, aching inside in a way she'd never known before. How could a mother do that, to her own son? Either of them? No wonder everybody said she was never the same after Douglas died—but they were wrong about the reason. It wasn't grief, it was guilt.

And I hope it ate at you every day of your life, Alison said silently to the departed woman. *The way it ate at your real victim. Douglas was beyond further harm, but Lake . . .*

"I . . didn't kill him."

It wasn't a question, but nor was it said in the tones of a revelation. It was flat, even, as if he'd lost the power to feel anything. His gaze was unfocused, dark, hollow.

"No. You took all that blame, all that guilt, for nothing. You were innocent, Lake. It was your mother who committed murder, not you."

"I didn't kill him."

This time there was an undertone she recognized beneath the words. And when she put the name to it, it frightened her: despair.

"Lake, what's wrong?" she finally asked. "Aren't you glad to know it wasn't your fault?"

He shook his head slowly. "I . . should be. Should be glad."

Her breath caught at the broken sound of his voice, the vagueness of the words. He was far beyond shock, even for the kind of news she'd delivered. It was as if this tough, strong man were crumbling before her eyes. Of all the things she might have imagined her news would do, she never would have guessed it would somehow crush him.

Without a word he got to his feet. He swayed slightly,

which frightened her even more; he'd barely had a glass of wine. He looked around as if confused about where he was. When someone opened the front door to come in, he focused on it and started that way. He walked slowly, as if he were concentrating on every step. Heads were turning, as they always seemed to when he passed. Although she thought that might happen anywhere; he was just the kind of man people looked at.

Hastily Alison dug into her wallet and tossed enough for a decent tip down on the table, and started after him. She caught up with him at the door. The light from the restaurant's sign angled down onto his face, and her breath caught a second time.

He looks desperate, she thought.

He pushed past an older couple making their way in. Alison nearly groaned aloud when she saw it was Mr. and Mrs. Grimes, and that the woman was looking down her nose at Lake, contempt and anger tightening her already pursed mouth.

Lake ignored them and kept going. Alison nodded at the couple, seeing by the woman's expression that she'd about run through her quota of newcomer tolerance. *You'll be singing a different tune when this gets out*, she promised the sour-faced woman.

Then she dodged outside, catching at Lake's arm. He pulled free. He looked down at her as if he didn't even recognize her. He backed away from her.

"What is *wrong*?" she asked. "You should be relieved, after all this time thinking you were responsible—"

"I didn't kill him!" he said for the third time.

She stopped in her tracks, frozen not by the words he'd said before, but by the way he said them. It came out as if ripped from somewhere deep inside him, a cry of anguish unlike anything she'd ever heard. He turned sharply and began moving away. She started to follow, but within three strides he was running. Running so swiftly he was a good distance away before she could react.

She started after him, then stopped. What was she going to do, chase him down the street? Wouldn't the good folk of

Jewel love to have that image to discuss over their morning
coffee . . .

Let him be, she told herself. *You've just changed a large
part of his history, it's going to take time for him to get used to
it.*

She turned slowly and walked back to her car. She drove
home to the small house she rented, having sunk all of her sav-
ings into the gallery. She changed into soft, worn jeans, a
sweatshirt and heavy socks, made herself a cup of cocoa she
didn't really want, and sat down in the darkened living room,
curling her feet up under her.

"It's done, Colin," she whispered into the shadowy room. "I
just hope it wasn't a mistake."

She sat there for a very long time before she finally went to
bed.

Where the hell was the bastard?

*Joplin barely suppressed a furious snarl. He wanted to
break his cover and stomp up and down the few streets of this
laughable little burg, demanding that McGregor come out. But
to do so would sacrifice the advantage of surprise; McGregor
didn't know yet he was here, and he wanted to keep that edge.*

*He thought he'd seen him once, a couple of days ago, but
that local cop had been with him, and he hadn't dared to try to
get a closer look. And small as this burg was, he couldn't
cover it all at once. But its smallness also made it impossible
for him to just sit and stake out the gallery; too many people
noticed things like that in little backwater places like this.*

*Angrily he got back in the driver's seat of the panel van
he'd rented. He was weary of having to sleep in such degrad-
ing places as that cruddy hotel room and the too-cramped
back of this van. He'd never had to spend so much time on a
job before, under such conditions; any other job and he'd be
relaxing in a five-star hotel by now, spending the result of a
profitable mission.*

*But never had a job meant so much to him, either. He could
put up with it for a while longer.*

*He drove back to the small RV park he'd found on the edge
of town, and put the van neatly in its allotted space. Jewel.*

What a stupid name for a place. He'd even seen in the flyer he'd picked up in the post office and pretended to read with great interest, to give him a chance to stay in one place and surreptitiously spy on the main street, that it had been named for one Jewel McGregor, wife of one of the town's founders. Old wimp must've figured that'd keep the old battle-ax happy.

He'd wondered if there was a connection between that old McGregor and the man he would soon be cutting into bite-sized pieces, but then he'd noticed a woman behind the counter watching him rather intently. He'd given her a wide smile and a wink, stayed just long enough to see the old bitch blush, then he'd headed back to the van.

Now, as darkness fell, he wondered again where McGregor was hiding. His absence didn't fit with what Joplin was sure was a ploy, this whole art show thing. It had to be a trick, a trap, and McGregor really thought he was stupid enough to come blundering in. But where was he? What good was a trap if you weren't around to spring it? He would have sensed McGregor if he was close, he knew he would, and that he didn't feel a thing, not even a twitching of the skin at the back of his neck, told him the man was nowhere close. And that made him nervous.

He climbed into the back of the van and began to go over his gear. He rechecked the magazines on all the weapons, made sure all the necessities for the plastic explosive were handy, checked the padded bag that held the baseball grenades. He picked up the most unlikely weapon, the one that would be his message, the one that would tell McGregor that his time to die was at hand.

Then he turned to his true love: he drew out the long, curved knife, running his fingers over the gleaming blade that could already split a hair. But he began to hone the edge anyway, taking a sensuous pleasure in the long, rhythmic strokes. When he was done, the edge would slice through silk without a whisper, he thought.

The repetitive motion lulled him, until he was rocking with it, almost humming under his breath. A slow smile spread over his face.

The smile widened as he imagined Lake McGregor's blood dripping from the blade.

*   *   *

Alison hadn't slept well for the last two nights. The look on Lake's face, that hollowness in his eyes, the unsteadiness of gait in a man she doubted had ever inadvertently stumbled in his life, ran like an endless video in her mind. She'd known what she'd told him would have a tremendous impact on him, it couldn't help but do that, but she'd thought it would be a positive impact. Instead, he'd practically crumbled before her eyes.

And she couldn't deny she felt responsible, even though she'd had no idea it would affect him like that. And no idea why it had. But she didn't think she'd ever forget the sound of his voice uttering what should have been a joyous revelation in tones of horror.

But what haunted her the most was that tiny glimmer of joy that had died stillborn. What had killed it? What thought or realization had made it impossible for him to feel what he should have felt, the relief and happiness that he hadn't killed his brother after all?

As late morning neared, she finally gave up on the idea of any more sleep. She got up and showered, all the while trying not to acknowledge that part of the reason she was so upset might well be that she was more attracted to Lake McGregor than she cared to admit. He was as complex as his work, and she was fascinated and intrigued by both, but it was more than that. It had to be, or she wouldn't be so worried about whether he was all right. She wouldn't be aching inside as if she'd inadvertently hurt a dear friend.

She stepped out of the shower and grabbed a towel. She rubbed hard with it, as if it could scrub away the grogginess and the persistent thoughts.

Think about what you have to do today, she ordered herself.

Yvette was handling the gallery, so all she really had to do was call the printer and okay the printing of the brochures, and make additional calls to some of her best repeat customers, urging them to attend. Assuming Lake hadn't taken off and there was still anything to attend, she thought, then yanked her thoughts out of the rut again.

The framing and matting was well on its way, and she had finalized the layout of the show yesterday. It would work, she thought, effectively channeling people through, while at the same time giving each painting its own private space. She'd decided to tie the paintings together with displays of the pencil and charcoal drawings in between, so that there was a sense of connection, yet no one painting would compete with another.

The portable display walls were already set up, thanks to Lake; because of his willingness to work she hadn't had to call Eddie Drake, her usual help with miscellaneous carpentry. Just as well; she'd about run out of patience with the natives of Jewel and their determination to be judge and jury without access to all the evidence.

And just like that, she was back on the subject she'd been trying so hard to avoid.

There's nothing more you can do, she told herself. She'd done as Colin had wanted, she'd passed on everything he'd wanted his son to know, and she'd even gotten Lake to believe it. And it hadn't been easy. So she couldn't be expected to do anything more. There *wasn't* anything more she could to.

She thought of the stack of sketches he'd brought. She'd seen others he'd done, Colin had shown her several from Lake's school days. But the difference in the two sets was obvious, sharp, and distinct. The early ones had been mere examples of a budding talent, quick, clever drawings of friends, family, and even a pet or two, interspersed with scenes of the mountains, animals, and local settings done with an eye for both detail and mood. The others, the later ones, were . . . haunting. Even in simple shades of gray and black on white, the haunted feeling was there. They were stark, sometimes grim, and utterly compelling.

And she didn't have to ask what had caused the difference.

So why hadn't he rejoiced to find out it hadn't been his fault, that his brother hadn't died at his hands? Why hadn't the news lightened that darkness he'd been wrestling with for all these years?

And why did she feel this compelling urge to search out Lake McGregor and make sure he was all right?

Maybe she'd just take a drive out Silver Creek Road. It was a pretty drive, and she'd never been all the way to the end, she had the afternoon to herself, so why not? And in the process she could just reassure herself that she hadn't truly destroyed the man by carrying out his father's last wish.

"Right," she muttered, knowing she was reaching. "Tend to business," she ordered herself. After dressing quickly in jeans, sneakers, and a soft, bright blue sweater, she left her hair down, running a brush through it quickly, then sat down to make her phone calls.

She was done in less than an hour, with the printing arranged, and promises from at least five of her best customers to attend and bring a friend, despite the short notice.

Then she gathered up her keys and her large purse, and headed for her car. The little blue sport utility didn't get driven all that much; her house was less than a mile from the gallery, and she usually walked unless weather prohibited it. And apparently she should continue, she thought wryly, considering what had happened to it the last time she'd left it at the gallery.

She let out a breath of relief when she rounded the corner and saw Phoenix apparently intact. She didn't think anything really bad would happen, but after the painting episode, and her car, she was well aware many of the residents of Jewel weren't happy about this show; they expressed sympathy, but in such a way that she knew the subtext was that she'd asked for it.

She found Yvette not alone, but not with a customer, either; instead she was talking animatedly with Ray Tinsley as she unpacked a crate that held some new stands Alison had ordered.

Alison hesitated, thinking she should tiptoe back out and leave them alone, but Ray spotted her and gestured her over.

"I was about to go to your house, Alison. I wanted to talk to you."

Surprised, Alison walked over to them. She glanced at Yvette, who gave her a shrug and a smile to indicate she shouldn't feel bad.

"What about?" she asked Ray.

Ray glanced at Yvette, looking torn, as if he hated the idea of asking her to leave them alone, but didn't want to tell Alison whatever it was in front of her.

"I'll go enter these into inventory," Yvette said, taking the hint and picking up the packing list from the crate.

Alison sighed inwardly, wishing she hadn't come in just now, thus interrupting what could have been a promising conversation. Matchmaking was obviously not her strong point. And Ray didn't look happy either as he watched Yvette walk away.

"If you don't ask her out soon," she told him, "I'm going to be reduced to something blatantly obvious like arranging a blind date."

He looked at her sheepishly. "I will. Really I will. I'm just . . ."

"Taking too much time," Alison finished when he paused. "She's a patient woman, Ray, but she won't wait forever. And she shouldn't have to."

He nodded, staring down at his hands.

"You had something to tell me?" she prompted after a moment of silence. His head came up quickly.

"Oh. Yes." He still looked doubtful, and she wondered if Yvette's presence hadn't been the only reason for his hesitation. "I . . after we spoke, I made some calls. Talked to some of my old buddies, from the Rangers."

Alison went suddenly on alert. "Is this about Lake?"

Ray eyed her. "I heard you'd progressed to first names. And you're really doing some kind of a show?"

"We are."

"He's really got paintings, and you're going to show them, at one of those champagne kind of things you put on?"

Was that all this was about? she thought, relieved. She could deal with this; Ray wasn't like so many others in town, didn't want her run out on a rail because she'd dared to not toss the town bad boy out on his ear.

She leaned against the wrapping table Yvette had been using. "Yes, it's true. A real champagne kind of showing. His paintings are quite wonderful. You've seen the one that was in my window."

Ray looked bemused. "I guess I never really believed that was his. Most people here don't, you know. But he always could draw. Back in school, he used to sketch stuff so quick it amazed me. He did a drawing of old man Murphy that—" Ray broke off, reddening. "Well, it was funny. But paintings. That's real stuff."

Alison didn't bother to try to educate him on the reality of other forms of art; Ray was one of those people who had probably walked by Lake's painting in the window with merely a glance. It made her wonder about any future he and Yvette might have, but she always calmed her misgiving by telling herself it was none of her business, and Yvette wasn't as . . . wrapped up in art as she herself was.

"He has a tremendous talent. His work is not . . . comfortable, but it's very, very powerful."

"Hmm," Ray said, in the tone Alison had come to recognize as indicating he had no real interest and was just being polite. She heard it occasionally. There were such people in the world, she knew, and some of them were perfectly nice people, hard as it was for her to believe.

"What was it you wanted to tell me, Ray?"

His mouth twisted slightly, and he hesitated, as if not sure where to start.

"Who did you talk to?" she asked, hanging on to her patience with an effort. Ray dealt quite well with issues of law, was a peacemaker in the best sense of the word, so obviously this was personal; that was the only time he was so awkward.

"Some old army buddies. And eventually, my old CO. He retired last year, so it took me a while to find him."

"And he said . . . ?"

When he finally spoke, it was in the rushed way of one jumping into cold water. "He said he knew Lake. Or rather, knew about him. After he left the Rangers."

Alison let go of her straw. She wasn't going to like this, she thought. She could sense it.

"He said that the covert team Lake joined up with was called the Wolf Pack. They weren't government, but had government sanction. They were the ones the feds called when they couldn't—or wouldn't—touch a mission. And they got them done, whatever it took. They never failed, the entire time they existed."

He'd already told her this, although not in such detail, so Alison knew this wasn't the point.

"Okay, so they were the Mission Impossible guys in reality."

"Sort of. From what my contacts said, they were on the side of the angels, as it were, doing things that needed doing but that political correctness or diplomacy sometimes got in the way of. Rescuing hostages, stopping chemical or biological weapons from being used, that kind of thing."

Hero stuff, Alison thought, feeling a certain sense of relief and, oddly, pride; Lake's toughness had been used in good causes.

"So they were tough, but still the good guys." But she knew there had to be more, or Ray wouldn't be so nervous. "And . . . ?" she prompted.

"They each had . . . code names, which is what they were solely known by. My CO only knew Lake was one of them because the guy who put the team together called him to check on Lake's service record. They were friends, and the guy told my CO they were looking for people with no ties, so he had to verify Lake had really had no contact with his family for years."

"Why? Why did they want—what did you say the other day—orphans?"

"No leverage," Ray said bluntly.

Alison blinked. "You mean . . . nobody that could be used against them, like as hostages or something?"

He nodded. Alison felt the chilly brush of a reality she'd never really confronted before, the unsettling knowledge that things like this went on, regularly, in that underside of the world she had never seen. That it couldn't all be dismissed as the product of Hollywood and the authors of the latest thrillers.

"After their leader, the man code-named Alpha Wolf, was lost on a mission, they broke up. That was about ten years ago. Up until then they were the perfect team, each man having at least one specialty, and between them they had all fronts covered. One was the explosives man, one was the tracker, one the computer expert . . ."

"And Lake?" she asked softly, knowing he was the one left out by the grim look on Ray's face.

"Lake was the weapons expert. And," he added in a tone that matched his expression, "the assassin. In my CO's words, 'He was the Gray Wolf, the best, coldest killer that ever walked.' "

Chapter 13

She was, without a doubt, Alison thought, losing her mind. Why else would she be just sitting here instead of phoning all over to call off this whole thing?

After Ray had dropped his bombshell, she had been too stunned to do anything but make her way into her office and collapse into her chair. She'd needed desperately to be alone, and had virtually ordered Yvette and Ray to go to lunch. And then she turned the closed sign around in the window, and locked the front door.

Lake was the assassin . . . the Gray Wolf, the best, coldest killer that ever walked . . .

Ray's words rang in her head, making her shiver. She knew Ray wouldn't lie, but it seemed so impossible. Lake had been here often in the past week, and she hadn't seen anything dark and evil lurking behind those pewter eyes. If she hadn't seen his anger that first day, she would have thought it impossible for such a charming man to be so angry.

But she had seen it. And now she felt like somebody around a beautiful and well-mannered dog—but carrying the memory of that dog snarling viciously.

Except that Lake McGregor was no house pet.

She still couldn't quite believe it was true, what Ray had said. She was wary of Lake, but never frightened, and surely she'd be frightened of a man capable of the kind of cold-blooded killing Ray had spoken of?

"He could kill a man and walk away as if he'd just stepped on an ant, with no more feeling, no more concern," Ray had told her. "My CO said that's what made him invaluable, that he could kill without qualm, yet be utterly trusted. He was as much a weapon for that Wolf Pack as any rifle or grenade."

She sat there for a long time, staring at the paintings that were sitting in her office, waiting for the two high school boys she hired occasionally for heavier work to arrive later today, and put them in the storeroom out back so she could finish the framing; the frames were done, it was simply a matter of finish work, putting the canvases in them and sealing the backs.

Right now they were in wooden holders, each designed to hold several canvases carefully upright and apart. The front canvas in the first rack was the original, the one that had started it all for her. Next to it, fronting the other set, was the one of the doomed buck.

Had she been a fool, to look at his art and think it couldn't have been done by a man who held human life so lightly, who killed without cause or remorse? Was she being misled by her love for the work, by her fascination with the artist?

Once more she studied the differences in the two paintings, thinking she must truly be crazy, to be turning to the source of the problem for distraction. But art had been her salvation more than once, and it was instinctive to turn to it now.

The subject matter was darker, grimmer in the later works, she couldn't deny that. But other than that, the difference was mainly in technique and assurance; the brush strokes were more definite, less studied in the later work. This was a common progression, as a young artist learned, as the techniques became second nature, requiring less thought, thus freeing the artist to concentrate on the emotions.

What hadn't changed at all was the underlying feeling of the work. She'd noticed when she'd first seen the other pieces that there was just as much emotion and complexity and layers to find in these.

Just as much, she thought.

Maybe she had it backward. Maybe what she should be noticing was that there was just as much emotion in the first work as there was in the later work.

How was that possible, if it was true? If he was the killer

Ray had said he was, how could it not show, how could there
not be a change, a difference in the work he'd done at seventeen and the work he'd done after he'd killed . . .

After he'd killed . . .

Her breath caught, and she sat up straight. Her gaze flicked
from the work of the boy to the work of the man. More ma-
ture, yes, in technique and approach, and subjects chosen
with the vision of a man who had been deep into the shadows. But the under-layers, the raging emotion hidden in dark
corners of the work, were there in both. As if whatever wa-
tershed had brought him to this level had already happened.

"Of course," she whispered. "At seventeen, he already
thought himself a killer."

*At seventeen, he already thought himself a killer. And he
hadn't been relieved to find out it wasn't true.*

Wild thoughts and speculations continued to race through
her mind, reasons, meanings, and above all that horrid sense
of responsibility. It was too much, and she knew she had to
get out of here.

She was back in her car and moving before she could
change her mind. She wasn't sure where she was going,
knew only she couldn't stay in the room with those paintings
another minute.

The sight of Ray's sheriff's car, with Yvette in the passenger seat, startled her out of her mindless fleeing. Hadn't they
just gone to lunch? She watched them turn onto Snowcap
Drive, curiously.

Snowcap Drive. Where Colin's house was. Without much
forethought, she followed. She saw the unit slow as it
reached mid-block. Her heart began to race when she saw it
turn into the driveway. Only then did she realize there were
several people clustered out in front. She slowed, her hands
tightening on the steering wheel. And then she saw.

The house had been trashed. Front windows broken, plants
trampled and dug up, the dirt thrown over walls and the
porch. More red paint slashed across the walls, and a large
puddle left on the steps, looking eerily like a pool of blood.

Hastily she parked, heedless of the angle of her car. She
scrambled out and headed toward the house, trying to dodge

the group of onlookers who were chattering away; she could hear enough to know they were expressing the same kind of sentiments she had heard directed at her—that this was only to be expected now that *He* had come home. In fact, he'd probably done it himself, they were saying. It would be just like him.

Then they saw her and a hush fell over the group. She could feel their stares digging into her as she worked her way past them. They moved out of her way, but slowly, as if each wanted to have their chance to look at her, so they could spread it around later how she'd looked and acted.

She caught up with Ray just as he was coming out of the house.

"Is he there?" she asked breathlessly.

Ray shook his head. "No sign." She let out a relieved breath. "Inside's a match for this," Ray continued, gesturing at the mess.

Yvette, who had immediately come to stand beside Alison, and tossed more than one glare at the crowd out on the sidewalk, asked, "Who on earth would do this?"

Ray studied Alison for a moment. His gaze flicked to the pool of red paint, then back to her.

Alison's eyes widened. "You think it's the same person who did my car?"

"And your front window, which you never told me about."

Alison looked at Yvette, who shook her head. "Not me, girlfriend. You said you didn't want it reported."

"Lake told me," Ray said, startling Alison.

"He did?"

"Yes. And speaking of Lake, I'll need to talk to him about this. Any idea where I might find him?"

Here it was, the excuse she didn't know she'd been looking for until Ray had handed it to her. "I'll tell him," she said, avoiding a direct answer; she didn't think Lake would appreciate Ray turning up on the doorstep of what was apparently his sanctuary.

Of course, he wasn't likely to appreciate her showing up either.

Ray looked at her steadily, and she knew she hadn't fooled

him, that he knew perfectly well she was dodging the question. But he also let it pass, adding only, "Make it soon."

You are certifiable, she told herself as she ran back to her car.

She was, no doubt. But she was still going up Silver Creek Road.

It was a longer drive than she'd realized; remote, she thought, was barely the word for it. She was already on the edge of wilderness. And at times, it seemed, on the edge of the world; there were too many unexpected sharp, steep drop-offs for her comfort. Of course, wilderness was a relative term; there were those who considered the concrete fields and canyons of L.A. a wilder place than any mother nature had provided.

And both certainly had their share of predators, she thought.

The question was, was Lake McGregor one of them? One of the rare predators who could stalk through both kinds of wilderness with equal deadliness?

They were tough, but still the good guys . . .

Her own words came back to her. Ray had said it was generally agreed that this Wolf Pack was on the right side—which, she realized, depended on your point of view—so there was nothing for her to be afraid of. The Mission Impossible guys never hurt any innocent bystanders, after all.

With an uneasy feeling that she was more naive about some of the darker sides of the world than she'd ever realized, she drove on. And up. And on. Until the road ran out.

She sat at the dead end, staring at the white barrier and the yellow diamond sign that bluntly told her ROAD ENDS.

"Well no kidding," she muttered, staring at the abrupt edge of the asphalt.

She got out and looked around. This wasn't quite high country, but it was getting there fast. She remembered when she'd first come to Jewel, how she'd had trouble with the thinner air, and had had a string of bloody noses until she'd adjusted to the dryness. Now it seemed normal, and the period of adjustment a small price to pay for the sheer beauty of the place.

The south facing side of the low mountain rising up on her right was covered in grasses, shrubbery, and other fairly low foliage. On the other side of the road rose the north facing side of a slightly higher mountain, covered thickly with fir dotted with spots of aspen. It was like being caught in some strange duality; if you looked at the side that got so much more sun, it seemed like nothing more than a mountainous high desert; the other side was lush and green and rich-looking. And you could see both with nothing more than a turn of your head.

The aspens weren't that obvious now, but would soon turn to pure gold and draw thousands of tourists to gaze at the brilliant color, and put a few dollars in the pockets of enterprising ski resort operators who had realized they could make some money running their lifts long before the snow hit, taking people up for panoramic views of the natural wonder of the changing season.

She could use one of those lifts right now, to see if she could spot the McGregor cabin. She wondered if John had been wrong about the location; she looked in all directions and saw no sign of habitation. The only sign that man had ever set foot beyond the end of this road was a narrow gravel track to the left of the road's end barrier. Past the white guardrail it curved off to the left, up the hill—a hill that would be a mountain anywhere but in Colorado—and quickly disappeared into the trees.

She walked over to the start of the gravel track. She glanced back at her little sport utility, gauging its width against the space between the trees that seemed to be closing over the narrow drive. His lower rental could do it easily enough, she thought, but she'd be bringing some leaves, if not branches, home with her.

But then, she thought with a grin, that was the point of this kind of vehicle, after all. Although she wondered how many supposedly "off-road" cars ever really left the government-maintained roadways. Not that hers hadn't sustained damage enough sitting politely in its place at the gallery.

She'd try it for a mile or two, she decided. If it went that far. And if she didn't find him, she'd smother this stubborn sense of responsibility and go home. Which she should probably do anyway, she thought ruefully.

The best, coldest killer that ever walked . . .

Ray's words echoed in her mind yet again and sent a tiny shiver racing down her spine. The muscles between her shoulder blades contracted reflexively in response.

Her mind still couldn't make the jump from the man who produced those paintings to the cold-blooded killer Ray had described.

Sure, she muttered to herself as she climbed back into the driver's seat. *As if talent exempted him from the possibility.*

But her inward chiding didn't take; the man who had painted those pictures might indeed have been an assassin— she had to accept that Ray's information was probably accurate—but there was no way she would believe the cold part. He may have killed, but he had not done it with emotional impunity.

And he was one of the good guys, she reminded herself. Rescuing hostages and the like. Not that that made her any more comfortable with the idea, but at least she could be fairly sure he wouldn't turn on her, that he wasn't just some crazed maniac who would kill her without provocation.

She heard the crunch of the gravel beneath her tires and the brush of tree branches on her roof at the same moment as she carefully steered onto the narrow track. She was grateful for the concentration it took; it kept her mind off the silliness of what she was doing. It was her mother's fault, she thought. She'd been the one who had instilled in her the notion that if you hurt someone, even unintentionally, it was up to you to make it right.

"Darn you, Mom," she muttered. Then took it back hastily; she had no right to complain about her mother, who was loving and generous despite her tendency to try to run her only daughter's life. No right to bemoan teachings that, in her heart, Alison knew were good and right. No, she had no right at all to gripe, not when there were mothers like Cora McGregor around.

She found herself hunching down as she went farther and the trees seemed be closing in, brushing her windows now. It seemed only a matter of distance before they quit brushing and started scratching. But she kept going; this track had to be here for a reason, she thought.

And then she came to a fork in the road. Actually more than a fork, almost a T, as the gravel track split into two, one leading to her left at a right angle, and staying at this level, the other rather steeply up the hill a little to her right.

She sat for a moment, considering. And then, with a wry twist of her mouth, started up the more difficult path. It just figured, she thought; nothing else about this had been easy.

She was a hundred yards along before she realized she'd trapped herself; if she didn't find his place, or at least some-place wide enough to turn around, she was going to be stuck backing down this track, which suddenly seemed narrower than a deer path. And much steeper than it had looked. And you just never knew when a stand of trees hid a precipice that could be deadly if you misjudged.

She glanced back down the hill, wondering if she could even do it, and wondering more than ever why she'd gotten herself into this in the first place. Then something belatedly registered, some glimpse amid the trees of a shape with the regular lines of something made by man, not nature. She looked back, not certain exactly where she'd seen it, only that she had.

It took her a moment to spot the small, rustic-looking cabin almost obscured by the trees. It had to be just up the hill a bit farther, and she pressed on. It looked like just the type of place she'd expect, isolated, secluded, and hard to get to.

Like the man himself, she thought, *in more ways than one.*

It was another two or three minutes until she was proven right, until she could see the rear of the rental car protruding from a covered carport that was an extension of the cabin's steeply pitched roof. It was parked at an odd angle as well as not being all the way inside the carport, as if he'd parked hurriedly. She wondered if that meant he hadn't calmed down much by the time he'd gotten here.

She pulled into the small driveway area, although she supposed it didn't matter since this branch of the gravel track appeared to end here. She got out and walked toward what appeared to be a front door, although the small porch was dusty and looked like it hadn't been used in a while.

She knocked. And waited. Nothing. She looked for a doorbell of some kind, even a mechanical chime to ring, but there was nothing. She knocked again.

After several minutes passed, she decided to look for whatever entrance he obviously used. She made her way through the trees, and around the first corner of the cabin. The outside wall was solid except for two medium-sized windows, and she kept going. It was cool here in the shade, and when she saw a sunnier patch up ahead she picked up her pace.

She reached the corner and stopped dead in her tracks, her eyes widening.

"Oh," she murmured in surprise.

Sunlight poured down through the clean Colorado air, seeming to flow across the small meadow before her like a liquid, golden stream. Through some quirk of the hillside's—to heck with it, it was a mountain to her—formation, she could see the towering peaks of the Rockies beyond, and knew the cabin had been placed here, at this angle, just for that reason. It was, she realized with a slight acceleration of her pulse, the meadow in the painting of the doomed buck. And faced with the reality, the simple, clean, sunlit reality, she realized full force the talent of the man who had turned it into a place of bloody sacrifice.

No wonder he stayed here, she thought. The house in Jewel was nice, but this . . . this was spectacular. And he would need this, she thought, this openness, this wildness.

Not to mention the light, she thought, her artistic instincts kicking in. Now, long shadows were falling across the meadow as the sun fell to the west. But in the morning this place must have light to die for.

Instinctively she glanced at the cabin, and saw that indeed, a little farther down the wall, a huge picture window faced the meadow. It reflected the sunlight in a gleam she'd bet

could be seen for miles, from the right angle. A thought
struck her and she stepped back a little, peering toward the
roof of the cabin. And found what she'd half expected . . . a
skylight, to allow in even more of the glorious light. She
doubted they'd even been thought of when this cabin had
been built, so it had to have been added later. By Lake, no
doubt, who had known what a treasure he had here; light was
a painter's tool as much as the paints and brushes and canvas.

There was also a long porch that ran the length of the
cabin on this side, and she guessed he'd used it more than
once, to paint outside. Perhaps even to paint *Sacrifice*.

Then she spotted a door to the right of the picture window,
and guessed this was the entrance he used. She went up the
two steps to the porch, and crossed it to the door. She
knocked.

Again nothing.

Maybe he was out, hiking or something. Maybe he'd
needed the solitude of the woods to deal with what she'd told
him. Or maybe he was inside, refusing to answer. True, it
had been nearly two full days, but what she'd told him had
totally changed *years* of his life; he had a right to some time
to adjust.

She knocked again. When there was still no response, she
began to think about leaving a note. It was an unsatisfactory
idea; she wanted to know that he was all right now, didn't
want him to learn about what had happened at the house
from a note, and didn't have too much faith that he'd call her
if she asked him to—if he even had a phone way out here—
but short of breaking in, she couldn't think of anything else
to do.

She turned and looked out at the meadow once more, once
more struck by its simple, serene beauty. What a counterpoint his work was to this; his paintings held all the bright-
ness and peacefulness, and at the same time all the darkness
and chaos that was its antithesis.

She didn't know how long she stood there, just looking,
soaking in the view, breathing in the sweet, clean air, but
when she at last turned to go, the sun wasn't quite so glaring

as it reflected off the window. She could actually see inside from here, she realized. Curiosity drew her, overpowering her qualms about snooping, and she walked toward the window.

The small living-room area had obviously been taken over as a studio; there was painter's equipment everywhere, cloths, jars with brushes and other bits of equipment, and a couple of empty easels folded closed and leaning against the far wall. There was a heavy canvas drop cloth on the floor beneath an easel that held a canvas she could only see the back of. He'd taken the time to protect what was probably the original wood plank floor; she could see the pegged end of one of the boards near the edge of the cloth, just beyond—

She froze.

She leaned forward, staring at what she'd seen, praying that she was wrong.

She wasn't.

She recognized the distinctive watch, the strong arm, and the long, finely muscled fingers. The rest of him was obscured by the sofa that had been pushed to one side to make room for the easel, but his outflung arm was in sight. Motionless.

Horror shivered through her as the possibilities raced through her mind. One loomed over all, and she hated it.

She didn't want to believe that Lake McGregor was dead.

She made herself reach out for the door. It was unlocked.

Alison stood there for a moment, a little nonplussed; with his background, he left the door unlocked? She'd expected to have to find some way to break in—even envisioning having to shatter that beautiful window—had been gearing up for the task, and now the door had simply opened at a touch.

Then she came back to herself and stepped inside.

It was cold. Much colder than outside. As if the chill of the coming night were here early, or that from last night lingered. As if he'd done nothing to warm the place, even through the night; it was late summer, yes, but it still got nippy at night at this altitude.

She hurried across the room, barely noticing the small oak

dining table that had been shoved to one side and now apparently served as a storage place, dodging the cockeyed sofa.

He was facedown in front of the sofa, his long, lean body sprawled awkwardly. Papers were strewn about, both beside and under him. A small end table lay on its side, the brushes and jars and paint-stained cloth it had apparently held sent in a spray of clutter across the floor. One of the jars had held water, which now puddled on the plank floor.

It seemed clear he'd fallen. And the water was not yet dry, so it couldn't have been that long ago. She went down on her knees beside him, her eyes searching for some sign of what was wrong. Her gaze skipped to the floor beneath him, and it was only after a moment that she realized she was looking for blood.

She shuddered. He wouldn't. Surely a man as strong as Lake, a man who'd been through all he'd been through in his life, wouldn't kill himself? He must have been through awful things, surely he wouldn't take the easy way out now? But he was also an artist, and while she didn't subscribe to the popular theory that that made him inherently unstable, she also had to admit he was unlike anyone she'd ever known before.

She reached out to him, knowing she had to know, had to find out. Her hand was shaking, and she was honest enough with herself to admit it was partly because if he was dead, she was going to carry the burden that she'd played a part in it for the rest of her life.

He was alive. She knew it before she actually touched him, because she could feel his warmth. Still, she slipped her fingers beneath his jaw and pressed; his pulse was steady, strong, if slow.

She let out an unsteady breath of relief. For a moment she simply stared down at him. The silver hair was tousled, but pushed back from his face as if he'd shoved his hands through it several times. There were bruised-looking shadows beneath his eyes, so dark that the black sweep of his lowered lashes no longer stood out like smudges of the charcoal he used for his sketches.

She touched his face; he felt warm, even more so than usual, but not badly feverish. She sat back on her heels, considering. He'd apparently been painting when he'd gone down; there was a brush lying next to his outflung hand. For the first time her gaze went to the canvas on the easel, what he'd apparently been working on.

She stifled a cry.

He'd finished it before collapsing. There was nothing to be added. Nothing could possibly make this any more powerful, any more haunting. Any more horrible.

She stared, unable to look away even though it made her tremble. A long figure, sprawled across a rock in a helpless position that made her think of the rack of ancient times. And above him, in the night sky, faces. Ethereal, ghostly faces, each etched into the layers of paint with thin lines that dug down to a lower layer of pale color in a way that made them seem ephemeral, yet with such exquisite detail that they were undeniably real; Alison didn't doubt she'd recognize any one of them if she ever saw them.

But one face in particular drew her eye; it was the face behind the trapped figure, away from the others, and it was looking at that helpless man with an expression of such sadness it made her throat tighten. That face drew her for more than the simple fact that it was exquisitely drawn, and wrenchingly beautiful.

It was Douglas McGregor. Frozen in time, and in childhood, the same face she'd seen in Colin's photo albums. Douglas, whose life had ended at the hands of the one person in the world who should have protected him most, and whose death had been laid at the door of his brother.

His brother, who had carried the guilt ever since. His brother, who had poured his torture out on canvas.

His brother, who was the man on the rock, trapped, pinned, held by things out of his control. There was no mistaking it, the swipe of silver paint over the hair, the dark brows scrunched together in agony. The figure that was Lake stared up at the sweetly sad face of his brother, while the other ghostly faces hovered apart, as if waiting their turn to torment him.

Their turn.

She gasped, realizing now what she was seeing.

It was true. What Ray had said was true. Lake had been that assassin. And the horror of it was all here, in this canvas that he'd apparently painted in a frenzy of work over the past forty-eight hours. She knew that layering technique took time, that even with acrylics the paint had to dry before the etching. What had he done, hovered over the canvas until it was dry enough to proceed?

She stared at the small figure of the man, trapped, held helpless before the onslaught of ghosts. She didn't understand the connection, why had he only now done this painting? Was it somehow connected, was what she'd told him somehow responsible for this outburst? For that's what it was, clearly, an outburst, a veritable scream from a tortured being.

She shuddered, and made herself look away from the painting. It was too intense, far too intense to look at for any length of time. It frightened her, more even than his reaction to her news had. Besides, right now he needed help.

She put a hand lightly on his shoulder. He didn't stir. She shook him, gently.

He erupted into motion. Alison gave a short, sharp scream as he knocked her aside with a sweep of his arm across her chest. She sat down hard. He was in a crouch without her quite seeing the movement. And he was staring at her. His eyes were wide and gleaming like molten metal. A vivid image flashed through her mind; was this what those faces had seen, in their last moments? This man, running on instinct, feral and absolutely deadly?

It took him a moment to focus on her, and that alone told her how far gone he was; she doubted it ever took him more than an instant to come awake knowing his situation exactly. The wildness faded, the deadliness vanished. He sat back down in an awkward tangle of long legs.

"Ali . . . Alison?"

Oh, God, she thought. He sounded . . . bewildered. Lost. It was so at odds with the man she had just seen, it wrenched at her.

"Are you hurt?" she asked.

"I . . . don't know."

He looked dazed. He tilted his head slightly, as if he still wasn't certain she was there. As if he wasn't quite certain of anything. He glanced downward, as if surprised to find himself on the floor.

"I must have passed out," he muttered.

"When?"

"I . . . don't know. It was light out."

"Have you slept at all? Eaten?"

His brows furrowed as he looked at her. "We had dinner."

"Lake," she said gently, "that was two days ago."

He looked at her blankly. "It was?"

He looked around again, this time taking in the fading afternoon light coming through the large window. It reflected off the spilled water, and she saw his gaze take in the strewn brushes. And he went very still.

After a moment he slowly raised his head, to look at the canvas above his head. It was as if he'd only now remembered its existence.

She could almost feel the tension pouring back into him. His body went rigid as he stared, his hands curling into fists. And then, as if that small strain was too much, he sagged back against the floor of the sofa, his head lolling back on the seat cushion, his eyes closing. The very limpness of his body told her he was exhausted, and she guessed he truly hadn't slept since they'd parted.

"I'm sorry I woke you, but I was . . . worried."

"Had to finish." His voice was weary, so incredibly weary she could almost feel the sense of enervation herself. "They wouldn't leave me alone."

She glanced up at the hovering, haunting faces; she didn't have to ask who *they* were. Silence reigned for a minute or two, and he lay still, eyes remaining closed. And then, abruptly, as if it had just occurred to him, he sat up and looked at her.

"What are you doing here?"

She hesitated; it didn't seem the time to tell him about the house. He might not care about the property, but the continuing meanness behind it was something he didn't need to think about right now. "I told you, I was worried," she said instead.

He lifted his head. "Worried?"

"You weren't . . . exactly yourself when you left the other night."

He stared at her. "You were worried about *me?*"

She wasn't sure if that was astonishment or disbelief in his tone, and decided she didn't like either possibility.

"I'd have been worried about anybody who looked the way you did that night."

His eyes narrowed. "Worried enough to come all the way out here?"

"Why not?" she retorted, stung by his suspicion.

He studied her for a moment. "You do have an investment of sorts to watch out for, I suppose."

"Right," she said, exasperation kicking through her, "all I care about is the showing."

He seemed surprised by her tone, and that irritated her even more. Was it only moments ago her heart had been pounding as she looked in at his unconscious body, terror filling her?

"I wouldn't care at all if you'd been dead, as long as I have the paintings to show, is that it?"

"I didn't say that."

He sounded almost contrite, but Alison was on a roll now, her usual tact and diplomacy vanished. "In fact, it'd just up the value of your work if you'd been dead, wouldn't it? No, better yet, murdered. Nothing like a juicy murder to escalate fame and prices."

"Thinking about doing it yourself?" His tone was so mild it took some of the fervor out of her.

"Maybe," she muttered.

"You'd have to stand in line," he said dryly.

And then, as if just hearing his own words, he drew himself up straight, his eyes going oddly metallic, and unfocused, as if he were looking inward, or a memory had just come to him.

"You've got to get out of here," he said, using the arm of the sofa as a brace to lever himself to his feet.

"Look, I didn't mean it, you just made me angry—"

"Alison . . ." He swayed on his feet slightly, and she scrambled up to steady him. To her surprise he didn't shrug her off. "You can't stay here, it's not safe."

She lifted a brow at him. "Safe enough that you left the door unlocked."

"I wasn't expecting you."

She gave him a sideways look. Was that some twisted insult, that if he'd been expecting her he'd have locked it, or did he mean he'd been expecting someone else he'd left it open for? Or was he just so tired he wasn't making any sense at all?

"Who else knows this place even exists," she asked, "besides you and John Thompson?"

"That doesn't matter," he said, and she knew she wasn't imagining that he was gradually leaning more against her, more than she ever would have guessed he would let himself. "He'll find me." She felt a tremor go through him. "He might even have followed you, you've got to leave."

"Who might have followed me?"

"It doesn't matter," he repeated. "But it's me he's after, he won't bother with you if you just *go*."

It's me he's after . . .

This was crazy, she thought. She was standing here propping up a man who normally probably could have carried her up that mountain track she'd driven. She was listening to rather wild statements she normally would have dismissed as the ravings of a clearly exhausted mind.

But there was nothing normal about this. Even if Ray hadn't told her, there was something about this man that made such things seem frighteningly real. And possible. Things far beyond a trashed house.

"Who is it, Lake?"

He shook his head sharply, and the effort almost took him to his knees. She eased him down on the sofa, and sat beside him.

"Is it . . . something to do with one of them?"

He saw her gesture at the painting, but he didn't look at it. Instead he stared at her face, as if stunned.

"You know? Who they are?" he whispered.

"I guessed. They're your ghosts, aren't they?"

He gave a harsh, short laugh. "You have no idea," he said. "You couldn't." It was barely audible. "You couldn't know, not and stay in this room with me."

With a tremendous effort, and fighting the common sense that was screaming that he was exactly right, she forced her voice to stay even and quiet.

"I know, Lake. I know what they have in common."

He denied it again. "You can't."

She took a deep breath. And then she said it.

"They're the faces of the people you've killed."

Chapter 14

McGregor had to be playing some kind of stupid mind game, Joplin thought, staring into the darkness of the back of the van, listening with no small irritation to the too-happy family camped in the next space.

That was the only thing that made sense. McGregor must be thinking that if he stayed out of sight, then he would do something stupid. McGregor had always bought into Russell's bullshit about patience, when in truth he probably just didn't have the balls to go out and make something happen.

But he did. And he would; he wouldn't play that coward's waiting game. It didn't matter that he didn't know exactly where his quarry was. He would find him. That it had already taken longer than it should have only prodded him harder. He refused to admit McGregor's seeming vanishing act could be so effective; he just knew there had to be a trail, somewhere, that somebody in this damn, godforsaken little zit of a town had to know something.

And he was going to find that someone. No matter what it took. Hell, he'd taken groups of hostages as big as half this town; there'd been nearly a thousand kids in that school he'd taken over to convince that mayor with delusions of grandeur it wasn't wise to mess with the cartel. He'd gotten what he'd wanted then, and it had only taken a half a dozen dead kids. He could handle this little place, even if he had to take them one by one.

Not that he thought he would. He'd gathered enough on his careful trips into Jewel to realize any one of them would hand McGregor over to him without a qualm. And he might just have to resort to that.

But he had a couple more ideas to try first.

* * *

He was so damned tired he couldn't think, Lake realized. So
tired he could hardly move. So tired he didn't know what he
was saying. Except that he was saying too much.

Or was he? Sometimes it seemed like he didn't have to say
anything to Alison; she seemed to guess more than he ever
would have told her.

But how the hell had she known who they were, those
faces?

The obvious answer hit him belatedly. She knew, because
she knew who he was. What he was. And there was only one
way she could know that.

"So," he said, suddenly even more exhausted than he could
ever remember being, "I was right in the first place. You are in
on it."

Even as he said it, he still couldn't believe it. It just didn't
seem possible that the woman he'd spent so much time with in
the past several days could be hiding something like that.

"In on it?" she asked, looking for all the world utterly innocent.

"What's Joplin's plan?"

"I think you need some rest," she said. "Badly."

"It can't be Duran, there's nothing left of him. He—"

"Lake, stop. You're not making any sense. Why don't you
lie down—"

"And go to sleep? Is that the plan? You drug me, and he
comes in when I'm helpless?"

"Drug? What are you—"

"I know he wouldn't let you kill me, he wants that pleasure
for himself, so—"

"Kill you?" she yelped. "You think I . . . what on earth *do*
you think?"

He'd never been much of a gambler—except, perhaps, with
his life—but he would have bet just about anything that her astonishment was genuine. And if it was, then that meant he'd
been right and she wasn't in league with Joplin or Duran. But
then how did she know about the ghosts?

He lifted a hand, rubbing at his gritty eyes, fighting the fog
that seemed to make it impossible to think. He'd gone longer

without sleep before, and he'd done it while traversing the roughest of terrain, so why the hell was he so wiped out when all he'd done was paint a picture? True, he'd felt drained before, when finishing a painting after a mission. Finally he'd had to admit that the process was as much emotional as anything else, although he was reluctant to acknowledge that he even had such emotions, let alone that they had so much power over him.

But he'd never, ever felt anything like this.

He had to think. He had to decide, if he'd been right or wrong, if he could trust her or not. Once he would have trusted his life to the gut instinct that was saying she wasn't part of this, but that was ten years ago, when all his instincts had been operating at peak efficiency. When he could manage to open his eyes again, she was looking at him. Steadily, thoughtfully. "I'm going to assume you're just too tired to think straight. Do you have any food here?"

He shook his head as if it would rid his brain of this haze so he could deal with what seemed to him like a non sequitur. "I . . . yes. I think so."

And then she was gone, leaving him feeling a bit dizzy. He should move, he thought. While she was gone, he should do something. He just couldn't think exactly what.

He wasted fruitless minutes trying to think, and then she was back, something in her hands. She sat down beside him on the sofa, holding a mug out to him. A savory aroma rose on the steam from the contents, and in almost the same instant it reached his nose his stomach growled audibly.

"You probably need something more solid, but soup was quick and I figure a good start."

For a moment he just stared at her. Then his stomach growled again. He looked from her to the mug and back again. He couldn't believe she'd try to poison him. If she really was in on it, that wouldn't be her style; Alison would look him in the eye and blow him away. But there was still the question that had taken over his mind.

"I assume that you like that kind, since you had—"

"How did you know?" he asked.

She took the jump in subject without a blink, although it

was a moment before she answered, as if she was considering whether or not she should. "Ray."

"Ray . . . Tinsley?"

She nodded. "He was warning me. About you."

He frowned. "Until I came back here, I hadn't seen him for years. Since before I—"

He stopped himself, closing his eyes and stifling a groan as he realized he'd been about to give himself away. He didn't know how much she knew yet, and there was no point in handing her any more. But he was so out of it he was liable to really trip up if he didn't shake off this sluggishness.

"He made some calls."

"About me?" He thought about it for a moment. He supposed it was possible, now, ten years after the Wolf Pack had disbanded, that the ex-Ranger might have known somebody who would know something, and tell him. Ray had always been personable enough, people liked him, even the army brass . . .

"He was just concerned. He'd heard rumors . . . and thought I should know, since I was essentially working with you."

"Rumors?"

"About what you did after you left the Rangers. About the Wolf Pack."

God, she knew about the pack. How much? "What—exactly—did he tell you?"

"Does it matter now? It was ten years ago, wasn't it?"

He rubbed at his eyes again, wishing it would clear his head. If Ray had told her that, then chances were he'd told her the rest. And surely she wouldn't lie about it, not when he could so easily check her story with Ray.

He heard a small sound that could have been a sigh. "I'm sorry. That was a foolish thing to say." He looked up and saw her staring at the painting. "Obviously it still matters a great deal."

The pure, warm sympathy in her voice seemed to weigh him down, even more than the weariness, but in a better way, a warmer, almost comforting way. And he knew, in some small part of his mind that seemed to be still functioning, just how badly off he was by the simple fact that he was thinking like this. He'd never searched for, in fact rejected sympathy, and accepted comfort only when injured severely enough to require it, and from those paid to administer it.

She turned to look at him, and all the warm solace in her voice was there in her eyes. He tried to look away, knowing that he couldn't afford this. But he couldn't tear his gaze away from her face, from the soft gentleness in her expression, the concern in her eyes.

Stop it, he told himself sharply. He'd already risked too much by succumbing to the need to paint. God, he'd lost two days, if what she'd said was right. Two days where he'd completely lost track of his surroundings. Two days when Joplin was likely here already, and behind the damage done. Two days where he had no recollection of what he'd done, his only memory the fierce, unrelenting drive to finish the painting of the faces that haunted him.

And now that it was done, they still haunted him. The painting had seemed imperative, essential, even crucial at the time, but it was done and nothing had changed, the ghosts had not been exorcised. And he was so tired his head was spinning.

"What happened, Lake?" she asked softly, so softly the words didn't even seem spoken aloud. "What was it about . . . what I told you?"

He didn't have to tell her. He could just tell her it was none of her business. Better yet, say nothing at all. But she just sat there, looking at him like that, and somehow that look was more effective than any torture he'd ever endured. And he'd been gone at by experts, a time or two. He'd withstood mental and physical torment she could never understand, but he was about to buckle under the pressure of her gentle gaze.

"I thought you would be happy, or at least relieved, to know you hadn't killed Douglas. Instead, it threw you into chaos. Why?"

He shook his head once, slowly. He took in a gulp of air, then another, aware he was having to remind himself to breathe. He swallowed tightly, then shook his head again. He didn't know if he was indicating he wouldn't tell her, or that he simply couldn't speak; the latter seemed most definitely true, he couldn't get out a single word.

"I know it's awful to think that your mother did it, and let you take the blame all these years, but still, isn't it better to know that your brother didn't die at your hands?"

"No." It came out as a rasp of sound, barely a whisper. He gestured a little wildly at the painting. "Because they *did*."

"But your brother—"

"He was the *reason!*" It burst from him, his voice suddenly at full strength, despite the shivers that he couldn't seem to stop.

"The reason . . . you killed them?"

"The reason I could."

She was silent, and when at last he looked at her, she was studying him, warily. He couldn't tell what she was thinking— maybe simply that he was crazy—and for some reason it seemed imperative, as imperative as the painting had been, that she understand.

"Don't you see? I killed my own brother, so I knew my soul was already lost, forever."

Alison's eyes widened. "You mean you thought it didn't matter if you killed the others, since . . . your soul was already lost?"

"I've lived with that knowledge ever since the day Douglas died. So when I joined the Wolf Pack, I . . ."

He heard her take a quick, audible breath as comprehension dawned on her face. "So you decided if there was killing to be done, you'd do it?"

He lowered his eyes and studied the mug in his hands— when had he taken it?—noticing that the liquid was rippling. He must still be shaking, although he wasn't really aware of it.

"It was all I could think of to do, to atone," he said dully, aware as always of the pitifulness of any effort at atoning for the greatest transgression. "I'd . . . killed my blood brother, I had no soul left to lose. But I could save the men who were like brothers to me from losing theirs."

"By killing so they didn't have to," she whispered, and he knew from her voice that she understood at last. And now she would realize she shouldn't be here, she would go, escape, leaving him to pull himself together and prepare for the battle to come, the battle only luck had saved him from when he'd

been too frenzied to know anything but the brush in his hands
and the canvas before him.

But she didn't go. She still sat there, so close he could smell
the sweet peach scent of her perfume, the scent that made him
wonder if she would taste as good as she smelled. And knowing that she probably would.

And now, as he sat here shaking, his defenses in shambles,
unable to find the strength to put up even the simplest of barri-
ers, he admitted to himself that he wanted to know that taste.
Admitted that he, who had held himself apart for so long,
wanting no one, needing no one, would surrender what was
left of his godforsaken life to know it.

"My God, Lake, I'm so sorry."

Her words and the pain in her voice brought his head up
sharply. He stared at her in surprise.

"Sorry?" *What did she have to be sorry for?*

"I thought what I had to tell you would . . . save you, after
years of thinking yourself guilty. But instead I've taken away
the very foundation of your life, haven't I? I've destroyed the
rationale that let you keep functioning at all."

That she saw it, and so clearly, rattled him. That she felt
badly that she'd done it, even unknowingly, awed him.

"It wasn't . . . You didn't know."

"Neither did your father, Lake. All he knew was that you'd
carried the blame for Douglas all these years, unjustly. When
he was dying, it was the only thing he could think of, that you
had to be told . . ."

His father. Now the change in the will made sense, the leaving him everything. He shuddered, almost violently. The hot
soup sloshed in the cup. He lowered it to rest on his knee,
afraid he'd spill it and humiliate himself further.

"Drink that," Alison ordered briskly. "You need the food,
and the warmth."

She waited until he raised the mug for a sip. The warmth
was like a shock to his system, and he had to admit it felt
good. He took another. And another. The soup was gone before he realized it, and the warmth spreading out from his
stomach lulling. He set the mug on the table carefully.

"Good," she said. "Now I'll fix something more solid for you. And then you sleep."

Sleep. God, he needed it. He'd hit the wall before, dealt with crisis after crisis until the last reserves were gone, but he'd never felt like this, empty, shaky, without an ounce of grit left in him.

"I can't," he said, sure of the truth of that even if he couldn't quite remember why at the moment.

"You're about to collapse," she said. Then, gesturing at the floor, "You *did* collapse."

"I can't," he repeated, fighting through the befuddlement he couldn't seem to shake. "Have to stay awake."

"Even you have limits, Lake."

Joplin, he thought suddenly, relieved. That was the reason. "He'll find me, I have to watch, and be ready."

For a moment she just looked at him, an odd expression on her face. Then, softly, she said, "I'll watch, Lake. I promise."

And then she touched him, put a hand on his shoulder, and he shivered again.

"You have to rest, Lake."

He wanted to touch her, to take that hand and hang on. For an instant he felt as if his very life depended on it. And then he was doing it, putting his hand over hers on his shoulder. He closed his eyes and let his head fall forward. She didn't pull away. And after a moment he dared more, he let his head loll to the side, capturing both their hands. But it was only hers he felt, only hers he drew warmth from, only hers he never wanted to let go.

And then she was close beside him, he could feel her, wanted more than anything to reach out and hold her, but couldn't find the strength, and then she did it for him, putting her arms around him, urging him to lie down, whispering soft words in his ear, words of rest and ease and trust.

And for the first time in longer than he could remember he trusted. And let himself go, sliding into the beckoning darkness, thinking that if he never woke up it would be worth it for these few moments of her closeness.

*   *   *

Yvette flipped a long, curly strand of her hair back behind her shoulder. She was very glad that man had come in, even if he was only browsing. She needed the distraction; she was worried about Alison. It wasn't like her not to be here by now, and she'd called her at home and gotten no answer.

And she couldn't get yesterday out of her mind, when Ray had had something to tell Alison. Something he hadn't wanted Yvette to hear.

She sighed inwardly. Darn Ray anyway. Every time she thought he was going to actually, finally, make a move, and get beyond the casual chat that hinted he wanted more but never came out and said it, he either retreated or something happened to interrupt and he never got back to it. She didn't blame Alison, or anybody else. Except Ray.

He must not want it very badly, she thought, *or he wouldn't let that keep happening. So maybe I should just quit wasting my time.*

The customer—browser, she corrected herself—was walking along the mantelpiece wall, but Yvette stayed where she was, double-checking the menu the caterer had sent over for the show. One of Alison's cardinal rules was to let people look as long as they wanted. Only when they focused on a particular piece, or gave that look around that signaled they were looking for someone to answer questions, were they approached. She wasn't into hard sells.

In fact, she'd once said, she wasn't into selling at all. She was in business, yes, but her goal was to find the right person for the right piece and vice versa, not sell art as if it were cars or cookies. Yvette had teased her about it, saying that instead of selling art, she put it up for adoption. Alison had responded by retitling her invoices "custody papers."

And all she wanted, Alison had told Yvette when she'd first come here, was to make a living doing it. "I'm not looking for fame or a name or big bucks," she'd warned her. "I just want to have a little to spare after I buy food and pay the rent."

"And my salary," Yvette had said blithely. She knew this was exactly what she'd been looking for after the hectic pace of the advertising firm she'd left, after four years of banging her head on a glass ceiling that was doubly thick for her, being both female and with a Hispanic surname.

So Alison had welcomed her, and they'd done well. Alison had welcomed the help, Yvette had welcomed the trust and responsibility she soon gained. And she'd gained a deeper friendship as well; sometimes she felt closer to Alison than she did to her own sisters. Of course proximity was part of it, they were still back in Los Angeles, but—

She interrupted her own thoughts when she realized the man who had come in had stopped near the front window. He was looking around as if trying to find something, and Yvette knew that was her cue. She headed that way, smoothing her skirt as she went.

"If you have any questions, I'll be happy to answer them," she said as she got close. Another of Alison's preferences; never, ever use that trite sales phrase "Can I help you?"

The man turned, and Yvette suddenly realized he looked vaguely familiar. She didn't think she knew him, though, and hoped he wasn't a prior customer she should remember. Or worse, a local she should know by name.

"I was wondering," he said with a smile that was quite charming, "last time I was here, there was a painting in the window. A rather . . . dramatic one."

Ah, so he had been here before, but didn't live here. She should have realized that; very few locals wore such tidy jeans. She smiled; tourists she could be forgiven for not remembering.

"Ah, yes, the McGregor," she said.

"The McGregor?"

She gave a light chuckle. "Sorry, that's the artist's name. I got in the habit of calling the painting that, before it was named. It's *Layers* now. If you like that piece, you might be interested in the show we're having of his work. I'd be happy to get you a flyer."

"Yes, I'd like that, please." He followed her back to the counter. "Miss Carlyle, is she still here?"

"She still owns the place, yes, but she's not here now." *And I wish I knew where the girl was,* Yvette added silently.

"She'll be in later, I'm sure. She's got a lot of details to tie up before the showing."

"I'm sure she does. I believe she told me this artist is from here in Jewel?"

"Yes," Yvette said, and left it at that. She tended to agree with Alison that the town of Jewel hadn't been very kind to Lachlan McGregor, and wasn't about to spread the ancient scandal to a tourist. "He doesn't live in town anymore, though. I believe he has a place up near Silver Creek."

The man nodded as if that was more than he wanted to know. "I'm sorry I missed her, but perhaps I'll see her at the show."

Maybe that was where she was, Yvette thought as the man thanked her graciously and left. Maybe she was with McGregor. She'd been teasing Alison when she'd said she'd been half in love with the artist before she ever met him, but perhaps it had held a grain of truth. Now that would be a nice change, Alison Carlyle enjoying herself with a man instead of wrapping herself up in the gallery business so tight she barely had room to breathe, let alone actually have a life.

She liked that idea. Alison was a wonderful woman, and she'd been alone for too long. And a good hot fling with a prime piece of male like McGregor might be just the thing to get her started really living again.

The door chimes rang sweetly again, and Yvette lifted her head. And smiled despite her earlier irritation with the man, for there stood Ray, in civilian clothes, nice ones, looking almost new, and shiny cowboy boots that looked like he'd just taken them out of the box.

But more importantly to her was what he wasn't wearing: a hat. She knew how sensitive he was about his receding hairline, and that that was why he was almost never seen without his uniform hat or a baseball cap on. That he didn't have either on now seemed significant to her.

"Hello, Ray," she said, putting as much welcome into the smile as she could.

"Hello, Yvette," he said. And then just stood there, looking at her. And for once, she resisted the urge to make it easier for

him, to fill the silence with meaningless small talk. She simply
looked right back at him.

He shifted his feet, and she saw him take a deep breath. But
he didn't speak. Finally, in irritation, she gave up.

"How on earth can a man who's been an Army Ranger find
it so hard to simply talk to me?"

He blushed, but to his credit he didn't dodge her exasperated look. "Because," he said, "nobody in the Rangers was
ever as pretty as you. Or mattered as much to me."

He'd deflated her sails completely. She didn't know what to
say. And found she was blushing a bit herself. "I . . . thank
you."

"Besides," Ray went on, "I never asked any of them on a
date."

She laughed. "I'm glad to hear that." Then, as his meaning
registered, she added, "Are you asking me?"

"Yes."

"Well, at last," she said.

Ray blushed again, but he didn't look particularly embarrassed this time. "Does that mean yes?"

"I believe it does, Mr. Tinsley."

He smiled so widely she forgave him all his shyness and
hesitancy. "I'll pick you up here after closing, then."

She started to say "Fine," then frowned instead.

"Is that a problem?" Ray asked.

"No," she said quickly. "It's just that . . . Alison hasn't
shown up today, and she didn't leave a message and doesn't
answer her phone."

Ray frowned in turn. "That's unusual, isn't it?"

"Very. Even when she takes time off, which is rarely, she
usually stops by at least once." Yvette sighed. "If she doesn't
turn up, I'll just close and lock up as usual, I guess."

"She didn't say where she was going?" She shook her head.
"Have you seen her since she left to try and find Lake?"

"No." Yvette lifted a teasing brow at the man who had taken
months to work up the nerve to ask her out, "I hope that's
where she is, that she's with her artist having a wonderful
time."

Ray went still. "*Her* artist?"

"Yes." She eyed him quizzically. "You've never said . . . are you one of the burn Lake McGregor at the stake crowd?"

"No, I'm not," he answered, firmly enough that she was impressed; it wasn't an easy stand to take in Jewel. "But he . . ."

"He what?" she prompted when he trailed off.

"He's got a history that isn't the . . . purest."

"You mean besides what happened here?"

"Yes. But please don't ask me any more, Yvette. I can't tell you."

"But you told Alison?"

He looked uncomfortable. "Yes. Because she has . . . other connections to him."

"Her friendship with his father, you mean."

He nodded. "I'm sorry, but I just can't say any more. It wouldn't be right."

She looked at him, hearing the finality in his tone. He truly wouldn't tell her, for the simple reason that he thought it unethical, unfair, or against his principles.

After a moment of her silence he sighed. "I suppose you're mad at me now."

"Quite the contrary," she said softly. "Be here right at six, all right?"

The smile that curved his mouth was thanks enough, but he said it anyway, and she liked that. And as he left, she thought today was turning out much brighter than she'd thought it was going to be.

If only she knew where Alison was.

Chapter 15

Alison awoke in a bed with absolutely no recollection of how she'd gotten there. She gradually became aware of the soothing warmth that seemed to surround her, she sleepily realized Lake McGregor was in that bed with her, beneath a thick quilt. That they were both still fully dressed only muddled her further.

Odd, she hadn't shared a bed with a man since Steve had died, but this felt natural, and she found herself snuggling into that warmth, that comforting, soothing heat he generated and was kind enough to radiate her way. The room was chilly, if the tip of her nose was any gauge, yet she felt cozy and warm and not at all like moving.

But she did open her eyes. Slowly, tentatively. The faint light of dawn was showing, gray and misty, at the small, uncurtained window a few feet away from her. She closed her eyes again, thankfully; it was far too early in the morning to even think about getting up.

Early? In the morning?

It suddenly got through to her, all of it. It was morning, the night was past, and she was in a bed with Lake McGregor. She went rigid, her heart suddenly fully awake and hammering in her chest. Slowly, very slowly, she turned her head.

He was behind her, and that warm, heavy weight she'd felt at her waist was his arm. She was dressed, as was he, but his heat still seemed to sear her. He was sleeping, deeply she thought; at least his breathing was deep and even. She could see his face in the growing light. Even in sleep the shadows seemed to hover; there was no boylike softness about him except for the brush of his lashes against his cheeks.

The dark, bruised circles beneath those lashes seemed to have faded slightly, she saw with some relief. He'd gotten enough sleep for that, at least. Probably not as much as he'd needed, if he'd been up and working for as long as she suspected he had been.

And then she remembered the rest, that she'd arrived here before dusk, and what she'd found. And that he'd fallen asleep on the sofa, after pulling her down beside him. She'd stayed there, wide awake, for the longest time, her gaze shifting from his face to the canvas on the easel and back again, one emotion after another tumbling through her.

She hadn't had the heart to wake him for something more substantial than the soup, but had eventually gotten up to fix herself a sandwich with the peanut butter and honey she'd found in a cupboard, and a couple of slices of bread that were barely on the edible side of stale. Then she must have fallen asleep herself, in the big chair opposite the sofa.

Everything she'd learned last night came back to her in a rush now, and with it came the chilling weight of responsibility. Ever since Colin had wrested that promise from her, she'd pictured herself as some sort of angel of mercy, delivering him from years of guilt and self-blame, and instead, she'd destroyed him.

She turned away from him again, staring out the window, the mystery of how she'd gotten here forgotten for the moment. Funny, she thought, that it was what the truth she'd told had done to him that disturbed her, and not the fact that she'd learned beyond denial that what Ray had said was true. Lake McGregor was a killer.

He had killed, she amended silently. And he'd done it in the line of duty, as it were, judging from what Ray had said. Did that excuse him? Did it make a difference?

Of course it did, she told herself. Many men had killed in the line of duty, and many of them were declared heroes. And they hadn't had the . . . impetus Lake had had. It wasn't his fault he was living with a horrible past he should never have had to carry, a past that had led him down a lethal path. He'd justified it in his own way, a way she found oddly noble, considering the deadly results.

"Alison?"

She nearly jumped when he spoke sleepily. As it was, the rough, gravelly sound of his voice, saying her name, and the feel of his warm breath brushing her ear, sent a shiver down her spine.

She steadied herself, then turned once more toward him. His eyes widened, as if he hadn't quite believed it was her.

"I thought I was dreaming," he whispered.

The implications of that sent fire racing through her. He went very still, and she wondered if her reaction had shown in her face. Her eyes widened as he moved toward her, his hand, so warm and strong, coming up to cup her face.

"God, you're beautiful," he said as he rubbed his thumb gently over her cheekbone.

"Lake," she said; it came out a breathy little rush of sound.

He moved again, and her eyes closed involuntarily as he tilted her head slightly. She knew, she could feel it coming, but she still gave a little start when his lips touched hers.

He was hot and strong and powerful, and it was as if he were pouring every bit of all three into this kiss. Yet it was re-strained, and she thought again, inanely, of that wolf on a thin leash.

And then he swept the tip of his tongue over her lips, and thought about anything else fled. All that was left her was sen-sation, rippling out from beneath his mouth, careening down to breasts, hips, even toes, making her suddenly aware that with his other hand he'd pulled her close against him.

Not even with Steve, whom she'd loved with all her heart, had it been this hot, this fast. Their loving had been gentle, warm, and occasionally silly, and nothing like this sudden, fierce flare of intensity and heat.

But she would not have expected anything less from this man; she knew from his work that his passions ran deep and swift, and it only made sense that that would translate to this.

She heard him make a low, rumbling sound, and it sent a shower of sparks arcing through her. Emboldened by that sound of need, she returned the caress of his tongue with her own, and was rewarded by a repeat of that sensual sound.

He probed farther, deeper, teasing her with hot swipes over

her lips and tongue, and tracing the ridge of her teeth. He shifted, putting a leg over hers, and she savored the weight. She realized her fingers were clamped on his shoulders, not to push him away but to pull him closer, ever closer.

God, it had been so long, so very long since she'd even wanted a man to kiss her.

She wanted Lake McGregor to do a hell of a lot more.

And then, suddenly, he was gone. He pulled back from her sharply, and she nearly cried out at the loss.

"What the—?" he muttered.

She opened her eyes.

He wasn't even looking at her. He was looking around the room, and appeared as puzzled as she had felt upon awakening.

"I . . . how . . . ?"

"I was about to ask you the same thing." *Before you kissed me like no man ever has.*

He frowned. "I was . . . on the sofa." She nodded; although she wondered how he could even think after that kiss. "Did I . . . ?"

"You must have," she said, smiling crookedly, "because I surely couldn't carry *you*."

He looked, to her amazement, sheepish. He rubbed at his face, and she heard the faint scratch of his hand over his unshaven jaw. Irritation bubbled up inside her; was he going to act as if that kiss had never happened?

Then the motion stopped, abruptly. His hand came down. He raised up on one elbow and looked down at her, recollection blazing in his eyes.

He'd remembered yesterday, she realized.

"Why are you still here?" His voice wasn't just morning raspy now, it was hoarse. "I told you to get out."

"I promised to watch," she said simply, ignoring the bluntness of his words, although she felt a little off balance from the sudden change from loving, sweet-kissing bedmate to blunt rudeness. "Besides, you needed someone."

"I think you have me confused with someone else," he said, his voice still hoarse, but as cold as the room now. "I don't need anyone. Ray told you what I am."

"Yes," she agreed. "Now why don't you tell me?"

His brows lowered, dark beneath a fringe of tousled, silver hair. "Me?"

"Tell me," she repeated. "What you *were,* what the Wolf Pack did."

"I'm sure whatever he told you was close enough."

"Was it? It all sounded pretty glamorous, real heroic stuff—"

"Glamorous?" He practically spat out the word. "It was anything but. Sweating in the jungle, drying out in the desert, expecting to be caught every second . . ."

"Saving hostages," she said, remembering what else Ray had told her. "Stopping biological weapons from being used on innocent civilians. And—"

"Ray talks too much." He grimaced. "Half the time they didn't call us in until so many had already died we couldn't bury them all."

She suppressed a shiver at the stark words. And made herself answer evenly; she was surprised he was telling her this at all, and she didn't want him to stop. The kiss . . . well, that could wait. For now.

"But you saved them. The survivors."

"If we were lucky." He seemed to see what she was thinking, and as if he didn't want her rationalizing his role in things, quickly went on. "The rest of the pack got them out, or to safety. While I . . ."

"Did the real dirty work."

He stared at her, as if he couldn't understand her reaction. She wasn't sure she understood it herself; she could see the necessity for the ends, but the means bothered her greatly. She knew she wasn't the first one to ever wrestle with such a dilemma, but it was the first time for her on such a personal level.

"Tell me," she asked after a moment, "was there any other way to accomplish what you did?"

"Nothing that hadn't been tried. We were the final option," he said. She noted that there was no hesitation in his answer, no doubt. This, at least, he was sure of.

But he moved then, slumping back on the pillow behind

him, as if he was too weary to go on. She wondered if he was having second thoughts about what he'd already told her, if he'd decided he'd told her too much. Then he asked, "Did Ray tell you what our name meant?"

"The Wolf Pack? No. I thought it was just a name."

"It was an acronym. W.O.L.F. The guys who called on us, they like that kind of thing. Helps them hide what they're doing. Or hide from it."

"And W.O.L.F means?"

He said it quietly, but it was no less ominous for his soft tone. "Without Option . . . Lethal Force."

Her breath caught as realization struck. "And you were . . ."

"The lethal force," he finished when she couldn't. "That was our bottom line. What made us different. We had the sanction to use lethal force when we had to, on anyone, without orders. No checking in first, no channels, no chain of command, no limiting it to military targets . . . just kill if necessary."

And he was the weapon. The morning light was filling the room now, and Alison sat up. The quilt fell back, but she was no longer conscious of the chill of the room. She looked down at him, but he didn't meet her eyes. He was staring intently at the ceiling, as if he thought the wooden beams were about to give way.

"Was that . . . also the final option? Killing?"

"Most of the time," he said. "We avoided it if possible. The team was for the good, Ian saw to that."

"Ian was . . . the Alpha Wolf?"

He looked surprised. "Ray knew that much?"

"He didn't know his real name. Or he didn't tell me," she amended.

"Ian and his then father-in-law dreamed up the Wolf Pack, to do the things that should be done but that nobody had the guts to do, for fear of being labeled politically incorrect, or damaging our diplomatic relations with some country who's a bit lax on human rights."

Worthy goals, she thought. And perhaps there really was no other way to achieve them, not in the darker corners of the world.

"And he led you, as well?"

"Ian Russell was the heart of the pack. We trusted him, and he never, ever let us down. And in the end . . . he died for us."

His flat, even voice was a startling counterpoint to words packed with emotion, even pain. Even as the daughter of a cop, her life had been more sheltered than she had ever realized; to her, this was the stuff of fiction, of movies. Her father had protected her from such reality. Her fears had been much smaller, she'd grown up knowing about theft, burglary, assault, occasionally murder, but nothing like this kind of wholesale slaughter.

But Lake had lived it, with all its ugliness and danger. She wondered how many there were like her, who lived every day in their relatively safe, peaceful world, never thinking about what it took to keep it that way. And who it took. Men like those in the Wolf Pack. Men like Lake.

"I'm sorry," she whispered.

He turned his head then, looking at her again at last. "Don't romanticize it, Alison. Or me. I was the killer wolf."

"Did it . . . have to be done?"

"I didn't decide that, I did as I was told. And sometimes I did it on my own, when there was no other way."

He wasn't going to cut himself—or her—any slack at all, she realized. He wasn't going to let her sugarcoat any of it; he was going to make her face it, in all its ugliness. Her natural horror at the kind of life he'd led, the things he'd done, was hard to overcome. She wasn't one of those extremists who said there was never, ever any excuse for ending a life, but neither did she take it lightly. But she had the feeling that, no matter what he said, neither did Lake.

"Did you ever kill . . . just to do it? Because you liked it?"

His eyes widened. The metallic sheen was strong now, in the morning light. "No," he said after a moment. "I never liked it. Or hated it. I never felt a thing."

The best, coldest killer that ever walked . . .

"And now? Do you feel anything now?" she asked, almost afraid to hear the answer.

"Now?" His expression changed somehow, shifted, and for

a moment something ancient and weary looked out of his eyes. "Now I don't know anymore."

The phone rang about five minutes after the roses were delivered. Yvette read the card again, the sweet, simple thank you, before she reached for the receiver.

"Phoenix," she said.

"Good morning."

To her own amazement, she blushed. "Hi. The roses just came. They're beautiful, Ray. Thank you."

"You're beautiful."

Her color deepened. "Thank you," she repeated, a little amazed at herself; compliments weren't so very rare that she should be so flustered.

When she got herself together, she told him again what a wonderful time she'd had last night, thinking how true it was, even though they'd only gone to dinner. Of course, they'd closed the restaurant down, sitting and talking for hours after they'd eaten. One of the advantages of being with the local law, she supposed; nobody came along and threw you out.

"How about tonight?"

She'd been hoping he'd ask. "I'd love to."

"Can you get off early? I was thinking we'd go up to Carbondale and catch a movie."

There was no movie house in Jewel, and the theater miles away, almost to Interstate 70 out of Denver, was the closest option. She hadn't been in a while, and liked the idea, but Ray's words brought the nagging worry of the day back to her.

"I don't know, Ray. I still can't find Alison."

"What?"

"She hasn't come in yet, and she's always here by nine. And she's still not answering her phone."

"You've heard nothing from her at all? Not even a phone message since she left the McGregor house?" His tone was no longer soft, flirting, it was sharp and brusque. And she knew that in the space of a split second she'd gone from talking to her shyly charming companion of last night to the cop.

"No. I went by her house this morning, because I was afraid she might be ill. When she didn't answer the door, I used the key she gave me in case of emergencies. But she wasn't there."

"Any sign of anything wrong?"

"No, everything looked like it usually does. She's pretty tidy."

"Nothing knocked over, no food left on the table, no signs of a hasty departure? Nothing like at Lake's father's place?"

She struggled to keep her voice as businesslike as his. "No. I even checked her closet. Her clothes are there, and her suitcase."

"Good thinking."

Warmed by the praise, she added, "And I checked the garage. Her car is gone."

"That saves me a trip," he said.

She felt a chill sweep her. She'd been worried, but she hadn't admitted to herself how worried until now, when she heard how seriously Ray was taking this.

"Ray," she began, but couldn't think what to ask first.

"We'll find her," he assured her. "And then you can chew her out for scaring us."

She liked that *us*. Liked that he was already thinking that way. It was too early, of course, but she was honest enough to admit she preferred him to be in a rush rather than her.

"And you can bet I will," she told him.

"I wouldn't take that bet," he said, and she could almost see him smiling. Then he was silent for a moment before asking, "Were you serious, when you said she might still be with Mc-Gregor?"

"I was only . . . theorizing."

"So you have no real reason to think she would be? That she wouldn't have just told him about the house and left?"

"Only that she's . . . fascinated by him."

"Women always were," Ray said, and Yvette suddenly realized that Ray had known McGregor, from before. And despite her worry, she was curious.

"What was he like? Before, I mean."

"He was . . . normal. All-American kid. Everybody liked him. Captain of the baseball team, solid player on the football team, good grades, the whole thing."

"So," she said thoughtfully, "it was that much more awful for him when he lost it all."

"I suppose it was," Ray said. "You sound like you feel sorry for him."

"I feel sorry for the boy he was," she corrected. "I don't think anybody could feel sorry for the man he is now."

"He certainly doesn't invite it," Ray agreed. "But do you think Alison is . . . fascinated enough to be with him?"

"Even if she's not, there's the showing coming up. She still had things to talk to him about. I suppose she could be with him for that, but . . ."

"Where? There's no sign he was staying at the family house, unless you believe he trashed it himself."

"I don't. That's far too childish, from what I've seen of him. And Alison mentioned something about a place back up in the hills, on Silver Creek."

"I remember that. His grandfather had a cabin up there. Lake and I went fishing up there a couple of times." Ray sounded thoughtful. "What about her other friends?"

"I've called the ones I know of. No one's heard from her since I last saw her. And I called her mom in Denver. I pretended I wanted something else, because I didn't want to scare her . . . but she hasn't heard from her, either."

"Seems like you've done most of my work for me already," he said.

This time the praise wasn't enough. Her hand tightened around the receiver. "Ray? Do you think . . . God, you don't think something's happened to her?"

"I don't know. It's way too early to panic, honey. But I'm going to start checking. Alison doesn't strike me as the type to be careless about letting her friends worry."

"She's not. She's the other way, in fact. I think it's because of how long she waited, worrying, not knowing, when Steve was killed."

"Then we'd better get serious about looking for her. I'll start by having the local deputies keep an eye out for her car. You don't happen to know the license number?"

"I . . . can probably find it. I think she keeps the registration in her file cabinet here." Yvette smothered the trepidation that rose in her at the thought of Alison maybe out there alone, possibly hurt in an accident. And refused to let her mind even touch on the grimmer possibility.

"Do that, and call me. And if she hasn't turned up by noon, we'll file a missing persons report. That'll get other agencies involved. She's an adult, free to go and do where and what she pleases, but if this is so out of character for her . . ."

"It is," Yvette said softly. "In the ten years I've known her, she's never just . . . dropped out of sight like this."

She felt a little better after she'd hung up. Ray was taking action, and he knew what to do.

She would have felt a lot better if he'd been able to reassure her that Alison was safe with Lake McGregor.

Chapter 16

He'd told her far too much. Lake had known it even as he'd been doing it, but he couldn't seem to stop the words from coming. He tried convincing himself that he'd done it to scare her off, but even he wasn't buying that. It might have been a small reason for the spate of words he hadn't been able to stem, but it wasn't the main one.

The problem was, he didn't know what the main reason was. Or didn't want to know.

He sat staring out the picture window, his back to the kitchen, where he could hear her still bustling about. And to the canvas he couldn't bear to look at.

He tried to analyze why he'd told her so much coolly, dispassionately, as was his habit and—or so Ian had said—his greatest strength. Of course, Ian had also said that if there was anything he could change about Lake, it would be that coldness, because eventually it would cripple him.

Ian had known about Douglas. When he'd first been interviewed for the Wolf Pack, Lake had told him, bluntly, that he'd killed his own brother, and had refused to answer anything else, figuring this would get him bounced right from the get, so there was no point in spilling the rest of his miserable life story. Ian had never blinked.

He'd found out in his final interview that Ian had had the incident investigated, and had found the circumstances "acceptable." Lake had been stunned, wondering how anyone could find fratricide acceptable.

But he hadn't done it after all.
He hadn't killed Douglas.
The indelible image that he'd carried for so long, of his

brother's lifeless face, bruised by his fist, rose in his mind. His mother had made him look, had ordered him to look at what he'd done. She'd made him sit with Douglas, until they came to take him away. He'd killed her baby, she'd screamed, her most precious son. He was evil, nothing less, and because she was a good Christian woman she would pray for his soul, even though it was already lost, gone beyond saving . . .

And all the time, he thought now, almost numbly, she'd known. She'd known she had committed the most unnatural of acts, known that she was the true killer, the worst kind of murderess, the kind that dealt death to her own child. And had not only let her only remaining child take the blame, but had stoked the fires against him, leading an entire town in their denunciation of him . . .

And he had spent his life believing it. Believing himself damned beyond redemption. Believing that his soul had already been condemned, so it didn't matter what other crimes he piled upon it; what was one more sin when you were looking at hell anyway?

But instead he'd blackened an innocent soul.

He felt torn, clawed at by hot, angry talons—he hadn't killed Douglas, but he had killed all the others. He'd been relieved of blame for the very death that had allowed him to function as the killer the Wolf Pack had had to have. It didn't seem to matter at the moment that most of them had deserved killing, that the world was a better place without them, didn't count that he'd helped save ten times that many. He'd traded the most personal kind of guilt for a more universal, but no less intense guilt. And it was squeezing him inside in a way he'd never known, twisting, ripping at him, in a way he didn't know if he could stand.

He'd always figured he was as tough as he needed to be; he'd withstood some pretty ugly treatment on occasion. But all the physical pain he'd ever endured was nothing compared to what he was feeling now. The physical pain had been endurable, because he knew there would be an end to it—it would stop, or he would die. But this . . .

"Hope you're up for steak. I found these in the icebox. And

toast is about the only side dish I could come up with, but I sprinkled some parmesan cheese on it."

He turned to look toward the kitchen, doing so, he noticed wryly, in a way that assured he didn't have to look at the painting. He should just cover it up, he thought. Throw a drop cloth over it. Except that it seemed somehow right that he should leave it open, so he would have to dodge it, as if it were some sort of punishment.

"It was all I could find, other than chili, and that seemed a bit much this morning."

Right now, to him, anything seemed a bit much. But he knew he had to eat, he'd gone too long, he could tell by the weakness in his legs and the steady, pounding headache centered at the top of his head. And he couldn't afford to be in this condition, not now. It was only a matter of time before Joplin found him, and he had to be ready.

And he had to have Alison out of here.

She'd be safe enough back home, or in the gallery, where the connection to him was tenuous enough that Joplin would believe her if she told him she didn't know anything. Joplin would never believe Lake had been foolish enough to tell her anything, let alone as much as he had. Even he couldn't believe it.

But he had been that foolish. And he didn't know why.

What he did know was that he never wanted to spend another night like last night. He'd slept, he'd been too exhausted not to, but his sleep had been full of dreams unlike any he'd ever had before, even in the first, hormone-heavy days of budding adolescence.

And swimming to the surface on occasion throughout the night and realizing he truly was holding the cause of it all in his arms hadn't helped any.

If she knew how he'd been dreaming of her, she would have been long gone. And if she had any idea about the hot, erotic images that had populated his dreams, images of her wanting him as much as he wanted her, images of her soft and warm and naked and ready, images of her atop him, beneath him, beside him as they explored each other endlessly, she'd have slapped him before she left.

"Lake?"

It came out low and husky, and his entire body tightened at the sound. He looked at her, and read in her eyes that his thoughts had been all too clear on his face. He was, it seemed, rusty in more ways than one.

"You have your car here?" he asked.

She nodded, looking a little disconcerted at the ordinary question. If his expression had been half as hot as his thoughts, he couldn't blame her.

"Then you'd better get your cute little butt in it and get out of here."

Her expression changed, became cool and unreadable to him, and he doubted it had anything to do with his reference to her anatomy. Although he wasn't sure; funny, the worse he got at hiding his thoughts, the better she seemed to get.

"Do you mind if I eat first?" she asked, her tone bland. "I'm rather hungry."

So am I, he muttered inwardly. *Hungrier than I've ever been. And it couldn't happen at a worse time.*

He opened his mouth to tell her again to leave, had the words on the tip of his tongue, but found himself agreeing she could stay and eat first instead.

He wondered about that bad timing as he walked toward the small table where she'd cleared a space amid the clutter for two plates. All these years, and he hadn't had more than an occasional passing interest in a woman, and then only for the temporary treatment of urges grown too strong to suppress.

And now, when he could least afford it, when distraction was the last thing he needed or wanted, into his life walked the one-of-a-kind Alison Carlyle.

He shifted his chair so that his back wasn't to the window; she was where he'd usually sit, facing the expanse of glass, but it wasn't worth the explaining it would take to get her to vacate the seat. He'd just be more alert. As he would have to be from now on; he'd laid out the bait and it was only a matter of time before the vermin took it.

He was halfway through the steak when she hit him with it.

"Are you going to let me have the painting for the show?"

He stared at her. "What?"

"Seems a reasonable question. And a good idea. A sort of pièce de résistance, and an unexpected bonus for the customers."

"You don't really mean you want to . . . display that?"

"Why not? It's the most powerful thing you've done, even more than *Sacrifice*."

He swore, low and harsh and heartfelt.

"I know, Lake." All matter-of-factness had vanished from her voice now. "I know it would be like . . . ripping yourself open for the world to see, and I know how frightening that can feel—"

"Then how can you even ask?"

"Because that's what great art is."

Great art.

He nearly laughed out loud, but stopped it because he was afraid it would come out as a moan.

"So who's after you?" He barely managed to swallow, and sat staring at her. "Is it something connected to the Wolf Pack? Somebody out for revenge or something?"

She said it mildly, as if it were an everyday topic of discussion for her. Compared to this tone, she'd been hysterical when she'd finally told him the old house had been wrecked. He searched his admittedly shaky memory of last night, trying to remember if and what he'd told her. She studied him across her plate, her expression as bland as her tone had been.

"Alison—"

"I think if you're throwing me out because of him, I have a right to know, don't you?"

"No."

"So it is a him?"

His brows lowered. "Don't play games with me, Alison. You'll lose."

She lowered her fork to her plate. And she glared at him. "I am *not* playing games. I don't. I asked a simple question."

"Stay out of it."

"No."

She said it in exactly the same noncompromising tone he had used, and it took him aback slightly.

"Why?" he asked, before he even thought about it. "Why

won't you just leave it alone?" *Why won't you just leave* me *alone,* he added silently.

"Because I'm incapable of merely observing life. Because I love your work. Because I want more of it in the world." She eyed him levelly and fired the last blast. "Because I care."

He dodged the declaration instantly, vehemently. "You may love my painting, but you don't know a damn thing about me. And the world would be better off without my kind of work."

"I disagree," she said calmly. "And I believe you left out the last one."

His jaw tightened as he went on. "And if you care, it's because of my father. You liked him, so you're trying to like me. Well, don't bother."

"I did like your father. He was a kind, gentle man. And he was hurting so much, over you."

"Right."

"He was," she insisted. "I know. I listened to him, as he lay in pain and dying, tell me how horrible he'd been to you, how he should have helped you more, no matter what your mother said or did. That he'd wanted to look for you, when you first ran away, but . . ."

"I'll bet my mother threw a fit at that idea."

She nodded, her expression so sad he couldn't doubt her sincerity. "He argued with her. Said this way they'd lost both their sons. But she said . . . you were dead to her anyway and she was glad you were gone. He thought it was because you'd . . . killed Douglas, but all the time it was because she couldn't stand to have you around as a constant reminder of what she'd done."

He still couldn't quite absorb it all. What was ironic, he supposed, was that he wasn't having trouble accepting that his mother had killed Douglas, only that he hadn't. He could believe it of her, but he found it much harder to think of himself as free of that sin.

"You can't quite believe it, can you?" she asked softly, reading him so perfectly it made him nervous. "All these years you blamed yourself, and now all of a sudden you find out you're innocent . . ."

"Hardly innocent. I've got more than enough sins to replace that one with."

He felt her eyes on him as he took another bite of the steak he could barely taste anymore. "Would you have committed the others, if you'd not thought yourself guilty of this one?"

And just like that, she'd dug down to the crux of it, and hit home.

"I don't know," he whispered, hating the way the words sounded, as if they'd been torn from him against his will. As perhaps they had been.

He couldn't look at her, didn't want to see her face. She would either be looking at him with repugnance, or with sympathy, and he didn't want either one from her. For a long time she said nothing, and he began to think—to hope—that she was going to let it end here. At last. He could get her out of here, before it was too late, before she got caught up in—

"What about the rest of the Wolf Pack? Where are they now?"

He still didn't look at her, but supposed it couldn't do any more damage than was already done. "Jess—he was the Lone Wolf, the tracker—is on his honeymoon."

"Really?" She sounded surprised.

"He married . . . Ian's widow." He stole a quick glance at her, and saw her expression. "They had a thing going, way back, before she married Ian. But she wouldn't marry him."

"But she did now?"

"Jess said . . . there were things he had to learn before he was right for her."

"Jess," she said slowly, "sounds like a wise man."

"Maybe. Now."

"And the others?"

"There was only one other, besides Ian. Rob Cordero."

There was a pause before she said gently, "Was?"

"He's dead." *And for that you'll pay dearly, Joplin. I promise you that.*

"I'm sorry. You all must have been very close."

"Closer than . . . brothers." An odd sensation filled him as he said it. He'd used the words before, but never, ever without the deep, tearing bite of vicious irony tearing at him. Until now.

"Tell me something, Lake," she said in a conversational tone that made him wary. "If someone thinks they have a terminal disease, and goes a little bit nuts because of that, and then later they find out they aren't sick at all, do you blame them for what they did when they thought they were going to die?"

"When it's murder?" he asked, knowing that for all her kindness, all her bleeding-heart tendencies toward him, she was too gentle, too humane to accept that.

"You're determined to hang yourself for this, aren't you?"

"The thought has crossed my mind," he said wryly.

She stared at him, and he saw her expression change as she realized he'd meant that literally.

"It wasn't your fault, Lake. None of it was your fault."

Why she cared was beyond him. Surely this went far past any lingering responsibility she might feel, either to his father because of her promise to him, or to he himself because what she'd thought would be cause for rejoicing had instead cast him into turmoil. And he wasn't fool enough to read much of anything into what had happened between them this morning. They'd both been half-asleep, had awakened in unaccustomed intimacy, he'd wager they'd both been alone a long time—it was just a simple chemical, hormonal reaction to the situation, to be expected between two people who found each other attractive.

He wasn't sure how he knew that, but he did; Alison Carlyle would never have kissed a man she didn't want, not like that. And the very thought of her wanting him, in an intimate, sexual way, threatened to rip loose what self-control he had left. He grasped for a diversion.

"You're ready to forgive me for everything, aren't you?" he asked.

She crossed her knife and fork on her plate, and pushed her chair back from the table. "The only person who has to forgive you," she said, "is you."

She rose to her feet and picked up her plate. She reached for his, but he stood up and took it himself before she could. She turned to head into the small kitchen.

He heard a sharp sound.

Unmistakably breaking glass. Then an odd thump.

In an instant the old instincts kicked to life. He dived for Alison. She gave a little shriek as he hit her, hard, and took her down. Her plate hit the floor, an oddly muted echo of the glass-breaking sound. He cushioned her fall with his body. It knocked a bit of wind out of him; she was not a tiny woman. Then he rolled over, taking her with him. And then again, until they were in the small kitchen.

"What are you—"

"Quiet." It hadn't been a bullet; not only had there not been a sound—even from long range—but there hadn't been the distinctive *thwap* of a round burying itself in the wood of the walls. Something had hit the floor, and although it hadn't sounded like any canister or grenade he'd ever known, he wasn't assuming anything.

"Are you cra—"

"Alison, shut up," he hissed.

Whatever it was, it hadn't blown up. Yet. He knew up the hill to the west was the best line of sight on the cabin, something he'd been aware of for a long time, ever since he'd come to think of life—and death—in such terms as line of sight and cover and ambush potential. But for somebody to get something through the window like that, they had to be a lot closer. And the glass hadn't shattered, as it would for anything big enough to carry enough explosives to take them out. Nor had anything come in after, to indicate the first was merely the preparation break to make the hole.

Alison opened her mouth again, but closed it without speaking. He didn't know what had changed her mind, but he welcomed it. He twisted around so he could look through the doorway to the picture window. He found what he was looking for.

Dead center, he thought.

A small, fairly neat hole. Too big for a bullet, too small and tidy for a grenade, or tear gas canister, or a flash-bang.

And nothing was happening.

"Stay here," he ordered, and got to his feet. It could be a de-layed fuse, he knew, in which case he should send her outside, but if she went outside, then she could run right into whoever had done this.

"Lake—"

"Just stay. I'll be back in a minute."

He edged carefully into the other room. Pressing himself against the wall, he inched his way to the large table that held his painting supplies. He reached out and beneath a pile of rags, and pulled out the lightweight Glock he'd kept loaded and at hand since he'd arrived. Slowly, keeping low and as much out of sight of the big window as he could, he moved into the main room.

He saw it right away. Lying amid the brushes and scrapers he'd sent flying when he passed out and hit the table. Small, and innocent-looking.

A smooth, nearly round rock, no more than an inch and a half in diameter.

A floorboard creaked behind him. He whirled, in a crouch, slamming the pistol into firing position.

Alison smothered a gasp. He yanked the weapon to the side, in case his trigger finger didn't get the message to stop in time.

"Damn it, Alison, I said stay put!"

"You didn't come back—"

"So you decided to come see why? Maybe run into our visi-tor?"

"All right, it was a mistake."

"I could have killed you!" He straightened up, secured the Glock, and jammed it into his waistband at the small of his back. The adrenaline was still coursing through him, and he wasn't quite ready to let her off yet. She didn't argue with him, which almost irritated him; he wanted a fight. With somebody.

"Your reflexes are . . . pretty impressive," was all she said.

"Why the hell do you think I live alone? I could kill some-body without even intending to."

She paled slightly, but said steadily enough, "But you didn't."

"Sheer luck."

"I doubt that."

He had to give her credit; she'd obviously been scared, but she was determined not to let it show. She looked at the window, at the hole, and frowned. Then she lowered her gaze, and he saw it stop on the floor.

"A rock?" she asked, incredulously. "This was all over some kid throwing a rock through your window?"

"It was no kid," he said.

He walked over and picked up the round stone. He hefted it, remembering. It had been during a guerrilla warfare simulation, when he and Joplin and the rest of the Wolf Pack had been "dropped" behind enemy lines with minimal equipment—and no firearms, only a single grenade each and a supply of the paint balls used in war games to show captures and kills, paint balls they would have to get close enough to use hand-to-hand, since they only exploded with considerable impact.

The mission was to take out a well-guarded munitions dump. Joplin had gotten himself marked as a kill early on, after he insisted he could take the guards out with a knife. But the guards had been battle-veteran Green Berets, and while Joplin had taken out one, there had been two more on top of him before he could apply the red "kill" paint.

Lake had taken a simpler route. In fact, he'd gone back to basics. David and Goliath, to be exact. He'd fashioned a sling out of his knit shirt, and nailed the three remaining guards in the back of the head with the paint balls, hard enough to prove that had he been using rocks, they would have been stunned at the least. If he'd been using a gun, they'd be dead. As it was, they'd gone into defensive posture, scanning the underbrush the attack had come from.

And then he'd neatly lobbed his grenade over their heads and into the bunker the same way.

The game had been over, the bemused guards were wiping paint out of their hair, and Ian had been both laughing and pleased at Lake's unorthodox but effective approach.

And Joplin had been furious. Humiliated and furious at being the only man marked as a kill. He'd had some choice words about Lake's use of a child's toy in a man's game.

"Better than a child's tantrum," Lake had said.

That night a rock much like the one he now held had crashed through his barracks room window.

Message received, Joplin, he said to himself.

The game was on. Only this time, neither of them was playing, and the red wouldn't be paint, but blood.

Chapter 17

"I want you right behind him," Lake said as Ray turned to go back to his unit.

Alison never moved. She simply stood there, arms folded in front of her, looking at him. She'd been shaken when he'd dived at her, and more than shaken when he'd drawn down on her, but there was no sign of it now. Part of it was that she'd seen the rock and written it off as another kid's prank, and part of it may have been Ray's reassuring presence, but he knew that wasn't all of it, that it was her own strength that had enabled her to recover quickly.

She walked over to the broken window. She carefully stuck a finger through the hole, then removed it and looked at him.

"That's double-paned thermal glass." He didn't answer what wasn't a question. "You don't just toss a rock that small and have it go through both panes. You'd have to . . . shoot it with something."

He lifted one shoulder in a half shrug. It didn't stop her from going on.

"You reacted like you were still under fire in a war somewhere. You had a gun ready and at hand, like you were expecting an attack. And you went out hunting with it, after the rock was thrown, when the logical assumption was that any kid would have run like hell. What's going on, Lake? Who did you leave your door open for yesterday?"

She was too damn smart, he thought, but he tried to head her off anyway. "Training. Reflex."

He reached for the Glock Ray had studied with interest, all the time eyeing Lake suspiciously. Alison watched him, apparently unmoved.

"Not impressed, are you?" he said, waggling the lightweight but very effective weapon.

She imitated his one-shoulder shrug. "My dad was a cop, and I worked three years at a youth shelter in South Central L.A., where gangs are a way of life. I saw a lot of guns. And a lot more damage done by them."

He didn't know much about L.A., but he didn't have to guess South Central wasn't Beverly Hills. When he'd first seen her, she hadn't looked the type to get involved like that. But now . . . now maybe she did, dressed in jeans and a sweater the same bright, clear blue as her eyes, a sweater so soft-looking it made his fingers itch to touch it again, to feel it under his fingers, as he had this morning when he'd kissed her, when he'd wanted so much more than that kiss—

"And I didn't forget my question. What's going on?"

Of course you didn't forget, he thought. But in fact he was glad of the interruption to his wayward thoughts. He wasn't used to having his imagination take off with him like that, that was a part of him he'd thought long dead.

"It's personal, so drop it. Please."

She looked at him intently. Then suspicion flared in her eyes. "You said somebody was after you. Is it somebody from town? One of those narrow-minded old—"

He'd said that? He must have been truly out of his head. He let out a weary breath. "No, it's not, Alison. I can't—and won't—explain. Will you please just go?"

"Did the men in the Wolf Pack desert as soon as there was a threat?"

"That," he said in irritation, "has nothing to do with this."

"I could have been standing at that window, could have been hurt," she pointed out. "Not to mention you almost shooting me yourself. I think that makes me involved, Lake."

"Little girl, you have no idea what you're dealing with."

"And if you think insulting me is going to change my mind, you're wrong."

No, it would take a lot more than that, he thought as he set the pistol down within easy reach. She was tougher than she looked.

He resisted the urge to rub at his eyes, as if refusing to give in to it would somehow make him less tired. Or distracted. Or whatever he was that had enabled Joplin to get so close without him sensing it. True, judging from the force necessary to send that rock through both panes of glass—as Alison had quickly figured out—he must have been using a powerful slingshot, which meant he could have been some distance away, but still, there had been a time when an enemy couldn't have gotten within a mile of him without him knowing it. Ian had joked that he must be able to smell them, and asked if he had Native American mixed into his Celtic ancestry.

"Do you think he's gone?"

"Probably."

"Probably?"

"He wouldn't want to risk Ray seeing him. He's good, but so is Ray, and he would have guessed that."

"How? Is there some kind of secret signal you special forces types give off?"

He shrugged. How did you explain the subtle signs, the way of moving, the awareness, the instinct that told you that you were dealing with one of your own, someone who had walked the same ground, balanced on the same edge?

And then he suddenly realized he'd as much as admitted who the man was, all but name. He stared at her, trying to figure out just how she'd managed to manipulate that out of him. Was she that good, or was he that out of it?

"I guessed," she said, reading him so perfectly it unnerved him. "You said it's not somebody from Jewel, and it figures there would be some grudges left behind, from the kind of work you did."

If you only knew, he muttered to himself. But he had to head her off, minimize this, or he had the feeling he'd never be rid of her. She'd camp out here, and get herself hurt. Or worse.

"He's probably gone," he repeated aloud. "It's safe for you to go."

"Well," she said calmly, "if he's gone, then there's no need for me to rush, now is there?"

He stared at her. She'd so neatly trapped him again that he was a little stunned.

"Are you crazy, or just lacking in good sense?" he finally asked.

"I've been accused of both at one time or another," she said.

"Alison, please," he said.

As the words echoed in the room, he was stunned anew. Was he actually pleading with her? Why? Because of one shared, hot, fevered kiss?

The memory of those moments shot through him again, burning like a bullet would have, carving him up inside. Her mouth had been as soft, as warm, as sweet as he'd imagined. More so. Her flesh beneath the soft blue sweater had been hot and tempting. And if she hadn't looked up at him, with her heart in her eyes, he might have done a lot more than kiss her.

He suppressed a shiver at the desire that shafted through him like a white-hot iron. His body clenched around it, acknowledging its need no matter how much his mind tried to deny it.

He turned away from her, unable to meet that steady gaze any longer. He'd been stared down, he, Lake McGregor, the Gray Wolf of the Wolf Pack, had been stared down by a woman who didn't have the sense to get out of here and away from him when she had the chance.

"Who is it, Lake?" she asked. "Somebody who . . . didn't like something the Wolf Pack did?"

He gave a wry chuckle. "You might say that. Look, it's just . . . harassment, Alison. That's all. It'll be over soon."

"Tell Ray."

This time there was genuine humor in his laugh. "And he'll do what? Protect me?"

She flushed, as if the irony of an assassin needing protection had just occurred to her. And he wondered if she was fooling herself, pretending he wasn't what he was, if she'd forgotten. But as soon as it occurred to him he discarded the idea; he doubted Alison fooled herself much. She was too quick to see the good, too quick to forgive, but she wasn't a fool. Not by a long shot.

And if he didn't watch himself, he was going to fool himself into something stupid. He already admired her; he'd be worse than a fool to let it go beyond that.

And if you're tempted to forget that little fact, he told him-self, *just think of Joplin out there with a sniper rifle instead of a slingshot.*

"Go, Alison. Your friends are worried about you." His mouth quirked. "If they knew you were with me, I'm sure they'd be worried even more."

She eyed him levelly. "How do you think Ray knew to come looking for me here?"

His brows lowered. He knew that's what Ray had been doing, and had just happened to arrive shortly after Joplin had delivered his message. "I assumed he was just checking here because he knew about our connection."

The last two words gave him a strange sort of feeling even as he spoke them. He should have thought of another way to say it. Not that the words mattered; there was no connection between them, at least not one that would last beyond the mo-ment when he finally got to Joplin.

Or Joplin gets to you, he thought.

"Yvette sent him."

"Yvette? Why would she do that?"

"Because she thought I might be here."

"And that worried her, I'll bet."

"Not in the way you mean. She's an amazingly fair-minded person, and she doesn't share the prejudicial view of you half this town seems to have."

"Only half?" he asked wryly.

"I think you'd find a lot of the people your own age aren't quite as convinced you're the devil incarnate as your mother's contemporaries are."

"Their mistake."

"Uh-uh," she said easily. "That shoe doesn't fit anymore, remember?"

Again the shock of realization hit him; it truly was ingrained gut-deep, that reflexive assumption and acceptance of guilt. For an instant he felt the heady lift of freedom, before the flip side to his release drove home once more.

"It fits," he muttered. "It's just on the other foot."

"If you insist on equating things you did that needed doing, as part of a job that needed doing, with mortal sin, then that's your problem, Lake McGregor. Don't expect me to agree with you when you're wrong."

"You take a lot on faith," he said.

"Was your precious Ian a fool?"

"No," he snapped, stung.

"Was he evil?"

"No," he repeated, much less vehemently, seeing where she was headed.

"You trusted him?"

"With my life," he whispered.

"Then why shouldn't I?"

He'd been neatly outmaneuvered, and he knew it. He couldn't refute anything she'd said. But he couldn't help feeling as if he should. It couldn't be that easy. Shouldn't be that easy.

He made himself look at the painting. Made himself look at the faces. Faces he'd carried around in his mind and his heart and his gut for years before he'd ever committed them to canvas. Faces he would never, ever forget, even if he never looked at this haunting piece of work again.

He hadn't just lost his soul, he'd thrown it away.

If you insist on equating things you did that needed doing, as part of a job that needed doing, with mortal sin, then that's your problem.

He shook his head once, sharply. She was tangling him up, at a time when he could least afford it. It was bad enough that it had been proven so resoundingly that he was as rusty as he'd feared; with what she'd told him—and she herself—on top of it, he'd be lucky to survive to meet Joplin face-to-face.

He strode across the room and grabbed up a drop cloth. He threw it over the painting. This distraction he could eliminate, at least.

"Go home, Alison," he said tiredly.

"I'm not sure I want to go charging out there, if you're not positive that man is gone."

"That's why I wanted you to leave with Ray," he pointed out. The edge in his voice rose out of the knowledge that since he'd apparently lost whatever instinct Ian had thought he had, she could well be right, and Joplin could still be out there. He had to get her out of here; Joplin was just crazy enough that he'd decide to come ahead. And if he did, she'd be just a witness Joplin would have to kill.

And he realized in that moment how much doubt he actually had in his own capabilities. It had been a very long time since he'd had to think like this.

"Well, it's too late now," Alison said, "so I might as well—"

"Take the painting."

She blinked. "What?"

"Take it. Load it up. Visibly. Make a production of it. Then get out of here."

"Why? Why did you change your mind?"

"Does it matter?" he asked wearily.

"Yes," she said after a moment. "It does. It matters a lot."

"Just take it and go. If he is still around, he'll think that's all you came for."

Her forehead creased in puzzlement. "Why would he think that? He doesn't even know who I am." When he didn't answer, her eyes widened. "Does he?"

Lake's stomach knotted. He didn't want to tell her Joplin no doubt knew who she was. That he was behind all the vandalism. Worse, that Joplin knew about Phoenix. That that was why he was here. But most of all, he didn't want to tell her it had been planned that way. By him. He told himself it was because he couldn't risk her having any second thoughts. It had nothing to do with worrying about what she thought of him.

"It doesn't matter," he finally said. "You're not in danger from him. Like I said, it's just harassment, aimed at me. It won't last."

He wouldn't let himself consider what would happen if he was wrong, if Joplin had already gone over that edge Ian had known was there, and no longer discriminated between the intended target and anybody who got in the way.

It was true this rock had only been an announcement. A trumpeting of Joplin's presence, and a warning. Next time, it wouldn't be a rock. Next time, it would be for keeps.

He had to get her out of here while she still thought this was fairly harmless. And he would simply have to keep her safe. And for starters, he had to get her out of here, back to town, if he had to go with her himself. In fact, he would go with her, just to get her back among people. She'd be safe there; even Joplin didn't make public moves.

He hoped.

"You're certain she was all right?" Yvette asked worriedly.

Ray nodded. "She was fine. Lake looked like hell, but she was fine."

He'd decided not to mention the hole in Lake's front window. It would only worry her, and he supposed Lake's story of more vandalism could be true. It all sort of fit, although it would have taken a hell of a strong arm to get that rock through double-paned glass. And Lake wasn't acting like a man dealing with some simple malicious mischief.

"Was he sick? Is that why she stayed there?"

"That's what she said. That he'd been feeling a little off the other night, and he hadn't been in touch since. And when she got there, he was completely out of it, on the floor."

"Oh, no," Yvette said, immediately sympathetic. "Is he all right now? Does he need a doctor?"

"Don't let any of the old-timers hear you worrying about Lake McGregor," he said teasingly.

"Phooey on them," she said. "From what I've heard, they should all be ashamed of themselves. He was just a boy when all that happened, and it's not like he *meant* for it to happen."

She said it determinedly and rather fiercely, and Ray smiled. "Good for you," he said.

He did like this woman, he thought. She had the courage to make up her own mind about things, and to leave a fancy job in the big city, a job many would envy, to come to tiny Jewel and help a friend.

He supposed his admiration must have shown in his face, for she colored slightly. "Will she be coming back today?"

"I'd say so. Lake didn't look too happy with her being there."

Yvette sighed. "That's my girlfriend. She's not like me, I like men who are what they appear to be. Even if it takes them a while to get things moving."

Ray nearly blushed at the pointed look she gave him. "Thank you . . . I think."

She laughed, telling him without words that yes, she'd meant him. It warmed him, and his worry about what had happened this morning began to fade.

"But no," Yvette went on, "Alison has to go and fall for the dark, complex type."

"Steven wasn't exactly dark and complex," Ray pointed out. He'd met Alison's late husband on several of their trips to the area before the mountain road accident that had taken his life. He'd found him open, friendly, good-natured, and eager to soak in everything about the area he'd come to love. Ray had even once taken Steve and Alison on a local tour, to some of the spots the tourists never saw.

Steve had been, Ray realized now, just about what you'd have expected Lake McGregor to become, had not tragedy derailed his life.

And he had been very much in love with his wife. As she, it seemed, had been with him. Since she'd come to Jewel, she'd been seen at various town functions and social occasions, and eventually had been invited to even the most snobbish of local affairs, but she always came alone, or with someone like frail Mrs. Langley, who wouldn't have been able to make it by herself.

Through these generous acts, and others, she had become a part of the fabric of life in Jewel, gradually, walking just the right line between being outgoing and suitably restrained for a newcomer. Of course, she was still a newcomer to the old guard, and always would be. Anyone who moved here after adulthood was so termed; apparently children got some sort of special dispensation.

"No, Steve wasn't dark and complex," Yvette agreed, "but he wasn't a challenge to her, either. I know she loved him, but Alison's a very smart woman, and I think she needs a man who will do that, keep her on her toes."

"Just how involved do you think she is with him?"

"I don't know, really." Yvette lifted a brow at him. "Do you think it's a problem? Should I warn her off?"

Ray sighed. "I don't know."

And it was the truth; he was wary of Lake, but at the same time he didn't feel that gut-deep edginess he felt when confronting someone who was as twisted as the old guard around here would like to believe Lake was.

"Well, she might not listen to me anyway," Yvette said. "She pretty much makes up her own mind about things."

"Like you do."

"Most of the time. I like to do my own thinking."

"Then what do you think about lunch?"

She smiled, widely. "Why, I'd love to." Then, looking troubled, she added, "But I'm not sure I should close up—"

"Don't worry. I'll bring lunch to you. You like Chinese? That new place opened up on Saturday, out by the highway."

"I love it, all of it, and that would be sweet of you."

"I'll bring a bit of a lot of things, then."

Alison might be heading down a difficult path with Lake, Ray thought as he drove away, but he couldn't help seeing his own road unrolling in the sunlight before him. Yvette seemed to like it here in Jewel, yet she had no illusions about some of the very people who made his job a misery sometimes. They had a great deal in common. And were finding more every hour that they spent together.

Life, he thought, was good.

Chapter 18

It seemed to Alison almost as if that shocking moment had never happened, as if she'd never been knocked sideways by a flying tackle, as if she had never faced a loaded gun in the hands of a man she barely recognized. It hadn't been Lake McGregor she'd faced, it had been the Gray Wolf.

She shivered at the memory of what seemed impossible now. The rest of the day had passed peacefully and uneventfully. She had given Yvette the rest of the day free, and sent her off with Ray, after delivering a sincere apology for worrying her. Then she had nearly finished the framing this afternoon, with some help from Lake, who had reluctantly come down to town with her after taping over his broken window.

He had refused to speak of anything that had happened. He wouldn't even go by and see the damaged house. If it wasn't for his slight edginess, she would have thought he'd completely forgotten the rock, the tackle, and the moment when he'd turned his gun on her.

He also seemed determined to pretend that what else had happened between them had never occurred at all.

Not, she told herself, that that wasn't the wisest course. But still . . .

It was probably no big deal to him. He was probably used to waking up with women in his bed, and kissing them, and probably a lot more. Any man with his striking looks would be.

She knew even as she thought it that it wasn't fair, and likely not true. Lake McGregor had too much of the loner about him, he wasn't used to having anyone around, let alone women.

She had saved the painting she had named *Ghosts*—he'd

named none except *Sacrifice* himself, he'd told her—for last, half expecting him to change his mind and pull it back, since giving it to her had clearly been a ruse to get her off his mountain. It had stung a little that he would think he had only to offer it to her and she would leave without a second thought, but the desperation that had been in his tone and manner had made her tiny hurt seem unimportant.

And in the end, she'd won, she supposed; he'd given in and come with her. She just wasn't sure exactly why he had. Or what it meant.

"I'll do this one, if you'd like to . . . go for coffee or something," she said quietly, lifting the haunting canvas up to the table.

They'd been working in the storeroom where she did framing, the small, separate building that sat in the rear parking area of Phoenix. And Alison had never been so aware of how small the ten-by-twenty room was until today. Or maybe it was just that Lake seemed to fill it so completely.

"Do you want coffee?" he asked, as if he'd seen through her feeble subterfuge.

"No," she admitted. "I just thought you might not want . . ."

"To look at it?"

"You don't seem to like to. And I can understand that, really, I—"

"Can you?"

His voice was suddenly tight, harsh, the easy manner she'd seen all day from him, but hadn't quite believed in, vanished now. He slipped off the stool he'd been seated on. He leaned over the framing table, palms down on the surface, one hand near the mat cutter that ran along one edge, the other near the stack of frame pieces she'd been using.

"Neturu," he said sharply, jabbing a finger at one of the faces. "He murdered the ruling family of an African tribe—all except the female children, whom he kept to rape and torture and then sell as sexual slaves to anyone who had the price."

Alison's throat tightened, but she doubted she could get any words out anyway.

He jabbed at a second face. "Challesco. A warlord in the mountains of Central America who decided he was ruling by divine right, and set himself up as emperor. He set out to slaughter any of the native population who didn't go on their knees to him soon enough. And he used their children to do it, imprisoning them so their parents would try to rescue them— and when he'd killed the parents, he threw those children into a pit and left them to die a slow, starving death, eaten alive by rats and insects."

Alison shuddered at the too-vivid image. This was what he felt guilty for killing? For ridding the world of such monsters?

"Lawrence," he said sharply. "Blew up a busload of senior citizens, in the British countryside, when it looked like the peace talks with the Irish might be working. He didn't want that, not because he gave a damn about Irish freedom, but because it would greatly curtail his arms trade. He let the IRA take the heat, when for once they hadn't done it." For an instant his eyes closed, and she wondered what he'd thought of. And then he told her, and she wished he hadn't. "He knew about the bus, and where it would be . . . because his own aunt was on it. She lingered for three days, in agony, before dying."

"My God," Alison whispered.

He went on, giving her the story behind each face, tales of horror and ugliness that went far beyond her admittedly limited view. And with each one, she read the reality in his face, that there was a price for every death at his hands, and he'd paid it. Perhaps he'd not acknowledged it, or let it surface until now, but it was there, in his eyes, in his voice, in the tightness around his mouth.

When he finally stopped, she didn't know what to say. Or what he expected from her. Because he was looking at her as if he expected something, although she couldn't imagine what she could say that would give him ease.

"It's ugly, horrible, all of it, Lake. That people like that exist in the world. That they so often get away with what they do."

He lifted his head and stared at her. Silently. And she realized the depth of the battle he was fighting, had been fighting since she'd pulled the entire justification of his life out from under him. She took a quick breath and went on.

"The only thing that makes the knowledge bearable is

knowing there are men like you, and the others, willing to risk your lives to stop them."

She thought she saw a tremor go through him, but it vanished so quickly she couldn't be sure. "You believe that?"

She nodded. "I only wish you could." She was sure of the tremor this time. "You must have, at the time, Lake. You must have believed in what you were doing."

"I . . . did."

"Then nothing has changed since then. Not the rightness of what you did, not the need for it . . . nothing except your view of yourself."

"I wish I . . ."

His voice trailed off. She could only imagine what he might wish. That he could still believe in what he'd done. That he could still believe in himself.

She glanced once more at the painting, lying there on the cold metal table, stark, compelling. She looked back at the man who had created it, the man who had lived it. The man who wasn't, as she'd first thought, temperamental, but driven.

I think you've been half in love with him ever since you laid eyes on that painting of his.

Maybe it really was true. At the very least, she'd been fascinated before she'd ever known him. And now that she did . . . she didn't know if she could deal with his history—she didn't know if he could do that himself—but she did know she couldn't seem to fight the growing attraction she felt for him. Perhaps it was partly guilt, that she wanted to make up for what she'd inadvertently done to him. Or that she wanted to heal him, as Colin had hoped the revelation about Douglas would do.

But that wasn't all of it, and she was honest enough to admit that. In fact, not even most of it, she thought as she studied his profile as he looked at the canvas on which he'd poured out his soul, the soul he didn't believe he had any longer. But it was there, she thought as she shifted her gaze back to the painting. It was there, in all its painful, tortured clarity.

"No frame," she said suddenly.

His head came around. "What?"

"No frame. Absolutely nothing to detract from the painting. And on an easel, with brushes at hand . . . just as I first saw it."

He looked at her, at first quizzically, then with a hint of amusement. "I hope you don't want me passed out on the floor beside it."

That trace of humor sent a little thrill through her. Hope soared; if he could joke, surely he was coming to accept, wasn't he?

"Not necessary," she said lightly. "I'll come up with some other kind of floor decor. A drop cloth under it, maybe. A used one, that people would instinctively avoid stepping on. That would keep people at the right distance for viewing."

"Use the actual one. It's conveniently messed up with perfectly matching colors," he said dryly.

The humor, wry though it was, seemed to be holding. And that gave Alison hope, although she wasn't exactly sure for what. "That would be the easiest, of course. Thanks for the offer. After the showing, maybe I'll frame it up, too."

She said it deadpan, and for an instant he looked startled. Then he must have seen a glint in her eye, or the way she was barely able to keep her mouth from twitching, and he laughed.

"I've seen worse things passed off as art," he said.

"So have I," she agreed, smiling.

Then the companionable moment was lost when Yvette called her to the telephone.

"Ray said what?" Lake asked; Yvette had told him who the caller had been, and he'd been waiting for Alison to hang up.

"He said he found the kid who painted my window, and damaged my car and your house," Alison repeated, setting down a stack of newly printed forms on her desk.

That was impossible, he thought. It took a moment before he could get the question out. "Kid?"

She nodded.

"It really was a kid? All of it? He's sure?" He couldn't be right. It couldn't be that simple, that innocent.

"Yes," Alison said, her tone almost carefree; she clearly believed Ray had indeed found the culprit. "Mrs. Langley gave him away."

He knew he was gaping at her, but he'd been so utterly convinced it had been Joplin, and that the game had been launched. Could he have been wrong? *That* wrong?

He gave himself a mental shake. "Old Mrs. Langley, the piano teacher?"

"The same. She'd heard about the window, and remembered a boy who had shown up for a lesson with red paint under his nails and in his hair. She called Ray, bless her, and he snatched up the kid."

He remembered the woman who had seemed old even when he'd lived here; she had to be pushing eighty now. But apparently she hadn't slowed down any, at least mentally.

"Ray said he broke on the spot about painting the window, once he realized Ray was dead serious, and could prove he'd bought the paint. And then he confessed about the car, too, before Ray even asked."

Lake sat back in the eagle chair, feeling a bit stunned. He'd been so positive, sure his bait had worked and Joplin was here, and was just toying with him, with all this childish action. But if it truly *had* been a child . . . Ray said the boy had confessed, and it was even . . . logical, if not reasonable.

But if this kid had done the damage, then was Joplin here at all? Had he been so completely, utterly wrong? Jess had warned him about rust, but could he be *that* out of it, to blow it so completely?

"A kid," he muttered, still not quite able to believe it.

"One of Althea McCray's great-nephews, at that," Alison said. "Looks like I wasn't that far off when I asked her if she'd taken up graffiti."

Startled, Lake stared at her. "You asked the Iron Matron that?"

"I ran into her shortly after the window was done. She called you . . . that word."

"I'm not surprised," he said, "but still . . ."

"It seemed a reasonable question at the time," she protested. "And as it turns out I was sort of right. Her brother's grandson got in some bad trouble with his dad down in Pueblo. Willie's been staying with Althea."

Willie. He remembered the boy from the drugstore, the one

Melinda had said was her nephew. The same boy on the street who had made the comment about being glad Lake wasn't his brother. It fit. God, it all fit. It made perfect sense, and if it was true, it meant he'd been worse than wrong, he'd been stupid. He wasn't rusty, he was incompetent.

"Anyway, he'd been hearing nothing but her . . . ranting for weeks about you and the showing. So he was inspired to some kind of campaign against both."

"Both," Lake murmured as she pounded home his idiocy.

As if she'd followed his thoughts, Alison spoke softly, "Maybe that's who it was with the rock, too, Lake. Maybe it wasn't . . . whoever you thought after all."

"I . . . maybe."

Lord, could it be? Had it been simply a kid with a powerful slingshot, carrying out some kind of vendetta inspired by his aunt's hatred? Had there been no message at all there, no significance in the choice of weapon other than what a young, small-town boy had access to?

"Ray said he was going to take another look near your place. The kid's only transportation is a bike, and he might have left some tracks somewhere."

Lake was still reeling, and had to fight to even think rationally about what she was saying. "Ray thinks the kid got up there on a bike?"

"It's a mountain bike, a good one—the best, of course, because Althea bought it for him—and Ray thinks it's possible. The boy is familiar with the area. He said that and the bike would explain . . ."

She trailed off awkwardly, catching his full attention now. "Explain what?"

"Why you, of all people, hadn't heard anything."

Lake laughed, low and harsh. "I think you know why I didn't hear anything. I was too screwed up to even see straight, let alone hear."

"Lake—"

"Never mind." He waved her off, not wanting to discuss those lapsed two days any further.

"It's a relief to know it was just one kid," she admitted. "I thought the whole town had turned on me."

He forced himself to shut off the useless speculation about Joplin for the moment. He would have to analyze it later, when he had time to go over everything in his head, and see where he'd gone wrong. Which, it seemed, he had in a big way.

"I'm sorry they took my presence out on you. Jewel is—"

She cut him off. "It's not your fault they're a bunch of narrow-minded, judgmental jerks."

Her fierceness warmed him in a way he couldn't quite write off to simple amusement. "Jewel's judgmental jerks?"

"Never make it as a rock band, would they?" she said with a laugh that made him shiver.

"No, they wouldn't." Then, before he realized he was going to say them, the words came out. "Will you let me take you to dinner?" She blinked, clearly surprised. "To make up for the last one," he added. "I sort of . . . ran out on you."

"You had reason," she said softly.

"Is there anything you won't forgive?" he asked lightly, hoping it sounded as if the answer meant nothing.

"Yes," she said. "Throwing innocent children into a pit, or selling little girls, or—"

She stopped when he held up a hand. "I get the drift. Thank you." *For much more than what you said,* he added silently.

"You're welcome," she said quietly, softly. And as if she'd heard the words he'd only thought.

He wouldn't be surprised if she had. This woman upset his equilibrium unlike anyone ever had. He was so off balance that it seemed entirely possible that he'd mistaken everything, that the string of petty attacks had been the work of a bored kid who'd listened once too often to Althea McCray's venom. Possible that his bait hadn't worked at all.

Had he been so long away from the Wolf Pack's world that he couldn't judge anything anymore? Couldn't tell a concerted campaign of a trained fighter from the acts of a malicious child? Or was it still too close, making him see threats behind every tree and magnify them?

He didn't know. The only thing he was sure of was that if his judgment was this shot, then he shouldn't be relying on himself to keep Alison safe.

But was there anything to really keep her safe from?

He had no answer. All he could do was wrestle with the seeming fact that Joplin had had nothing to do with the things that had happened.

That maybe he wasn't even here at all.

Chapter 19

"Has anybody else ever seen your work?"

"No." A pause. "Yes."

"I see," Alison said, smothering a smile as she picked up her wineglass for the last sip.

Dinner had been pleasant, sliding along on the surface. Avoiding the topic of the kiss she'd never expected and couldn't forget. Ironic, she thought, that the topic that had once been so volatile had suddenly become preferable. But what surprised her was that he seemed willing to talk about his work. But he'd been acting rather odd ever since she'd told him the boy who had defaced her window and damaged her car and his window had been caught. As if he had something to think about that took priority even over his desire to keep his work to himself.

He made a wry face as he explained his contradictory answer. "I gave a piece away, but they don't know it's mine. I mean, that I painted it."

This surprised her, a lot. As private as he was about it, he'd given a painting to someone? "What a wonderful gift. They must be very special to you."

"Yes."

She thought a moment, something tickling the back of her mind. Then she had it. "The other man from the Wolf Pack, who's still alive—Jess, is it? You gave it to him?"

He drew back slightly, staring at her. "How did you know that?"

"Simple—I just couldn't think of anyone else who would mean enough to you to risk the exposure."

"Simple," he muttered.

"So . . . was it a wedding gift?" He gave her a sideways look, as if he were wondering how she knew that, too. "You told me he'd married Ian's widow. It's a logical assumption."

"Oh. Yes. It was."

"Tell me about it, the painting."

"What?"

"Describe it."

He shifted uncomfortably in his seat, and she wondered why. She'd seen all his other work, even the haunting *Ghosts,* so why would he be hesitant about this one?

"I . . . it's a lake, in the mountains."

She was going to have to work at this, she realized. He wasn't any more used to talking about his work than he'd been to showing it to anyone.

"Season?" she asked.

He blinked. "Spring. After a storm."

Spring. The beginning of new life. "A bad storm?"

"Yes," he said slowly. "A bad one."

"But it's over?"

"Yes," he said again, his eyes going slightly unfocused, and she realized he was turning inward, remembering. "The dark clouds are still on the horizon, not quite gone. But the sun has broken through . . . it's shining on the lake, it's quiet, peaceful."

"Peace after chaos," she said softly. "What a beautiful gift for a wedding."

"It's what I wish for them," he said, still looking at whatever was in his mind's eye. Then he came out of it; she could see him snap back to the present. "Jess deserves peace. And Beth even more."

And you don't? she asked him silently, already knowing what his answer would be.

"You didn't sign that one, either?"

"No. They think I bought it somewhere."

They may not for long, Alison thought. If this show went even half as well as she hoped, there would eventually be art dealers all over the region who would be able to spot a McGregor from thirty feet away. But she decided it wiser not to point that out to him just yet; sometimes she thought, because he had little faith in the value of his work, Lake really had no idea what he'd started, or how big this snowball could become.

She realized he was watching her rather carefully, and lifted a brow at him.

"Aren't you going to ask?" he said.

She didn't pretend not to understand; she knew what he meant. She'd asked him about signing any paintings that sold at the showing, and he'd at first said a flat, emphatic no, then, when she'd explained the necessity of a signature for authenticity and valuation reasons, that he'd think about it.

"You said you would tell me when you'd decided," she answered simply.

He looked at her as if he wasn't at all comfortable with her knowing him well enough to know when not to push. But after a moment he let out a short breath and said, "I'll sign them. Not that I think any of them are going to sell."

"They'll sell, Lake. Thank you."

"You're welcome."

His voice sounded strangely husky, and she wondered why. Was it that the idea that his art had value still seemed so impossible to him? And he was looking at her so oddly, as if he wanted to say something, but couldn't find the words.

"Alison, I—" He broke off sharply. Whatever it was, he'd clearly decided not to go ahead. Instead he finished hastily. "If you're finished, let's go."

"All right."

She got to her feet, wondering if this man would ever be able to open up to anyone, if he would ever get over the habit of keeping everything locked inside. She was certain it was a habit born long ago, on the day his own mother had accused him of the murder she herself had committed, and no doubt nurtured by training and years in a job requiring the utmost secrecy. The question was, was it a habit he could break? And would he even try? Could she ever convince him he should?

And when did it become your job to convince Lake McGregor of anything? she asked herself as they stepped outside, into evening air that held the faintest hint of the fall briskness to come.

But she knew the answer. It had become her job not when Colin had handed her the huge responsibility she didn't want, not when she'd learned he had been viciously and unjustly treated by those who should have loved him unwaveringly, but when she'd looked at his painting and fallen in love with the mind who could paint such ugliness and such beauty in the same image, who could see life's grim side yet also its glory.

She knew he would argue with that, that he would say he had painted the dark truth barely hidden by the gloss of sunlight and civilization, but that was simply a matter of point of view. It could just as easily be an image of the beauty overcoming the ugliness, the sunlight winning at last in this dangerous game he played.

He would probably laugh at her if she said it, she thought as they reached her car, but he couldn't stop her from thinking it. And believing it. You couldn't paint the light so beautifully if you didn't believe in it, if you didn't know its power.

"I'll drop you off at the gallery for your car," she said as they got inside.

He shook his head. "That's out of your way, isn't it? Yvette said you lived on the west side."

She laughed lightly as she turned the key. "Jewel is only five miles long in any direction, you know. No place is really out of the way."

"Just go home. I'll walk to the gallery. Yvette said you often do."

"Not at ten o'clock at night." She let the motor idle and looked at him. "You and Yvette seem to have had quite a chat."

Rather endearingly, he looked embarrassed. Something she imagined did not happen to him often. "She seems to think you . . . that I . . . she was worried about you," he finished awkwardly.

"Friends worry," she said neutrally.

She put the vehicle in gear and eased away from the curb. It was a rather silent ride; he didn't even protest when she headed for the gallery and his car instead of her home. She wondered what he was thinking, what had silenced him. For once she wished Jewel were a little bigger, or had more traffic at this hour; as it was they were sitting beside his rental car within three minutes.

She didn't like the idea of him going back up the mountain, and staying there alone, even if he insisted it was nothing but someone's effort at revenge for some old, petty slight. She had the feeling there wasn't much petty anything in his world, or his past, but she couldn't think of any way to stop him.

He barely said good night, and she had the feeling he was already a million miles away as he got out of her car and into his. He'd been so . . . distracted, all evening. With a smothered sigh she backed up so he could open the door, and so she could make a U-turn to head to her house.

She was in the middle of the maneuver when it happened. She heard the sound, a loud report cutting through the night. It echoed for a moment, then faded.

She knew what it was, there was enough hunting around here that she'd grown familiar with the sound of rifle fire. But it wasn't usually heard here in town, and certainly not this late at night.

She glanced back at Lake's car, to see if he'd heard it too, although she knew he must have.

She cut off her own sharp scream.

There was a bullet hole in his windshield.

That should have finally gotten his attention, he thought as he surveyed the scene in the street from his safe rooftop. He'd half expected McGregor to come after him after he'd sent that unmistakable message with the powerful slingshot, but he knew he would now. But the Gray Wolf would find nothing, not until he decided to let him.

The Gray Wolf. McGregor himself had chuckled when Russell had hung the name on him, saying he'd seen it coming for weeks. McGregor had always had the annoying habit of laughing like that, as if there were nothing in the entire world that could move him to any strong emotion.

"You'll find out different," he muttered as he stared down at the chaos in the street. "And it'll be a long, hard lesson."

He watched the woman, curious. She was reacting strongly, but females got hysterical over the stupidest things. He was going to have to figure out how she fit into this now. They seemed together, yet not together. Simply a business arrangement, with the woman an unwitting dupe, being used by McGregor? Or had it evolved into something more, something that explained the slight tension he sensed between them? Or was it just McGregor himself who was radiating the tension? He did have that silly aversion to using civilians. But clearly he was using her.

He'd been surprised when he'd seen the second vehicle parked at the isolated cabin, the day he'd made his first move, but when he'd seen her he'd begun to wonder. He had watched carefully that day, as the woman loaded something covered with a cloth into her car. A painting, presumably, for this show she was putting on.

He wondered what she saw in McGregor's silly dabbling that made her think he was a real artist. But apparently she saw something—or else McGregor was making it worth her while. That made more sense, that he was paying her to do this. It sure made more sense than believing he had some kind of artistic talent.

He didn't wonder why. He knew why McGregor had suddenly decided to go public. It wasn't any coincidence that he'd done it now. But it didn't matter. Even if it was intended as a trap, he was too smart to get caught in it. And wouldn't McGregor be surprised when he found himself caught in his own snare?

A black-and-white sheriff's four-wheel drive arrived, and a man in uniform got out. He lifted the rifle, and peered through the scope.

It was the same man he'd seen up on the mountain, he thought. Not the usual college-boy cop who'd never seen real violence. This one was different. Older. Tougher. He moved like a man who'd been in hostile territory. Like a man who knew what was what.

His finger caressed the trigger. He'd never killed a cop. He wondered what it would feel like. Wondered if he could center punch that shiny badge from here.

His finger tightened. The urge was strong, almost irresistible. And the idea amused him. McGregor had always been

*so self-righteous, never wanting to make a kill unless it was
necessary, always having to be sure they were in the right. Oh,
he could do it well enough, he was smooth and slick and quiet
and effective—if he was sure the target needed killing. Or deserved it. Even in training it had been there, that ridiculous
moral streak.*

*The killing of a cop would not sit well with McGregor's
overactive conscience. It might just put him off guard, force
him to make a move. But he didn't want him off guard. He
wanted him armed and ready, so there could be no doubt who
the winner was.*

He eased his finger off the trigger.

He would wait. So it would be perfect, he would wait.

"You all right, Alison?" Ray asked.

She nodded. Or meant to; she wasn't sure if the intent had
translated into motion. Ray's arm was warm and solid around
her shoulders, but somehow she wasn't comforted. Right now
she wasn't sure anything could comfort her.

"I've got to go talk to him again."

"Fine," she muttered. "Go ahead. See if *you* can get anything out of him."

She would never forget as long as she lived that shattering,
horrid moment before Lake had moved. That moment when
she'd sat there staring at the starburst of broken glass, unable
to see through it, unable to see him, and wondering in horror if
she should be grateful for that fact.

And then, at last, he had moved, rising up from the front
seat, where he had apparently dived for cover.

And the first thing the idiot had done was *yell* at her, for
God's sake. Yelled at *her,* for not flooring the gas pedal and
getting the hell out of here. Like she was supposed to just take
off and leave him there, not knowing if he was hurt, or
dead . . .

They'd shouted at each other for a couple of minutes before
the shock had set in, and she'd begun to tremble. He'd
stopped then, and in the ensuing silence she realized how
ridiculous they must have sounded. But before they could say
any more, Ray had arrived; whether via the grapevine or po-

lice radio, he always seemed to know what was going on before the dust settled.

By then people were starting to appear, people who lived
close enough to have heard the ruckus, maybe even the shot,
and had decided it was now safe to emerge and gape. Ray
shooed them back to the other side of the street, but he couldn't
make them leave. And they weren't about to when they realized that one of the players in this drama that had interrupted a
quiet night in Jewel was the town scandal.

Ray had called in his one deputy and they'd searched the
area Lake had indicated, although how he could tell that was
where the shot had come from was beyond her. Ray turned
back to Lake, who was sitting sideways on the driver's seat of
his rental, the door open, intently picking bits of safety glass
out of the gray sweater he wore. Alison watched, trying to sort
it all out, trying to figure out if it was all related, or just attacks
from several sides.

"Feel up to some more questions, Lake?" Ray asked.

He didn't even look up. "She should go home."

"She's a witness," Ray said.

"You got her statement, didn't you?"

"She told me what she saw and heard, yes."

"Then send her home. She—"

"—is tired of being talked about in the third person when
she's standing right here!" Alison snapped.

Ray, at least, had the grace to look chagrined. "Sorry."

She turned on the more recalcitrant male. "So I'm supposed
to go home like a good little girl, and forget all about the fact
that somebody just tried to kill you?"

"If he'd meant to kill me, he'd have done it," Lake said,
sounding tired. Then he grimaced as if he wished he hadn't
said it.

She lifted one arched brow at him. "He would have?"

"This is way out of Willie McCray's league," Ray said.
"You have some idea who this was, Lake?"

Alison stared at him, as if she could force him to answer just
by the force of her look. *So help me, if he tries to deny what's
so obvious, if he tries to turn* this *into nothing . . .*

He looked up at her, and grimaced again, as if he'd read her every thought. She didn't care if he had.

"This wasn't meant as a kill shot," he said wearily.

Ray looked at the bullet hole once more. Now that she was a bit calmer, Alison could see it was closer to the center of the windshield than to the driver's seat. Of course, she could also see that it had plowed right through the seat back, and into the rear seat behind it, so it didn't make her feel all that much better. All she could think of was what it would have done to Lake's body. And his seeming lack of concern jabbed through the chill of shock that enveloped her.

"How do you know he didn't just miss?" she asked acidly.

Lake shook his head. "He wouldn't miss."

"He's that good?" Ray asked.

Lake hesitated, then said at last, "He's the best sniper I've ever seen."

"Even better than you?"

"Yes," he said shortly.

"So you do know who he is?" Ray asked softly. "Is it somebody else from here?"

"No," Lake said, not even reacting to the repetition of the thought that somebody from Jewel might hate him enough to kill him. "And it's between him and me. Don't get in the middle, Ray."

"He's shooting rounds off in my town, endangering my people. That makes it my business. Especially," he added, holding something out to Lake, "when it's rounds like this."

Lake looked, but didn't touch the cylindrical object on Ray's palm. Alison could see it was some sort of bullet casing. It looked longer than any she'd seen before, but didn't understand Ray's tone or inference.

"You know," Ray said, almost idly, "some out-of-town hunters have gotten real determined since they raised the fees on hunting licenses a while back. Some have gone to bigger guns, thinking the old .308 isn't sure enough. But I've yet to see one go deer hunting with a high-velocity, long-range round like this. No point, since it could go right through a buck and not drop it unless you got lucky and made a heart shot."

"Deer season isn't for two months yet."

Ray ignored that. Just like it deserved, Alison thought.

"Now this," he said, hefting the casing, "looks to be a two-twenty-one round. The type used in a lot of military weapons. Sniper rifles in particular."

Lake said nothing.

"I suppose if I searched you or your car for weapons, I might turn something up?" Ray asked.

"If you were in the mood to violate the Fourth Amendment," Lake muttered.

"I'm not sure I'd consider it an unreasonable search, but I'm not going to push you. Besides, this town's still open carry."

Lake gave him a lopsided, halfhearted grin. "You never know when the next Ted Bundy might escape from jail and you'll need the locals and their weapons to round him up."

"That was Aspen. I don't plan on declaring *posse comitatus* anytime soon." Ray held out the bullet casing, and Lake knew he hadn't been diverted. "Don't suppose you'd know why somebody as good as you say would be sloppy enough to leave this behind?"

Again Lake said nothing.

"Calling card, perhaps?" Alison put in, her shock and terror finally turning to anger. He'd nearly been *killed,* for God's sake, and he was acting like it was nothing, like it happened every day . . .

But it once had, for him. Once, every day had been full of things like this. Maybe he was callused in the literal sense; it just didn't get to him anymore, not through the thick, insulating layer of experience.

She watched numbly as Ray finished up what investigating there was to do, which included, apparently, impounding Lake's rental car as evidence.

"And don't leave town without telling me," Ray said as Jewel's single tow truck arrived and began hooking it up. "You're going to tell me who's behind this, Lake. And soon. I'm not risking the people of this town getting in the way of some old vendetta you've brought with you."

"Oh, by all means, protect the good people of Jewel," Lake said. Alison's head came up at the bitterness in his tone; she hadn't heard that from him before.

"It's my job, Lake. To protect them. And you, too. I'm going to do that job. And if you don't like it . . . tough."

Alison saw something flicker in Lake's eyes, something like respect, and it was in his voice as well when he spoke.

"Touché, old friend," he said. "I wish you'd been sheriff twenty-five years ago."

Coming from Lake McGregor, that was a sizable compliment, and Alison saw by Ray's expression that he knew it.

"Where are you going to be?" Ray asked, his tone gentler.

"Around." When he saw Ray stiffen, he added, "I mean it, Ray. I'm not going anywhere. I'll check in."

"See that you do," Ray said, sounding slightly mollified. He signed the form the tow-truck driver stuck in front of him, told the last few straggling onlookers the show was over and sent them home, then went back to the sheriff's unit and left.

For a moment Alison just stood there looking at the sparkle of glass on the asphalt.

"Don't suppose you'd loan me your car," Lake said dryly.

Her head came up. "No, thank you. I just got it repaired, if you recall."

He shrugged. "The walk'll do me good."

"Walk?" It struck her what he meant. "Back to the cabin? Are you crazy?"

"Probably."

"You can't walk that! It's miles away, most of it uphill, and there's some nut out there with a gun. My God, a . . . a sniper, who's already taken a shot at you!"

"I suppose this isn't the time to say 'Been there, done that'?"

How on earth did he do this? An hour ago she'd been terrified he was dead. Now she wanted to kill him herself, for his smart-ass attitude.

"Maybe it's too bad he missed!"

"Maybe." He didn't even blink. "But like I said, if he'd wanted to kill me with that shot, he would have."

"So what was the point of this? What are you supposed to do now?"

"Wait."

"Oh, wonderful," she said, her jaw tightening.

"I'd better get started," he said, as if he was actually going to do it.

"You can't go back to your place anyway," Alison pointed out. "He knows where it is."

He said nothing, and turned his face away as if he were afraid she'd read his thoughts. She stared at him for a long, silent moment. And then it struck her.

It's between him and me. Don't get in the middle, Ray.

"You're not just waiting for him to come back, are you?" she said in shock. "You *want* him to come back."

He wouldn't look at her, and she knew she was right.

"That's what all this is about, isn't it? He's not trying to kill you now, because you've got some stupid, testosterone-induced idea of fighting it out man-to-man, don't you?"

When he turned to look at her then, a shiver ran down her spine. *He was the Gray Wolf, the best, coldest killer that ever walked.* As he stood there, awash in moonlight, the eerie glow turning his hair to pure, gleaming silver and his eyes to molten metal, she could believe it.

"You're going to kill him, aren't you?" she whispered.

He gave a weary sigh, lowered his head, and he was Lake once more. "I'd be very foolish to admit that to you, you being so close to the local law enforcement."

"If you think Ray wouldn't connect a dead body with you at this point, then you're underestimating him."

For some reason she didn't understand, he smiled. A genuine smile, not one of the ones that sent a shiver down her spine. "No, it wouldn't do to underestimate Ray."

"Don't go back," she said suddenly. "Come to my place. You can stay there. He won't know where it is."

He looked startled. "Your place?"

"I've got plenty of room."

"Ah. Your place, but not your bed."

Blood rushed to her cheeks, heating them despite the late night chill.

"I just like to be clear on things," he said mildly.

His tone was light, but Alison had the strangest feeling that behind the surface, his mind was racing, gauging, judging, and that it had little to do with what he was teasing her about. She

should have known he'd be thinking of . . . other things, that
the other was . . . just a joke. He'd as much as admitted he expected to have to kill this man who was after him.

And she supposed that meant she should run like hell, from
him and the insanity he seemed to live with. And run just as
hard from the crazy feelings he stirred in her. But she couldn't.
She'd never been a runner, she'd always been a doer. She
knew she couldn't run even as she considered the idea, and
considered retracting the invitation she couldn't help feeling
would put them at some sort of crossroads she wasn't ready
for.

"Go home, Alison," he said softly. And despite the gentleness of the tone, perhaps because of it, she knew there was no
point in arguing. So he wasn't going to come. She should be
relieved. But she wasn't.

When she at last pulled into her own driveway, she stifled a
yawn. It had been a long night, and was only going to get
worse; she would never get to sleep. And she knew it wasn't
solely because he was out there, somewhere, with some maniac with a high-powered rifle or something, hunting him. It
was also because, once the unexpected words of invitation had
left her lips, she'd been swamped with images that had only
been heightened by his teasing.

For the first time since Steve had died, she was curious
about what it would be like to be with another man. More than
curious, she admitted, recalling some of the very uncharacteristic and heated dreams she'd been having of late. All of them
featuring Lake McGregor in a very intimate starring role.

She wasn't anywhere near sleepy, although she felt exhausted. She knew her mind was racing far too fast to let her
relax, so she busily fixed a large pot of hot chocolate, hoping it
would soothe her, and knowing it would take the whole pan to
do it.

She started a fire, out of a need for comfort more than
warmth. She sat for a long time, the only sound disturbing the
quiet night the occasional pop as the resin in the wood heated
to the point of explosion.

It reminded her of the sound of that shot, and she almost
wished she hadn't done it. And the chocolate wasn't working,

even the second cup. How could you be so tired, and yet not sleepy? she wondered. Her body felt battered, as if she'd played a daylong game of football, but her mind refused to shut down.

She hated thinking of him out there, alone, even knowing that he was used to it, that it was what he did. Or had done; she realized with a little shock she'd never asked him what he'd been doing in the years since the Wolf Pack had disbanded. Somehow it hadn't seemed important, since obviously in the future he'd be painting. He probably wouldn't even be able to keep up with the demand, if things took off as she thought they would. Not that that would be a bad thing; more demand than supply was always a good situation for the seller. He could—

She froze, her muscles tensed, before her mind realized why. It played back, like a recording, the sound she'd just heard. It hadn't been the fire, nor one of the normal settling sounds of the house; she'd lived here for five years, and she knew every sound the place made.

This wasn't one of them.

And she thought it had been outside anyway, she thought as she played it back in her head once more.

Somehow that wasn't comforting.

Slowly, she got up. She thought of calling the sheriff, but Ray had had a tough night already, and the other deputy, Charlie Arpel, was not her favorite person under the best of circumstances; small-minded and cruel, he'd once made a pass at her so crude she'd rejected him rather publicly, and he'd never forgiven her.

Besides, it was probably just the local wildlife. An owl, perhaps, making his nightly rounds, or maybe even a deer; it wasn't unheard of that they wandered through town, especially at the end of a dry, hot summer.

It was only her overactive imagination that was trying to connect this somehow to what had happened tonight. And this morning.

The realization that it had only been this morning that the rock had come bursting through Lake's window—that it had only been this morning that he'd kissed her and kindled a fire like nothing she'd ever felt—rattled her. It seemed ages ago, and yet so vivid in her mind that she could still almost taste him on her lips.

She shivered, and got quickly to her feet, wrapping her arms around her. She'd just peek out the kitchen window into the backyard, she thought. That's where the sound had come from, she was sure of it now. And she could double-check and make sure she'd locked the door that led from the small dining nook to the outside, too.

She made her way toward the kitchen, only halfway there thinking to wonder why she was tiptoeing if she was so sure the sound was outside.

She pushed open the door. She stepped into the kitchen.

She ran into something tall and solid and alive.

She screamed.

Arms grabbed her, held. And a hand came around and clamped over her mouth.

Chapter 20

This was probably the stupidest thing he'd ever done in his life. He'd tried to talk himself out of it all night. He'd barely been able to concentrate on his search, barely been able to maintain enough efficiency to assure himself Joplin was no longer in town; the rest of his mind had been tangled up in this idea. He could list a dozen reasons why he shouldn't have done it—endangering her being at the top—and only one reason on the other side.

And in the end, that one reason had won out, over all his common sense, all his instincts, all his training.

That scared him. He was completely off balance, and he couldn't seem to right himself. He'd gone from being sure Joplin had been here to being almost certain he was not, and back to being certain the instant his gut had yelled at him to dive for cover in the car the instant before the bullet had plowed through. Somehow that he'd been right in the first place didn't ease his confusion.

At this point there was only one thing he knew for sure; he knew this was wrong, knew it was worse than foolish, but here he was anyway.

And he had just terrified Alison.

"Alison, hush, it's me."

He felt her go still and knew she'd heard him. He let go of her, taking his hand from her mouth and his arm from around her waist.

It was a mistake. She slugged him.

"You . . . you . . . turkey! You scared the hell out of me!"

"Shhh. I know," he said, rubbing at his ribs; she was no

weakling. "I'm sorry. I was going to call out when I got to the doorway. I didn't expect you to walk in here."

"And I didn't expect you at all." He thought her teeth must be clenched, from the sound of her voice, although she'd lowered it. He could see, even in the dim light, that she was glaring at him.

"I didn't say I wasn't coming," he pointed out reasonably.

"No, you just told me to go home, and stopped just short of patting me on the head."

"Does this mean you rescind the invitation?" She didn't answer right away. He could see her still looking at him angrily, could sense the tension in her body. "Alison," he said softly, "I would never condescend to you. You're too smart, too strong, and too . . . stubborn to put up with it."

It was a moment before she responded to that. "Thank you. I think."

He knew she hadn't quite forgiven him yet. "I just wanted you safe. I had to be sure."

"Sure of what?" This time he didn't answer right away. But he didn't have to; she figured it out quickly enough. "That he was gone . . . that's what you've been doing, isn't it? Looking for him, whoever he is?"

"I couldn't come here until I was sure I wouldn't be seen."

"And I suppose that's the reason for the cloak-and-dagger entrance, when I have a perfectly serviceable front door?"

"Yes. I can leave, if you want, and nobody would ever know I was here."

"I would," she said. "I'm not about to send you back out there, even if you are sure that nut with the rifle is gone."

Was that it? he wondered. Was it simply the shock of the ambush, the high-power rifle being fired at him? Was she feeling responsible again? He wondered all those things, but knew he couldn't ask. And then, before he could stop himself, he was doing just that.

"Is that the only reason I'm here, Alison?"

She hesitated before saying, "No."

"What's the other?"

As he'd come to expect from her—unlike most of the other women he'd known—she answered him honestly, without dissembling, without any coy lowering of her eyes. "What happened this morning."

He reached out, unable to stop himself, and grasped her shoulders. "You don't mean that rock through the window, do you?" he asked softly.

"No," she said, still honestly, but he felt her trembling beneath his hands.

He pulled her close, his mouth searching for hers, hungrily, almost desperately, and he only now realized how much he'd wanted this, how much he'd needed it. Her lips parted at his first touch, and he barely took time to savor the softness before he had to, simply had to probe into the warm, welcoming depths of her. Her tongue twisted, meeting him stroke for stroke. And when he retreated, teasing her every bit of the way, she followed.

The moment she took his lure and probed past his lips with her own tongue, the moment he felt the tip of it flicking over flesh that had never been so sensitive, he groaned, unable to stifle the sound as blood hammered through him in hot, heavy beats. The result was inevitable, and within moments he was tightening fiercely, his body clamoring for her with a swiftness that shocked him.

He tightened his embrace, aching for the feel of her against him, from head to toe. She was tall enough that he felt a satisfying length of taut, warm flesh, yet still it wasn't enough, he wanted more, he wanted all of her, he wanted them skin to skin, he wanted all of him inside her, he wanted them in every position he could think of and a few he'd only heard about.

Her hair was down, falling in soft, flowing waves down her back, and he tangled his fingers in it hungrily; he'd known it would be beautiful down, that it would feel like silk, but he hadn't known it would stroke him like some sinuous, sensuous living thing, hadn't known just the feel of it on his skin would fire him to the point of madness.

With a tremendous effort he broke the kiss, and for a moment he just stood there, because it was all he could seem to do. He heard his own breathing, harsh and quick, thought he could even hear the pounding of his heart in time with the

pulsing of his blood. He felt the insistent ache of aroused
flesh, and only the last shred of his will kept him from lifting
her up on a kitchen counter and taking her right here and
now.

"Lake?"

Her voice was tiny, shaky, and so sweetly husky he almost
lost that last bit of willpower.

"Too bad it doesn't snow here this early," he muttered.

"Snow?" she said, sounding puzzled.

"I need to cool down."

He thought he heard her laugh, a low, pleased sound. He
wondered if she was the kind of woman who liked getting
men all hot and bothered over her, then discarded the
thought; she wasn't the type.

"And here I was about to invite you in to sit by the fire and
drink hot chocolate."

So that was what he'd smelled in the kitchen. It was such a
simple thing, and such a warm, cozy image . . . but it wasn't
for him. He didn't deserve such warmth, such happiness, not
when Douglas—

He cut off his own thought. He hadn't killed Douglas. He
hadn't killed his brother, and this woman in his arms was the
only reason he knew that. She'd cared enough to keep her
promise to a dying man. And it hadn't been her fault that it
hadn't had quite the effect she'd expected.

But she'd been there then, too, when he'd felt so lost and
adrift. She'd been tireless in defending him from his harshest
judge, his own mind. She'd refused to blame him, refused to
let him blame himself, and she'd made the life he'd lived
sound reasonable, sane, and if not clean, then at least necessary.

And there were times when he even believed it, when he
believed what he'd done had been necessary, when he'd believed he'd done more good than harm in the long run.

"Lake?"

"Hot chocolate," he murmured. "I haven't had that
in . . . decades."

She laughed softly. "Come along, Methuselah. I'll get you
a cup."

He walked through her house almost gingerly; it had been a long time since he'd spent much time in a home. And this was a home, there was no mistaking that; there were touches of Alison everywhere, in the sensual plush of the deep blue carpet, the blue and gray and white plaid of the comfortable-looking sofa before the fire, the deep, rich contrast of forest green in pillows and the throw over the back of the sofa, thus capturing all the primary colors of this land.

And most of all it was in the little touches, the small statue of a whimsical bear cub trying to figure out water, an earthenware pot painted and fired in the glowing colors of a mountain sunset, the striking, powerful lines of a soaring eagle captured in a few quick swipes of charcoal on a stark white, linen finish paper, the piece cleverly mounted without being framed, the ragged edge of the heavy sheet only adding to its uniqueness.

"This is nice," he said, finishing rather lamely. "Really nice," he added, trying to make up for the inanity of it.

"Thank you. I like it."

"It's . . . very much yours," he said. "Did you buy it when you moved here?"

"Actually, I rent it. All the cash went into Phoenix. But my landlady's a love, and we get on well, so I've just stayed."

And made it all her own, he thought. When she told him to sit down and make himself at home while she went back to the kitchen, he wondered if he dared. He wanted to, wanted it so badly it scared him, wanted it more than he'd ever wanted anything except to see Rob get up out of that hospital bed, or Ian come home alive.

Neither of those had happened. Rob had died, and Ian had come home in a box. So how could he risk this?

Make yourself at home.

Didn't she understand? If he did that, he'd never want to leave. She was offering him what he'd ached for in some deeply buried part of his gut for what seemed like forever. He knew she didn't mean it that way, that she just meant for now, but how could he take even this little bit when his heart was crying out for it all, for a place to belong, someone to belong to?

God, was he whining?

It was true, Lake McGregor was whining. Whining for what he could never have, what he thought he'd given up on long, long ago. How pitiful could you get?

He heard her coming back, and sat down hurriedly. The fire snapped, the heat of it gradually wrapping around his chilled body. Too bad what really needed warming was buried much, much deeper. Even if Alison was right, and he still had his soul, it was no doubt shriveled and dry, and utterly beyond saving. He'd never known how to pray for redemption anyway.

"Here, try this."

She was there before him, holding out a mug with steam rising from it. He took it, and couldn't help the quirk of his mouth when he looked at it.

"You don't like marshmallows?"

"I do," he said, looking at the thick, sweet, white coating on the steaming chocolate. "It's just been a very long time."

"I suppose it's been a long time for a lot of things," she said, sitting down on the sofa beside him.

His head came up sharply. He searched her face, saw, here in the light, the color and slight swelling he'd kissed into her mouth. "Was I that rusty?" he asked.

Her eyes widened, and color flooded her cheeks. "I didn't mean . . ."

He hadn't really thought she had, but he'd wanted to see her reaction. It had been nicely satisfying. "But was I?"

"No," she whispered. "Not at all. Or at least, no more than I am." She lowered her eyes, staring into her cup as if the marshmallows were forming words she had to read. "There . . . hasn't been anyone since Steve died."

Five years, he thought. He couldn't say that. There'd been the occasional brief fling, but—

He suddenly realized this was what scared him most. That Alison wasn't the kind you had a fling with and walked away, the itch scratched, and with no lasting effects. Alison was like Jess's Beth, the kind of woman who would demand your all . . . but give all of herself in return. The kind of woman he had no right to, the kind of woman who would—or should—have nothing to do with a man like him.

But here he was. And here she was. And neither one of them was running. He couldn't seem to find the strength to leave; he didn't know what her reason was. Or didn't want to know.

He looked at her, looked at the twin sweeps of thick, dark lashes that shaded the rich blue of her eyes from his view. It would take an incredible mix of blues to match that color; ultramarine, cerulean, a touch of Prussian, highlighted with some high gloss . . . and then ivory tones for her skin, with just a tiny hint of liquid acrylic in . . . apricot, he thought, for the blush. And her hair . . . he'd use Mars black, with a touch of raw umber for the highlights . . .

She raised her head then, looking right at him, and with a smile he added to his mental list pure white, for the marshmallow mustache on her upper lip.

An urge came over him, sudden and powerful, too powerful to resist. He set his mug on the sofa table behind them, and leaned forward. She looked puzzled, but didn't pull away. Then heat sparked, caught in her eyes, and he realized she thought he was going to kiss her again.

And he was. Oh, yes, he most certainly was. But first . . .

He flicked his tongue over her upper lip, gently licking the sweet residue. Fire as hot as that on the hearth shot through him, and he knew he'd never be able to see a stupid marshmallow again in his life without thinking of this, of how it tasted on her. Someday he'd make her toast and eat a bag of them, just so he could kiss the taste from her lips.

Someday . . . God, he was thinking as if they had a future, as if there were a string of nights like this awaiting them . . .

He heard her give a nervous little laugh when she realized what he was doing. It was what he'd been waiting for without realizing it, and he took her mug from her, set it beside his, and pulled her into his arms.

She didn't resist, but rather sagged against him with a little sigh, as if she'd been waiting for him to do just this. The idea sent the fire within rocketing along nerves that were already humming, already alive with sensations that were shockingly new and intense.

He wanted her pressed against him as she'd been in the kitchen, but he didn't want to get up to do it. So he leaned back on the sofa and pulled her down beside him. He half expected her to call a halt, but she was blessedly silent, kissing him back, probing and tasting his mouth as if he tasted as sweet to her as her lips had to him.

He felt her hands on his chest, not to push him away, but rather flexing, testing, as if she liked the feel of him. And he wished more than anything in that moment that he didn't have this damned thick sweater on. And then she moved, sliding her hands down to his waist, then up again, beneath the sweater. Over his hot, too-hot skin.

He sucked in a harsh breath as every muscle in his gut tightened. She stopped, and he groaned.

"Don't stop," he rasped out, lifting himself against her hands. The movement slid her fingers over his nipples, and he nearly cried out at the blast of sensation that shot through him. "Stop."

At that, she lifted her head and looked at him. He shook his head ruefully at his own absurdity, then let it loll back on the sofa cushion, closing his eyes.

"You have to stop," he said when he thought he could trust himself to say what he meant to say, instead of what his body was screaming at him to say. "Because if you do that much longer, I may not be able to stop."

"And your reason for wanting to stop would be . . . ?"

Startled, his eyes came open and his head came up in a rush. She was looking at him expectantly, calmly, as if she'd asked if he wanted more cocoa. He suppressed a shudder at the implications of the question, and struggled to say something sensible.

"For one, I'm not exactly . . . prepared to go any further. I doubt winding up pregnant is on your agenda."

She gave him an oddly intent look, a look that had him wondering what on earth she was thinking. "Not at the moment," she agreed. "But I can handle that. Thanks to Yvette."

He blinked. *Not at the moment? What the hell did that mean?* "Handle . . . what?" he managed to get out.

Alison grinned. It took his breath away, the easy familiarity of that smile seemed as intimate as any touch, any kiss, and more intimate than most of those he'd had in his life.

"She gave me a bouquet for Valentine's Day this year. Each flower was a condom." He stared at her in disbelief. She laughed. "Sometimes subtlety is lost on Yvette. Or maybe she thought it was lost on me. She said her only wish for the year was that I need to use them."

He didn't know whether to laugh, or bless the absent Yvette. But he knew it wasn't that easy, that having protection at hand didn't make the decision.

"Alison . . . are you sure? That you want . . . this? Want . . . me?"

"This is not something I take lightly, Lake. Yes, I'm sure."

"Why?" he asked, mystified. Why on earth would a woman like her want to give herself to a man with his tangled, ugly past?

"I don't indulge in charity sex," she said bluntly, looking hurt.

He winced, and closed his eyes. He hadn't thought of how that would sound to her, and wished he hadn't said it, at least not that way.

"Lake," she said softly, "would you like to know what I see when I look at you?"

"I'm not sure."

"I see a man who has unjustly had a lot of pain and guilt and grief piled on him, but has gone on in spite of it. A man who found a way to turn even that grim, ugly evil he didn't deserve into something worthwhile."

He drew in a breath, but it was cut short when he felt her hand touch his face. His eyes snapped open, and the moment he looked at her he knew that was what she'd wanted.

"But that's not why I want him," she said in the same soft voice. "I want him because he makes my heart soar and challenges my mind with his work, and did long before I met him. And now because he turns my blood to fire and my knees to water, and that's never happened to me in my life. Not like this."

He simply stared at her, awed by the power and simplicity of her words, and the honesty and pure courage it had taken to say them. He still felt he didn't deserve her, but now it was for a very different reason, one he'd never felt about anything before in his life; he wasn't sure he was man enough for her. Wasn't sure he should take the precious gift she was offering.

But he was going to take it anyway.

She hadn't known this was coming, hadn't planned it. But the moment he'd kissed her again, so hungrily, so urgently, she knew it had been inevitable.

As he stood naked in the glow of moonlight from the window, she again thought of the Gray Wolf. Only this time she thought of his strength, his power, his muscled beauty. Thought of the fact that wolves—and men like this—were rare these days. Thought that he even wore the scars of a wolf, battle scars, marks that only accentuated his power because he was still alive to carry them.

And then she thought of what she'd read once, that wolves mated for life.

She shivered, brushing off the feeling those words gave her. She wasn't a fool, she wasn't going into this thinking she would bind this man to her for life. She wasn't thinking of binding him to her at all. All she was thinking of was that he was the first man in years to make her feel anything, to make her need, to make her want. She'd been afraid it would never happen again.

She'd never expected it to be like this, like fire and ice together, like the sun blazing down on a snowfield, hot and cold at once, and the melting was coming faster and faster with every breath she took, with every moment that she looked at him.

Then he turned, toward the fire, and she gasped as the flames painted him in light and shadow, giving his silver hair a molten look, and showing her just how aroused he was. She shivered, but it wasn't from cold or her own nudity, she could feel the warmth of the fire. Nor was it from hesitation; it had been a long time since she'd stood naked before a man, but she'd never been looked at so hungrily.

No, it was simply from need; she needed him, desperately, all of him, she wanted his touch, his kiss, and his strong body, wanted him inside her in the place that was aching beyond bearing.

She held out her arms. As if he'd been waiting for the signal, he came to her, murmuring her name, touching her as if she were fragile, stroking her as if she were some beautiful sculpture and he a blind man, seeing in the only way he could. His long, artist's fingers caressed her, molded her, until she was trembling.

"God, Alison," he breathed against her ear.

She couldn't say a word. She ran her hands down his back, her fingers tracing every curve of muscle, every scar that spoke of some fight won in a dark, distant place. And at last she cupped his taut buttocks, savoring his low groan as she pulled him against her until his erection was caught between them.

His hands came up and cradled her breasts, and he lowered his head to kiss them. His tongue crept out and swept over her nipples. She cried out at the sudden burst of fire, and cried out again when he caught first one taut crest and then the other between his lips and flicked them with his tongue. Her hips moved involuntarily, stroking him in the process. On and on it went, the heat rising, spiraling, until she was barely aware of anything except the melting sensation that was overtaking her. She sagged against him heavily, unable to stand.

"Now," he said hoarsely, and before she realized what he was doing he had lifted her in his arms. She wasn't a tiny woman, yet he did it as easily as if she weighed nothing at all. He took her down to the floor gently but quickly, and came down atop her with an urgency that couldn't be misread.

"I'll apologize now," he said, his voice tight, "because this is going to be too fast and too rough, but God, Alison, I can't stop."

A shudder rippled through her, at the images his words evoked. For an instant she was afraid, and all the darkness this man had lived, seen, and sometimes created hovered above her, ominously. But then she looked at him, at the tautness of his mouth, the heat in his eyes, and the sheer need reflected in his face in the firelight, and she knew that the man she was thinking of, the man he thought he was, would never have apologized, he'd have taken, no quarter given.

Lake wasn't that man. He was the man who created beauty out of chaos. He deserved the warmth of the fire, not the chill of the moon. And there was only one way for her to show him he was the man she saw, not the man he thought he was. "We'll do nice and easy later," she said huskily, and opened herself to him with a readiness she didn't—couldn't—hide.

It was awkward at first, it had been so long she was afraid she'd forgotten how this worked. But Lake reined in his urgency and calmed her, until she relaxed.

He slid into her, her own eagerness easing his way, yet at the same time leaving her feeling a deliciously stretched fullness. She clutched at him, moaning his name. He grasped her shoulders and pressed into her to the hilt, and she felt him shudder, almost violently. He whispered her name, low and rough, followed by a curse that was somehow amazed and joyous.

And suddenly she wanted it, what he'd said, rough and fast. And hard and wild and frenzied, like she'd never had it before. She whispered it to him, in broken fragments that were all she could manage as the fierce need overcame her embarrassment.

"God, yes," he rasped out, short and heartfelt words. And then he was moving, quickly, fervently, driving himself into her with a force that stole her breath and roused an answering franticness in her that made her claw at him in return, wanting more, ever more.

She felt the building of sensation, the rising tension, and knew that it was she who was going to be the fast one; nerves that had been dormant for five years roared back to life as if they were making up for that lost time. And when he shifted his body slightly, when he said her name in a worshipful voice she wouldn't have thought him capable of, she clutched him to her and wrapped her legs around him as if he were the only thing that could anchor her in the storm she knew was coming.

It broke over her in a huge, hot, undulating wave, and she cried out his name as her body clenched around his. Through the haze of pleasure she felt him drive deep once more, twice. Then a guttural cry ripped from him and he went rigid, arching himself against her. She opened her eyes, saw the beauty of passion in his face, touched with wonder, and prayed that they had seared away his ugliest memory with their own heat.

He collapsed upon her, gasping. He trembled in her arms, not trying to hide it, and Alison felt tears stinging her eyelids.

For a long time the only sound in the room was the snap of the fire, the sound of a log that had burned through collapsing, sending up a shower of sparks. The smell of the wood, clean and smoky at the same time, mingled with the scent that was already imprinted indelibly on her mind as Lake's. They dozed, not speaking, as if neither one of them wanted to risk words.

She opened her eyes much later to the faint light of the dying fire and Lake watching her, as if he'd been waiting for her to wake up. He moved his head, leaned over to whisper into her ear, "Want to try for that nice and easy now?"

She laughed, breathlessly, eagerly. It began again, and she found that while different, nice and easy with Lake had its points as well; the flight was longer, more languorous, but no less intense. And this time, he drove her off that edge twice before he allowed himself to follow.

Logic told her it was the five years wait that made it so spectacular. But her heart and her body knew differently. It was this man, the man who had begun seducing her before she'd ever laid eyes on him, with a few layers of paint on a canvas.

Finally, he shifted his weight off her, slipping to one side, and lifted his head. He looked at her, and she could swear there was bewilderment in his eyes. It could have been the flickering of the firelight, but when he lowered his eyes and swallowed tightly, she thought she might just have been right.

"There's . . ." He stopped, and swallowed again. And began again. "There's no hiding from this, is there?"

Alison's throat tightened as his almost awed words told her everything she could have wished to know, proved to her that this had been as extraordinary for him as it had been for her.

"No," she whispered. "And no pretending it didn't happen, or wasn't what it was."

He shook his head, slowly. "Alison, I . . ."

"Let's leave it at that for now," she said, not wanting to hear anything that would take away from this moment, and from what they'd found, not wanting to hear that it couldn't last, that he'd be leaving after the showing, going back to . . . wherever it was he'd come from.

Her earlier thought came back to her now, and she blushed to realize she'd just made love with—

Oh, be honest, she chided silently, *you just had hot, unequaled sex with a man you don't even know the most basic things about, his address, his job . . .*

But she knew the most crucial things, she told herself. She knew his heart, knew his mind, knew the pain he carried, and even the hope he'd kept hidden . . . until those moments when he'd trembled in her arms and she'd seen it in his face.

He let his head drop to her shoulder. She reached up and ran a hand over the silver hair that she'd found was not coarse like some gray hair, but rather smooth, like heavy spun silk. She stroked it, liking the feel, and when he nuzzled closer, as if he liked her touching him, she smiled into the firelit darkness.

After a while, she finally asked, "Where do you live, Lake?"

He went still. "Feeling a little reckless after the fact?"

Her color deepened, and she was grateful that the fire was providing the only light in the room. "I have no regrets, if that's what you mean." He took a breath, and she realized he'd been holding it, as if a great deal had depended on her answer. "I just realized I don't even know what you do," she explained, "or where you do it. Besides paint, I mean."

"I only paint here. At the cabin."

It wasn't an answer to her question, but it surprised her enough to ask, "Then . . . you've been back here?"

"Several times."

"But everybody said—"

"I always came in on foot, from Hotchkiss. Nobody saw me, or ever knew I was there."

She didn't doubt that; she imagined he was quite able to remain undetected if he tried. She almost asked if not even his parents had known, then realized it was a silly question. So she went back to her original query.

"And when you're not here, painting, what are you doing?"

He grimaced. "I thought the questions came the morning after."

She felt a pang at his words, but knew he was floundering, trying to protect himself, and couldn't quite get angry.

"Call me single-minded," she said.

He sighed. "Nothing," he said.

"What?"

"I travel. Stay a while here, a while there." He smiled, but it was a rather lopsided one. "I'm the nonproverbial, non-starving artist, I guess."

At least he was admitting he *was* an artist, Alison thought. That was something. "So you're . . . what, a permanent tourist?"

"Sort of."

He looked at her like he wished she would drop it, but she merely waited, silently. At last he sighed again, and spoke.

"I got paid pretty well for the seven years the pack ran. And I didn't spend much. Ian invested most of it for me. I don't have to work unless I want to."

"And do you ever? Want to?"

He shrugged. "Sometimes. If I find a place I like, and want to stay awhile. But eventually I'll get an idea, an image that sort of takes over my mind . . . and I have to come home."

She doubted he realized what he'd let slip with that one

simple word. *Home.* After everything that had happened, he still thought of this as home.

"It's like that for—"

A huge jolt cut her off. The windows rattled fiercely, and she thought she felt the floor jump. She gasped, her head snapping toward the front window, half expecting to see it broken. She scrambled to her knees and stared out into the night. Movement to her right caught her eye. Lake was already on his feet and moving, yanking on his jeans, reaching for his shoes.

"Was that an explosion?" she asked, not quite able to believe the obvious.

"I'd say so," he answered grimly.

He was pulling on his sweater, and she suddenly realized she should be doing something similar. She had her sweatshirt and jeans on and was reaching for her boots when he headed for the door.

"Lake, wait!"

"You stay here, I'll—"

"I will not stay here!"

"Alison, that was an explosion. Which means maybe a bomb. Stay put."

A bomb? The idea boggled her, here in small, quiet Jewel. As if to punctuate his words, there came the distant sound of a siren. She crossed the room swiftly, catching him just as he was reaching for the doorknob.

"I'm not going to sit here waiting and wondering," she insisted.

"Yes, you are," he said.

She drew herself up and faced him. "May I remind you I have the only car here?"

"So I'll walk."

"Fine. Then I'll drive."

He let out an exasperated breath. "I should take the car myself."

"Then I'd walk."

"Alison, damn it, it might not be safe!"

"Of course it will," she said sweetly. "You'll be with me."

He stared down at her for a moment. "You're a real piece of work, you know that?"

"What I'm *not* is fragile, Lake. Let's go."

He gave in at last, grudgingly. But three minutes later she felt more fragile, more brittle, and closer to breaking than she ever had in her life.

They rounded the corner onto Aspen Street to see the smoking ruin of what had once been a gallery called Phoenix.

Chapter 21

He'd done this to her. There was no avoiding the truth of it. Lake looked at her, sitting huddled on the curb. One of the fire crew that had finally given up trying to save Phoenix and settled for keeping the fire from spreading had put a blanket over her shoulders. Ray had been paged and was on his way, they'd been told, and he hadn't been happy at the news.

Lake knew he would never forget the sight of her, when it had sunk in that all was lost. He'd had to grab her, restrain her from running into the center of the conflagration when they'd first arrived; she'd been out of the car and moving the instant she'd realized it was Phoenix.

But then she'd seen the truth of it, and he never wanted to see anything like the blank hollowness in her eyes again. It hurt too much, reminded him of all the shocked, glazed eyes he'd seen over the years.

He would have given just about anything not to have to face her, but he knew he couldn't run from this. Not from her.

He stared at the blazing building. He couldn't do anything until he could get inside the place and look anyway. And that wouldn't be for hours; it was too hot, and would smolder for a long time after they got it out.

He walked over to the curb and crouched down before Alison. He wasn't sure she even knew he was there. He'd known in his head how much Phoenix had meant to her, had known how much of her life she had poured into it, but until he saw it in her eyes he hadn't known it in his gut. He did now.

"God, Alison, I am so sorry." She made a tiny sound, the only sign that she'd heard him, was even aware of him. "I should have guessed this might happen, should have gone after him instead of waiting for him to come to me."

The fact that Alison had been with him both times Joplin had made a move, and he hadn't dared to leave her alone with Joplin close by, didn't balance the scales in his merciless mind. By that very refusal to abandon her, he'd probably sealed her fate; Joplin would have seen she was important enough for him to protect, would have realized she was the reason Lake hadn't come after him immediately. Not knowing about the vandalism attacks, that was the assumption Joplin would have to make; he knew how the Wolf Pack had always been about protecting the innocent, and that Lake would be committed to keeping her safe even as he used her. No matter what she meant, or didn't mean to him.

Lake knew he hadn't been seen or followed last night when he'd gone to her house, but that didn't matter. What he'd already seen was all Joplin would have needed to know where to strike next.

In his effort to protect her, he'd instead doomed her to this heart-wrenching loss.

Only the thought of how much worse it would have been had Joplin seen him last night, had he known just what she did mean to him . . .

Just what *did* she mean to him?

It had to be just the ethic of the Wolf Pack driving him, nothing more, he told himself. He couldn't afford to care, not now, not with Joplin escalating things to this level. He had to be focused, utterly, on taking the man out. Nothing could distract him from that task, not even Alison.

And last night? some small voice in his head asked. *What did that mean? Nothing?*

He quashed it ruthlessly. Not now. He couldn't think of it now. It was as if some part of him knew he wasn't going to be able to convince himself it meant nothing, so he didn't dare even look at it at all.

He couldn't afford to care.

And besides, he didn't know how.

Slowly, her head came up, and he saw the struggle to com-

prehend in her face. She was in shock, he knew, fighting
through the fog that clouded the brain at times like this.

"He did this?" she whispered. "The man who shot at you?"

It hadn't even occurred to her, he realized. She didn't live in
that kind of world, his kind of world. At least she hadn't until
he'd come along and forced it upon her. She still didn't quite
believe it, he could see it in the way she was looking at him.

"But why?" she asked, sounding bewildered.

It would have been easier to let her think it wasn't true, to
let her believe it was just a mishap of some kind. It would
have been easier to make up some accidental source of an explosion.

It would have been easier to tell her the building had been
struck by lightning.

"To get to me," he told her instead, wondering how he'd
lost the ability to lie to her face, and knowing deep down he
hadn't lost it, she'd taken it away from him with her warm,
generous spirit. "To let me know he was through playing. To
let me know that he'll make . . . others pay if I don't face him
now, when and where he wants."

Especially anyone I care about, he added grimly to himself,
before that cold, logical part of him could remind him that he
wasn't thinking about that now.

Alison looked at the flaming ruin that had been her pride,
her joy, and the most beautiful thing she'd ever created. "He'd
do . . . that?" Her voice was shaky, but still disbelieving.

"And much worse."

She stared at him. "Who is he, Lake?"

"Alison—"

Her eyes flashed dangerously, and he welcomed the sign of
returning life even as he dreaded the position it put him in.

"I have the right to know, Lake McGregor, and don't you
dare tell me I don't. He's ruined . . . everything I have, everything I've worked for—"

Her voice was rising, quivering, and as if she'd heard it she
stopped herself. It shook Lake more than he wanted to admit
to see her this way, when she'd always been so strong, so calm
and collected. Even now she maintained strength enough to realize she was escalating out of control, and do something

about it. She didn't deserve this, didn't deserve to have a vicious predator like Joplin brought down on her.

It would end. Now. He would see to that. He had to. Jess had almost done it, but he'd had to protect Beth and Jamie, and Joplin had gotten away. Just as well; it was he, not Jess, who was the killer. And just because the reason he'd been able to do it and keep functioning had been yanked out from under him, it didn't change that. He still had it to do.

He should have done it before. Before this. He couldn't even look at the inferno behind him.

"Who is he?" she repeated, even now refusing to let him dodge answering.

"The less you know, the safer you'll be," he said.

"Safer?" she said incredulously.

"You're still alive."

"And if I'd been inside Phoenix?" she said, her voice calm now, too calm. The anger he'd seen flash before was growing into a steady, fierce rage. "I want to know, Lake."

There had been a time when he would have been able to deny her. A time when nothing would have moved the Gray Wolf to say anything he didn't want to say. But that was before Alison Carlyle had come into his life and literally turned it upside down. That was before he'd made love to her and it had been unlike anything he'd ever known or dreamed of.

Now he looked at her and saw only that she was right. That she did deserve to know who had done this to her. That she had the courage to deal with knowing.

And that she had the right to ask it of him.

"His name's Joplin," he said suddenly, still not happy with himself for being unable to resist the plea in her eyes and the stubborn firmness in every line of her body. The body he'd held, and that had held him, in the most intimate healing of ways.

"And?"

"He was part of the Wolf Pack up until we went live. Ian cut him on the last day. Apparently he's been carrying a grudge ever since."

"For . . . what has it been, seventeen years? That's a long time to hold a grudge for losing a job!"

"That's one of the reasons he lost it. Ian thought he might be . . . capable of this kind of thing. He told us he was afraid Joplin would lose it one day, forget that the goal was never to sacrifice innocent civilians. Or that he'd go on some kind of rampage if the wrong kind of situation arose."

"Then how did he get on the team in the first place?"

Lake shrugged. "He's smart. He hid it well. And it only came out under pressure. We suspected, but Ian was the one to call it, to say he wasn't just ruthless, he was vicious."

"But if Ian fired him, why is he after you?"

"It isn't just me."

Her forehead creased. He could almost see her thinking it through to the truth she probably would have guessed in an instant before. Then her eyes widened, and he knew she'd gotten there.

"The other one, the one who's dead, Rob . . . he killed him?"

"He did. And he tried to kill Jess, too. If Jess hadn't been too good, and if he hadn't underestimated Beth, as he usually does women, they'd all be dead, including Ian's son. Joplin would have killed him without a second thought. And he wouldn't even have thought of it as extreme measures."

"He wants to kill all of you? All for getting fired?"

"He was prodded. He was bankrolled and fed information by somebody else, the man who once ran the Wolf Pack, but had political aspirations and decided we were a liability."

She was watching him intently, and he wondered what she was seeing. "And decided you all had to die?" He nodded. "I presume," she said, rather too casually, "that he's dead too, now?"

Lake grimaced. "No. I went after him but there wasn't much left. He'd lost everything he ever wanted, everything he ever was. Taking his life seemed . . . anticlimactic."

Her expression changed oddly, in a way he couldn't define. It made him uneasy, so he added quickly, "Now do you see why you have to stay out of this?"

She laughed, high and sharp and humorless. "Stay out of it? You want to look behind me, and tell me how? Do you have any idea what Phoenix meant to me?"

His mouth tightened. "Yes," he said, his voice soft and hoarse with the pain he was trying to suppress, pain that he'd done this to her. "I'm so damn sorry, Alison. I never meant for you to be hurt like this. I should have found another way."

He knew the minute the words came out they'd been a mistake. A major mistake. If it were anyone but Alison, he would have hoped the significance wouldn't register, but he knew she was too sharp, too quick, and too smart, even in shock, to miss it. He thought of leaving now, quickly, before she put it together, then wondered when he'd become such a coward.

And then she looked directly at him, and he saw in her wide, shocked eyes that she had it.

"You never meant for me to . . . Another way . . ." She shook her head as if it would change the conclusions she'd reached. He knew the feeling, and knew it wouldn't help. Nothing would help. "My God," she whispered. "It makes sense now. The big turnaround, when you were so furious at first . . . why you changed your mind and decided to do the show . . . why you wanted the publicity when it seemed so out of character . . . you *planned* this!"

"Alison—"

"You did, didn't you, damn it! You planned this! You used me, and Phoenix, to bring him here, didn't you?"

Deny it, damn it, what's wrong with you? His common sense, his training, everything he'd learned about successfully running a mission, clamored at him. He'd always hated using civilians, but he'd done it. And lied when he had to. But he couldn't now.

Getting soft in the head because you screwed her?

He could hear Joplin saying it, gloating in his voice as the pale, black-rimmed eyes seemed to sneer. He also knew it was true. He hadn't been thinking straight since he'd met her, and the hours they'd just spent together had lit a fire under his confusion. They had him thinking about things he'd never dared think about, wanting things he didn't dare want.

And now, before those thoughts and wants had had time to become anything more than glimpses of possibilities, he was going to lose them. And some part of him was laughing,

laughing in the same sneering manner Joplin had in his mind, at himself for even letting such foolish wishes cross his mind.

He heard a vehicle approaching, the sound barely audible over the shouting of the fire crew and the incredible whoosh of the flames. His peripheral vision, always excellent, told him it was Ray's marked unit. Alison didn't even glance that way; perhaps she didn't even notice, or more likely she was too hurt by what she'd just figured out to pay any attention.

He made himself look at her, made himself meet that level, deep blue gaze, and knew he'd answered by not answering.

"You did," she whispered, and she looked as if she'd just seen Phoenix in ruins all over again. "You used me to advertise your presence so he would come here and find you."

"Alison . . ." He stopped when it came out little more than a croak. He swallowed and tried again. "I had to. I've been hunting him for weeks."

"You *had* to?"

"He murdered Rob, one of the gentlest, kindest men I've ever known. And he almost killed Jess. He hurt Ian's son, and would have killed him, and Beth too, if he'd had time. I have to stop him. And I'm the only bait he'll take."

"And you had to use Phoenix to do it?"

"It was the only thing I could think of to do, to go so public it would lure him out in the open."

"You had no real interest in a showing, you didn't believe a word I said about your work, did you?" she said. "You were using me, and my gallery, as bait, and you didn't even have the decency to tell me?"

"Tell you what? That I was hanging out a lure for a killer? Maybe ask if it was all right if I used Phoenix to do it?"

"Yes!"

"I couldn't ask you to do that. But I couldn't lose this chance at him. He had to come after me, not go after Jess again. Jess has something to lose now, he's got Beth and . . ."

He stopped when he saw the look on her face, and realized that he'd done it again.

"And you don't, do you." Her words weren't a question. "You don't have a damn thing to lose. Not a damn thing in the world you care about."

"I didn't mean it like that," he said lamely.

"Oh, really?"

Her sarcasm bit deep. "I didn't," he insisted, but with the feeling he was fighting a losing battle. "Alison, listen. I had to do this. The plan was to be in and out, and you'd never have to know."

"Use her and dump her, is that it?"

"No! I never meant to . . . You weren't supposed to . . ." He was losing it, he could feel it. He couldn't remember the last time he'd had to fight so hard for calm, had to work so hard to keep his voice even. "You weren't supposed to matter, not like this. I never expected you to be . . . you. I never expected not to be able to just . . . walk away. That I'd—"

"Alison!" a familiar female voice cried.

Alison looked up. He did as well, and saw Yvette running toward them, wrapped up in what looked like Ray's heavy uniform jacket. His mind noted the fact idly, that they'd apparently been together when the call had come in. And judging from the state of her hair and makeup, quite possibly indulging in the same activity he and Alison had been.

The images shot through his mind, fierce and hot and painfully erotic.

And painfully impossible. He quashed them again, and in some small, sane part of his mind registered the fact that the effort nearly made him groan aloud.

Alison got to her feet as Yvette neared. She was steadier now; he supposed her anger gave her the strength. She started toward her friend, then stopped. She looked back at him.

"I probably would have helped you, if you'd explained. But you never even tried." Her expression was stormy, but her voice was utterly cool. "Your friend Joplin isn't the only one who underestimates women."

She walked away. He lowered his head, unable to watch the two women console each other over the loss of a dream.

But at least their dream had existed, for a while. He'd lost his before he'd even realized it was there.

"I ought to lock you up," Ray said angrily.

"Got a charge in mind?" Lake asked wearily.

"Creating a public nuisance, for starters. Or maybe on general principle, for endangering citizens, wanton disregard for life and property."

Lake studied the man for a moment. Ray had been a friend, once. A close friend. They'd played baseball together, ridden their bikes over half the county, even gone fishing up by Gramps's cabin a few times. And Ray had been one of the few to stand up for him, in the face of his mother's public diatribes. For a moment, he wished he could tell Ray the truth, that he hadn't done it, hadn't killed Douglas.

But that would take time, and time was a luxury he couldn't afford right now. Ray was by the second looking more and more like he was seriously considering doing just that, throwing Lake in a cell.

"You can't lock me up," he said quietly.

"And why not?"

"Because if you do, he'll go after her."

He didn't explain what her he meant, and from Ray's expression he knew he didn't have to. It got chillier, and sterner. After what he'd told him, about Joplin and his nearly two-decade quest for revenge, Lake wasn't surprised.

"I told you I didn't want to see her hurt."

"Neither do I."

"I think you're a bit too late for that."

Lake winced inwardly. "I know." His gaze flicked to the building that had once been Phoenix. "I got . . . tangled up when that kid admitted he'd done the vandalism, because I'd been sure it was Joplin. Then when he took that shot . . . I just didn't think he'd go this far that fast."

"If you think that's the only thing hurting her, you're blind and stupid to boot."

Lake's head snapped around. "What?"

"Yvette warned me Alison was falling for you in a big way. You always did have a fascination for the females."

Lake gaped at him. He ignored the latter words; he didn't believe them anyway. "Yvette . . . said that?"

Ray nodded. "Said she saw it coming a mile away. Said that painting of yours had her half-hooked long before you got here." Ray shook his head. "I just wish you'd picked a tougher one."

Although he was still a bit stunned by Ray's words, Lake couldn't stop the rueful smile that curved his mouth. "She's a lot tougher than you might think."

"Not right now, she's not."

Reality crashed back in, wiping out any bemused gratification he might be feeling about the idea of Alison being hooked—half or otherwise—on him.

"That's why you can't lock me up, Ray. He won't stop. He won't ever stop. And if he can't get to me, Joplin will go after everybody around me."

Ray's voice went icy. "I wondered why a man with your past was suddenly going so high profile. You knew this would happen, didn't you? You brought him here, like some kind of plague. What is this, your revenge on Jewel?"

"No!" He surprised himself with the fierceness of his denial. "No," he said again, quieter this time. "I never thought . . . nothing was supposed to happen here. I was going to stay up at the cabin, and nobody in Jewel would ever have to know anything had happened."

"Until we found the body? Or bodies?"

"You wouldn't have. I would have seen to that."

Ray lifted a brow. "If you won."

Lake's mouth quirked. "No faith in me, Ray?"

For a long moment Ray studied him. "You're asking me to have a lot in a man I haven't seen for seventeen years."

Lake knew they were no longer talking about him winning. "I know, Ray," he said softly. "I can only tell you . . . it has to be this way. You were in the Rangers, you know that sometimes guys go haywire. And that when they do, there's nothing more dangerous, because they have all the training to carry out damn near anything."

"Is that what we're dealing with here?"

"Worse," Lake said. "But he's only after me. Just me, Ray, nobody else. And it will end there, if you let it."

"One way or another?"

"As far as you're concerned, yes."

"Meaning either you'll kill him, or he'll kill you and leave?"

"Yes."

"Lake," Ray said, his voice low, "you know I can't do this. It's my job to prevent killing, not . . . encourage it."

"There's only one way to prevent it. If you toss me in jail, he'll kill whoever he has to to get to me. And he won't be picky."

"And if I don't, you kill him."

"He's got it coming," Lake said.

"Is that how you did it, all those years? Told yourself they had it coming?"

Lake's breath left him in a rush, as if Ray had delivered a blow to his gut. He felt himself pale slightly, and wondered when it had begun to matter, when words that had rolled off him for years had suddenly regained the power to hurt.

"I'm sorry, Lake," Ray said. "I didn't mean . . . I know what you guys did, pretty much. You went into some ugly parts of the world, and you did things that needed doing. If you say they had it coming, then they probably did."

"Forget it," Lake said, rather sharply, unwilling to betray how much Ray's words meant, and feeling he'd already betrayed quite enough tonight. "Just give me a little time. That's all I need, just a little time."

Ray frowned. "How much time?"

"Twenty-four hours. You can stall things that long before you even have to admit it was arson."

Ray glanced over his shoulder. They had the fire fairly well knocked down by now, and were just searching for hot spots. "I will have to call in an arson investigator," he said. "And if they have to come in from Denver, it could be afternoon before they get here."

Lake let out a breath. "Thanks."

Ray turned on him again. "I didn't say I'd keep your name out of it. I'm going to have to tell them about that round you nearly took last night. And who you are."

"I know. But take your time, will you?"

Ray sighed. "It'll take time anyway. Red tape, paperwork. That's half of what I do. But damn it, Lake, letting you walk away, knowing you plan on killing a man—"

"Want me to knock you out and escape?"

Ray grimaced. "Not really." He took in a deep breath and looked at Lake straight on. "You swear to me this is the only way?"

Lake nodded. "People—truly innocent people—will die if I don't get to him first." He gestured at the skeleton of Phoenix. "That was just a calling card."

"And if he gets to you?" Ray asked. "What if he wins, Lake?"

"Then he's gotten what he wanted, and—" His mouth tightened as he thought of what else that would mean. "If he wins, Ray, you've got to do something for me."

Ray looked startled, then curious. "What?"

"There's one of the Wolf Pack left, besides me. Joplin's already tried for him, but Jess beat him at his game. But if I can't stop him, he'll go after Jess again. And he's got a wife, and a son now."

"You want me to warn him?" Lake nodded. "How?"

Lake's mouth quirked. "Put an ad in *The Wall Street Journal*. The Marketplace section."

Ray gaped. "What?"

"It's how we all agreed we'd contact each other, if we ever had to. It's how Joplin lured us out into the open in the first place."

"You mean that kidnapping you told me about?"

He nodded. "Jess has Beth and the boy safe now, but he'll have to be warned if I . . . don't make it. Just say . . . the Lone Wolf is really the Lone Wolf now. There won't be any need for code by then. And Jess . . . he'll understand."

Slowly, Ray nodded.

He was going to do it, Lake thought in relief. *Ray was going to give him that twenty-four hours.*

"You . . . need any help?"

The unexpected query startled Lake. "I . . . no. You're better off as far out of it as possible. The less you're involved, the more you can deny. Just . . . watch out for Alison. Keep her safe."

Ray nodded as if that went without saying. And Lake suddenly realized it did; his old friend took his job very seriously, and a big part of that job was protecting and watching over the people who lived in his little town.

"You're doing well here, aren't you?" he asked quietly.

"I like it."

"It shows."

The sky in the east was beginning to lighten as dawn came to the Rockies. It would be a while longer before it reached down to Jewel, but Lake knew it was time to get moving.

"Take care of her, Ray," he said. "I never wanted to hurt her. Like this"—he flicked a glance at the smoldering ruin—"or any other way."

Ray looked at him steadily. "Do you love her?"

Lake paled. "I . . . don't think about things like that. I don't dare."

Ray clearly wasn't in the mood to be merciful. "Do you?"

Lake, for one of the few times in his life, looked away from a challenge. He stared down at his feet, realizing inanely that they were cold without the socks he'd left behind in his rush.

The silence spun out tensely; Ray was giving no quarter. He must have been a hell of a Ranger, Lake thought. Then, when he knew he could dodge no longer, he gave in.

"If I ever could . . . love anyone . . . it would be her," he whispered.

"You'd better tell her that yourself."

Lake shook his head. "She won't listen."

"Not now. But later. Alison's not one to hold a grudge."

Lake looked at him then, gave him a crooked smile. "Thought you weren't sure I'd be around later."

"I find I have more faith in you than I thought. I doubt I'll have to place that ad."

"I hope you're right," Lake said fervently. He turned to go, then stopped and looked back. "Thanks."

Ray nodded. "Take care, buddy."

The friendly appellation, given by a man he respected, meant more to Lake than it should have, more than he could admit. He left before Ray could read it in his face.

And wondered why it was now, when he could very well

die before the next sunrise, that he found he missed something as simple as having a friend.

And wondered if, had things been different, he could have learned to love the way other people did.

Chapter 22

"I hate him."

"Of course you do."

"He used me."

"Yes, he did."

Alison looked up at Yvette, who was sitting serenely at her kitchen table, sipping coffee. She was more than at home in Alison's kitchen, and hadn't wasted any time in asking what she wanted, had just taken over and done it.

She had listened to Alison's rather confused tale of revenge and plots and bait without interruption, and had hugged her comfortingly when the loss of Phoenix began to close in on her again, bringing on an ache that she wished she could relieve with tears. But she couldn't, they wouldn't come, she could only bear the horrible pressure.

She felt as if she'd lost much more than a business, as if she'd lost a large piece of herself, and the last piece of Steve. She could picture everything that she'd lost, every bit of genius that was destroyed forever, because the creator had trusted her. It wasn't just things that had been blown away in that explosion, it was bits and pieces of light and brilliance the world could ill afford to lose.

"How can you be so blessed calm?" Alison asked Yvette, barely aware of the warmth of the mug in her hands. "We've lost everything, we're supposed to have a showing in less than a week, the . . . *artist* we're showing is a . . . a retired secret agent or something who uses people like paint rags, and it's his fault Phoenix is in ashes—"

"I wouldn't say exactly that. He didn't set the bomb himself, after all."

Something about Yvette's manner was at last getting through to Alison. She was concerned, yes, upset, and worried, it was all in her face. She was even angry, although not as angry as Alison felt; she had a much smaller investment in the place, although Alison had given her a percentage when she'd come to work there permanently.

But there was something else, a sort of serene calm beneath it all.

Like a video, the memory of when Yvette had arrived at the scene played back in her mind. And things that had not registered then, in her state of shock and fury, registered now. She'd arrived with Ray. And wearing Ray's police jacket. And looking just as she did now, a little tousled and very much kissed.

Alison's eyes widened. "Yvette?"

"Hmm?"

She even had the dreamy look in her eyes, despite everything. "You . . . you and Ray?"

Yvette blushed. And lowered her eyes, something the direct, open woman rarely did.

"We finally . . . got it together," she admitted shyly. "And it's . . . wonderful."

"Congratulations," Alison said, meaning it.

"Thank you," Yvette said. "Your matchmaking finally paid off."

Alison managed a smile. "I wouldn't have meddled if I hadn't thought you were genuinely interested. And that you two would make a good match."

"We do," Yvette said simply. Then, "Now that I've confessed, how about you?"

Allson's head came up, her eyes widening as the unexpected query caught her off guard. "What?"

"Honey, unless you've taken to wearing men's socks and drinking cocoa out of two mugs at a time, I'd say you've had an interesting night yourself."

"I . . . he just . . . it wasn't . . ."

"Uh-huh. You want to float that boat, next time shove your bra out of sight."

Alison blushed furiously. She didn't even bother to look;

in her mind's eye, she could still see the telltale blue satin
garment Lake had tossed aside in his hurry to caress and
touch her breasts, lying where she'd left it on the sofa in her
hurry after the explosion.

She stared down at her cup of untouched coffee. Her body
reacted to the memories fiercely, heating, shivering. Her
heart reacted with the ache that had been hammering at her
for hours. Her mind reacted with the anger she'd been stok-
ing for that same amount of time, ever since she'd looked at
his face and realized what he'd done.

"I hate him!"

"Uh-huh. And you love him. A hell of a place to live, my
friend."

"I don't!" Alison denied instantly.

"Don't you? You look me in the eye and say that, and
maybe I'll believe you."

Alison raised her head. "I don't," she said, but it came out
a shaky whisper even she didn't believe.

She jumped when the phone rang, and sank back down
gratefully when Yvette picked it up. It appeared to be yet another person calling with condolences. She was surprised at
the number that seemed sincere. True, many had called out
of sheer curiosity; the rumor that Lake was somehow involved in the explosion was running amok, it seemed. But
some had been genuine, and Alison had been moved by their
concern.

She only half listened to Yvette assure someone else, as
she had been doing all morning, that Alison was fine. Instead she tried to think about Yvette and Ray finally getting
out of the starting gate. She was happy for her friend, she
truly was, she told herself again. Yvette was a sweet, wonderful, smart woman, and she deserved a nice, decent,
straight-arrow guy like Ray, who would treat her well.

So why couldn't she stop these pangs of envy? It was nobody's fault but her own that she'd been stupid enough to
fall for an impossible man. For fall she had; she knew that
now. She knew it because it hurt so badly. And what could
hurt so badly except love and the end of it?

This was why she'd stayed alone, after Steve. This was

why, because she knew how awful it was when it went wrong. She'd thought death the worst blow love could take. But it wasn't. Lord, it wasn't.

The knock on the door made them both jump. Alison let out a weary breath; she didn't think she was up to visits in person. Yvette was still on the phone, so she had no choice. She crept toward the door quietly, thinking perhaps she could pretend not to be here. But when she looked through the peephole and saw a now neatly uniformed Ray, she knew that option was gone.

She pulled open the door, surprised at the flood of sunlight from the west; she hadn't realized it was afternoon. Nor had she realized there was a sheriff's unit parked in front of her house. Or at least it had been, it was leaving now, pulling out from behind Ray's four-wheel drive. What was truly odd was it wasn't Charlie, the other local deputy, but someone she didn't recognize.

"Who was that?"

"He's on loan," Ray said. "Things have been a little busy around here lately."

Alison's mouth tightened. "I noticed." But then she also noticed the shadows beneath Ray's normally warm brown eyes. "I'm sorry, Ray. You haven't gotten much sleep, have you?"

He blushed, and Alison suddenly remembered he'd had more than her troubles keeping him awake. She couldn't help smiling.

"Come on in. Yvette's on the phone. I assume that's why you're here?"

"Partly," he admitted.

She frowned, wondering what other reason he could have. He surely couldn't have any more questions for her; she'd answered them this morning for hours. But before she could ask Yvette had hung up the phone, and was headed toward them, the smile on her face warming Alison's heart despite her own misery.

But she didn't know how much of it she could take, that cozy, brand-new intimacy between them, so she went to her purse and picked up her keys. She needed to go talk to her insurance agent, and she'd need copies of the reports. She had a copy of the latest inventory here, thank God, but she—

"Alison? What are you doing?"

She turned to look at Ray, puzzled by the sharpness of his tone. "I have to go see Frank Mason about my insurance, and then—"

"Not today."

It sounded suspiciously like an order. Alison looked at him, brows furrowed. "Why?"

"You're tired," Yvette said, "you need some rest, and some food—"

"We just ate an omelet," she pointed out. "What's with you two?"

"Just leave it until tomorrow, will you?"

"But the insurance is going to be a nightmare, I need to get it started." It was going to hurt, a lot, to have to list all the things she'd so loved that had been destroyed—God, the waterfall, and the lily—but it had to be done.

"Alison," Ray said, much more gently now, "not today. Just stay home."

She stared at him, saw him and Yvette exchange a quick glance. "What's going on?"

"It can all wait, really, Alison," Yvette urged.

Something was up, she could feel it. "Why? What *is* going on? Why are you both so anxious to keep me here?"

They both shifted uncomfortably. She crossed her arms in front of her and set her jaw.

"Uh-oh," Yvette murmured. And Ray, who could read body language as well as anyone, let out a sigh.

"You could be in danger," he said.

Alison blinked. "Me? Where'd you get that—" She stopped as the obvious answer hit her. "Lake."

"He told me to watch out for you. Keep you safe."

Her brows lowered. "Watch out for me? Safe? Is that why that other deputy was out there? What was he, out there all morning? Am I a prisoner in my own house?"

"Of course not. Just wait until tomorrow, okay?" Ray said soothingly.

Alison wasn't soothed. "Why? What happens tomorrow?"

There was an instant, before Ray's professional mask came down, when she saw something flicker in his face. Guilt. Worry. Some combination of both.

"What happens tomorrow, Ray?" she asked again softly.

"Nothing," he said firmly.

She considered this thoughtfully. Then rephrased her question. "Then what happens between now and tomorrow? What happens that will make it okay for me to go out then, when it's not now?"

"Just trust me, Alison. Please."

Ray's voice was urgent, persuasive. And she was almost persuaded. Almost.

"What did Lake say?" She got his name out without hesitating, which pleased her; she'd been afraid her voice would break. "Why are you supposed to watch out for me? That bomb was meant to get to him, not me."

"Honey," Yvette said, "don't you see? Something happening to you would get to him worse than anything."

"I don't believe that for a moment," she snapped. So much for her calm about the subject, Alison thought wryly.

"You should," Ray said quietly.

"He used me. I was just a means to an end to him."

Ray looked at her for a long, silent moment, as if considering his next words very carefully. Finally, to her surprise, he reached out and put a gentle hand on her shoulder.

"He may have used you, but you're much more than that to him."

"I doubt that. He—"

"He told me, Alison."

She blinked. "What?"

"He told me if he ever could love anyone, it would be you."

Alison stared at him, stunned. "He . . . said that?"

Ray nodded. "He also said he didn't think about things like that. That he didn't dare."

Something tightened deep inside her, knotted up until she could barely breathe. She needed to think. And she needed to do it alone, without the two of them hovering.

"I'm going to take a shower," she said, turning on her heel, hoping they hadn't read too much in her face.

Mechanically she peeled off her clothes, trying desperately not to remember how they had come off the last time, only hours ago, how for the first time in her life she hadn't been shy about being naked with a man, but eager. And just as eager to see that man naked, to touch, to learn, to kiss, to taste . . .

She stood in the shower for a very long time, her confused thoughts racing through her mind faster than the hot water running over her body.

It was just too much, all of it. From the moment she'd seen *Layers* for the first time, she'd known the man who painted it would be complex, even difficult. But she had never imagined he could be a liar, and a user.

But what Ray had said haunted her. Had Lake really said that? Or was Ray being kind? She didn't think he would make something like that up; he'd been the one to warn her about Lake's background in the first place.

Lake's own words came back to her then. *You weren't supposed to matter, not like this. I never expected you to be . . . you. I never expected not to be able to just . . . walk away. That I'd . . .*

That he'd what? Fall in love with her? Had that been what he'd been about to say?

She shivered, despite the hot shower beating down on her. Maybe she was a fool, but she couldn't bring herself to truly believe last night had been a lie. That his touch had been merely seduction, some way to assure her continued cooperation in the plan she knew nothing about, or some way to distract her from things he didn't want her thinking about. If she had to doubt that that had been real, if she had to doubt he had truly felt anything during those long, lazy hours, and in the moments when he'd shuddered in her arms, then she might as well give up, because her judgment was absolutely worthless.

But even if it had been real, even if he'd really said that to Ray, that didn't change the fact that he'd used her, and Phoenix, for his own ends. And Phoenix was now in ashes, and she didn't know if she had the courage to make it rise again. Or the courage to face what Lake had done. Never mind that he thought he'd had to do it. Had to do it to stop a man who was capable of carrying the most lethal of grudges for seventeen years.

He wasn't just ruthless, he was vicious.

He murdered Rob, one of the gentlest, kindest men I've ever known. And he almost killed Jess. He hurt Ian's son, and would have killed him, and Beth too, if he'd had time. I have to stop him. And I'm the only bait he'll take.

She thought back to those moments when he'd named the faces in *Ghosts.* When he'd told her the stories of those faces, the atrocities they'd committed, she hadn't hesitated to agree that each of them deserved the fate meted out to them by the Gray Wolf. Had, despite her own ignorance of that kind of dark, seamy corners of the world, come to see that perhaps the methods of the Wolf Pack were indeed the only recourse when up against minds like those.

Funny how it changed when she was the method being used.

And that, she admitted, seemed the tiniest bit unfair.

So how did she feel? Was her assertion that she hated him more or less than a declaration based in pain and hurt feelings? Did she really hate him, or just what he had done? Was she expecting too much for him to believe that she would have helped him if he'd only asked?

He didn't even know you, she told herself. *How could he trust you to help? It goes against logic, let alone years of training.*

But he knew her now, and he still hadn't told her. And she blushed to think of just how well he knew her. To think of how he'd made her body soar, of how she'd become a wild thing beneath his touch, and how he'd seemed to love it, urging her on with hot, erotic words she'd never heard before, telling her what he wanted to do to her, and wanted her to do to him.

And in those moments afterward, he'd seemed utterly, totally quiet, and Alison had felt she'd been given a gift beyond measure, that of this dangerous, tortured man at peace at last, in her arms.

She didn't know how she felt, not really. Hurt, yes, angry as well, but both emotions were mixed up so thoroughly with so many others that she wasn't sure what the sum total was. Only that it made her sick inside with its intensity.

She gradually became aware that the water was turning cool. She automatically turned off the taps, slid back the shower door, and reached for a towel, but her mind was still churning.

He told me to watch out for you, Ray had said. And *just wait until tomorrow.*

Her own words came back to her, oddly, as if she were hearing herself speak them all over again. *What happens between now and tomorrow? What happens that will make it okay for me to go out then, when it's not now?*

She dried herself quickly, then lifted the towel to her head.

He told me to watch out for you.

While he did . . . what? She rubbed at her hair with the towel. And then stopped as more words echoed in her head.

I've been hunting him for weeks.

I have to stop him.

I couldn't lose this chance at him.

She clutched the towel to her, staring unseeingly at her reflection in the mirror.

What happens between now and tomorrow . . .

She knew just what was going to happen between now and tomorrow. Lake was going to kill again.

Or be killed.

It had worked. As he'd known it would. McGregor had reacted strongly and swiftly. He'd always known that the man's ridiculous streak of rectitude about using civilians could be used against him. And he'd done it, perfectly.

In fact, it had been almost too easy. All he'd had to do was endanger the woman, and McGregor, fool that he was, had immediately taken action. He'd turned her over to that cop who'd had people on her all the rest of the night and so far today. And right now, he was probably sitting up in that cabin of his, waiting.

It appeared he had truly abandoned the Carlyle woman to the cop's care, so perhaps she wasn't quite as important to him as he'd thought. Or perhaps he'd already grown bored with her; there certainly wasn't a woman alive who could keep a real man interested for long. Even a looker like this one.

And she was that, he thought as he watched the house with the sheriff's vehicle parked in front. In fact, perhaps he'd sample her when it was over. It would be more fun to do it now, so he could taunt McGregor with the knowledge that he hadn't been able to stop his unknowing civilian assistant from falling prey to the very man he had used her to lure here.

But he didn't want to risk it. The cop was there, and he had the look of a man who could fight if he had to. And there was no sense asking for trouble; unlike McGregor, he had his priorities in order. McGregor first, then the woman, if he was still interested. Which, he conceded, he might not be; she was only useful as a tool to use against him. Just as McGregor had used her as a tool to get him here. Or so he thought . . .

He nearly laughed out loud. Fool, he thought, you think you're running this show, McGregor, when you're just one of the monkeys. And you're dancing to my tune and you don't even know it. But you will. Before you die, you will.

Chapter 23

In fresh clothes and with her hair now dry and free of the lingering pall of smoke, Alison felt a little better. Padding down the hall in her stocking feet, she paused in the doorway to the living room. It was quiet in there, except for the occasional rustle of movement, and she wondered if she would create a monumentally embarrassing moment for all of them if she stepped inside.

She leaned forward and peeked around the corner. Tears stung her eyes at what she saw; Ray stretched out on her sofa, his head in Yvette's lap, sound asleep. Yvette was simply watching him, a soft, warm smile curving her mouth.

Alison sighed, the tightness in her chest ratcheting in another notch. She backed into the hall and stood there, needing the wall for support, hating herself for envying her friend the simplicity of what she'd found. Then grimaced at her own thoughts; no matter that it was in quiet Jewel, loving a cop was no easy thing. Who knew that better than she? She'd grown up with a knowledge other children didn't have, that someday her father might not come home.

And the horrors of life could reach even into this tranquil place; Joplin was proof of that.

She gave a start at a sudden squawk of noise, then breathed again when she realized it was Ray's portable radio set. She heard the voice of Denise Cox, the dispatcher at the local office, then mutterings as Ray stirred, then sat up to answer the call.

She could go in now, Alison thought, and not feel guilty for disturbing that loving tableau. She'd try again to tell Ray she had to get out of here, as much because she was about to go crazy as because she had things to do. She should be exhausted she supposed, she hadn't gotten much sleep—and she refused to think again about why—but instead she was restless, antsy, and—

". . . near Silver Creek. Resident up on the ridge says it sounds like it was about three-quarters of the way down the mountain, toward the end of the road."

She tuned in suddenly to the disembodied voice coming tinnily through the small speaker. And her breath stopped in her throat at Ray's clipped response. And then again at the weary, resigned, but not at all surprised look on his face.

"How many shots?"

"Two, he thinks. He thought at first it was poachers, but then decided not from that direction. Anyway, you said you wanted to know about anything from up that way."

Shots. Near Silver Creek.

"I'm on my way," Ray said, and reached for his equipment belt. He had the radio in its holder and the Sam Browne on and buckled before Alison recovered enough to step into the room.

"I'm going with you," she said, before she even thought about the words."

Ray wheeled around, startled. And shook his head at her. "No way."

"I'm going with you, or right behind you," she told him, crossing the room and jamming her feet quickly into the boots she'd discarded at the door, boots that were still dirty with ash and soot.

"Alison—"

"Honey—"

Ray and Yvette both began their protests in the same instant, and Alison ignored them both.

"You're not going out there," Ray said warningly.

She grabbed up her keys again before he could get some idea about hiding them. "I'm going," she said.

"Alison—"

"And on the way, maybe you can explain why this didn't surprise you."

Ray drew back slightly, looking guilty.

"You knew, didn't you?" Alison asked. "This is why everything was going to be all right tomorrow."

"Listen—"

"You let him go back up there, knowing that maniac was after him?"

Yvette was looking a bit puzzled; Ray hadn't told her everything, it seemed. But Alison couldn't worry about her friend right now.

"How did he talk you into it, Ray? I know he had to, you're too conscientious to just let it happen. What did he use on you?"

Ray let out a weary breath. "You."

She blinked. "What?"

"He said if I locked him up, the guy would come after you. And then come after him anyway, no matter where he was. And no matter who or how many he had to come through."

She suppressed a shiver. "So you . . . turned him loose?"

Ray winced. He held her gaze for a moment, then said in a voice that told her he knew full well the risk he'd taken, "He asked me for twenty-four hours. I gave it to him. Unofficially."

Twenty-four hours. Twenty-four hours, to kill a man or be killed.

"And if Lake's the one who's killed?" she asked bleakly. She heard Yvette's gasp, but didn't look at her.

"He swears the guy will leave."

"So your little town is safe, one way or another." She couldn't help the bitterness in her voice. "They threw him out, but now he could die to keep them safe. He's doing the dirty work again. But this time it's a damned self-sacrifice."

"And you're safe, Alison. That's what he cared about most." She bit her lip, not sure she was ready to believe that. "And don't underestimate him," Ray added. "I have a feeling if there's anybody really in danger out there, it's the man fool enough to cross Lake McGregor."

"I'm still going," she said stubbornly. She wasn't sure how she felt about all this, but she was sure she wanted to see this through. "That man destroyed everything I've worked so hard for, damn it, I have a right."

"To get yourself maybe hurt or killed? You lost a lot last night, Alison, but you're alive."

Just what Lake had said. You're still alive. Meaning it could be worse. Could get worse.

And he was up on his mountain, trying to make sure it didn't get worse. For her, or anyone else.

"I'm going," she insisted. "Do I go with you, or drive myself?"

Ray set his jaw. "Do I have to lock *you* up?"

"If you want to stop me, yes. But I warn you, I'll fight. You'll have to hurt me."

"She means it, Ray," Yvette said quietly. "I don't know what's going on, but I know that look in her eye."

Ray swore, and for an instant Alison felt badly for putting him in this position. Then, abruptly, he gave in.

"You ride with me. But you stay in the unit until I tell you, until I have a chance to check things out, understand?"

It was as good as she was going to get, she thought. And she had no desire to confront a madman; she wasn't about to go wandering around when he was loose up there. But she had to know if Lake was alive. She wouldn't let herself think of why she had to know, or what she would do if he wasn't, but she had to know.

"Understood," she said quietly.

"You'll call me as soon as you can? Both of you?" Yvette didn't look very happy at being in the dark, but she could obviously see the urgency and didn't demand an explanation. She didn't appreciate her friend nearly enough, Alison thought.

"Soon as I can," Ray promised, while Alison just nodded.

They were halfway to the end of Silver Creek Road when Ray finally spoke to her. There had been some chatter on the radio, mostly about the other deputies and backup. Charlie Arpel was on an injury traffic accident, and the loaner deputy was coming from some distance. Ray had acknowledged he was on his own, hung the microphone back in its rack, and driven on in silence.

Until he glanced at her and said, "Decide you don't hate him after all?"

"I don't know," she said frankly. "But if I do still hate him, I want him alive so I can tell him."

Ray chuckled, and she knew he'd forgiven her. "He's not . . . an easy man to understand. Or be around, I imagine."

Perhaps he understood her mixed feelings. "You sound as ambivalent as I feel," she said.

Ray shrugged. "Maybe. But whatever he is, or has done, it wasn't his choice. He wasn't left many choices, since he was seventeen."

The truth leaped to her lips; she wanted so badly to tell Ray, to tell everyone that Lake hadn't killed his brother. But it wasn't hers to tell, it was his; only he could decide if he wanted the world to know it was his unnatural mother who had murdered her own son.

All the images, everything he'd told her, careened around in her mind as they drove. She was in more of an internal uproar than ever. But as they got closer to the dead end and the gravel side track, she found it hard to think of anything but what might be up the hill.

"I'm going to park at the last curve before Lake's cabin." Ray's voice sounded different, and it took Alison a moment to realize this was the cop talking, not her friend. "And you're going to stay put, like you promised."

She nodded. And meant it. She had no desire to come face-to-face with a cold-blooded murderer. That there were those who would call Lake that occurred to her, and she supposed she should feel a sense of irony, but she didn't. Whatever Lake had done, it hadn't been cold-bloodedly no matter what anyone thought.

Including using you?

The question hit her with unexpected power. And she began to play back in her head once more what he'd said to her, began to remember the choked sound of his voice.

Then they rounded the last curve, and she saw the sign in the distance. DEAD END.

She hoped it wasn't prophetic.

*   *   *

Lake held his breath, listening. He knew Joplin was still out there. He didn't need to see him, didn't need to hear him, didn't even need the sudden hush of the forest noises to be sure.

He could feel him.

The old instinct was back as if it had never left him. He could feel the edginess in his hands, the readiness in his legs, the tension at the back of his neck, as if his hackles were rising.

It had taken him a minute to recognize it. He'd been, despite his efforts to concentrate, unable to fight off the vision that constantly haunted him. Not of the faces he'd portrayed in *Ghosts,* not of the children they'd found in that pit, not of Ian's battered, tortured body coming home in a box, not even of Rob hooked up to machines, hanging on until Jess told him they knew the truth. None of these had the power right now that a simple memory had—Alison staring bleak-eyed at the ruin that had once been the pride of her life.

He wondered how long that picture would haunt him. But deep down he knew the answer. Forever. He'd added another to the long string of horrible memories, and this one was somehow worse because he'd done it himself.

The image of that loving gentleness of hers, that had warmed him, saved him, given him a peace he'd never known before, turning to anger and disgust and hate nearly crippled him.

Until he'd felt that strange, skin-crawling sensation, until he'd felt the hair at the back of his neck rise, until he'd known Joplin had finally come and the showdown was at hand.

He'd had his weapons ready since he'd been here. Now he made his final decision. He put away the long guns; Joplin wanted this up close and personal, and Lake doubted he'd get a shot at him from a distance. He went for the Glock, tucked into a clip holster at the small of his back. He put two extra magazines in the right hip pocket of his jeans. He slid a small .38 revolver into a holster at his ankle; it would be useless at any distance, but if Joplin got that close, he might need it. He slid a large, razor-sharp hunting knife into a sheath on the left side of his belt and snugged it tight at an angle where he could reach it with his right hand if necessary. Then he stopped. If he needed more armament than this, he was in big trouble.

He left his jacket slung over the back of the sofa; he didn't want it interfering with his hands. But he pulled the knit ski cap out of the pocket and pulled it on, making sure as much of his too-visible silver hair as possible was hidden. It was not his old black watch cap, the one he'd used on countless nighttime forays, but rather a brown one, a color that would blend amid the greens and browns of the forest outside, as would the traditional green camouflage pants tucked into his lace-up boots. The brown thermal knit long-sleeved shirt he wore was chosen for both warmth and color and snugness; he couldn't afford any loose fabric getting in his way. He wished he had his Kevlar vest, but he hadn't taken the time to get it out of storage, and there certainly wasn't one to be had anywhere near Jewel.

It had been a very long time since he'd suited up for confrontation, he realized. And he suddenly thought he hadn't treasured the years of peace since then nearly enough. And that it should happen now, when for the first time he'd found something he dared to even think about wanting—

He was yanked out of his dangerous reverie by some gut-level awareness, screaming at him to pay attention. He took in a deep breath, warning himself that he had to pay attention here or he was going to wind up dead. Joplin would have won another round.

He set his jaw and strove for focus; he didn't want Ray to have to place that ad telling Jess he was all alone now.

He wasn't sure how long he'd been crouched here, fuzzy-brained, so he tentatively tested his legs, wondering if he could even move. They seemed responsive enough, so he looked ahead, picking his path through the thick underbrush.

He took one step. Two.

The shot hit him high on the left shoulder. It pushed him sideways. He shoved off with his legs, propelling himself farther in that direction, tucking and rolling until he came to a halt behind a large blue spruce. He felt the burning, and instinctively tried to block it. Jaw set, he reached up with his left arm, making it work despite the pain; he didn't dare occupy his gun hand. He inspected the area, not from the front, but from the back, and was relieved to feel an exit wound; the round had gone through, tearing the muscle above the collarbone.

He wondered for an instant what Joplin was using for ammo; it hadn't seemed to have done much damage. He could still move his arm, still feel his fingers.

Of course, he muttered to himself. *He wants you to die hard, not easy. No copper jackets, no superdestructive, tumbling, tearing bullets. Just nice, clean, through and through wounds that would bleed, not taking you out, just weakening you until he'd got you cornered. Then he'll cut your heart out, just like he promised . . .*

He shook off the thoughts, tried to shake off the pain. Joplin had left a clear, unmistakable message for him. When he'd gotten back to the cabin that morning, there had been a bundle for him waiting on the sofa. A small bundle, wrapped in one of his own shirts. The cloth was soaked with blood, so much blood that it had seeped into the sofa cushion, telling him it had been there a long time, probably since shortly after he'd left to follow Alison yesterday.

He hadn't wanted to unwrap it, but had known he had to. And when he had, to find the tiny heart of some hapless small creature, marked gruesomely with human teethmarks, he'd known what the message was. Joplin had taken the heart out of this animal, he'd taken the heart out of Alison by destroying her dream, and he'd take the heart out of his quarry and eat it.

It won't make up for not having one of your own, Lake had thought to himself then.

And now he realized, as he crouched there fighting to ignore the pain in his shoulder, that he was aware for the first time in a very long time that he had a heart himself; he'd thought himself as much without one as Joplin. But his was still alive, still functioning. He knew, because it was aching. He knew because he thought it was going to tear apart in his chest every time he thought of Alison and what he'd done to her, how she must feel about him now, finding out he'd used her—especially after the night they'd spent together . . .

He shivered, knowing he didn't dare dwell on that, not now. He let himself think of Alison one last time, but the image overlapped with the knowledge that Joplin was here, and merged somehow into an ugly, horrible vision of her in Joplin's hands. As that tortured little creature had been, whose heart had been cut out simply to send a message.

And suddenly it was back, that cold detachment, as if a switch had been clicked, turning off the emotions churning inside him. For a split second he wondered why, wondered if it had been the thought of Alison in trouble that had enabled him to regain some kind of control, but he knew he couldn't spend time in speculation. Not now.

Summoning up the discipline he'd learned in his years with the Rangers and had honed to a powerful force with the Wolf Pack, he cleared his mind of all but one thing—the man out there. He didn't think of the pain, didn't think of what that man had done, who he'd killed, or the reason he was here. He didn't even let himself think of him by name, he was simply the target now.

He knew he was going to take more fire the instant he moved; with all his woolgathering, the target had gotten a bead on him, knew just where he was. He coolly assessed his condition; he could take a couple more shots like that one before it started really hampering him, as long as the target didn't change his tactics. He doubted he would; killing from a distance wouldn't satisfy his need for revenge. He'd taken this to a very personal level, and that's where it would be to the end.

Lake moved then. He took another two steps. As expected, another shot shattered the quiet. But this time he was ready; he'd already changed direction, diving forward to the cover of even thicker brush, and the bullet merely nicked his right calf. In the same motion he rolled to his feet. He made a quick move back the way he'd come. Then he scrambled right, allowing himself to make just enough noise. Then he cut left, low and silent, dodging shrubbery and barely making a sound.

He was clear by a foot when the next shot kicked up dirt behind him.

The hunt was on again. Only this time, Lake was in the game. The Gray Wolf was back.

Alison froze when she heard the shot. She'd seen enough of handguns in her years working in the L.A. youth shelter, and on the range with her father, but she knew little about them other than their deadliness. She guessed that shot had been from a pistol, not a rifle, but she couldn't tell any more than that.

Not that it mattered; how did you decide which was worse, being stalked from afar by a maniac with a rifle, or being so close to him that a pistol would work?

She shivered, wondering if she should have taken Ray's well-meant order and stayed home. But that image of Lake sprawled on his own floor as she'd found him that day had somehow, in her mind, become an image of him lying dead in a pool of his own blood, a victim of the life that hadn't been his choice.

She had to know. She'd decide later what she'd do about it, but for now, she just had to know.

Another shot. She gave a little start, and shifted restlessly in the seat. It had sounded like the same gun, but what did she know? And if there was still shooting going on, then it wasn't . . . over, was it? Lake had to be still alive, either shooting or being shot at . . .

She laughed at the irony of the sound of gunfire close by being a good sign. She knew it was a dangerous kind of laugh, knew it rose out of that wild, panicked feeling that was building in her.

Please, please, please, she found herself chanting under her breath, her hands curled into fists, and she begged she wasn't sure who for she wasn't sure what.

She hated this. Hated just sitting, waiting, when in her life she'd always *done.*

Another shot. Her breath stopped again. Silence.

Her head snapped to the left as a crackle came from the radio on the center console.

She heard Ray's voice come over the speaker. Tight. Strained. As if through clenched teeth.

"Shots fired, officer down."

Chapter 24

"Oh, God," Alison whispered.

She sucked in a breath as Denise came back instantly, her voice calm but her words sharp and quick as she confirmed the location. Ray answered, but slowly, sounding groggy.

"Copy, unit one. Ambulance on the way, and backup is now code three."

Alison supposed that meant with lights and siren and all the speed possible. But would it be in time?

Ray started to acknowledge the transmission, but his voice faded away and the radio went silent. Alison stared at it, willing Ray to finish, to say he was all right. Denise called again. Nothing. Her voice came over the radio again, strained this time.

The silence continued.

For a moment she sat there, shaking. Ray was hurt. Lake could be hurt, too. Or already dead; Ray was no fool, and if Joplin was good enough to get him, he might just be good enough to get Lake. ·

She felt helpless, trapped. Her heart was hammering in her chest as the silence continued.

Do something, do something, do *something!*

The silent order seemed a scream inside her head. But what could she do? Her gaze fell upon the shotgun in the up-right rack next to the center console. Even if she could fig-ure out how to unlock the rack, she didn't know the first thing about shotguns. She'd probably end up shooting her-self.

God, you're like those women in movies you always hate,

*that sit cowering in a corner and screaming uselessly while
men kill each other.*

She was *not* going to be like that. She never had been, and
she wasn't going to start now. She looked around rather
wildly. The only thing she could see was the police baton
stuck into a holder on the driver's door. She grabbed it; it
was better than nothing. And she had taken a self-defense
class her dad had signed her up for once. Too bad the only
thing she remembered that might help was to jab with the
end of the stick, not swing it like a bat.

She opened the door and slid out, telling herself her legs
weren't really that weak. Then she heard another shot, and
knew she was kidding herself.

But she was going to do something. It had never been
more important in her life that she do as she always had:
take action. Of some kind. If nothing else, she could find
Ray, maybe help him.

*And pray that the killer had left him where he'd fallen,
that he wasn't waiting in ambush, for some idiot like her to
stumble along looking for him.*

She tightened her grip on the polished wood of the baton.
She felt like a fool as she crept up the hill. She headed for
the cabin because that was the way Ray had gone, and she
didn't know what else to do. Just before the cabin came into
sight, she had the thought that she should get off the gravel;
her footsteps were crunchingly audible. She stepped off the
track and into the softer dirt. Dodging the frequent outcroppings of rock, she made her way slowly closer to the cabin.
Goose bumps broke out on her skin, and she was breathing
in quick, shallow pants; she was scarcely aware of either.
She was straining to see, to hear, in a way she'd never done
before.

She didn't find Ray along the way to the cabin. He must
either be at the cabin, or have continued his search from
there into the woods. She continued, slowly, trying to be
quiet. She got to the cabin and waited what seemed like forever, listening. There wasn't a sound. She tried the side door
she'd seen the first time she'd come up here; it was locked.
She crept toward the corner, afraid to look out at the

meadow, afraid of what might be there. But she made herself do it.

The meadow was empty.

It was also silent, which bothered her. No birds, not a sound but the occasional rustle of leaves from the slight breeze. She could smell that distinctive end of summer smell. The sun shone down on the expanse of grass and wildflowers, just beginning to wilt after a hot summer. No movement, no signs of life.

When she could stand it no longer she edged onto the porch and toward the door. It was unlocked, as it had been before. She nudged it open, wondering if she dared call out.

No, she didn't dare. Her voice probably wasn't working anyway, she thought. Carefully, watching her every step on the wood floor, she inched inside.

More silence. The silence of an empty house; she knew he wasn't here. It looked much as it had when she'd left; the scattered supplies had been picked up, tubes and small jars of paint neatly aligned on the drop-cloth-covered table, brushes stowed in the jar beside them. The sofa had been moved, back into what was apparently its normal place opposite two chairs, its back to her now, at right angles to the window, so one could sit and look out over the meadow from it. Or could, before the window had been broken.

She shivered slightly, remembering the omen that had been. She looked out into the sunny afternoon, up at the towering peaks in the distance, then out at the small but lovely expanse of meadow. Instinctively she took a couple of steps toward the window, toward the warmth. For an instant she imagined it covered with snow, a pristine layer that would turn the landscape into the colors of her home, rich evergreen, pure white, the gray of the Rockies and the blue of a Colorado sky.

And then she shivered more fiercely, as if that snow had already arrived. What on earth was she doing, standing here like this, as if she had nothing else to do but admire the scenery? She turned to leave, knowing the house was empty.

She stopped dead, staring. Staring down at the cushions she could now see over the back of the sofa.

Blood.

She wouldn't have thought it would be so obvious, so undeniable. The stain wasn't red, it was a rusty brown, but she knew just the same.

The image that had haunted her came back full force, Lake, dead or dying, never having come to terms with his own innocence. She pictured a gravestone, set in the earth next to his brother's, and let out a low moan. Douglas had loved his big brother, Colin had told her. Had loved him with all the childish adoration that drove older brothers to occasional fury. He would have hated to know the burden his brother had carried.

Lake couldn't be dead, she told herself repeatedly as she stared at that ominous stain. He couldn't be.

Some part of her mind was telling her something important, something about her reaction to the idea, but before it could register another shot from outside spun her around on her heel.

A second shot drew her eyes to the woods rimming the edge of the small meadow.

That second one had sounded different from the first. She couldn't say how, just that it sounded different, like it might have come from a different gun. What the hell was going on? It had been at least twenty minutes since the call had first come over Ray's radio. Were they playing some kind of crazy game out there in the woods? Taking potshots at each other?

She leaned forward suddenly, squinting. Had something moved, out there across the meadow, in the trees? She held her breath, watching, for so long that she thought she'd imagined it.

And then she saw it again, the sudden movement.

A man, perhaps two men, she couldn't tell. But one of them appeared to be in green . . . Ray? Was he not badly hurt after all? Or was he hurt and trying to get to help? He was moving, so he wasn't dead, but . . .

She had to do it. She couldn't stay here and hide any more than she'd been able to sit in Ray's unit and wait, not knowing, imagining. She thought for a long moment, then gathered her nerve, took a deep breath, and made herself move.

Tightening her grip on her paltry weapon, she moved, not toward the door she'd come in but the side door, invisible from the meadow. She'd work her way around through the trees, she thought. It would take longer, but it would be better than marching across the meadow in full sunlight, asking to be seen.

It was easier in theory than it was in fact; the trees were thick and the underbrush occasionally impassable. It was taking too long, she was making too much noise, and every second of the way she expected to hear another shot, this time aimed at her. It wasn't at all hot, not up here, but she felt perspiration forming on her skin.

If she hadn't been watching where she was putting her feet so carefully, she might have missed him. But she caught a glimpse of an unnaturally solid green on the ground just off to her right, away from the meadow. She turned, and saw it was Ray. Down, and apparently unconscious.

Quickly she knelt beside him. She bit her lip on a cry of dismay when she saw the bloodied side of his face. She tried to hang on to some bit of conventional wisdom she'd once heard, that head wounds generally looked worse than they were, but this still looked awful. With a trembling hand she reached out to his neck, letting out a long breath when she felt a pulse beneath her fingers, fairly strong and steady.

She made herself look closer, to find the source of the bleeding. It appeared to be the side of his head above his left ear. She looked closer and saw, not the hole she'd feared, but a long, furrowed gouge in his scalp. And the blood she could see did not appear fresh, nor did he appear to still be bleeding.

She couldn't think of anything to do for him, with her limited skills, and since he wasn't bleeding at the moment, anything she tried might just make things worse. An ambulance was on the way, and while it would take a while for them to get all the way up here, they could do more for him than she could. She should just wait for them, and—

A shout jerked her head around. She heard a low, harsh

grunt and her heart leaped up to her throat. It had been close, barely twenty feet away. Instinctively she ducked, scratching herself on a low branch of a shrub she could only hope wasn't poisonous.

She could hear more sounds now, more grunts, and oddly muffled thuds. Slowly, with exquisite care, she raised her head above the underbrush.

Sunlight shafting through the trees caught Lake's silver hair, sweaty and tousled as if he'd been wearing a hat. He must have been who she'd seen; he was dressed in camouflage pants and a green shirt. He was on one knee, rising to his feet.

Or trying to, she thought, only then seeing the ominous dark stain on his back, the stain that made her think of the blood in his house. He got to his feet at last, and she saw more blood, on his leg, and even more running down his right arm and dripping off the hand that held the knife.

She thought her gasp at the sight of the unexpected and very personal weapon must have been audible even from her hidden spot, but Lake didn't react. Nor did the other man, the one she only now saw, as Lake moved in on him. Also in camouflage, the man also held a knife, a long, wicked-looking blade stained with what had to be Lake's blood.

The two began circling each other. They looked, she thought, like two wolves who had been fighting for too long, but would never give up. Like two wolves who would fight until one of them went down forever.

She caught a glimpse of Lake's eyes; they were glittering and hard, more metallic than she'd ever seen them. There was nothing of fear or even pain in them, despite his wounds, only a coolness as hard as the granite around them.

She watched, unable to do anything else, unable to even move. The grimness of it, the ruthlessness of it, stunned her; it was no less than a fight to the death. They were both bloody, both clearly exhausted, but still they kept on. It was ugly, elemental, primitive. Thrust and parry, dodging, sometimes crashing together like the bighorn sheep that lived in the higher elevations. Again and again they clashed as Alison watched helplessly.

And then, for the first time, she got a clear look at Lake's deadly opponent. Got a clear look at the other man's face.

Dear God, she thought.

She knew him.

But that was impossible. She must be mistaken.

But she wasn't. She knew she wasn't.

The thoughts began to tumble through her mind in a rush. Memories cued other memories until the probable course of events was undeniable. The sense of external heat vanished; an inward fury boiled up in her as she stared at the man. What Lake had done seemed like nothing compared to what she was guessing at now.

The second man charged Lake. They came together with a thud that explained the earlier noise she'd heard. They went down together. They rolled away from her, each fighting for position, to come out on top. First Lake, then his opponent, then Lake again. She heard a grunt. Then a hiss of pain. Then, the other man was on top. His knee dug into Lake's belly. She heard his breath as it was driven out of him. Joplin twisted his fingers in Lake's hair, yanking his head back. She saw Lake try to shake his head. Saw him try to twist to one side.

And then she saw the silver glitter of a blade as it caught the sun. As if in slow motion she saw it start to descend. Saw the blood that already marked it.

Saw the intended target, Lake's bared, vulnerable throat.

She didn't think about what Lake had done. She didn't even think about what he'd told her this man had done. Or what she already knew he'd done, had known in the moment she saw his face and recognized him. She simply reacted. Instantly, and no doubt stupidly.

She charged out of the brush, her pitiful weapon held like a battering ram. The descent of the knife continued, and she screamed. The man looked up. He spotted her. She saw recognition flash in his eyes, then surprise.

It was that surprise that gave her the extra second she needed to get within reach. With the full force of her body and her momentum she rammed the butt end of the baton into his ribs. He yelled, then swore. He swung his arm around, trying to bring the knife to bear on her.

At the sight of the huge blade arcing toward her, she instantly forgot what she'd learned about using a stick as a weapon. Instead she swung it as if she were aiming for the left field bleachers.

She got lucky. He was twisted so that the blow came down on his back, just over the kidneys. A squeal of pain escaped him. He sagged slightly. Alison glanced at Lake. In his eyes was something that hadn't been there just moments ago: fear. It startled her. She didn't understand.

Then she heard the low, hoarse whisper that was all he seemed able to manage.

"Ali, no . . ."

He was afraid for her. Not himself, her.

Before she had the chance to absorb the realization, her moment of inattention cost her. Joplin recovered enough to grab at her. He caught her elbow in a crushing grip.

She sensed another movement. Lake was recovering, trying to help. His leg came up, and he managed to knock the man sideways. Off of Lake now, the man scrambled precariously to his feet. Lake rolled over, but only made it to his knees, his breathing still labored. The man lunged at him with the knife, letting out a furious snarl.

Alison swung wildly this time. Her hands were sweaty, the baton slipped. She didn't hit him so much as he ran into her blow. It caught him across the forehead. The impact of wood against solid bone reverberated up into her hands. Blood flowed over his face, making her stomach turn. He staggered back. Lake got to his feet, swaying but upright. She heard him suck in a breath, then another. But before he was recovered enough to move, the relentless enemy came at him again.

Alison steeled herself for another try. The knees, she thought frantically, wasn't that a good place? She didn't have time to think about it. She swung again. Either he couldn't see for the blood she'd drawn, or he hadn't expected the lower blow. She hit him solidly across the knees.

He shouted in pain, and staggered back again. And began

to flail the air as the ground seemed to give way. Lake swore and lunged forward. He grabbed the man's arm just as, oddly, he seemed to disappear.

It was only then that Alison realized they were on the edge of one of the many granite outcroppings that dropped off sharply here in the Rockies.

And she'd just sent a man falling over one.

And Lake was hanging on to him by one arm, muttering in a language she'd never heard before. Still she knew he was swearing; some things didn't change no matter the language.

She edged toward him, warily, still clutching her surprisingly effective weapon. Her breath caught at the unexpected sharpness of the dropoff; it was practically a cliff, and a good fifty feet of sheer rock face. Deadly.

And the man she had struck was now dangling over it, his sole link to life the man he'd been trying to murder.

And Lake was trying to save him, she realized with a little shock. His first instinctive thought had been to save, not destroy. Even this man he hated.

He was sprawled flat out on the ground. His right hand was clamped around the man's left forearm, his own arm stretched and twisted over the rocky edge.

"Hold still, damn it!" Lake exclaimed, trying to get better purchase.

"Fuck you, you bastard!"

Even as he spoke, the man's free arm came up. He still had the knife. The blade glittered as he drove it home.

It dug into Lake's right hand, cutting deep. Lake cried out, recoiling. Losing his grip on the man's arm.

And Alison could have sworn that the cry she heard as the man fell to his death was one of triumph.

Chapter 25

Left leg.

Right side of his rib cage.

Left shoulder.

But the worst, Lake thought, was his right hand. It was throbbing, fiercely. Enough to make him wary of opening his eyes; he wasn't sure he wanted to see what was left of it.

He kept his eyes closed, thinking, trying to fight his way through the remnants of whatever drug they'd pumped into him to work on him. He searched for the last thing he remembered, but all he could come up with was the sound of a siren. Whether it had been the ambulance coming up the mountain, or going down toward the small clinic with him in it, he couldn't recall.

But he hadn't been in it alone.

Ray, he remembered, smothering a groan the pain hadn't been able to wring from him. He closed his eyes tighter as images floated back to him, of Ray pale beneath the blood that covered half his face. They'd told him Ray would be all right, but who knew better than he how head injuries could go sour in a hurry?

His fault, he thought. Ray had tried to be fair, had always tried, and it was his fault. Joplin had fired the shot, but—

Joplin.

The image came back to him in a rush. His right hand flexed in response to the memory of trying to hang on, and his shock when Joplin had stabbed the knife into his flesh, making him let go, making him send the man down the lethal drop. Just as Joplin had wanted; it had been written on his face that he

would rather die than owe his life to the man he hated so in-
tensely.

Pain shot through Lake's hand and up into his arm, and he
couldn't quite stop the groan this time.

But he was alive. The pain told him that. He was alive, and it
was a damn lucky thing. Joplin had been a madman, absorbing
blow after blow, bleeding from even more wounds than he
himself had been, and yet he'd been damn near unstoppable.
They'd run through all their weapons, gotten down to the
knives. Joplin had almost had him more than once, and that last
time, if it hadn't been for—

His eyes shot open.

"Alison."

It came from him on hushed breath as the memory flooded
back, of her dashing out of the trees like some kind of avenging
angel, refusing to be cowed, refusing to give up, not running
even when Joplin had turned on her with that knife . . .

He sat up abruptly. His shoulder screamed a protest, and his
ribs weren't any too happy about the idea either.

"Slow down."

The soft warning came from beside him, and his head
snapped around.

She was there. She was there, apparently unharmed, and
looking down at him with an expression he couldn't begin to
describe or even comprehend.

"You're . . . all right?" His throat was impossibly dry, and it
came out like a croak.

"I'm not hurt," Alison said as she reached behind her and
picked up a glass with a straw, then held it for him. He let her,
not sure he wouldn't drop it if he tried to take it. He managed a
swallow or two of water, then, more slowly, swung his legs
over the side of the gurney. He felt himself wobble, but the unsteadiness cleared after a moment.

And then what she'd said—and hadn't said—sank in. She'd
said she wasn't hurt, but not that she was fine. The one memory he'd been missing flashed to life, and he saw it as vividly
as if it were happening in front of him, Alison taking that wild
swing at Joplin's knees, sending him careening over the
precipice . . .

Joplin had made his own choice when he'd used his knife, Lake thought, but Alison had still delivered that final blow. It was this that he saw in her eyes, he guessed. And he felt that heart he'd only recently discovered he still had tear a little.

"You saved my life," he said quietly. "Thank you."

She lowered her eyes. "I . . . didn't even think about it. I just did it."

"If you hadn't, he would have killed me. And then you."

She looked up quickly, and he saw by the sudden widening of her eyes that she hadn't thought of that, that once he'd been dead, Joplin would have turned on her.

"I wish you hadn't risked yourself," he said gently, "but once you were there, you did what you had to do." Then, although he was almost afraid to ask, he did so to divert her thoughts. "Ray?"

"He's going to be fine."

Relief flooded him. Ray was okay, Alison was unscathed, physically at least . . . perhaps fate had decided to cut him some slack this time.

"It took a couple dozen stitches," Alison went on, "and he's got a moderate concussion so they're going to keep him awhile, but there was no fracture and he's going to be all right. Yvette's with him, babying him I'm sure."

"Good."

"And you," she added, "should be babying that hand."

He glanced down at his right hand, encased in a plastic cast assembly that held the last two fingers stationary. The wound that had been delivered last had been the worst; the nick in his leg was barely a sting now, his cracked ribs would heal quickly, his shoulder a bit slower but it would still heal.

But Joplin's blade had gone nearly all the way through the outside edge of his hand, they'd told him, doing damage all the way. A couple of tendons had been nearly severed, and there was nerve damage. He would never again, the doctor had told him grimly, have full use of his ring finger, and probably none at all of his little finger.

"Funny," he mused, barely aware of saying aloud, "once I would have been happy I could still use my trigger finger. Now, I'm just happy I'll still be able to hold a brush."

He sensed rather than saw Alison's sudden stillness. He closed his eyes, not wanting to see her face, knowing she must be thinking about everything she'd lost. Because of him.

"I want out of here," he muttered, sliding to the floor, steadying himself with his left hand on the gurney.

"I don't know if they're going to release you—"

"I don't give a damn. I'm gone."

She drew back as he snapped. "Fine," she said coolly.

"Sorry. I just hate hospitals. Even small ones."

"I doubt anybody likes them much, from this side."

He made his way fairly steadily to the doorway and snagged the first white uniform he saw in passing. He raised enough of a fuss that the doctor finally appeared. After getting over his surprise at seeing Lake upright, and delivering several stern warnings about the care of his injured hand, he at last gave in to Lake's nonnegotiable stance and released him.

"You'll be with him for the first twenty-four hours, Ms. Carlyle?" he asked as he filled out the form on the metal clipboard. "He shouldn't be alone."

Alison blinked. Lake opened his mouth to protest he didn't need anyone, then shut it again without speaking. He wasn't at all sure that was the truth anymore.

"I . . . guess so," she said, but she didn't sound happy about it.

He couldn't blame her, not after the destruction he'd brought into her life. She probably wanted him gone for good as soon as possible. He couldn't blame her for that, either.

They went by Ray's small room as they left, but he was asleep. Yvette's jacket and purse were there, but there was no sign of the woman.

"My place," Alison said briefly as she opened the passenger door of her blue four-by for him; at some point she'd obviously gone home and gotten it. "I'm not going back up on that mountain."

He nodded in understanding. It was a silent ride, and it didn't change when they got to her house and went inside. Without a word she walked him into her room, gestured him to the bed, got him a sweatshirt that fit fairly well to replace his worse-for-wear shirt, and pillows to prop him up and to place under his injured hand.

He'd never expected to be in her house again, let alone her bed, even alone. Not after she'd learned how he'd used her. And especially now, after she'd been touched by such horrors as she had been today.

"Alison?" he said, knowing they had to talk.

"What?"

"Will you sit down for a minute?"

She did, silently, on the edge of the bed, put poised to leave. As if she didn't want to get too comfortable, too willing to stay.

It took him a moment to find the words. "It's hard to deal with, I know. But you have to face it, it won't go away if you ignore it."

"Is that your expert opinion?"

The words stung. "Yes."

"I didn't mean it . . . like that." She smiled, or tried to; it ended up half-done and oddly self-mocking. "I couldn't let him kill you. There was never any question about that. And I know he . . . had it coming. He was ruthless, evil, in fact downright Machiavellian. So why am I feeling so ambivalent?"

"You've never . . . been even partly responsible for another person's death before," he said baldly. He didn't see any point in sugarcoating it; it was the truth, and he knew—more than ever now—that Alison was tough enough to take it.

"I've never even seen it that close before," she said ruefully. "Not that kind of death. Not . . ."

"I know," he said gently. "I won't lie and say you'll get over it. You won't. But you'll learn to live with it. Eventually."

For a long moment she just looked at him. "Thank you. For being so . . . kind about it."

"I've never forgotten what it feels like," he said. "And even when it's someone like Joplin, you still—"

"Joplin," she said suddenly, angrily. "You mean Peter Clarkson, don't you?"

"What?"

"That's the name I knew him by."

He sat up, heedless of the twinge in his ribs and the pain it caused in his hand. "You knew him?"

She nodded. "I didn't realize until I got a look at him there in the woods. That bastard, he planned it, all of it. He used Colin, he used me, and it was all a setup."

He frowned. "What are you saying?"

"Your Joplin," she said, her voice taking on an edge of cold fury he'd never heard in anyone before, and he'd seen some hard-edged people, "was introduced to me six months ago as a friend of your father's."

Lake drew back. "My father's?"

"Yes. Colin said Peter was a friend of yours, so I took it at face value. He must have convinced Colin he knew you."

"He . . . talked to my father?" Lake felt something sick begin to churn in his stomach.

"More than that," she said flatly. "He was the one who suggested Colin bring *Layers* to me in the first place."

Lake felt beads of sweat breaking out on his forehead. "That long ago?" Dear God, Joplin really had been here, setting himself up with his father, over six months ago? He'd hung *Layers* out as bait, just on the chance someday Lake would find out and bite? He'd known it was most likely a trap, but he hadn't expected this.

"And it was Peter-Joplin who suggested the ad in *The Wall Street Journal,* after John Thompson and I had tried everything else we could think of," she added.

"Son of a bitch," Lake muttered. Duran must have told him even that, he thought numbly.

"He orchestrated this whole thing, from the beginning. He set Colin up, then used Colin to set me up, and me to set you up. I was nothing but a stupid, unwitting pawn."

"Apparently," Lake said, his mind reeling a little, "so was I." And then, as something else struck him, he whispered, "My father . . . you said it was a fall . . ."

"Yes," she answered, sounding puzzled. "He was up on— Oh, my God. You don't mean . . . you don't think he did it? That he pushed your father, murdered him?"

"Dad was *never* careless with heights. Maybe Joplin got tired of waiting, or realized I wasn't likely to come back here on my own."

He saw her expression change as her mind moved from possibility to probability. "God, if he wasn't dead, I'd like to kill him all over again!"

It burst from her passionately, fervently. He saw the look in her eyes, the near wildness, and knew just how she was feeling, so full of outrage with nowhere to expend it. He'd felt it so often, when they'd confronted the atrocities committed in the name of politics or religious zeal, and there had been no one to blame, or no way to punish those responsible.

He reached out with his good hand and took both of hers. "Thank you for feeling that way. For my father's sake."

She stared at him for a moment, and he could feel the tremors rippling through her. He tugged, gently, on her hands. She seemed puzzled. He was afraid to ask, but knew he had to. She needed it. *He* needed it, something he never thought he'd ever admit.

"Lie down with me," he said tightly. "Just to . . . let me hold you." She drew back, studying him. Not moving. And he knew he had to give it all to her. He barely got it out. "And hold me."

A moment's more indecision and then she was beside him. She moved carefully, avoiding his injuries as best she could, and was soon snuggled up to his side. He wasn't above putting his right arm around her, knowing she'd be hesitant to move and jostle his injured hand.

He waited until he was sure she wasn't going to speak herself. Then he made himself say it. Say it all.

"I can't tell you how sorry I am. Not just about Phoenix, but—"

She lifted her head. "I forgot. Yvette said the storeroom wasn't burned."

He blinked. "What?"

"The paintings are all right. They're all that's left, but they're all right."

"All of them?"

She nodded. "No damage at all, that Yvette could see. So there's some good news."

"I guess."

He considered it for a moment. If it was true, and if she was right about their value—and he knew how good she was, he had to believe it, no matter how absurd it seemed to him—then there might be enough there to at least start to rebuild Phoenix. He'd have to fight her to take it, but he'd work on that later. In the meantime, he had to finish this.

"I'm sorry I got you into this, Alison. That I used you, without giving you any say, without giving you a choice. It was . . . SOP for the Wolf Pack, and I just followed it. It never mattered before, as long as the person didn't get hurt."

"Maybe . . . there's no other way to deal with that kind of person than to use his own methods."

"I never, ever meant to hurt you."

"You'd have to go some to match what that . . . bastard did," she said.

That bit of tentative understanding gave him a hope he'd nearly given up on. He tightened his hold on her, ignoring the pain it set up in his hand. He simply held her, wishing he were well enough to make love to her, wishing she would let him. But then she moved slightly, snuggling up against him in a way that made him think he might just settle for this, if he could have it for the rest of his life.

He felt weariness beginning to steal over him, fought it for a moment, then wondered why he was bothering. There was nothing he had to stay awake for, alert for, not anymore. And it felt so good just to lie here, holding Alison close, feeling her warmth, her softness, hearing the gentle sound of her breathing.

Lake felt something huge well up inside him, something warm and all-encompassing. It wasn't just concern for her, wasn't simply the admiration he already knew he felt for her courage, it was something more, something bigger.

And as he slipped off into sleep, it came to him what it was. His last conscious thought was he should be laughing at his own foolishness.

Love and the Gray Wolf just didn't mix.

He knew it was true when he woke up and the only sign that she'd been there in that bed with him was a note on the pillow. He picked it up gingerly.

Lake—
I can understand, and I can forgive, but no matter how much I want to, I can't fight your demons for you. I can't

*make you forgive yourself. It's not all ugliness, it's not all
darkness—sometimes the light gets through. It could be so
simple, if only you would let it.*

A.

He felt a tightness in his chest.

She was saying good-bye.

He blinked. And then blinked again. Something was wrong
with his eyes, they were stinging. He didn't realize what was
happening until he felt the wetness streaking down his cheek.

Lord, he was crying. The Gray Wolf never cried, but he was
now.

He forced himself to sit up. He wouldn't make this harder
than it already was. He would be gone before she came back.

Alison was glad Yvette was off with Ray today. They'd been
spending a lot of time together ever since he'd gotten out of the
hospital, and Alison was more than willing to give her the time
off; doing everything was keeping her mind occupied. There
wasn't much left to do, anyway, after better than a month of
wading through chaos.

She sighed wearily, wondering if she had the courage to start
again. She tried not to think of all the things she'd loved, the
crystal waterfall, the lily amid the carnations, the carved
mantel . . . Did she have the heart left to try to make Phoenix
rise again, literally from the ashes? She didn't know. She didn't
know if she had a heart left at all; there seemed to be an empty
ache inside her where it had once been.

She'd had to send out announcements postponing the showing, and had been touched by the outpouring of sympathy from
her patrons and former customers. She'd dealt with the insurance company, who was not happy with the concept of a piece
of clay having value into five, even six figures, but they couldn't
argue that she'd paid the necessary premiums. They were a bit
more recalcitrant about the building; it had been arson, after all,
and they weren't yet convinced she wasn't involved, although
Ray had said he'd speak to them and do what he could.

But what had stunned her the most was the reaction of the
people of Jewel, who had gathered round her and offered sup-

port as if she'd been native-born. A clean-up crew had arrived the first Saturday morning after the explosion. Lunch arrived in baskets from what seemed like every house in town, and the Silver Spoon. By the end of the weekend the shell was cleared of debris. A couple of pieces had even been found intact, and a couple more possibly repairable.

Even the ladies had expressed their sympathy, although none of them seemed too upset over the idea of the showing having been canceled. Even Althea had shown up briefly, to deliver a stiff, grudging apology for Willie's behavior, met with coos of admiration from the ladies present and a wry acceptance of the peace offering, insincere though it was, from Alison. But it had been the woman's look of barely suppressed triumph as she looked at the shell of Phoenix that made Alison's decision for her; she would rebuild.

She had also found her office wasn't a total loss, although the smell of wet ashes lingered; the blast had apparently been set to blow forward, taking out the gallery, but the back area was left almost intact. Which was also why the storeroom had been left virtually untouched. Along with Lake's paintings.

She smothered a sigh with the reflexiveness of long habit; since the day she'd left him that note, she'd been trying to re-sign herself to never seeing him again. She'd even tried to work up her anger at him again, but had failed miserably; she'd seen now the kind of enemy he'd been fighting, and realized he'd had little choice but to do what he'd done. And if they were right, and Joplin had had something to do with Colin's death . . .

No, she couldn't be angry at him. She knew, in her heart, that she'd forgiven him long ago. She'd forgiven him in the moment she'd known he was no longer the man he'd been.

She'd begun when he'd told her he'd left the man who had orchestrated Ian's death alive because he was too broken to kill. And she had forgiven him in the moment when, instead of watching his bitter enemy, the man who seconds ago had been about to slash his throat, fall to his death, he had instinctively moved to save him.

If only he could forgive himself.

She heard a noise and looked up, surprised; not many were

willing to enter the blackened building to make their way back
to where she was working in the office, filling out yet another
set of forms, affidavits, and explanations for the insurance
company.

She called out, but nobody answered. She felt a shiver of
sensation down her spine; the memory of the time when any
noise could have been a threat was never far away. Slowly she
got up and walked toward the doorway, peering out into the
blackened shell that had once been her gallery.

There was no one there. Her brow furrowed. She stepped
through the doorway, then stopped when something caught her
eye. A package, wrapped in heavy butcher paper, leaning up
against the charred outer wall. It was about two by three feet
square, and flat.

About the size of a painting.

Warily, she inspected it, then picked it up and carried it into
her office. She could feel through the paper that it was framed.
She set it on one of the surviving chairs and studied it for a moment longer, trying to keep her mind from making illogical,
fantastical leaps.

Then, disgusted with herself, she took her letter opener,
made a slit across the top, and tore the wrapping away in one
great pull.

Her breath caught, and her throat tightened. She stared, not
quite able to believe what she was seeing. There was no denying the hand here, the strokes were as distinctive as a signature,
the energy, the power as conclusive as fingerprints. It was
Lake, it had to be.

But it was unlike anything he'd ever done. And it was not
simply that it was a portrait, it was much, much more. It was a
painting that was free of the dark, ominous, disturbed undertone of all the others. It was a work of luminescence and
beauty, not the cry of a tortured soul. It fairly glowed, shim-
mering with a brilliant light that seemed beyond the capacity
for paint to capture.

It was a portrait of hope.

It was a portrait of her.

Her vision was suddenly blurry, and she almost missed the
small brass plate fastened to the bottom part of the frame. She

had to blink rapidly to read the two simple yet not simple at all lines.

Light
Lachlan McGregor

"Oh, Lake," she whispered, the tears overflowing now. He'd won. He'd won through at last. He'd painted the light, and he'd signed it.

She hadn't heard him, but some part of her must have known he was there, because she didn't even jump when he came up behind her. His hands came up to rest on her shoulders; she could feel the plastic of the cast that still supported his hand, but had obviously left the crucial fingers free to paint.

"I thought your note meant good-bye," he said. "I thought you must hate me."

"No," she whispered, not looking at him.

"Then I realized what you meant, what you were saying. You don't want to fight someone's demons for them because you hate them."

"No," she repeated, even more softly.

She heard him take a deep breath. She heard him swallow, as if his throat were tight.

"I love you," he said.

She shivered. She knew probably better than anyone what it took for him to say that, what he'd had to go through to reach this point.

"I mean everything that picture says, Alison." She felt the tug of emotion at the simple acknowledgment that he knew she would see everything he'd put into that incredible piece of work. "It's everything you've taught me. And I'll try to live it, if . . . if that's enough."

She turned then, looking up at him through her tears, slipping her arms around him. "It's enough."

"An old, broken wolf doesn't have much to recommend him," he said, his mouth twisting wryly.

"But he has me," she said. "I love you, Lake McGregor."

She felt him shudder. "Then he's the luckiest creature on this earth."

She held him, feeling his warmth, sensing that he believed what he'd said down to his soul.

She *would* rebuild, she thought. Phoenix would be even better than before. She could do it, she knew she could.

And Lake was going to be a star, whether he believed it or not. She was as sure of that as she was that she loved him.

And that the Gray Wolf, reconciled with his ghosts at last, loved her.

Phoenix Rises Out of the Ashes

by Erica Remington

ARTS Editor

JEWEL—This might be a small town, but it shone as brightly as its big brothers Aspen and Vail last night during the grand reopening of Phoenix, the popular upscale gallery that was destroyed in an explosion three months ago. Given the state of the place at that time, the glittering gala last night was little short of a miracle. But Phoenix owner Alison Carlyle has a lot of friends, including some nationally prominent artists she discovered, several socially and fiscally prominent art investors, and a lot of regular folks who value her unique vision.

Among the many artists present were world-renowned Jon Degroot, just in from his Paris showing, locals Jane Red Cloud, Martin Page, and Lourdes Blake, and the latest Phoenix discovery, Lachlan McGregor, whose singular and powerful work was the focus of the opening, and made him the star of the evening. McGregor is also Carlyle's fiancé, and several of tomorrow's wedding guests, including Carlyle's mother and matron of honor, Emily Carlyle, and best man Jess Harper, his wife Elizabeth and their son, arrived early for the opening.

Also in attendance were Denver businessman Charles Copeland, Aspen socialite Margaret Phillips, and mover and shaker George Gillespie of TechCorp, who purchased the centerpiece painting of the evening, McGregor's Sacrifice, for a price well into five figures.

McGregor's story isn't just one of hometown boy made good, it's much more dramatic than that. Wrongly blamed for the death of his brother over twenty-five years ago, McGregor, great-great-grandson of the town's founder, left Jewel never to return. Now vindicated through the efforts of his fiancée, McGregor has become the darling of Jewel society; no report yet on whether the reclusive artist will accept the town's overtures.

McGregor, who surreptitiously arranged for the afore-mentioned artists to bring a recent work to replace those lost in the explosion, and Carlyle will be leaving after to-morrow's ceremony for a lengthy honeymoon, while Phoenix remains open to tantalize those special visitors with the unique taste Carlyle has catered to for the past five years.